Murder Most Crafty

MURDER MOST CRAFTY

EDITED BY
Maggie Bruce

BERKLEY PRIME CRIME, NEW YORK

THE BERKLEY PUBLISHING GROUP
Published by the Penguin Group
Penguin Group (USA) Inc.
375 Hudson Street, New York, New York 10014, USA
Penguin Group (Canada), 10 Alcorn Avenue, Toronto, Ontario M4V 3B2, Canada
(a division of Pearson Penguin Canada Inc.)
Penguin Books Ltd., 80 Strand, London WC2R 0RL, England
Penguin Group Ireland, 25 St. Stephen's Green, Dublin 2, Ireland (a division of Penguin Books Ltd.)
Penguin Group (Australia), 250 Camberwell Road, Camberwell, Victoria 3124, Australia
(a division of Pearson Australia Group Pty. Ltd.)
Penguin Books India Pvt. Ltd., 11 Community Centre, Panchsheel Park, New Delhi—110 017, India
Penguin Group (NZ), Cnr. Airborne and Rosedale Roads, Albany, Auckland 1310, New Zealand
(a division of Pearson New Zealand Ltd.)
Penguin Books (South Africa) (Pty.) Ltd., 24 Sturdee Avenue, Rosebank, Johannesburg 2196,
South Africa

Penguin Books Ltd., Registered Offices: 80 Strand, London WC2R 0RL, England

This book is an original publication of The Berkley Publishing Group.

This is a work of fiction. Names, characters, places, and incidents either are the product of the author's imagination or are used fictitiously, and any resemblance to actual persons, living or dead, business establishments, events, or locales is entirely coincidental.

First edition: April 2005

Library of Congress Cataloging-in-Publication Data

Murder most crafty / edited by Maggie Bruce.— 1st ed.
    p. cm.
    ISBN 0-425-20206-2
    1. Detective and mystery stories, American.   2. Handicraft—Fiction.   3. Artisans—Fiction.
I. Bruce, Maggie

PS374.D4M8545 2005
813'.0872083527455—dc22

2004062731

PRINTED IN THE UNITED STATES OF AMERICA

10   9   8   7   6   5   4   3   2   1

Individual Copyrights

Contents

Introduction 1
Maggie Bruce

The Collage to Kill For 5
Susan Wittig Albert

The Gourd, the Bad, and the Ugly 25
Maggie Bruce

Call It Macaroni 47
Jan Burke

No Good Deed 69
Dorothy Cannell

If You Meet the Buddha 89
Susan Dunlap

Strung Out 105
Monica Ferris and Denise Williams

Oh, What a Tangled Lanyard We Weave 131
Parnell Hall

How to Make a Killing Online   161
Victoria Houston

The *M* Word   175
Judith Kelman

Bewreathed   205
Margaret Maron

The Deepest Blue   223
Sujata Massey

Waxing Moon   243
Tim Myers

Light Her Way Home   257
Sharan Newman

Ellie's Chair   279
Gillian Roberts

Motherwit and Tea Cakes   307
Paula L. Woods

Appendix   331

Murder Most Crafty

INTRODUCTION

§§

I love making things.

There's something magical about taking everyday materials and turning them into something that didn't exist before, a thing at once beautiful and useful. I've indulged myself in this passion by knitting, crocheting, and embroidering. I've hooked rugs, made pottery bowls, cups, and vases, and even built furniture. Once, on the way to a wedding, I finished sewing the borders of a quilt I was giving as a gift to the bride and groom. In the past three years, I've become obsessed with gourds and all the wonderful ways these humble fruits can be transformed using paints and dyes, feathers and pine needles, pyrography and carving.

I'm not the only one who finds that spending time working by hand with yarn or clay, fabric or paper, gourds or wood, brings a measure of peace, pride, and satisfaction that few other activities afford in this hectic and demanding world. Across the country, the popularity of crafts fairs, classes, instruction books, and specialized shops that sell a smorgasbord of materials attest to the abiding love so many of us have for an object well made, an appreciation for the skill and care required, and, for many, a desire to try our hands at something new.

Long before the twenty-first century, though, necessity used to govern such pursuits. Archaeologists and historians offer examples from all over the world and through all of history and prehistory of how people have made things by hand, devising systems to store seeds, roots, food, and clothing, creating utensils for cooking and eating, designing ways to cover our bodies and to light the moonless nights. Those hunters and gatherers of long ago sat around their communal fires carving water dippers from gourds, working animal skins into clothing, making adornments from stones and feathers to declare the uniqueness of the wearer. And as their hands worked, they told stories that explained the world, or entertained, or taught lessons about human behavior that helped tribal elders pass down wisdom and warnings.

So, crafts and storytelling have been around for a long time. But never quite in a collection like this. Murder, an altogether different kind of handiwork, is unsettling, and decidedly unlovely. When the fabric of everyday life is rent by crime, a craftsperson might respond with practiced precision and meticulous methods, as well as a deep understanding of human behavior, to repair the tear and set things right.

In each of these stories, fifteen writers who have artfully practiced the fine art of murder-on-the-page highlight crafts ranging from papermaking, gourd decorating, macaroni art, mosaics, fine sewing, knitting, lanyard making, fly tying, basketry, and wreath making to indigo dyeing, candlemaking, furniture finishing, and collage making. The appendix will help you find materials, instructions, and other folks who share an interest in crafts. And if you're like me, the instructions that follow each story will keep you busy for many hours trying your hand at the activities in these tales. Of course, the only how-to's we've included are the legal ones . . .

Enjoy!

MAGGIE BRUCE

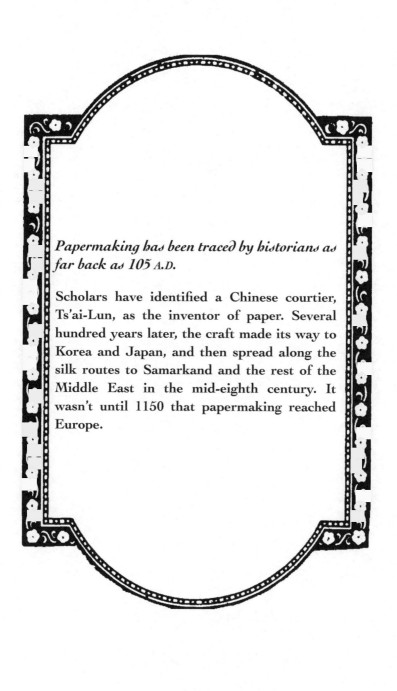

Papermaking has been traced by historians as far back as 105 A.D.

Scholars have identified a Chinese courtier, Ts'ai-Lun, as the inventor of paper. Several hundred years later, the craft made its way to Korea and Japan, and then spread along the silk routes to Samarkand and the rest of the Middle East in the mid-eighth century. It wasn't until 1150 that papermaking reached Europe.

THE COLLAGE TO KILL FOR

by Susan Wittig Albert

Susan Wittig Albert is the author of thirteen China Bayles herbal mysteries, most recently Dead Man's Bones *and a collection of short stories, as well as the Cottage Tales of Beatrix Potter, English village mysteries set in the early 1900s and featuring the beloved children's author/illustrator and her animal friends. Susan and her husband Bill Albert, under the pseudonym of Robin Paige, have coauthored eleven late-Victorian and early-Edwardian mysteries. The Alberts live in the Hill Country of central Texas.*

§§

AT THE TIME she died, I didn't know Mattie Long very well. We had connected rather casually about three or four years before, when we both took a class on how to make handmade paper with herbs and garden plants. I own my own growing business and have a husband and teenage son to take care of, so I needed a new craft about as much as I needed another head. (Another pair of hands, of course, would be welcome.) Still, I enjoyed it immensely, and even managed to develop some simple projects for a make-and-take class on papermaking that I teach at my herb shop a couple of times a year.

Mattie Long, however, was so inspired by the class that she went on to become a paper artist, creating her own paper, then using it to create things like collages, paper sculptures, origami, boxes, even lampshades. She sold these lovelies in art galleries and exclusive shops as far away as Houston and Dallas. Her day job (she was a receptionist for a local doctor) and her passion for paper art took so much of her time that we only saw one another when she dropped in to gather plant materials from my garden—lavender and rosemary, fresh rose petals and pansies—to incorporate into her paper. Some six months ago, though, I suspected that her artistry might be paying off, for she rented a studio on the third floor of the Craft Emporium, next door. I began to see her fairly frequently, going in and out, toting bags and boxes of supplies, stopping to chat with the other craftspeople—until I saw her for the very last time, lying dead at the foot of the stairs. It was definitely a shock, I'll tell you. You don't expect to discover a dead body on a quiet Tuesday morning, before breakfast.

But maybe I'd better back up and fill in some of the background details. My name is China Bayles. After I left my law career (I was a criminal defense attorney for a large Houston law firm) I bought a shop called Thyme and Seasons Herbs, in Pecan Springs, Texas, a small Hill Country town halfway between Austin and San Antonio. The shop is located in a hundred-year-old limestone building that I share with Ruby Wilcox, who owns the Crystal Cave, the only New Age shop in Pecan Springs. Ruby and I are also partners in Thyme for Tea, a tearoom that serves light lunches and afternoon tea and caters for special events. If you've never visited, you ought to consider dropping in the next time you're buzzing down I-35. You can't miss us— we're at 304 Crockett Street, just a couple of blocks off the town square, between the Hobbit House Bookstore and the Craft Emporium, a turn-of-the-century three-story Victorian that's been converted into a more-or-less-successful craft boutique. The people who rent space in the Emporium seem to sell enough of their crafts to keep going, while owner Constance Letterman, who has to pay the upkeep bills on the old place, is always moaning that it needs to be more successful (translation, more profitable).

As I said, I found Mattie Long's body early on a Tuesday morning, so early that none of the shops were open and nobody else was around. You see, Constance had given Ruby and me a key to the Emporium, so we could get in if there was an emergency. Now, you might not call running out of toilet paper an emergency, but Ruby did, and since she was the one in urgent need, I was the one who was deputized to take the key, hustle next door, and raid the Emporium's second-floor supply closet. Constance wouldn't miss just one roll of toilet paper, but it would take care of Ruby's immediate crisis and hold us until we could restock this vital necessity (and sneak a pay-back roll into Constance's closet) later in the day.

Which is why I was stumbling up the Emporium's first-floor stairs in the dark of a winter Tuesday morning, fumbling for the light switch at the top. And why, when the light came on just in time to keep me from stepping on a sprawled body, all thought of the immediate crisis totally vanished. Ruby would have to wait a while longer for her toilet paper. That was Mattie on the floor, her arms flung wide, her head bent at an unnatural angle, her neck clearly broken. It didn't take a rocket scientist to figure out that she had fallen down the steep, narrow, dogleg stairs that led to the third floor.

It's funny, the things that go through your mind at such a time. My first shocked thought was of Mattie, of course. The financial problems that had for so long plagued both her and her sister Caroline seemed to have eased, and Mattie had been excited and pleased about her new studio space— it was sad that this accident had to happen just when things were going right, for a change. I thought of Caroline, too, and of how close the two sisters were, and how much Caroline would miss her.

But I also thought of Constance Letterman, who owns the Craft Emporium, and fervently hoped that her liability insurance was up to date. An accident like this was bound to be costly.

At the time, I couldn't have guessed just how much it would cost, or who would ultimately have to pay.

I'VE OWNED THYME and Seasons for quite some time now, and you'd think I'd get tired of the hard work and responsibility. But that hasn't happened yet, perhaps because I enjoy the shop so much, not to mention the gardens around it. No matter how difficult things may be, I'm always cheered by the sight of chile pepper ristras and garlic braids hanging against the stone walls, gleaming glass jars filled with dried culinary and medicinal herbs, and shelves of handcrafted herbal vinegars and soaps and cosmetics and potpourri. Look anywhere in the shop, and you'll see bouquets of dried love-lies-bleeding and lunaria and goldenrod, and baskets of statice and artemisia and sweet Annie, an all-natural treat for the eyes and nose. Outside, the gardens are built around themes: a fragrance garden, a Shakespeare garden, a butterfly garden, and (Ruby's favorite) a medicine wheel garden. I come early and stay late, and love every minute of it, even when I'm weeding.

A few days after Mattie was buried, I was hanging the CLOSED sign on the door when I looked up to see Caroline Howard—Mattie's sister—coming up the walk. I called to Ruby, who came through the door that connects our shops just as Caroline opened the front door and came in.

"Oh, I'm so glad you're still open," she blurted out. "I wanted to get here earlier, but Tom needed me, and I couldn't get away."

From the look on Caroline's face, I knew she was worried about something. At Mattie's funeral, Ruby and I had offered the usual sympathetic formula: we were there for her if she needed us. We meant it, of course, but I hadn't actually expected her to take us up on it, and certainly not so soon. I didn't quite know what to say.

Ruby, however, is never at a loss. "Hi, Caroline," she said, in a tone that was at once casual and concerned. "How can we help?"

Caroline glanced around the shop, as if she wanted to make sure that we were alone. "If you have a minute . . ." she said nervously, her voice trailing off.

"Sure," I said, following Ruby's lead. "Take all the minutes you want."

The story came haltingly at first, then in a tumbling rush of words, and ended with a burst of tears. Caroline was deeply upset and not entirely coherent, but Ruby and I finally got it all sorted out. Some of it we already knew, and some of it was a surprise. Quite a surprise.

It seemed that Caroline's husband, Tom, had a serious heart condition that required several surgeries and frequent hospitalizations over the past several years. They'd been unable to get health insurance. Desperate, Caroline had done everything she could to scrape together enough money to pay the bills. But she couldn't do enough. The family ship was about to go to the bottom when, six months ago, Mattie had handed Caroline ten thousand dollars—in cash.

"In cash?" Ruby asked, widening her eyes incredulously. She's six-foot-plus in her sandals, her bright red hair springs out in tight ringlets, and she has the most expressive hands I've ever seen. When Ruby is incredulous, she's incredulous all over.

Caroline nodded. The first contribution had been followed by a second one, and then, just two weeks before Mattie's death, by a third. The grand total: thirty thousand dollars, every penny of it in cash. Mattie refused to say where she was getting it. She would only say that somebody owed her the money, and that there was more where that came from. Caroline was afraid that Mattie had been blackmailing somebody. And maybe, just maybe, the blackmailer had killed her.

"You have to tell Sheila about this," I said, reaching for the phone. Sheila Dawson, *aka* Smart Cookie, is our chief of police. This is considered by some citizens (Pecan Springs, by and large, is a conservative town) to be a most unsuitable job for a woman. Sheila is always running into trouble from the City Council, which has given her a great deal of grief over some recent unsolved crimes.

Caroline put a restraining hand on my arm. "No," she said. "I can't talk to the police, China—not right away, anyway. You know Tom. He'll be terribly upset if he suspects that the money we used to pay his medical bills was . . . well, dirty money." She bit her lip. "That sort of stress could kill him."

I frowned, biting back the temptation to say that one way or another, most money was dirty money. But it wouldn't help. Tom was born again a few years ago, and expects everybody to toe the straight-and-narrow. "But you're willing to tell the police about the money if there's other evidence that Mattie was murdered?" I persisted.

"I guess I will if I have to," Caroline said slowly. "But I was hoping that you could . . . well, look around. Without involving the police."

"Investigate, you mean?" Ruby asked, with an eager shake of her red curls.

Caroline nodded. "I'll be glad to give you the key to her apartment. You could start there. And her studio, of course." She frowned. "Actually, it looked to me as if someone had searched the studio. My sister was a very neat person, and there were quite a few things out of place."

"Of course we'll have a look," Ruby said in a reassuring voice, patting Caroline's shoulder. "We'll get started right away, won't we, China?"

I sighed. I could tell by the tone of Ruby's voice and the dancing light in her eyes that there was no point in arguing with her. When she decides to play Girl Detective, there's nothing left to do but go along. And I'll have to admit that I was curious, too. It was hard to imagine how Mattie Long could have laid her hands on thirty thousand honest dollars. The money that went to pay Tom's medical bills had to have come out of somebody else's pocket, and there had to be a reason for it.

What was the reason?

Who gave Mattie that money?

And had her death really been an accident, or had somebody sent her hurtling headfirst down those stairs?

WE STARTED WITH Mattie's condo, which was located in an upscale area of Pecan Springs. The place was large and very nice—much nicer than I would have thought, given her financial circumstances. A receptionist in a doctor's office doesn't earn a lot of money—although, as Caroline told us, Mattie had quit that job about six weeks earlier. She hadn't made a move to get another job, either. She'd told Caroline that she was going to concentrate on her paper art. It was time, she said, to turn her art into a career.

Caroline had been right. The condo was neat, obsessively neat—at least, that's how I would describe it. It looked like something Martha Stewart would be obsessively proud of, in fact. Ruby took the kitchen, bathroom, and living room; I took the bedroom, dining room, and the little hallway. Caroline told us that she herself had already done a careful search, looking for letters, notes, or any communication between Mattie and someone she might have been blackmailing. She had found nothing. But an examination of her sister's bank account had just revealed that Mattie had actually received *more* than the thirty thousand dollars she had handed over to Caroline—about twice as much, in fact. Which accounted, in part, for the condo and the nice furniture. And that amount of money couldn't have come from the sale of her crafts. She was good but not *that* good, at least to my way of thinking.

Like Caroline before us, Ruby and I finally had to admit defeat. As far as we could discover, Mattie had left no hidden diary, no calendar of clandestine meetings, no secret stash of letters, and not a single telltale clue to whatever monkey business might have led to her death. What she did leave, of course, were plenty of clues to her artistic passion: boxes full of art supplies and equipment, large portfolios containing her handmade papers, plastic bins full of dried herbs that she intended to incorporate into her work—hollyhock flowers, milkweed fibers, thistle, Joe-Pye weed—and other bins full of decorative paper, confetti, glitter, and ribbon, as well as old photos and printed materials. In the refrigerator, we found plastic bags of leftover pulp that she was saving. And on the wall, shelves displayed a collection of origami, fiber art, and small sculptures, made with her own paper. Each of these was beautifully unique, incorporating bits of photos, printed material, and handwriting, as well as Mattie's handcrafted papers.

"It looks like the place is clean," Ruby said in a resigned tone. "Not a sign of anything . . . well, crooked."

I had to chuckle. "Ordinarily," I said, "that would be a good thing. Just a quiet, clean, life, filled with her art and—"

"In a condo that she couldn't *ordinarily* afford," Ruby interrupted pointedly. "And with enough money left over to pick up her brother-in-law's hospital tab and finance a new career." She gave an exaggerated sigh. "There is something here that does not meet the eye, China—if only the eye could see it. Maybe we'll have better luck at the studio."

CAROLINE WAS RIGHT again. It was obvious that someone had searched the two-room studio, for things were disordered—not greatly so, but certainly in comparison to the order of Mattie's condo. Supplies on the shelves were disarranged, items had been pulled out onto the floor, and art hung crookedly on the wall. But it was a well-lighted, cheerful place, perfect for crafting, and I felt that Mattie must have enjoyed working there.

There was a long table in the center of the main room, filled with Mattie's work-in-progress. The old kitchen (the

Craft Emporium had been converted into small apartments at some earlier point in its checkered history) was now the work area where Mattie made her papers. This was where she kept her molds and deckles, felts, plastic buckets, scoops and strainers, and a kitchen scale. On the stove were several stainless steel pots where she cooked the plant fibers that eventually became paper. There was a large commercial blender on the counter, and a plastic vat stood next to the sink. In one corner, I saw a large paper press, and a clothes-line and boards for drying paper. If it hadn't been for the class Mattie and I took together, I wouldn't have known what all this equipment was used for. It was obvious that Mattie had gotten into papermaking in a big way.

But that was just about all that was obvious. Caroline said she hadn't given the studio a careful search, but since somebody else had (Mattie's blackmail victim, presumably, who might also have been Mattie's killer), it seemed important. So Ruby and I spent the next couple of hours going through everything—all the supplies, equipment, and finished pieces of paper art. Not knowing what we were looking for certainly made the job harder, but we did our best. We searched the work table, the shelves, and all the flat drawers where Mattie had kept sheets of paper, pulled out now, and the contents disordered. On one wall hung a number of paper sculptures, framed and mounted behind glass. On another wall hung half a dozen framed collages, creatively constructed of handmade papers and paper objects such as theater tickets, torn photos, torn pieces of maps, newspaper clippings, scraps of sheet music, calendars, bits of cloth, and the like. Each was organized around a theme, and titled: *The Opening, Sisters, Landscapes, Feels Like Home.*

We discovered our first clue on that wall. I took down one of the framed collages and, out of curiosity, turned it over. On the back, to my surprise, I saw another collage. Like the one on the front, it was also made up of artistically-arranged scraps of paper and bore a title: *Fragments of a Life I.* So it was the first of a series. As I looked closer, I thought

I recognized a photo that had been torn out of the Pecan Springs newspaper, the *Enterprise*, and incorporated into the design. I blinked and looked again.

"Ruby," I said urgently. "Come here."

"What have you got?" she asked, stepping around the table. "Something interesting?"

I held up the collage. "Who's this?"

Ruby frowned at it. "Isn't that Alice Mason?" she asked in surprise. She peered closer. "And what's that, China? It looks like . . . like part of an obituary, out of the newspaper. Why, it is! Alice Mason's obituary."

Alice Mason, a pretty (if ditzy) thirty-something librarian at the Pecan Springs Public Library, had been found dead the year before—strangled with her own panty hose, her body dumped in a secluded area a few miles outside of town. There'd been an unexpected jolt when the autopsy report came back, for Alice (who had never been married) was three months pregnant.

Alice's murder had not been solved, which was one source of the City Council's discontent with our chief of police. In fact, Sheila and I had talked about the case just a couple of weeks before. She had told me that she knew who had committed the crime—a prominent local person whom she refused to name. But because the person was so well known in the community, the D.A. insisted on having more evidence before he would take the case to the grand jury. She was still pursuing the case, but the investigation was running out of steam.

"There's a piece of a handwritten letter in the corner," I said. "Hand me that magnifying glass, Ruby."

A moment later, Ruby and I were staring openmouthed at one another. The handwritten scrap appeared to be part of a torn love letter, written in a delicate hand on pink paper. All that was visible was part of the concluding sentence . . . *love you with all my heart and long for you every moment. Yours until death, Alice.*

"I don't understand," Ruby said, scowling. "What's this

supposed to mean, China? Why would Mattie Long make a collage out of Alice Mason's obituary?"

Why, indeed? Unless—

"Maybe there's more," I said.

I took down the next collage and looked on the back. Yep, there it was. This one was titled *Fragments of a Life II*. It was made up of another photo—this one looking as if it had been clipped out of the high school yearbook—and an overdue slip from the Pecan Springs Library, with Alice's initials on it, and a stamped number. The borrower's number, I guessed. There was another scrap of the same love letter . . . *will always remember last night, and our kisses and your lips on my throat* . . . And there was also something that looked like part of a prescription, with Alice's name on it, written in those illegible squiggles that doctors use so you won't know what they're instructing the pharmacist to sell you.

"A *prescription?*" Ruby squeaked. "What in the world—"

Yeah. What in the world. I reached for the third collage. This one was called *Fragments of a Life III*. It contained part of a patient's record, with Alice's name at the top. And a casual snapshot of a smiling doctor, taken in his office. The photo was pasted partly over another clipping of Alice's obituary.

I stacked the three framed collages on the table. "Stay here and keep an eye on these," I said. "I'll be right back."

"But . . . but where are you going?" Ruby spluttered.

"To phone Sheila," I said shortly. "I think we've uncovered something she's been looking for. And maybe Mattie's murderer can be brought to justice without dragging Caroline into it."

"WELL, ARE YOU satisfied?" I asked.

"Not exactly," Sheila said glumly. She leaned against the counter in Ruby's shop. "But it saved the cost of the trial."

If you've met Sheila Dawson, you know that she does not look like your standard-issue police woman. No. She looks more like a Dallas deb in full bloom, or a Junior Leaguer on her way to the Alumnae Tea. Today, she was wearing her Monday-go-to-council-meeting garb: a pale yellow blazer over a creamy silk blouse. Her ash-blond hair was pulled back sleekly, and there were pearl earrings in her shell-like ears and a pearl necklace around her swan-like throat. If you didn't know that she was a blackbelt in karate, you'd never in the world guess.

"What?" Ruby asked in surprise. She put down the crystal ball she had been polishing. The shelves in Ruby's shop are full of things like crystal balls and magic wands and Tarot cards. "I would have thought you'd be happy to see Weaver put away."

"She'd be happier if there hadn't been a plea bargain," I said.

"Yeah." Sheila shrugged. "But I'll take what I can get. At least he's off the streets. For quite a while, actually."

Shortly after we'd discovered the three telltale collages, the grand jury had returned the indictment Sheila had been looking for. Two counts of capital murder against Dr. Richard Weaver, the prominent local gynecologist in whose office Mattie Long had worked for seven years. When all the plea-bargaining and legal bowing-and-curtseying was done, of course, the charges were somewhat less. That morning, Weaver had pled guilty to second-degree murder in the deaths of Alice Mason and Mattie Long. Judge Wooster, who is known in this county as a hanging judge, sentenced him to two twenty-year terms to be served consecutively. That was a surprise. Given the doctor's social position, everybody expected him to serve the sentences concurrently, with the probability of early parole. Maybe there's some justice in this world, after all.

Sheila looked from Ruby to me. "You know," she said, "I have a lot to thank you for. I could never have charged Weaver with the little I had—before you found those collages."

"Thank Mattie Long," Ruby replied. "She's the one who discovered that Weaver and Alice Mason were having an affair, and that Weaver had gotten her pregnant. And after Alice was murdered, she's the one who began putting the evidence together."

"Yes, but instead of taking her evidence to the cops, she cashed in on it," Sheila said darkly. "Definitely a no-no."

"But she paid," I said. "And a high price, too."

As part of the plea bargain, Dr. Weaver had been required to make a full confession. Mattie had indeed gathered evidence of his affair with Alice Mason—a couple of love letters, the record of her pregnancy—and assembled it in the form of the three collages we had found in her studio. She had made a photocopy of each collage and sent them to him, one at a time, with the promise to hand over the originals after he'd paid for them. But by the time the doctor had forked over sixty thousand dollars, he began to be afraid that Mattie would never be satisfied. On that fateful Monday night, he went to her studio and demanded that she hand over the originals. When she refused, he sent her tumbling down the stairs, where I found her when I went to look for Ruby's toilet paper.

"What about the blackmail money that Weaver paid?" Ruby asked. "Will Mattie's sister have to pay it back?"

"I doubt it," I said. "If Mattie were alive, of course, Sheila could arrest her on three counts of extortion. But she's dead. Her killer is in no position to demand that Caroline and her husband repay the money, and Mrs. Weaver isn't likely to want the negative publicity that would be stirred up by a lawsuit. Of course, I could be wrong. But I think Caroline's in the clear."

Sheila shouldered her Gucci bag and went to the door. "Thanks again, guys. Now I can tell the City Council to get off my back."

"Right," Ruby said with a laugh. "You can tell them that the Case of the Collage to Kill For has been solved."

I groaned. "Ruby, murder isn't funny."

"I know that, China," Ruby said indignantly. "But if we

can't have a *little* fun, life would be pretty bleak." She appealed to Sheila. "Wouldn't it, Smart Cookie?"

"You tell 'em, Ruby," Sheila said, and closed the door behind her.

§§

China Bayles's
Herbs & Flowers Paper Project

To make the mold, you'll need:

> fiberglass window screening, about 10" × 12"
> a wooden picture frame, about 8" × 10"
> staples or tacks

To make the pulp, you'll need:

> white or ivory paper napkins, or in other pastel colors
> white or pastel copy paper (with no printing)
> a blender
> water
> liquid starch (an optional sizing)
> a 1- or 2-quart pan
> rosemary leaves
> bits of fern
> tiny leaves of thyme, savory, southernwood
> petals from roses, marigolds, pansies, other small
>   blossoms

To make the paper, you'll need:

> a plastic dishpan, to serve as the vat
> 6 damp felts (12" × 14" pieces of light-colored felt or flannel fabric)
> a cookie sheet (on which to stack the post of felts and paper)

a damp sponge
a second cookie sheet (to press the post)

Instructions

1. **To make the mold**, stretch the fiberglass screening over the wooden frame and staple or tack it as tightly as possible.

2. **To make the pulp**, tear the napkins and paper into small pieces, enough to fill the blender about half full. Add warm water to within about 2" of the top. Start the blender at a slow speed, then increase the speed until the pulp is smooth and well blended, and you can no longer see bits of unblended material. If you are making writing paper, stir in 2 teaspoons of liquid starch. (The sizing helps to keep the ink from bleeding into the paper fibers.)

3. **To add the decorative materials**, remove stems from petals and leaves, and keep separate. Bring a quart of water to boil. Add petals and blanch for five minutes. Strain. Add both petals and leaves to the pulp and stir gently.

4. Pour the pulp out of the blender into the vat (the dishpan). Repeat this process twice more, until you have the contents of three blenders in the vat. Now, add enough warm water to fill the vat about three-quarters full. Stir this *slurry* with your hands to mix, and add more water or more pulp to make it the right consistency. Remember, the thicker the slurry, the thicker your paper will be.

5. **To create a sheet of paper**, pick up the mold by the short sides, holding it with the mesh side up. Dip the mold into the pulp-filled vat, at about a 45-degree angle. Scoop it under the surface of the pulp. Straighten it, then lift it steadily out of the slurry. This step should take just a few seconds. You're aiming to get a smooth, fairly thin layer of

pulp on top of the mold. If you're not satisfied, turn the mold over and slap it so that the pulp falls into the slurry—a process called *kissing off*. If the sheet looks okay, shake the mold left to right and back to front. (Pretend you're panning for gold.) The shaking locks the pulp fibers together and produces a smooth, uniformly thick sheet of paper. Shake until the water has drained and the fibers start to mat together. You may want to kiss off several times, until you get the hang of it.

6. **To couch the paper**, lay a damp felt on the cookie sheet. When the mold stops dripping, place one long edge of the mold on the felt, with the wet sheet of paper facing the felt. Gently lay the mold flat, so that the paper is lying directly on the damp felt. With the damp sponge, block the back of the mold to take up the excess water. (Wring it from the sponge back into the large plastic tub.) Then hold down on one edge of the mold, and slowly lift the other. The wet sheet of paper should remain on the felt. If it sticks to the mold, you may not have pressed out enough water, or you may have pulled up the mold too quickly. (Again, this takes a little practice.) Place another damp felt on top of the sheet of paper.

7. **To make additional sheets of paper**, stir the pulp with your hands and repeat from Step 5 above. If the first sheet of paper seemed too thick, add a little water. If the slurry begins to get thin by the time you've made your last few sheets of paper, you'll need to make more pulp. Stack the sheets of paper and the felts on top of one another as you work. (This is called the *post*.) Save the last damp felt for the top of the post.

8. **To press the paper,** carry the cookie sheet outdoors, or put it in the bathtub, so that you don't

have a mess to clean up. Then use the second cookie sheet to press the remaining water out of the post.

9. **To dry the paper,** gently separate the paper from the felts. The paper can be dried by draping it over a clothesline, or it can be laid flat on sheets of newspaper.

10. **To reuse your pulp,** dump the slurry out of the vat into a colander, or onto your mold, and let it drain. To save the pulp, put it into a plastic bag and freeze it, or roll it into small balls and let them air dry. Caution: don't pour pulp down the sink unless you like to clean clogged drains.

Please remember that papermaking is not a precise, closely engineered process. (If you want completely smooth paper with crisp edges and even coloration, buy it from the stationery store!) And there's no one right way to make a sheet of paper, just as there is no one right way to make a garden. The fun is in the experimentation. So experiment, play, admire your work — and above all, enjoy!

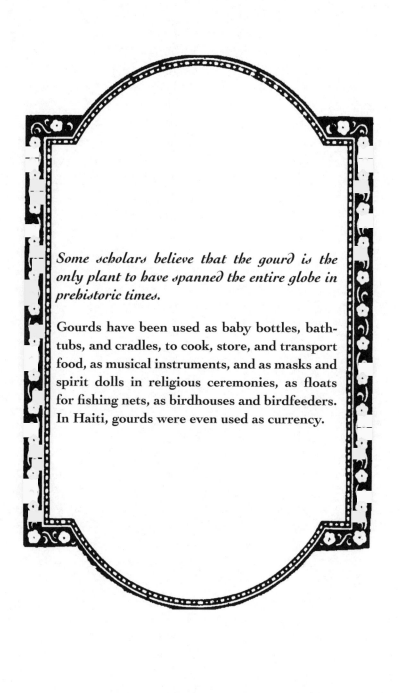

Some scholars believe that the gourd is the only plant to have spanned the entire globe in prehistoric times.

Gourds have been used as baby bottles, bathtubs, and cradles, to cook, store, and transport food, as musical instruments, and as masks and spirit dolls in religious ceremonies, as floats for fishing nets, as birdhouses and birdfeeders. In Haiti, gourds were even used as currency.

THE GOURD, THE BAD, AND THE UGLY

by Maggie Bruce

Maggie Bruce discovered decorated gourds on a trip through Kentucky, Tennessee, and North Carolina, and has spent many happy hours learning the craft and the art of working with gourds. In The Gourdmother, *the first Lili Marino mystery, Lili moves from Brooklyn to Walden Corners, and discovers that football, land disputes, and racial prejudice can be a deadly combination.*

ॐ

HE WAS GORGEOUS, and I was disheveled. Not a great way to make a good first impression, and letting my mouth hang open at the sight of his dark eyes and a smile that would brighten Finland in January was not going to change that. I stood my ground in the doorway and resisted the temptation to ask him to fast-forward about an hour so that I could shower and put on some mascara and a clean shirt.

"Yes, I'm Lili Marino. Have we met, Mr. Van Krief?" As though I might forget that face, and the warmth in his voice when he said my name.

"Oh, I'd remember if we had. Please, call me Leo. No, we've never met and I have to tell you that it took a little detective work for me to find you." Leo Van Krief flashed a dimple and shook his head, sending ripples through the thick waves of his gold-blond hair.

Why had this man taken the trouble to drive to the tiny

town of Walden Corners, make a left past the auto body shop, and climb the hill to my dirt road? I was suddenly acutely aware that no cars had driven past my cottage since his sleek blue Jaguar pulled up. I scanned the road for a sign that someone might be headed in my direction. It was a dry day, and a dust cloud would hover in the wake of a car braving the half-mile of unpaved road. Nothing hovered.

"I don't mean to be rude but I have . . . an appointment in fifteen minutes." Looking like this? Who did I think I was fooling?

"Okay, but I've come up from the city to see you. You're a craftsman, yes?"

I'd play. I nodded my assent.

"And that means you can reproduce something you've made before. You learn techniques of working with materials, you develop certain designs, and they're yours so you can do them over and over. Isn't that right?"

Wherever this was going, I couldn't stand here nodding like a bobble head. And an unkempt one at that. "Not really. No two gourds are exactly the same. I can make something similar but not exactly like one I've done before. Why do you—"

"You're the person who made this, right?" He pulled a photograph from his jacket pocket and passed it to me. The color image showed a small cannonball gourd decorated with one of my Native American motifs.

My heart thudded to a stop and I leaned against the doorway for support. I gathered my wits and said, "Why do you—"

"So you can make me one just like it, right?" Van Krief reached into the Dean & DeLuca shopping bag at his feet and pulled out a foam-wrapped object. His shapely fingers peeled back the tape, rolled away the foam, and steadied the gourd that sat nestled on the cushion. "I'll pay you, of course. But I need it in a hurry. I want to give it to a friend who saw the original and fell in love with it. So, can you do it? By tomorrow?"

My tension exploded into laughter. Of course. It was simple. The other person who had come here three days earlier and asked me to duplicate the same gourd was also a friend of the recipient-to-be.

"I'm sorry," I said, restraining the impulse to reach up and smooth his furrowed brow. "I don't want to spoil things for you. I thought you should know that I just finished making that same gourd for someone else. She picked it up three days ago."

His mouth opened, but nothing came out. He closed it, swallowed hard, and finally said, "A young woman with a Spanish accent? Ella? Ella Walsh?"

I nodded.

Color drained from Leo's face and his chest rose with a rapid intake of breath. I wanted to slap him on the back, dislodge the shock, perform an emotional Heimlich maneuver, but he regained his voice and said, "Perfect. That's really perfect. She thinks she can . . . Never mind."

Never mind? Was I supposed to not mind his confusion or his anger or the request to make another gourd? I was losing patience, no longer entertained by watching Leo prowl my porch in all his agitated feline grace. He stopped in front of me, and nodded once, as though he had made a decision and was confirming it to himself.

"My friend will love it that both of us thought of this," he said, his voice a little too loud. "Can you have it ready by tomorrow? You show me those new gourds and I'll pick one. But I also want an exact replica of this. I'll come by at ten tomorrow. It will be ready, right?"

"I really need two full days. I have to burn the design, apply the color, then wait twenty-four hours before I spray it with a fixative. If I don't, the colors might run."

"And the hole in the bottom. It has to have the hole in the bottom."

To duplicate the original, I would have to drill a quarter-inch-diameter hole in the bottom. I almost never did that, but I'd been playing around, creating sculptures with gourds, and had made the hole so that the gourd would rest on a stick. The whole enterprise turned out to be terrible art and no fun to boot, so I'd recycled the gourd with its holey bottom.

"Of course. Hole in the bottom." Or in my head for trying to rush this to fit his timetable. "Except, I really need more time. Thursday would be better."

"I need it for tomorrow." His beautiful face turned crimson. His voice dropped, and he leaned against the porch rail, hands in his pockets, the picture of nonchalance. "You're good. I know you can do magic, yes? Don't forget to show me the new ones you mentioned, too. I have the perfect place for one in my American crafts collection. Please say you'll do it."

As much of a sucker for dimples as I might be, the thought of a New York City collector being interested in my work was more seductive, as was the idea that I'd be a couple of hundred dollars better off by this time Wednesday.

"Okay, I'll do my best."

Leo Van Krief hugged me, and not in a brotherly way. He stepped back and looked into my eyes. "Thanks. I really appreciate this."

My warning flags were still fluttering as I shook his hand and then turned and pushed open the screen door. By the time I'd reached my workroom, the Rock Hudson–Doris Day scene I'd imagined had faded to black. First of all, what woman wants to be with a man who's prettier than she is? And, second, I got the feeling there was no "there" there. Just a slick surface, no heart, no messy longings or unsettling imaginings, not even any corny jokes or vehement opinions.

I stared at the photograph and then at the gourd. This was a fairly simple design, one that I'd done twice and would be able to reproduce fairly quickly. The gourd Leo had brought with him was the same size, and very nearly the same shape—round like the cannonball it was named for, but with a flatness at the bottom that allowed it to sit on a surface without rolling away. But it wasn't the same. This one had a slight bulge at the blossom end, a tiny declaration of difference that drew my fingertips to it. As much as I tried to explain that one of the things I love about working with gourds is that they're each unique, that they have personalities even before I do a thing to them, people who aren't familiar with them often give me that *whatever* look and then change the subject.

As I always do when I start a new gourd, I held it first, loving the smooth, hard surface, the surprising lightness, the pleasing roundness. With a soft pencil, I drew the lines for the design, then selected the fine-tipped stylus and turned on the woodburner. As soon as the hot tip touched the gourd surface, the unmistakable smell of charred gourd shell put me immediately into something akin to a trance state. Time didn't matter, bills didn't exist, and strange requests weren't bothersome.

For a while.

As I worked, Leo Van Krief and his silky voice and his entitled manner kept intruding on my thoughts, colliding with memories of Ella Walsh, who talked about growing up in Buenos Aires when she came to collect the gourd I'd made for her. This was surely the strangest set of commissions I'd ever had.

After two hours, the design was done, and I got out the dyes and brushes and spent another hour applying color. Working with leather dyes is a lot like painting with watercolors. They run, they streak, and you learn to either control them or use the serendipitous results to create magical effects.

Still, by dinnertime the triplet gourd was finished and drying, and I ate some leftover chili before sitting down at the computer to work on a corporate report that was due in a week, and that would pay enough to keep me in groceries for five months. It had taken a while to put the pieces together, but somehow, out of a near disaster of a love affair and a job that had been sucking the soul out of me, I had created a life I loved. I felt virtuous, but more than that, I was content.

*   *   *

AS PROMISED, THE gourd was ready at ten on Wednesday, and Leo Van Krief took it and a carved dipper, paid me more than I'd asked for, and then drove off in a receding swirl of gray-brown dust that turned to clay an hour later in a spring downpour that threatened to go on forever and ended up lasting four solid days. It rained so much I was afraid my asparagus would drown. It rained so much I was sure the field mice and the chipmunks would start building rafts and pairing up. With no chance to distract myself in the garden, half my daylight hours were filled with contacting potential clients to keep my freelance writing business afloat. The rest of the time I rewarded myself by starting new gourd designs. I ate when I felt like it, which was about every two hours, so mostly it was celery stuffed with peanut butter, hardboiled eggs, and the occasional adventure into bread making.

By Sunday, twinges of springtime cabin fever had erupted into a burning desire for actual human contact rather than merely the virtual kind. I decided to head for The Creamery.

Little ponds had sprouted in the café's driveway. The rain, gentler now, plinked into the puddles like tears. I tossed a glance at the leaky sky, then picked my way along the dry spots to the steps leading to the café, drawn by the brightness of the lights. Inside, three of the six tables were occupied by people I didn't know. My friend Nora stood at the counter, her back to me. Her bright red purse was slung atop a newspaper on an empty chair, and I sat down at the table and waited. One of the nice things about living alone is not having to engage in chatter when what you really crave is silence. Which, turned around the other way, is exactly the same as one of the sad things. Today, I was eager for a little harmless gossip, conversation about where a pal had been, who was there, what was said.

Nora's double take was followed by a huge smile as she made her way to the table. "Hey, you snuck in here!"

"Sneaked. I think the preferred usage is sneaked."

"Anyway, you're a nice surprise. I've been trying to come up with some way to keep my pies from turning into soggy bogs, but in this weather nothing works."

In high summer season, Nora, a former colonel in the army, exercised her perfectionism in her pies. She sold forty a weekend to the café, who then resold them to weekenders who kept trying to entice her into moving one hundred miles south to New York City so she could sell to high-priced food markets.

"Just make little cards that say that the pies should be popped into the oven for twelve minutes to crisp the crust."

"Twelve. Not ten. Brilliant. Makes me sound like a stickler." Her eyes narrowed. "I can even do it on my printer on those nerbly little cards. Thanks. You still working on that corporate report?"

"Four more pages and I can pay for my car insurance. I just needed a time-out."

Nora sighed and sipped her tea. "Wouldn't it be nice if someone plopped a million dollars into your lap? If only. What would you do?"

"Africa." I surprised myself with the answer, but my head swam with pictures of trees whose names I didn't know, with golden grasses waving in a breeze along rolling savannahs, with colors bleached by dry air and relentless sun.

"That should be my line. Check out the old country. So to speak." Nora's dark brown fingers grasped the white arm of the chair and she pulled herself to the edge of the seat, back erect and neck elongated. "Did I ever tell you that I'm of royal blood? The Princess of Zimbabwe, except that's not what it was called when my great great greats were taken away."

"Only a hundred times, Your Highness. So, if either of us wins a million dollars, we could go together. To Africa.

You'd look up the royal relatives, and I'd go visit all the calabash artists." Time, I thought. All that money would buy me a lot of time.

"I imagine we'd both enjoy it if a million dollars fell out of the sky." Her purely joyful laugh made the bespectacled man at the next table lower his newspaper and frown at her.

I laughed along with my optimistic friend. "Maybe if a wad of bills hit you on the head, it would knock some sense into you."

"I have sense enough to know I have to get back to my kitchen. Call me if you want to come to that auction tomorrow." Nora gathered her things, tossing the Metro section of the *New York Times*, which had been hidden beneath her purse, onto the table. I was about to throw it into the pile near the door when I noticed two familiar faces smiling out in black-and-white.

Leo Van Krief and Ella Walsh, along with a third man identified in the caption as Cliff Westwood, all lined up in what appeared to be a reception area. A sign behind them announced their names. To Leo's left, in a glass case, an object that looked like my gourd gleamed under a spotlight.

My chest nearly puffed with pride . . . until I read the headline above the photograph.

I shivered. After I forced myself to read it a second time, the shiver turned into a full body tremble.

"Architect Dies in Suspicious Accident," the headline screamed.

Oh, this was bad. Dreadful, in fact. Gourd pride vanished as I tried to catch my breath and force my eyes to focus on the words.

"What's wrong, Lili?" Nora's voice startled me, and I nearly jumped out of the chair. She scooted her chair next to mine and held one corner of the newspaper as she read. "You know him? Sorry. Wow, brakes failed . . . possibility of foul play . . . investigation underway . . . That's awful."

I scanned the article, my stomach clenching. Cliff Westwood was driving north on the FDR Drive in Manhattan

and apparently lost control of the car on the wet road when
his brakes failed.

Leonard Van Krief and Ella Walsh, partners of the deceased, were in shock over the accident, and over the investigator's assertion that someone had tampered with
Westwood's brakes.

The architecture firm, the news report stated, had floun-
dered in recent years but had postponed filing for bankruptcy because they had hopes of getting the bid on a new
performing arts center in Brooklyn. Mr. Westwood and Ms.
Walsh were the principal architects on that project.

A private funeral would take place on Tuesday, and the
memorial service for Mr. Westwood was to be held on
Thursday.

"How awful," I managed to croak out. "These people . . .
I saw them last week. I mean, they came to order gourds, I
mean . . ."

Nora bent down and hugged me. "Oh, Lili, I'm so sorry.
To lose a friend. That's terrible. No wonder you're so upset."

"Friend?" I pulled back, trying to calm my breathing
and slow the tumble of anxious confusion that clamored in
my head. "I never met the man who died."

*But his partners had each ordered identical gourds from me. Just
days before he died.* "See that gourd?" I stabbed at the picture.
"Those two partners each came to my house, *to my house,* all
the way from the city. Separately. Three days apart. And
they each had a photograph of that gourd and asked me to
make an exact duplicate. What do you think that's about?"

"What did they tell you?" Nora asked in her usual direct
fashion.

"That it was to be a surprise gift for someone who had
seen the original and really liked it. Leo was surprised to
hear that he wasn't the first to have the idea. I wonder if
Cliff is the one they had me make the gourds for," I mused.
"There's something fishy in the state of New York, and my
gourds are involved."

"I see that glint in your eye, Lili Marino. You've spent

too much time alone in that little house and now you're imagining things. You're bored? Write a corporate report. Rob a bank. Do not let that Sicilian blood get all excited over nothing, you hear me?"

Her words helped me cool the heat I'd inherited from my father, Dave Marino, to downright tepid. But it was my mother Ruth's genetic contribution that began to surface, a rabbinical drive for truth that made it impossible for me to let questions go once they presented themselves to me. The question wasn't how many angels could dance on the head of a pin; it was how many identical gourds it took to justify a suspicion that Leo Van Krief and Ella Walsh were the foul players.

The partners had been working on a new project, and they wanted to cut Cliff out of it. No, that didn't work. What good would it do to bump off the golden goose? Okay, the company insured all the partners and each would get a piece if the other died, and with Cliff gone, Ella and Leo would share in the proceeds.

Maybe, but what did that have to do with gourds?

The hole in the bottom—someone, Cliff perhaps, had hidden something in the gourd, and Leo and Ella were planning to play Three-Gourd Monte. Leo made it a point to ask about the hole. Ella had made me go back and put it in. But what was it that could fit inside a half inch-hole in a gourd that would be worth killing for?

"I'm driving down to New York City in two days to meet a corporate client anyway," I reasoned to my unreasonably cautious friend, "so I might as well drop in for the memorial service. Of course, the article says it's private. But maybe I can figure out a way to get invited."

Nora leaned in close and whispered, "I know I won't talk you out of this. So, as long as you're going anyway, you should watch their eyes. If someone looks up and to the left when he's saying something, that means he's lying. My Granny Ethel taught me that."

Her eyes were looking straight into mine when she passed along that bit of advice.

THE SKY GLITTERED like blue diamonds, the breeze was cool on my skin, and the quirky Tribeca shops gleamed in the springtime freshness. I walked down Hudson Street, peering nostalgically into store windows, watching the glorious variety of people, taking in the to-ing and fro-ing of New York City that was no longer part of my everyday life.

A tiny little squib in the newspaper that morning had said police had determined that Cliff Westwood's brake line had been deliberately cut. Why? Who wanted to kill an architect in a firm that was fending off bankruptcy?

Lost in my musings, I nearly walked past the storefront that housed Van Krief, Walsh and Westwood. But when I looked into the window, I stopped so short the man behind me, a bearded fellow with an eyebrow ring and a lizard tattoo running from his left ear down into his shirt, nearly plowed into me.

There, on a pedestal in a glass case that swam in a pool of buttery light, sat . . . nothing. No gourd graced the spot in which it had appeared in the newspaper photo. The case was empty. Nora's warning to stay away blared like a loudspeaker in my head, but I turned down the volume and pushed the door open.

Praying that Leo Van Krief or Ella Walsh wouldn't walk into the office, I cleared my throat. In seconds, a woman materialized from the dark hall, exuding an air of bored menace that reminded me of the *caribinieri* in the airport in Rome. She pushed her horn rims up on her nose, and said, "We're closing in ten minutes. Everyone's going to the memorial service."

"Oh," I stammered, "that's why I'm here. I lost my employer's announcement. You know Mr. Trump, he'll kill me. Do you think you could give me another one?"

Her eyes flitted over me, and then she started sticking stamps onto envelopes. "I have to get this mailing out and then go supervise the caterer. They already messed up. Brie. *Nobody* serves brie anymore. What about the manchego I ordered? I said. Next thing you know, they'll tell me they're serving seared tuna instead of dry-rubbed spare ribs."

I almost smiled at the thought that I'd been away from New York City long enough for the food fashions to change, but I caught myself in time. A memorial service was a solemn event, no matter how the spare ribs were prepared.

She peeled another stamp from the roll, and as she reached out for another envelope the entire pile of letters, about fifty in all, slid to the floor in a blizzard of white. The receptionist sucked air in through her teeth and pressed her hands to her forehead.

"Here, let me help with that." I knelt and gathered envelopes, not altogether altruistic in my offer. "I'm sure it will work out. It's good they have you to keep things on an even keel around here. Mr. Van Krief and Ms. Walsh must be so upset."

"Upset," she said scornfully. "That lady, she must think she's Evita, being from Argentina and all that. Which she thinks gives her the right to throw a tantrum. Over a foolish gourd."

Foolish gourd? Indignation nearly propelled me out the door, but the receptionist's next words stopped me.

"Him, too. Leo is usually so nice to me. But him? Yelled louder than she did when he saw the gourd was gone. Fourteen million dollars. He kept yelling those words over and over. Fourteen million dollars. What's so special about that thing, that's what I want to know." She slapped a stamp on another envelope. "The day poor Cliff died, too. You'd think they would . . . anyway, it was gone, and Leo was furious. Fourteen million dollars, that's what he kept shouting."

My gourds were good, but not *that* good.

Confused, I gathered two more envelopes that had slid under the desk. Whatever was hidden in the gourd was worth fourteen million dollars. I put stamps on the envelopes and looked at the receptionist. "That gourd, do you know where it is?"

"It was Mr. Westwood's. And he kept it locked in that case. And he had the only key." Irritably, she swatted the air with her hand. "He was a true gentleman. And now I'll never know."

Never know what? In her anger and anxiety, she was rambling. I might as well have been a doorknob. Or a *foolish* gourd. I peeled another stamp off the backing and stuck it on an envelope.

"He told me, 'Watch the television news, Milly. Friday the ninth.' I asked him which news, which network, and you know what he said? 'Any news. Next Friday.' Man died in that awful accident before I could find out what he meant." The last envelope flapped in the air as she fanned herself. "That's tomorrow. I like Sue Simmons. I'll watch Channel Four. I have to get out of here. That service has to start right at two."

"The address?" I asked.

The receptionist waved a small card in the air and held it out to me. "Pellegrino," she said. "They better have my Pellegrino."

"Thanks." I offered my sad-gracious smile as I glanced down at the card. The creamy, heavy stock announced that the wake for Cliff Westwood would be held at the Building Trades Union Hall, which had been designed by Ella Walsh, at two o'clock.

Ms. *Caribinieri* grimaced and muttered, "Whatever," before she hurried past me and held the door open, waiting for me to leave.

I roused myself and stepped outside, shocked back to my senses by the street noises. Why did Cliff Westwood tell the receptionist to watch the news this Friday? Where was the gourd that had occupied the place of honor in the glass display case? And, most important of all, what did any of this have to do with the accident that killed poor Mr. Westwood?

Maybe at the memorial service I'd learn enough so that the police wouldn't consider me a delusional country bumpkin wasting their time with talk about gourds and dead men.

THE CROWD MILLED about the wide lobby in clusters that seemed to be divided according to shoe style. The low-heeled crowd, mostly older and well-coifed, bent heads toward each other near the spiral staircase that led to a balcony, while the stilettos and sandals nodded and exchanged hushed confidences near the tall windows opening onto a courtyard featuring a huge granite wall down which blue-tinted water cascaded. Loafers huddled in groups of eight or nine, while the wing tips snagged wineglasses from the trays carried by two young women who were probably interns from Cooper Union.

Milly, the receptionist, fluttered around the damask-covered tables, straightening napkins and looking generally worried.

I stood in the doorway until I made out the mane of golden hair and followed my gaze to Leo Van Krief's pale face. Leo stood surrounded by beautiful women and a lone man in a pastel shirt, all nodding and paying the kind of attention that I thought only Bill Clinton could command. He smiled graciously, glancing around the room every once in a while to see who was watching him. When he spotted me, his eyes looked up and to the left. What, I wondered, would Nora's granny make of that?

In the corner, Ella Walsh, her dark hair pulled into a demure bun, was being handed a champagne flute by a white-haired gentleman sporting an ascot and a concerned, patrician air.

I heard whispers about the closed casket, the damage to Cliff Westwood's face from the impact, the genuine regard for his work. The whole scene made me itchy. What was I doing, intruding on their grief? This was not about gourds and tricks of craftsmanship but a personal gathering to mourn the loss of a human being. Ashamed that I'd brought my suspicions here, I was about to try to thread my way to the door when a woman bumped into me.

"Oh, I'm sorry." She blinked several times, her translucent skin wrinkling around the corners of her blue eyes. A cloud of baby powder wafted toward me, and I grabbed at her elbow to steady her. "I'm not usually so clumsy. I guess I'm just . . ." Her voice trailed off.

"No, no problem. Are you all right?" I steered her toward a chair, and she followed without protest as I pressed her gently to the seat. "Can I get you some water?"

She shook her head, gray curls bouncing. "I'm fine. I was just thinking he would be here today if not for . . . Oh, dear. He decided to quit the business a year ago, turn it over to the other partners, but they said he couldn't leave a sinking ship." She sniffled and dug into her pocket for a white, lace-trimmed handkerchief.

That *he.* Cliff Westwood. Completely abject now about the fraud I'd been in coming here, I patted her hand. "I'm sorry for your loss," I murmured.

But she didn't seem to hear me. "They said that he had to stay around and help get the business back on its feet, even though those two were the ones who . . . But just the other day, he told me that he'd waited long enough. That it had taken almost a year, but he'd prepared the harbor and his ship was coming in. That's what he said. And he told them that he was going to his lawyer in Westchester to get the dissolution papers. Imagine that, married to the man for thirty-six years and I'm to blame for . . ."

My heart wrenched at the depth of her pain and the power of her misplaced guilt. Entirely sure that this nice woman's husband had been murdered by his business partners, and completely uncertain about why, I kept my focus on Mrs. Cliff, who seemed to need to talk, even if I was a stranger. Maybe, especially because I was a stranger.

"If he had left on time, he wouldn't have been in such a rush. You know how it is some mornings, dear. You wake up

all warm and there's this lovely man beside you. Cliff and I
got to snuggling and then, well, we got so we forgot the
time, and oh, it was lovely, after thirty-six years, you know
we do have a little practice, but it's still so magical to be
with a man who wants to . . . oh, dear, you must think me
terrible to be telling you all this at my own husband's wake,
but you seem to be such a nice person. I wish I could take
that morning back." Her pale, lined cheeks flushed with
color, and she dabbed at her eyes.

"Please, Mrs. Westwood, you mustn't blame yourself."
She must have known about the police report concerning
the tampered brakes, but this wasn't the time to bring up
facts. "Can I get you something?"

She shook her head. "Maybe I'd better sit down. The service is going to start soon. I'd better find Milly. She promised to sit next to me."

I led her to another seat and slipped out as quietly as I
could and headed into the sunshine. I could suspect from
now until Thanksgiving—unless I could come up with
something more tangible than an anxious flutter in my
stomach and three identical gourds, I would sound like I'd
inhaled too many fixative fumes if I tried to explain to anyone else.

Maybe, I thought, I should go over to the First Precinct,
just a couple of blocks away, and tell them everything I
knew and let *them* figure it out.

The receptionist's story about Cliff telling her to watch
the news on Friday was odd. The three identical gourds
were odd. Leo's reaction to seeing me at the wake was odd.
Mrs. Westwood's talk of Cliff's ship coming in was oddest of
all, but still, zero plus nil added up to nothing.

LIKE THE SERENDIPITY of applying colors to gourds, it
sometimes takes just the right piece of information to make
sense of a puzzle, and that piece came to me three hours later
as I watched the local news in my friend Joyce's apartment.

I was staring at the screen, not really paying attention until the local anchor, a woman with too many teeth, said something that brought me out of my daze.

"Fourteen million dollars, folks. One more day, that's all that's left. If no one comes forward with the winning lottery ticket by tomorrow, the prize money goes back into the pot. So if you're out there, you have thirty hours left to claim your fourteen million dollar prize."

Fourteen million dollars.

The famous unclaimed lottery ticket. It had been on the news last summer. Fourteen million American dollars. Enough to keep Dave and Ruth in any kind of eggs for the rest of their lives. Enough to buy me centuries of time. Enough to kill for.

If Ella and Leo found out that Cliff had the winning ticket hidden away in a gourd for fifty-one weeks . . . if they planned to steal the gourd and substitute an empty gourd so that Cliff would be lulled into believing the ticket was safe . . . if they'd killed him to prevent him from protesting when they claimed the lottery ticket . . . if the gourd wasn't where they expected it to be after all that hard work and the lottery ticket still was not safely in their possession . . . then that sweet, distracted lady with the lace handkerchief might have it, and that would surely put her in danger.

I punched 911 on my cell phone as I rummaged for the program from the memorial service. There it was, a box outlined in black, asking that cards be sent directly to Maxine Westwood at an address on Franklin Street. I told the skeptical person who answered the phone that I had information about a murder and asked them to send a cop to Maxine Westwood's.

The thought that I might be the one to tell Cliff's wife about the gourd and the lottery ticket warmed me. Her widowhood would be a bit more manageable, at least the financial aspect of it, when she claimed all those millions of dollars.

I told the doorman that I had a package for Mrs. Westwood and then rode up in the slow-moving elevator and found apartment 3C and pressed the buzzer. Maxine Westwood, deep circles pouching her tired eyes, opened the door.

"Mrs. Westwood, I am so sorry to bother you at a time like this, but I have something important to tell you."

Gracious in her bewilderment, she motioned me inside. I followed her into a sunny room devoid of furniture, except for two well-worn leather recliners that faced a blank wall where I could imagine a big screen television sitting. The walls were bare, the floors were, too. The only other objects were lined up in melancholy array on the fireplace mantel: a clear glass vase, two reproduction Lladro statues, a blue and white jar with an arabesque lid, and a wood box with an intricate Art Nouveau design carved on its top. Not a single gourd in sight. Maxine Westwood sat primly, her hands folded in her lap. I wondered briefly if she was on some drug to help her get through the difficult first weeks of mourning, and I noticed a tremor in her cheek. My message seemed even more important, now that I saw her circumstances.

"This may sound strange," I began, "but do you know where your husband's decorated gourd is? The one that used to be in the office, I mean."

Maxine's features sharpened, as though responding to a sudden alert. "That gourd. He loved it. It was really special to him."

"There *is* something special about that gourd, Mrs. Westwood. It's—"

But she went on as though I wasn't even there. "It was his wish, he gave me the gourd the night before he left, the night before he . . . died. He said I shouldn't let anyone else have it. Well, he said not Leo and not Ella. God willing, it's with him now. I saw to that."

I tried to follow her meaning. "He's . . . you mean, the gourd is with him?"

She nodded, and I had a fleeting vision of Leo and Ella digging up the casket, frantically shoveling dirt until they hit the hard wood with a ping, scrabbling through the soil as their fingernails turned black and loamy.

"You mean, you buried the gourd with him?"

"Oh, yes," she said, her voice calm and clear. Having fulfilled his wish obviously brought her a measure of peace. "Well, no. I mean, it went into the casket with him, you see."

With a deep sigh, Maxine Westwood pushed out of her chair and walked to the fireplace.

"Mrs. Westwood, I have reason to believe that the gourd may be more important than you know. This may take a while to explain. Where is Mr. Westwood buried?"

She just shook her head.

I was afraid I was losing her, and I didn't quite know what to do. Should I bother her until she was forced to come out of her grief-induced fog and go through the unpleasant business of digging up her husband's casket to retrieve a lottery ticket worth approximately fourteen million dollars, but only if she could produce it by tomorrow? Walk away and leave her to her private feelings?

There was only one right answer.

"Mrs. Westwood, I'm really sorry to disturb you, but this is important. Can you tell me where your husband is buried?"

She shook her head again, and I realized that her gesture was meant to show me something. She ran her hand lightly over what I'd taken to be a blue and white ceramic apothecary jar.

"He's always right here with me. Cliff, his wedding suit, and the gourds," she said, patting the urn. "Just like he asked. It was the least I could do."

I wished her well and slipped out the door. Maxine Westwood would learn about her bad luck when Leo and Ella went to trial. That was time enough for her to join me in knowing that the words "up in smoke" would never again have quite the same meaning.

๛

Gourd Ornament

You can create your own gourd ornaments for special occasions with a few easily purchased supplies. Cleaned gourds are available in a dizzying variety of sizes and shapes at gourd festivals across the country or from online suppliers. For this project, I use nest egg gourds, which are, as the name implies, about the size of a large egg.

To make a hole in the top of the gourd to insert a hanger, I use a rotary tool, but an ordinary drill will do. A large "eye" of a hook-and-eye door latch works well. As you drill and as you insert the hook, take care not to squeeze too hard, or give up too soon. Gourds can be fragile; on the other hand some gourds have thick shells, and it may take a while to screw in the hook. Once the eye hook is inserted, it's time to decorate the gourd.

You can experiment with different kinds of color. Acylic paints will give rich, opaque coverage, while leather dyes produce a more translucent effect. Colored pencils, shoe polish, furniture polish, oil pastels—I've tried all of these and loved the results. Your design can be copied from a picture you like, traced from a template, or made up as you go along. Again, I've done all those things and each has made for a happy gourd day.

After you've applied the color, be sure to let it dry for at least twenty-four hours. Then, you can spray it with polyurethane or use a varnish to seal the color. Apply sealer lightly to avoid thick, globby bumps and ridges. Hang the ornament to dry, then add a loop of ribbon or chain, and *voila!* A gourd ornament that's unique and personal.

Yankee Doodle, who stuck a feather in his cap, wasn't calling it a type of noodle. Nor did he originate macaroni art by dyeing noodles and attaching them to his hat.

The song was sung by British soldiers in derision of the motley colonial troops they fought in the American Revolution. In the eighteenth century, an English macaroni was a dandy who affected Continental manners and dress, especially a fancy style of Italian clothing. As out of place with sophisticated dress as Irene Kelly is teaching a crafts session, the American colonists in the song were farouche fellows, bumpkins who considered themselves dressed up with a mere feather in their caps. But soon the song was picked up by the colonials themselves, and made into an anthem sung in a defiant spirit.

CALL IT MACARONI

by Jan Burke

Jan Burke is the Edgar®–award winning author of Bones *and ten other novels, including the standalone thriller* Nine, *a collection of short stories entitled* 18, *and, most recently,* Bloodlines. *Creator of newspaper reporter Irene Kelly, Jan was born in Texas and has lived in Southern California most of her life.*

§§

LET'S FACE IT: no one with a sibling believes in either nature or nurture. My sister looks too much like the Maguires—my mother's side of the family—for me to be certain that we have the same father, but alas, my parents were so devoted to each other, I can't bring myself to seriously entertain the notion that Barbara is related to a milkman. My search for adoption papers—hers or mine—never bore fruit, so I've come to believe that although each Kelly sister spent her childhood under the same roof and grew from zygotes created by the same gene donors, they were simply fated to be nearly polar opposites.

Which is not to say I don't love her. Or that I wouldn't try to help her out of a fix. She feels the same—one of the few things we have in common.

One recent Friday afternoon, she helped me out of a fix. My car was in the shop, my husband was at work, and I needed a ride home from the mechanic's. I was going to ask my neighbor for help, but Barbara called just as I was on my way over to his place. When I tried to excuse myself from talking to her by telling her about my errand, she offered her help instead.

In a momentary lapse of good judgement, I accepted. Life can go so wrong in mere seconds.

Started out okay. We were in separate cars, and she followed me without getting lost or rear-ending my car or forcing me to pull over more than once when she got stuck at a red light.

On the return trip, I was on my best behavior. She only had to toss her head a few times before I realized that she had new earrings—long silver twists, each with an emerald set at the end. I pretended to be suitably impressed. I cooed over her new Kate Spade bag. I did not make faces when she nattered on endlessly about the new Oriental rug that graced her living room, or when she smugly predicted that the "Crafts Ladies"—as the group of project enablers that meets at her house every so often calls itself—would admire and envy that purchase when they met at her house on Sunday. She was especially looking forward to the reaction of Elizabeth, who had apparently started something of a rug craze among the Crafts Ladies. Barbara did tell me not to be sarcastic when I said that I thought the Crafts Ladies ought to be hooking or weaving or otherwise making their own rugs.

As she talked about these women, I realized that there was a certain degree of mutual Jones-ism within the group: they tried to keep up with one another in the material goods department. Whatever one bought, two or three others went shopping for within a week. Elizabeth seemed to set the pace for Barbara. Elizabeth also had new earrings, and a new Kate Spade bag. I was tempted to tell Barbara that Elizabeth had taken a vow of silence, but I didn't think she'd believe me.

I reminded myself that she was doing me a favor, so I made my own little vow of silence and kept other comments to myself. I heard the latest news of Susan, Sally, Carol, Connie, Dina, Doris Ann, Margery, and Marianne—the Crafts Ladies. I barely managed to refrain from asking if they shouldn't invite someone named Bonnie to join them, so that Barbara could have a first-name-initial pal, then realized that Elizabeth probably went by Beth. That scared me into remaining silent when Barbara started singing "Reunited" to herself as she drove, a song which has become something of a personal anthem for her ever since her semi-ex-husband Kenny moved back in with her. It replaced "I Will Survive" and "I Am Woman," her favorites after the divorce. Fool that I am, I had left my iPod at home.

She stopped singing to tell me that the craft of the day on Sunday was going to be resin casting. The Crafts Ladies were going to make placeholders for dinner parties out of dried flowers and resin.

Let the record show that I didn't immediately lose my temper when, two blocks from my home, she turned in a direction that led away from it.

"Other way," I said.

"No, this is the right way. I just need to stop by Crafty Fox."

"Oh, no!" Really, it was almost an involuntary reaction.

"Don't make a fuss. It's on the way."

"We were on the way before you made that turn."

"I had to take this street to get to your house, didn't I?"

"Yes, the store is on this street," I said in exasperation, "but it's six miles in the opposite direction of the turnoff to my place."

"It's on the way now," she said, apparently referring to some special inner map that shows all roads leading to Barbara and what she wants, then added, "It will only take a minute." She has a special inner clock, too.

"When in your lifetime have you spent 'only a minute' in Crafty Fox?"

"It's not going to kill you to go with me. We're sisters. We should do things together once in a while."

"I thought you planned these group crafts projects out months in advance. You're just now buying supplies for Sunday's meeting?"

"Of course not!" she said, highly offended. "This is for two months from now."

I knew it was useless to point out that there was, therefore, a lack of urgency to make this trip now. I kept asking myself why I had ever mentioned to her that I needed a ride. Knowing how long it would take her to browse through the arts and crafts supply store, I realized I could have walked the ten miles from the mechanic's shop and been home sooner than I would be now that she had hijacked me for a shopping expedition.

I don't have anything against the Crafty Fox itself. I am not immune to its charms. When we walked in, I gazed about me in wonder: here were gimcracks and gewgaws out the yingyang.

I was in the modern equivalent of the medieval woman's witch's hut: everything for anything, and the knowledge that men really didn't approve of it. For the modern woman, it was a combination toy store, hardware store, and magic shop. It even smelled like an herbalist's place: fragrant soap-making crafts employing essential oils and dried flowers were enjoying a vogue. The resident sorceress and owner of the establishment was a friendly, charming woman whose nickname was Fox. Today she wore an awe-inspiring vest covered with hundreds of tiny buttons sewn into mosaic patterns of cavorting foxes.

It was she who cast a spell on all who entered.

The spell? It makes you say this to yourself. "I have the time, patience, and skill to complete any project. The process will be fun and frustration-free. Friends, neighbors, and total strangers who encounter the discreetly placed finished masterpiece in our home will eye it covetously and ask, 'Where did you buy this?' They will be amazed when I answer, 'I made it.'"

In Fox's store, I suddenly find myself wondering what the

bathroom would look like if the wastepaper basket was covered in a material that matched the curtains, the tissue box, the soap dispenser, and toothbrush holder. I think about how lovely it would be to present Frank with a sweater knitted from the eye-catching, soft yarn in certain bins. I envision creating endearing decoupage portraits of our pets. I imagine painting, in whimsical but attractive ways, figurines I have cast with my own hands, then setting them out in the garden to delight my guests. I think of sitting by the fire and cleverly plying my needle and colorful threads over an intricate and pleasing design held taut by a hoop.

Then reality rears its unfeminine head and grasps me in its clumsy fingers, and I am forced to accept that these fantasies are akin to those I used to have on the first day of every new school year. I never got straight A's or the good citizenship award, either.

I am, alas, not craft-enabled. One must face facts.

Barbara, on the other hand, enters pillows, jams, place settings—or whatever else she's into that year—in the county fair and wins ribbons for them.

Fox adores her, of course. After all, Barbara has started a coven of craft women who buy all their supplies at Fox's store. The nice thing about Fox is that on those rare occasions when I accompany her acolyte, she doesn't ignore me, even though I stopped buying crafts supplies years ago. It isn't because she thinks I'll write about her for the newspaper, either—she knows that in all my years as a reporter, I've never worked for the business section or features, or in any other department that might do a story about an establishment like hers.

After asking Barbara about the new rug, which told me that Barbara had been in the store fairly recently, she directed my sister toward the supplies for making something that involved big eggshells covered with tiny glass beads and ribbons—all very delicate, as I understood it. Barbara walked toward that aisle with the gait of a sleepwalker caught in an especially delightful dream.

Fox talked to me while Barbara wandered out of sight. So much for sisterly togetherness.

Fox was in the middle of a hilarious story involving an encounter between her dog and a skunk when Barbara yelled out, "Fox, do you have a ladder?"

"Yes, I'll be right with you."

I walked with her as she went toward an aisle on the other side of the store to fetch it. It was a big, rolling safety ladder, the kind that looks like a metal staircase on wheels. I squeezed past some boxes and got on the far side of the ladder to help her maneuver it. We had just started to roll it when I heard Barbara say "Uh-oh . . .". This was followed in quick succession by a tremendous crash, a scream of pain, a sharp thud, then silence. Fox and I stared at each other wide-eyed, then Fox ran toward Barbara. I squeezed out from behind the ladder and followed.

It was a lucky thing for me, but not for Fox, that I was second in this brief footrace, because I'm sure the same thing that happened to her would have happened to me. She turned the corner onto Barbara's aisle, hit some of the thousands of glass beads that were scattered all over the floor, and took a nasty fall.

In a Keystone Kops movie, at this point, everyone would have stood up brushed himself off, and climbed back on a racing paddy wagon. Nobody stood up. There wasn't anything funny at all about the sight before me.

Barbara lay passed out on the ground, very pale, and bleeding from her arm, which was broken in a way that almost made me lose my lunch. I glanced back at Fox, who was holding her ankle. "Never mind me!" she said. I pulled myself together, took out my cell phone, called 911, and followed instructions about my sister and her arm.

At some point during that short but seemingly interminable wait for help, I noticed that an emerald had been dislodged from one of Barbara's earrings. I mentioned it to Fox.

"It's probably among these beads somewhere," she said. "I'll sift through them for it when I get a chance to clean up."

FIVE HOURS LATER, I was driving Barbara's car away from the hospital and back toward the Crafty Fox. Frank— my husband—followed in his car. The doctor had decided to keep Barbara at the hospital overnight for observation. She had a bump on her head, a sprained ankle, a compound fracture of her right arm, and lots of bruises. I don't think she'll ever try the Darwin-Award-worthy bit of climbing up the shelves in the store again. Kenny, her semi-ex-husband, was still at her bedside when I left, and I have to admit he was being a comfort to her.

Fox's own fall had resulted in a broken ankle. I took her keys and drove Barbara's car back to the store, which I had hastily locked up before I followed the caravan of ambulances to the hospital. Frank, who's a homicide detective, helped me to do a few favors for Fox: we emptied the cash register and put the money into her safe, then put a note on the door saying that the store was closed but would reopen on Monday. "Do you know Betsy—Elizabeth?" Fox had asked me. "She's one of Lydia's Crafts Ladies. She sometimes covers for me so that I can have an extra day off or a week's vacation. She was upset to hear about my fall, but said she'd be free to help me out next week."

Frank and I also tried find the missing emerald, and told ourselves that although we failed at that, by sweeping up glass beads (which are the very devil to get out of seams in linoleum), we probably prevented other crafters from meeting their dooms in the beading aisle. I saved the beads and sweepings in a plastic grocery bag and put them in Fox's office, determined to come back and look through them again. We mopped up the bloodstains, which made me feel a wave of pity for Barbara. Then, following Fox's instructions, we set the alarm.

From the Crafty Fox, Frank followed me to Barbara's house so that I could drop her car off. From there, at long last, I got a ride home.

BARBARA CALLED AT the ungodly hour of seven on Saturday morning, screeching at me just after I said "Hello." She was on her cell phone. Kenny was taking her home. I managed to sort through the hysteria and figured out that she was in a panic because the Crafts Ladies were going to be at her house on Sunday. Although she would be home, she would be in no condition to lead the crafts group in embedded resin casting.

"So cancel it," I said.

You would have thought I had asked the Pope to cancel Easter. After a few minutes of half-listening to her rant, I found myself thinking that all this freaking out couldn't be good for someone with a head injury, which led me to say the fateful words: "Barbara, I'll do it for you. I'll come over to your house and welcome everyone and do the whole bit."

There was a promising moment of silence, then she said, "You can't."

"Sure I can. I don't have anything planned for tomorrow afternoon."

Frank, who was awake now, and listening to my half of the conversation, rolled his eyes, seeing our rare day off together going straight to hell.

"You'll have to come over today," Barbara said. "I'll try to teach you how to do it."

Glancing at Frank, I said, "I'm busy this morning, but I'll be by this afternoon."

Staying in bed with him a little longer turned out to be the only good idea I'd have for most of the rest of that day.

MY MULTIPLE ATTEMPTS to learn how to do embedded resin casting were unqualified disasters. Since each stage took twenty to thirty minutes, and there were four stages, I shot the whole day doing nothing but causing my sister to get more and more upset with me at two-hour intervals. If it wasn't trouble with air bubbles, the gel wasn't firm enough to support the embedments. The flower petals I tried to put into them bleached out as if I had put them in boiling water. I just couldn't get the mixture and the timing right. Every trial run produced goo.

I had a headache from the resin fumes, my fingers felt as if I had dipped them in Super Glue, and I was certain that one day a doctor would tell me that I had a rare disease only known to occur in three populations: headhunters, mummy-makers, and early twenty-first century crafters. The doctor would find it more likely that I was a mummy-maker than a crafter. By the time this diagnosis would be made, my sister would have been dead for many years, carried off by a strong fit of hysterics one Saturday afternoon.

"Barbara," I said, when her series of observations on ways I had ruined her life slowed enough to allow an interruption, "I obviously can't teach them this craft. I'll teach them something that I'm good at, and you can teach them resin casting when you are up and around."

"What are you good at?" she asked sulkily.

"I'll surprise you."

"Yes, you will!"

Kenny came home just then, which is why she is still breathing.

I drove home, feeling dejected. Barbara was right. When it came to crafts, there really wasn't one I was good at. I tried to recall the last time I had completed a crafts project successfully. Childhood, probably.

In fifth grade, I had made a relief map of California out of a mixture of flour, water, food coloring, and salt. Before I could get the project to school, Southern California did what most of the population of Northern California has long been wishing for, and crumbled into little pieces somewhere below Santa Barbara.

I recalled whittling a recognizable horse-shaped form from a bar of Ivory soap when I was about nine. Would the ladies enjoy that? Would I need to round up pocketknives, or could Ivory be carved with a table knife? Maybe I shouldn't provide sharp objects of any kind to women who thought they'd be doing resin casting.

I started to feel amused at the idea of leading the Crafts Ladies in a project straight out of a Girl Scouts meeting. Maybe I needed to come up with something that would really allow them to be kids again.

Kids!

Suddenly, I had my craft in mind. Macaroni art. Biggest advantage? I had recently led a macaroni art session with Frank's very active nephews, a way of getting through a rainy afternoon without scars or furniture breakage.

The best thing about macaroni art is that if your local craft store is closed due to, oh, let's say, an unfortunate slip-and-fall accident, you can get all the supplies you need at any grocery store. So I picked up some bags of elbow macaroni and other uncooked pasta of varying shapes, some plastic food storage bags, rubbing alcohol, string, paper plates, white glue, a roll of aluminum foil, and some food coloring. Then I went home and downloaded a few danceable tunes. I was good to go.

An hour before liftoff, I arrived at Barbara's house with one grocery bag, and everything I'd need to play those tunes through my small but mighty portable speakers.

Barbara was sitting up in bed, twice as cranky as she had been the day before. Kenny had wisely decided he needed to be at work that afternoon, so as soon as I arrived, he took off. She was miffed at him for that. I refused to tell her what craft we would work on, which made her no happier, and when I told her that I would bring the ladies back to her room to show off the results, she became downright panicked.

I was given a series of orders that involved everything from straightening all the items on her dresser to brushing her hair for her, but fortunately macaroni art doesn't require a lot of prep time. She couldn't manage putting earrings in on her own, so I helped her with that. She asked for the ones with the emeralds, then remembered one was missing its stone and started to cry. I thought about how much pain she was probably in, and felt sorry for her again. I hugged her gently, got her to stop crying, and paraded a series of other choices. The diamonds were deemed to be too dressy for the occasion, so we moved on to pearls, gold hoops, and finally to some beaded ones. I had just put those on her when the doorbell rang.

"Oh, nuts," Barbara said. "Someone is here early. Probably the twins."

"Twins?" I asked, but hurried to answer it.

She was right. Doris Ann and Sally greeted me warmly. They dressed differently, or I don't think I would have been able to tell them apart. I was sure I was going to mix up their names anyway. Sally had a yellow shirt on, so I tried the mnemonic of "Saffron for Sally." Two minutes later, I had addressed her as Saffron.

She laughed it off. Whatever misgivings I had about the Crafts Ladies were immediately dispelled by these two. They were easygoing and bright and it didn't take long to discover that they shared a wicked sense of humor.

"How's the patient?" Sally said, then whispered, "Has she talked your ears off?"

"Be nice," Doris Ann warned, but when Barbara began a long monologue about her accident—including saying that it never would have happened if she hadn't offered me a ride—it was Doris Ann who tilted her palm to give a glimpse of a homemade pin she held. It looked like the kind of thing a teacher would give to a child as a reward, and said, "I'm a good listener."

My failed attempt to stifle a laugh produced a loud snort. I was only saved from accounting for this sound because the doorbell rang again.

Susan, Carol, Connie, Dina, Margery, and Marianne arrived over the next few minutes. They each took turns mollycoddling Barbara while the others fixed coffee and laid out various edible goodies they had bought. "The hostess is never allowed to cook on the day she teaches a craft," Connie told me.

I was relieved, because I hadn't even thought about that aspect of a gathering like this one. "The first half-hour or so, we just eat and gab and get comfortable," Marianne said. "Then we get to work."

I heard Dina say, "I'm so excited about learning this resin work. I can never get mine to set right."

I got lucky one more time with the doorbell.

Elizabeth—who preferred to be called Betsy, as it turned out—was the last to arrive. She looked a little pale when she beheld Barbara's new rug, but Margery said in a low voice, "Yes, Betsy, hers looks more like yours than any of the ones the rest of us bought, but if you are going to be such a trendsetter, you have to look on our imitation as flattery."

Betsy shook her head and said, "It's not that. I should tell you, Chet and I had a big fight. He's left me."

Margery looked shocked, but Susan, who had overheard them, said firmly, "Lucky you!"

This was apparently the majority opinion on Chet.

"He ruined the rug," Betsy said. "I'm going to have to throw it away."

"What?" Marianne cried.

"He spilled all my soap-making oils on it. The house would have reeked of them, except for the burning smell." Tears started to roll down her cheeks. "Said he hated all my crafts. Hated the way I decorated. He had broken almost all the things I made with you," she said, her voice breaking on a sob. "He had taken all my needlepoint and burned it in the fireplace! He was standing there, watching it burn when I came home. In the frames were just ashes."

This produced outrage on her behalf, several rather colorful expressions about Chet and his antecedents, and resulted in far more sympathy for her than Barbara had received over her injuries—which made me feel glad that my sister was bedridden and unable to witness it.

"Well," said Marianne, "let's start casting resin. Today is the first day of the rest of your crafts, Betsy!"

"Yes," said Carol. "Let the resin casting begin!"

They all looked toward me. Although a few minutes in their company had already convinced me that I wouldn't have any trouble getting along with them, I felt nervous. "The program has changed a little."

I looked toward Carol. "Barbara tried all yesterday to teach me resin casting, and I couldn't get it to work once. I just made goo."

Dina laughed. "What a relief! I'm so glad it's not just me!"

In the ensuing brief discussion, it was clear that only Betsy had experienced any success at it. "I could teach it if you'd like," she said, but without much enthusiasm.

Connie was watching me. "I have a feeling Irene has an alternate plan."

"I've got a craft for you," I said. "Macaroni art."

There was a brief moment of profound silence, followed by gales of laughter. But it was good laughter, not the mocking sort.

A few minutes later, I had covered Barbara's kitchen table with old newspapers (something I have no trouble acquiring) and the simple supplies were laid out before the crafters.

"You can choose to make a necklace of elbow macaroni, or a work of art on a paper plate, or both." It occurred to me that I should have had samples of the finished product to show off. They didn't seem to mind. "But this project requires cooperation. Here's what we're going to do. Each of you will take a plastic bag and some food coloring. You are going to put up to about one pound of macaroni in the bag, and add half a cup of rubbing alcohol, then you can add about fifty or sixty drops of food coloring. Less for lighter colors, more for more vibrant colors. You can mix colors from different bottles of food dye to make another color in the bag."

"Yellow and red to make orange," said Doris Ann.

"Blue and red to make purple," said Margery.

"Exactly," I said. "Experimentation is encouraged. Zip the bag shut and let me know when you're ready for the next step."

There was a little time taken over selecting pasta, and before long they had created a plastic-encased liquid-and-macaroni rainbow.

"Now, make sure those bags are well-sealed," I said. As they were checking them, I went over to the iPod, and selected the playlist I had put together the night before.

"Now, the next step is to shake it up good. So pick up those bags and dance with them," I said, as over the speakers Gloria Gaynor started singing "I Will Survive."

They didn't move at first, sort of illustrating the "petrified" line Gloria was singing. So I picked up my bag of red and started moving. They got the picture then, and started singing and dancing right along with me. We made a conga line of sorts and snaked our way out onto the back patio. I could see that Betsy was really getting into the lyrics.

We kept this up for about thirty minutes, with some slower songs here and there to prevent collapse. I run a few miles nearly every day, but it was clear to me that some of these women were a tad more sedentary. Betsy and Connie were doing fine, but almost every one else took little breaks as needed. I told them to pace themselves, no shame in resting. By the time the set wound up with "I Am Woman," most of us were ready to set the bags down. They carefully drained them while I laid aluminum foil over the newspaper.

"Okay," I said, "spread them out on the aluminum foil. We need to give them a chance to dry."

While this was going on we had another round of refreshments, and visited Barbara, who asked me if I had "Reunited" on my iPod. I didn't.

She eyed me skeptically, but was soon distracted by a question Susan asked her about her injuries.

We finished the afternoon by gluing the shapes onto the paper plates in designs of our own choosing. I also demonstrated the technique of putting a little glue on the end of a piece of string and letting it dry, to make the string easier to thread through elbow macaroni for bracelets and necklaces.

"Won't the dye rub off on our skin?" Marianne asked.

"No, that's why we added the rubbing alcohol to the food coloring," I said. "But do not ask me why that works. It just does."

These true crafters showed their artistic abilities. My paper plate art and necklace were undeniably far more crudely fashioned. We each made an extra necklace for Barbara, and put them around her neck like Mardi Gras beads.

She got all weepy again, just as she did when, after the crafters helped me clean up, her friends said good-bye.

When I helped put away her necklaces, she told me she wanted me to have one of them. She gave me the prettiest one, the one with the most vibrant colors. The one Betsy made.

I took it and thanked her, and helped her to settle on the pillows and bed, so that she'd be more comfortable if she fell asleep. She was drowsy by then, but asked me to bend closer for a kiss on the cheek. "Thank you," she said. She seemed to nod off, but her eyes opened as I sat in a chair near the bed. "You don't have to stay," she said.

"No, I don't," I agreed. I put the earphones for the iPod in my ears, and settled back to listen to a book I had downloaded. I found I couldn't concentrate on it, though, so I turned it off and watched her sleep.

AFTER WORK ON Monday, I drove over to the Crafty Fox. Betsy was with some customers, but she smiled and nodded at me. I walked back to Fox's office, to retrieve the bag of sweepings so that I could sift through it to look for Barbara's emerald. It wasn't where I had left it. The whole office looked neater. With dawning horror, I realized that Betsy had probably taken it out to the Dumpster behind the store. I pushed the back door open—causing an alarm to go off.

Betsy rushed back, but I had already entered the code and disarmed it. "What happened?" she asked.

I explained.

"Oh, yes, I saw that. I did throw it away. I'll get it for you." The phone started ringing. "Probably the alarm company," she said. "Would you please get that? I'll get the bag of sweepings."

I answered it, and sure enough, it was the alarm company. They wanted me to put Fox on the phone, which I said I couldn't do, so then they asked if any other authorized person was there. Praying that Betsy was authorized, I mentioned her, and they said, yes, they'd like to talk to her. I opened the back door again, and looked toward the Dumpster. To my surprise, Betsy was actually inside it. She looked very embarrassed, and said, "It wouldn't fit in the trash cans at my house, and I didn't think Fox would mind my using her Dumpster. I couldn't stand the smell anymore."

I had noticed by then that I was in the world's most fragrant alley. And that there was a rolled up carpet in the Dumpster. The one on which her husband had spilled soap-making oils.

I explained about the security company on the phone. Luckily, she had found the sweepings and handed them to me. I helped her out of the Dumpster, and she ran in to answer the phone.

I searched and searched through that bag, and Betsy helped me whenever she could get free of customers. "Do you want to just give her my earrings?" she asked.

"Thanks, but no, I couldn't do that," I said. "She can live without an emerald." I hesitated then added, "Have you closed out all your bank accounts and credit cards?"

She looked startled, then shook her head. "I don't think Chet will . . ."

"Betsy, if you don't believe me on this one, ask Barbara what an ex-husband can do to a bank account. If Chet comes back to you, no problem, you add him to the new account. But don't let your credit go to hell on behalf of a guy who would burn needlepoint."

She sighed. "I'm glad I talked to you. I wouldn't have thought of that. And to be perfectly honest, I know Chet won't come back to me."

So we talked for a while about her plans for the future. When I left her, she seemed to be in a determined mood.

THREE MONTHS LATER, I was riding in Barbara's car as a passenger again, on a visit to see Fox. Barbara was telling me that Betsy had sold her house and moved to Minneapolis. "She's completely cut herself off from all her friends here," Barbara said. "None of the Crafts Ladies have heard from her since she moved there."

I was about to say something in reply when my purse fell over on the car seat. I watched three dimes disappear in the seat fold. I wasn't too proud to stick my hand in there to pull them back out. I felt something roll back on my hand with one of them, something that I at first thought was a large pebble. When I saw what it was, I said, "Well, I'll be damned."

It was an emerald. Barbara was ecstatic.

"It must have fallen off before you went into the store." *When you were tossing your hair around, trying to get me to notice them*, I thought.

I enjoyed temporary hero status.

At the store, talking to Fox, I remembered the day I spent all that time sorting through the sweepings. "And Betsy offered to give you her earrings," I said to Barbara.

"She did? Wow." Barbara, I could see, was feeling guilty for being a little catty about Betsy.

"I wonder whatever became of her husband," Fox said. "I don't know if I told you, but he hasn't even been in touch with his own sister. She came by here one day to see Betsy. Betsy told her that she hadn't heard a word from him since the day he left. Said he didn't even give notice at work. I guess it's a real pain when someone just disappears like that. Betsy couldn't collect insurance or anything. Luckily, she owned that house before she met him, and so her house was in her own name, or she wouldn't have had a thing to live on."

"What about the rest of his family?" Barbara asked. "Maybe they've heard from him."

Fox shook her head. "His parents died a while back, and I guess this sister is his only sibling. I don't understand why he wouldn't have been in touch with her."

"Maybe they had a falling out," I said.

Barbara scowled at me.

"It happens," I said.

AT HOME THAT night, I kept thinking of rolled rugs. I didn't think the one I had seen in the Dumpster was big enough to hide a body, and even if it had been, it wouldn't have been easy for Betsy to lift the combined weight of man and rug over the walls of the Dumpster. Hard enough to put that much weight into the trunk of a car.

My curiosity kept nagging at me, and eventually I talked to Frank. I didn't think he thought much of my concerns, because I got a speech about how many adults disappear of their own volition, and how the police don't have time to look for people who haven't committed crimes and just don't want to be found.

But a week later he was telling me that the new owners of Betsy's house had allowed the crime lab to do luminol tests in the living room. The fireplace had been torn out and replaced, he was told, and the former "cottage cheese" acoustic ceiling had been scraped off and repainted. A small amount of blood had been detected near a baseboard. Not enough to prove anything.

He told me that Betsy's wanted for questioning, and Chet's officially a missing person. He said if someone ever has time to work the case, they'll probably look for her at craft shows.

I'm not sure I want them to find her. I'm not sure I want to know what she got away with, if indeed she got away with anything at all. I look at the fine work she did on the macaroni necklace, the artistic touch she gave a childish craft. I think of the fact that only two people I know can cast resin successfully. I think, too, of how my sister wanted to be more like her than anyone else. But that, of course, isn't the whole truth, either.

§§

Macaroni Art

Macaroni and other uncooked pasta shapes can be used in many ways for arts and crafts projects. Here's what you'll need for the crafts in this story:

> **Elbow macaroni and any other uncooked pasta shapes that strike your fancy (try ziti, penne, orecchietta, farfalle, rotini, conchiglie, ditalini, ruote)**
> **Food coloring (primary colors can be blended to make other colors)**
> **Several large Ziploc bags or other sealable containers**
> **Aluminum foil**
> **Rubbing alcohol**
> **Paper plates—flat-surfaced, thick ones are best**
> **String, cut in lengths for necklaces or bracelets**
> **White glue**

The amounts of each will vary according to the number of colors and amount of macaroni you wish to work with for your art project. To work with a group as in the story, use one pound of macaroni per bag, add a half-cup of rubbing alcohol, and fifty-five drops of food coloring for vibrant color. For a smaller project, use a cup of macaroni, five to six drops of food coloring and one tablespoon of rubbing alcohol.

Use a separate container for each color. Seal the container and dance around and shake it up. Give it about thirty minutes to really absorb the color, but if you are doing this on a smaller scale and are impatient (or your kids are), even after five minutes, some color will be absorbed.

When you are ready, gently drain the colored water from the pasta.

Some people dry the colored pasta on paper towels or newspapers, but aluminum foil won't bond with the starch in the pasta, so I prefer it.

Give it at least thirty minutes to dry.

The pieces can be glued onto paper plates in colorful mosaics, either in a recognizable form or an abstract design.

Those shapes with holes in them, such as macaroni and ruote, can be strung together to make a necklace or bracelet. You'll find it easier to thread the string if you put a drop of glue on one end to stiffen it.

The mosaic made in Barcelona's Guell Park by Antoni Gaudi may have served as inspiration for the later collages of Picasso and Dali.

The use of broken crockery and other found objects in addition to tiles added a new twist to the ancient art of mosaics, which can be traced backward through the ceilings and walls of majestic buildings of the Byzantine empire, to the floors of Greco-Roman structures, and all the way to Sumer, where terra cotta cones were pushed point first into clay walls to create interesting patterns.

No Good Deed

by Dorothy Cannell

Dorothy Cannell's first novel, The Thin Woman, *featuring Ellie Haskell, was published in 1984, and is still in print, along with nine subsequent books in the series. She has also written* Down the Garden Path *and* God Save the Queen. *Her short story "The Family Jewels" won an Agatha award.*

§§

CHERRY VILLAGE WAS a happy place until Mr. Moffatt retired. He'd always been the worst kind of bore. The sort of man to be avoided at all cost. The other residents had been known to cross into oncoming traffic or hide behind potted plants at social gatherings to avoid him. But during his working life, he'd had two things in his favor. His job, which had something to do with chicken feed, involved travel. It meant he was often gone for weeks at a time. And, making for the biggest saving grace of all was his wife, Alice.

Alice Moffatt was a marvel. A woman of infinite capabilities and extraordinary helpfulness. This could have made her as obnoxious as her husband. But unlike him, she was not puffed up by her own importance. She had a diffidence about her, an anxiety not to offend, or put herself forward where she wasn't wanted.

"Look at them!" Her neighbor Donna Watson stood back

to admire the sitting room curtains Alice had just produced for her in record time. "The workmanship is top-notch. They hang perfectly because she insisted on lining them. Amazing, isn't it? There's nothing that woman can't do, and yet nobody has the least desire to knock her off her pedestal."

"It might be different if she were beautiful or even moderately attractive." Evangeline Evans sank a fork into the sumptuous sponge cake Alice had brought round to Donna's house along with the curtains. "But she isn't. She's—I hate to be unkind—frumpy!"

"Does dowdy sound better?" queried Susan Dumas.

"What's interesting," Donna said, "is that she has such a marvelous sense of style and color when it comes to home decorating. One has to assume she was one of those plain girls who never saw the advantage to bothering about their appearance."

Donna, Susan, and Evangeline had all retained their good looks well into their fifties. Their divorces had been amicable. None of them were soured on men, but they were inclined to pity their married women friends for their lack of independence. And no woman was to be pitied more than Alice, despite Ernest Moffatt's frequent work-related absences.

"If only there were something we could do to make life easier for Alice." Evangeline meant this, but she was equally interested in her second slice of sponge cake. It would be the perfect dessert to serve the next time it was her turn to host an afternoon of bridge.

Susan's thoughts drifted to the oil painting Alice was in the process of completing for her. It promised to be a perfect likeness of her barrister son, his wife, and their two children. Perfect in the sense that it subtly eliminated Giles's weak chin, the steely glint in Mary's eyes, and the children's self-satisfied smirks. That was the wonderful thing about Alice. She always knew what was wanted without having to be told. The colors in the portrait blended beautifully with the sofa and chairs she had reupholstered for Susan the previous year. Within the next few weeks Alice would bring round a fire screen, worked in exquisite needlepoint. Next to arrive would be the lamps she was making out of a pair of eighteenth-century silver candlesticks she had found at a flea market.

Probably the very best thing about Alice was that she made it clear, in her hesitant, throat-clearing way, that she would be hurt, even crushed, if anyone suggested paying her for—as she put it—the little odds and ends she did for them. When Susan had suggested reimbursing her for the price of the candlesticks, Alice had stood firm. She had bought them for a song, on the spur of the moment, thinking they would do for her own sitting room. Once she got them home it was clear they were all wrong. Seeing she couldn't return them, she would have been stuck if Susan hadn't made room for them. The same was true of the curtains now gracing Donna's windows.

"I've had that material in my sewing room cupboard for over a year and had been feeling so guilty about not doing anything with it." Alice had been typically flustered a few weeks previously when she had brought it over for Donna's inspection. "I must have had the colors of this room in mind when I chose it. I've always thought yours one of the prettiest houses in the village. Who doesn't love a thatched cottage? And, if you don't think me too pushy, I do think this floral polished cotton would look far better at your latticed windows than at my plain ones."

Donna hadn't argued with her. It wouldn't have been kind.

"You would be doing me a favor by taking it off my hands. Ernest doesn't like green. And you just can't get away from green in floral prints. It's all those stalks and leaves." Alice had stood looking as if this were somehow her fault.

The man's name suited him down to the ground. He was the most appallingly earnest man ever to have set foot in Cherry Village. But Donna and her two friends had never once let slip to Alice that five minutes in his company made an eternity in hell sound like a Sunday jaunt. Somehow she managed to speak fondly of him. Wasn't it only common compassion to let her hang onto her pride?

"The house is so empty when Ernest is away," she had said when she delivered the curtains that morning. "After all these years I should be used to him being gone so much. His work has always required him to travel. But somehow it gets harder rather than easier. That's why I always keep busy. And people, especially you three, are so kind in making me feel useful."

Everyone likes to be appreciated. Donna felt good about herself in particular and Cherry Village in general, as she sat enjoying Evangeline and Susan's company. Alice had only stayed for a few moments after hanging the curtains. She'd had to hurry off to the mosaic class she was taking in the nearby town of Skettering. Grouped around the table Alice had French polished one afternoon when she was at a loss for something to do, the three happily single women looked their best.

Their faces reflected the warm glow that comes from brightening the lives of others. It was a pity that Alice wasn't much of a bridge player. Donna, Evangeline, and Susan had taken up the game with a vengeance after their divorces. There were plenty of fellow enthusiasts in the village, making it unusual for them not to play at least three times a week.

Alice had once mentioned that Ernest enjoyed bridge and hinted, in her bashful way, that should he be at home he would be glad to make up a table. No one need worry about not being up to his standard. Ernest was so good about making allowances.

Getting around that one had required some tact. Evangeline had regretfully explained that Mrs. Randall-Whitby from the Manor House was in charge of finding substitute players and, as Alice well knew, she was a woman who didn't take kindly to suggestions, let alone being told what to do. Following that small hiccup, Donna had given voice to the question that had occasionally popped into her mind.

"Could it be possible Alice really is fond of her awful husband?"

"Oh, come on!" Susan had exclaimed.

They'd ended up having a somewhat shamefaced laugh about it. Evangeline finished off a third piece of sponge cake, knowing she was in no danger of gaining an ounce. There was, however, no laughter—not so much as a quiver of amusement, when word leaked out that Ernest Moffatt had taken early retirement. Surprisingly, Alice hadn't come round to break the news to them in person. Susan heard it from the vicar's wife one morning at the bus stop.

"Such a shame," said that kindly woman, "on account of it being for health reasons I mean. Heart problems. Apparently, Dr. Johnson told him he has to slow down and get the weight off. But as we all know, that's easier said than done. So hard to stick to those stringent diets. I'm not sure I would want to go on if all I could eat for the rest of my days was a forkful of chicken or fish. Unfortunately, surgery isn't an option. He's already had one bypass operation. And he's in no fit state to survive another." Susan vaguely remembered Ernest being in the hospital a couple of years previously. She was almost sure that she, Evangeline and Donna had sent flowers, or perhaps it was a get-well card.

The bus came and went with the vicar's wife on it, but Susan was no longer in the mood to go into Skettering and search for new towels for the bathroom she'd had her heart set on having remodeled. The crowning glory was to have been the mosaic wall Alice had designed as part of her course. It was in a dispirited mood that Susan went home and rang up Evangeline and Donna. They came over immediately, and the three of them sat dolefully staring at one another.

"It's a blow," acknowledged Evangeline. "The possibility of bumping into Ernest Moffatt any time we set foot outdoors is going to take some getting used to. And for Alice's sake, we can't tell him to push off."

"We have to think positively," said Susan.

"He may drop dead before the week is out." There was no sponge cake to raise their spirits that day, but Donna had brightened a little.

"I don't see him sticking to a diet and exercising on a regular basis." Susan also beheld a small beam of light at the end of the tunnel.

Regrettably, this was extinguished a few days later when Alice finally turned up with the silver candlestick lamps, which were to have been delivered the week before. She apologized to Susan in her typically muddled fashion for the delay. The gist being that life was a lot different now that Ernest was retired.

"It must be a big adjustment for both of you." Susan dragged her eyes away from the lampshades that were missing the fringe Alice had promised. "What a worry it must be, this heart problem of his! But I imagine it doesn't do to dwell on what might happen between one moment and the next. Better to make the most of every day you have together."

"How right you are! That is our goal!"

Susan, who was not of a demonstrative nature, was preparing to provide a hug, perhaps even a kiss on the cheek, should Alice's eyes moisten. There was no need. She was looking into a face that was far from woebegone. More than that . . . it displayed a newly acquired strength. There was now firmness to the line of Alice's mouth, a sturdiness to her jaw . . . the light of purpose in her eyes. Despite her old plaid skirt, plump build, and carelessly combed hair, she didn't look as frumpy as usual.

"Doctors aren't gods. They don't know everything." She spoke comfortably, kindly, as if Susan were the one who needed reassuring. "Ernest's father had a bad ticker, as he called it, but he lived to be eighty-seven. And it was a perforated appendix that got him in the end. There were several uncles just the same, everyone was amazed that they made it from one year to the next, but they all went on to a ripe old age."

Susan pictured herself providing this encouraging news to Donna and Evangeline.

"The uncle that Ernest was named after soldiered on till he was ninety-odd. Now that makes for a wonderful omen, wouldn't you say?"

Susan could only nod.

"There was a common thread to extending those lives," Alice paused. For a moment Susan feared she was going to name each and every one of Ernest's relations who had beaten the odds. But she was merely gathering her thoughts. "What did the trick for those men was that they all had wives to coddle them—smooth out their worries, make sure they didn't overdo or rush about, whilst at the same time maintaining an interest in life. Encouraging them to take up hobbies of a nice relaxing sort."

"Very sensible," agreed Susan.

"And I have reason to feel particularly fortunate." Alice seemed to grow in stature. "All those years of taking classes and honing my skills in the decorating arts! Finally, I can put what I've learned to the best possible use. I can share my knowledge with Ernest, providing him with an outlet to replace the mental and physical stimulation he's missing now that his working life is over."

"So satisfying for you." Susan hoped she sounded appropriately enthusiastic. Mostly, she wished that Donna and Evangeline were present, so she could weep on their shoulders. On Alice's behalf, of course. Her courage was so poignant. Susan tried not to think about the candlestick lampshades that might never get their fringe. Alice was talking about encouraging Ernest to begin his own art project.

"Something simple, that's bound to turn out well and make him feel pleased with himself."

What the residents of Cherry Village found most objectionable about Ernest Moffatt was that he was always far too visibly pleased with himself. As she couldn't bring this up, Susan listened, with only a few sideways glances at the lampshades, while Alice brought up the subject of her mosaic classes.

"I'm sorry I won't be able to finish out the course; but it just wouldn't be right to leave Ernest three mornings a week. I know what people will be saying, that I need to do things for myself in order to be at my best, emotionally and physically, in order for me to do a proper job taking care of Ernest. But I'll get more than enough fulfillment cooking really tasty meals within the guidelines of the diet Dr. Johnson has prescribed. And . . . as I just mentioned . . ." Alice fussed with her clumpy curls, floundering with all her old confusion, trying to remember what she had been saying.

"You were talking about your mosaic classes." It would have been silly for Susan not to take the opportunity. "And I've just come up with a bright idea. Why don't you draw up a design and come over and practice on my bathroom? That way you won't be wasting what you've learned! No particular schedule. Just whenever you feel like getting out for an hour or so. You and I can have some of our nice little chats. Or if I'm off doing something, you can be all nice and quiet here by yourself."

How could Alice resist? Here was the golden opportunity to escape, if only now and then, from Ernest's raucous laugh, his booming voice, his fatuous commentary on every blinking thing that crossed what served for his brain. Susan stared in disbelief when Alice shook her head.

"You're so kind to think of it, but really I can't make any plans at the moment that don't involve Ernest. I have to live up to the example provided by all those women in his family who kept their husbands alive by the strength of their marital devotion. Oh, but . . ." Her voice floated off like a wisp of cobweb.

"Yes?" Hope reared its lively head.

"You've reminded me why I mentioned the mosaic classes. In our very first one we were shown how to decorate a flowerpot with broken pieces of china. Nothing could be simpler. And so pretty—as well as being cheap, because you can use old, cracked or chipped cups, saucers, and plates. I've talked it over with Ernest, and we decided to use this idea for his first project."

Alice looked at her watch, said she'd had ever such a nice time, but she did need to get home to prepare the omelets made without yolks that she had found in the *Hearty Hearts Cookery Book*. The moment the front door closed behind her, Susan reached for the phone, then remembered that neither Evangeline nor Donna would be home. They were playing bridge at the Manor House with Brigadier and Mrs. Randall-Whitby. Susan went to bed that night feeling put-upon, left out, and with a tickle in her throat that had her wondering if she were coming down with a cold.

It turned out to be the flu. Dr. Johnson came twice. She spent several days in bed, dragged around the house in her dressing gown for the remainder of the week, and generally didn't feel like herself for a fortnight. She had brief, hoarse discussions with Evangeline and Donna over the phone, but they didn't come 'round because they didn't want to catch her germs, and she didn't want to see anyone, not even her two closest friends. It was on the day that she decided she was really back to her old self that she went through her stacked-up post and found the invitation from the Randall-Whitbys. It was for a drinks party that evening. The ideal opportunity to step back into life as lived in Cherry Village.

Parties at the Manor House tended to be on a grand scale. On entering the drawing room, Susan was not surprised see two women in severe black dresses and crisp white aprons drifting between the clusters of guests. They proffered silver salvers piled with delectable looking canapés. A babble of voices and rumbles of laughter floated Susan's way. It was clear the party was off to a great start. Spotting Evangeline and Donna, she hurried to join them. They only got to chat for a few moments before their hosts hove up along side them.

"Have you seen our mural?" The brigadier was looking every inch the country squire.

"No? Then you must let us give you a personal viewing." Mrs. Randall-Whitby was all commanding affability as she edged the three women to her left. "There in that alcove." She waved a large hand. "As you see it shows the Battle of Trafalgar. There we have the dying Nelson, surrounded by grief-stricken members of his crew. Some people I imagine might find the subject matter morbid but . . ."

"Tommyrot!" The brigadier chortled dismissively. "Glorious moment in our history! Britain—Queen of the Sea, and all that!"

Evangeline, who knew quite a lot about art, drew a deep breath. "Marvelous!" The word hung in the air until Donna found her voice.

"Powerful!"

"And what a lovely choice of colors." Susan was wondering if something on a slightly smaller scale would be right for her sitting room. Perhaps a fishing boat with a seagull perched on it and, if it wouldn't spoil the mood, nobody dying. Sensing that she might not have struck quite the right note, she hastened to inquire who the Randall-Whitbys had commissioned to do the mural.

"We talked to several professional artists—all quite well known," replied the brigadier, "but none of them shared our vision, couldn't quite get to the heart of what we wanted, isn't that so m'dear?"

His wife inclined her head in agreement. "So disappointing, but then one morning I was standing next to Alice Moffatt at the butcher's counter. Just for something to say really, I told her about our little predicament."

Were Donna, Evangeline, and Susan surprised?

"As a result of that coincidental meeting," Mrs. Randall-Whitby gave one of her wide hand gestures, "everything fell happily into place. Of course, I'd no idea that Alice had just finished a course in landscape and portrait painting, or that she would adamantly refuse to take any money for her work. One doesn't like to feel one is taking advantage of people but . . ." Memories of what the professional painters had wanted to charge came flooding back. Both husband and wife had been put off their food for a week.

"Is Alice here tonight?" Evangeline peered over a group of heads.

"No . . . that is . . . in a matter of speaking, no . . . she isn't." The brigadier cleared his throat and started again. "Frightful spot to find oneself in, never felt such a damned heel in m'life! But if we'd invited Alice . . . well, there's no getting around it! He'd have had to come, too. Couldn't have told her to leave the confounded fellow at home. Not the sort of thing done in polite circles. And there's now that business of his having a wonky ticker. Should feel sorry for him, I suppose, but the thing is, once was enough! We did have them over for dinner right after Alice completed the mural. Had half a dozen houseguests staying at the time. Old friends. Go back donkeys' years. Easygoing lot! Didn't see a difficulty. But that chap Moffatt . . ." The brigadier's face was turning puce.

"Now then, Edward," his wife admonished, "it doesn't do to relive the experience. We have to move on."

But not, Evangeline, Donna, and Susan hoped, before they got to hear some of the details. "Was it really so dreadful?" They asked as one.

"Never endured such an evening in m' life." Brigadier Randall-Whitby showed no signs of calming down. "The fellow didn't stop talking from the moment he and that poor wife of his arrived, except when he was tossing cheese balls the size of walnuts down his throat and swallowing them whole."

"We'd put them out along with the before-dinner drinks." His wife placed a soothing hand on his shoulder. "For the odd nibble—you know how it is—but none of our other guests got even one. He stood hogging the plate, while talking interminably in that slow ponderous way of his—every syllable drawn out to excruciation, about his lifetime in chicken feed. On and on about how he thought free-range eggs were overrated. And then, right after we had

sat down to dinner he brought up—of all unsuitable sub-
jects," Mrs. Randall-Whitby swayed on her feet, "he went
into appalling detail about the . . . the bowel habits of laying hens."

"Surely not." Evangeline wondered if she should fetch
her a chair.

"Nobody touched their soup." The brigadier was working himself up to a new froth. "We had some hopes for the
fish course. But by then, Moffatt was telling a joke. Telling
it and retelling it every time he got lost in the middle because, of course, he went right on stuffing his fork into his
mouth between one syllable and the next. It was one of
those yarns about St. Peter and the pearly gates. Heard it
before. Who hasn't? The lorry driver and the nun and I
don't know who else dying on the same day. But that man
had to make his embellishments."

"The part about Jesus on a bicycle was certainly new."
Mrs. Randall-Whitby held onto her husband's arm for support. "One of our houseguests had just taken late-life holy
orders. I was surprised he didn't get up and leave the table.
He didn't mince words later. Blasphemous was the way he
put it."

"The evening only got worse as it went on." The
brigadier was about to expound further, when someone
tapped him on the shoulder, and the moment was lost.

"We must meet for a talk," Evangeline told Susan and
Donna. There was a grim purpose in her eyes. It was even
more apparent the next day when the three women sat
around the Queen Anne table that was one of Alice's refur-
bished pieces.

"It's time we did something about our friend." Evangeline had never before referred to Alice as a friend. But the
other two knew whom she was talking about.

"She was in her garden just now," said Donna. "I told her
we'd seen the mural last night. Making it sound as though
we were at the Manor House for bridge. I went on about
how impressed you'd been, with your knowledge of art. She

was her usual self-deprecating self, explaining how she'd traced the scene from an enlargement she'd made of a well-known painting. As though there was really nothing remarkable about it. She even managed to smile when she said that Ernest had called it painting by numbers."

"He would." Susan ground her teeth.

"It came to me as I tossed and turned in bed last night," Evangeline handed round cups of tea, "that we can no longer close our eyes to the situation. We cannot allow Alice's creativity to be stifled. It's the spark that lights her life. If we stand by and allow it to be extinguished, it would be the same as killing her ourselves."

"Yes," said Donna, "but when it comes down to it, what can we do about it?"

"We'll have to kill Ernest instead."

There was silence. Shock had become the dominant presence in the room.

Donna found her voice first. "Couldn't we send him out into the woods with a handful of breadcrumbs?"

Susan was thinking about Ernest's father and the uncles who had refused to turn up their heels until old age finally nabbed them. "I do see we have to do something," she sounded as croaky as when at her worst with the flu, "but the word *kill*," she struggled to explain herself, "is one of the nastier four-letter ones."

"Then we'll wash out our mouths with soap," responded Evangeline crisply.

"*Murder's* an even nastier word." Donna needed a second cup of tea.

"Then let's not use it." Susan was pulling herself together. "We have to realize that friends are sometimes called upon to make sacrifices for the better good. None of us likes being put in this position, but this is no time to think of ourselves. I've already accepted the fact that I'm unlikely to ever get my mosaic bathroom wall. And that I'll have to put the fringe on those lampshades myself."

"Absolutely. We're not looking for any personal gain.

That's what makes our chances of coming through this with minimal complications so good." Evangeline spoke like the teacher she had been, conferring praise on an apt pupil.

"You don't think we'll get caught?" Donna was beginning to feel better about the situation.

"Of course not. People don't usually get rid of people as an act of kindness. Also, we barely know Ernest Moffatt. I don't suppose any one of us has ever spent more than five minutes in his company. That may have seemed an eternity at the time, but it's a fact that now pays dividends. Besides, we're going to make it look like death from natural causes." Evangeline pressed her hands on the edge of table. "Now, let's get down to the means. Surely it shouldn't be too difficult, given his condition, to bring on a fatal heart attack. It's managed all the time in crime novels."

A silence that was not fraught with tension settled on the room. It was the thinking sort.

"I'm not sure where I heard it," said Donna. "Maybe I read it somewhere, but it was about that stuff men take when they can't rise to the occasion. If used by someone taking heart medication it can cause a massive, often fatal, attack."

"Sounds just the ticket." Evangeline smiled her approval. "But how do we get hold of it? One of us could go to Dr. Johnson with a fabricated story, but it might stick in his mind. And it seems to me, we'd be taking an unnecessary risk." She noticed the look on Susan's face. "What's on your mind?"

"There's some in my guestroom."

"Been saving them for a rainy night and a tall dark stranger?" Evangeline raised an eyebrow.

"I found them in the bedside drawer after Giles and Mary came for the weekend a few months ago. I didn't like to throw them out in case he remembered and looked for them on the next visit. He'd be embarrassed thinking his mother knew he was having . . . difficulties. But that's life," she reassured her two friends. "I won't put Giles's feelings ahead of what needs to be done."

An uneasy thought popped into Susan's head. "You don't think that Giles, being a barrister, might get to wondering if there might be a connection between his pills being gone and Ernest Moffat being dead?"

Donna laughed with genuine lightheartedness. "My dear, I'm his mother, is he going to imagine I'd help send anyone on his way to meet the Grim Reaper?"

They had the method. Now they had to decide how to administer the pills. Would they dissolve in a cup of tea? Wouldn't there be an odd taste? Then it came to them. The answer was bite-sized cheese balls. Like the ones Ernest had been tossing down his throat when invited to dinner at the Manor House. Hadn't Brigadier Randall-Whitby said the man had swallowed a plate of them whole?

"We'll invite him for an afternoon game of bridge," said Donna. "We know from Alice that he'll leap at the opportunity. She won't mind not being included. She's not keen, and of course we'll only have the one table."

"Better that she's not present. It really wouldn't be considerate." Susan was trying not to think that she might just get her mosaic bathroom wall. Alice would have a renewed need to stay busy with Ernest gone permanently.

"I'll have bridge," volunteered Evangeline, as though they were talking about an ordinary game.

"Let me bring the cheese balls," Donna was quick to say. "I have the recipe; it has to be the one Alice shared with us. I'll make a couple of dozen and pop some pills into a few of them."

"What a pity we won't be able to eat any." Susan pulled a face. "Of course we have to hope Ernest keeps tossing them down till he gets to the right ones. But I don't really suppose that will pose a problem. We'll have to check any that are left just to be on the safe side. It would be too awful if a policeman were to help himself to the one left on the plate and," she couldn't restrain a giggle, "immediately solved the case."

"Are the police routinely summoned in cases of sudden

death?" asked Donna. Neither Susan nor Evangeline had the answer, but they agreed it was well to be prepared on every point. It was also settled that they would arrange the bridge game for the following Thursday afternoon.

It was only a week away, but the days crawled. At times their nerves got to them. But there was no need. Things couldn't have worked out better. Ernest arrived promptly at Evangeline's door with his own deck of cards. Within five minutes he had removed any flicker of remorse the three women had been feeling. The Randall-Whitbys had not exaggerated the evils of having him as a guest. Everything about him, from his red face to his ponderous speech to his chuckling satisfaction at his perceived wit was enough to make one scream. Donna spared no time in handing him the plate of cheese balls and Susan dreaded to think that it might not all be over before the end of the first rubber. There was one iffy moment when he got off his chair with amazing speed, looking as hale and hearty as a man with a severe heart condition could. Was it possible their plan was about to fall apart? Was he about to rush home to Alice in the throes of chemically inflated passion? False alarm. He was only helping himself to another whopping glass of sherry. When he gripped his chest five minutes later and keeled to the floor, it was something of an anticlimax.

After that, things happened so fast they became a blur. One of them must have phoned Alice and Dr. Johnson because suddenly they were both there. Dr. Johnson said that sadly it was only to be expected. Time of death was established. Alice wasn't crying. Then she was. Evangeline produced cups of tea. Donna suggested contacting the vicar. Two men came in with a stretcher, bumping into Susan. And then, just like that, it was the next day. People who met Evangeline in the village commiserated with her for having something so unfortunate happen at her house. Word got out that Ernest Moffatt was to be cremated. The funeral service came and went. Alice wore black and held up well. The weeks began to pass. Life it seemed was returning to normal.

Or so Donna, Evangeline, and Susan thought. But it didn't turn out that way. Alice had sent them each a sweet letter saying how sorry she was that they'd been thrust into such a difficult situation, and how appreciative she was of their cards and phone calls. But when they went round to her house, she was rarely home. And only once or twice did she stop by to see any of them. They learned from the vicar's wife that Alice had joined a widows' group in Skettering.

"Of course it's what she needs," ventured that salt-of-the-earth woman, "there's nothing like being around people who are in the same situation as one's self. It will help Alice move forward. And she's bound to make some good friends. People always take to her, don't they? Do you know, it wouldn't surprise me if she decides to move to Skettering. A fresh start may be the very best thing."

She was to prove right. A few months later a For Sale sign went up outside Alice's house. It sold quickly and a pleasant family moved in. Donna, Susan, and Evangeline insisted to one another that they had no reason to feel ill used. They were glad that Alice had seemed content the last time they saw her.

"Although," Donna strove not to let a hint of bitterness enter her voice, "it has crossed my mind that maybe we didn't know her as well as we thought we did. Could it be that she had counted on someone or other getting rid of Ernest for her?"

There was no answer to that. But one thing was certain. Cherry Village was never again the happy place it had once been.

§♥

Mosaic Flowerpot

You'll need a clay flowerpot, some china or other pottery, and a grout/adhesive mixture, available at hardware stores or craft stores.

Select pieces of china in the colors and patterns of your choice. Spare dishes and chipped plates are ideal. Place these between two pieces of cloth and hammer gently to break into the desired sized piece.

Spread a layer of grout of sufficient thickness to secure the chips when pressed into place around a plain clay pot. Wipe with a damp cloth and leave to set. This should take about five or six hours, enough time to enjoy several nice cups of tea.

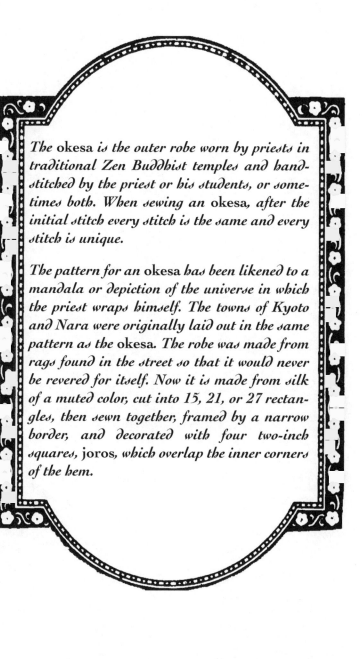

The okesa *is the outer robe worn by priests in traditional Zen Buddhist temples and hand-stitched by the priest or his students, or sometimes both. When sewing an* okesa, *after the initial stitch every stitch is the same and every stitch is unique.*

The pattern for an okesa *has been likened to a mandala or depiction of the universe in which the priest wraps himself. The towns of Kyoto and Nara were originally laid out in the same pattern as the* okesa. *The robe was made from rags found in the street so that it would never be revered for itself. Now it is made from silk of a muted color, cut into 15, 21, or 27 rectangles, then sewn together, framed by a narrow border, and decorated with four two-inch squares,* joros, *which overlap the inner corners of the hem.*

IF YOU MEET THE BUDDHA

by Susan Dunlap

Susan Dunlap is the author of eighteen novels, in three series fea-turing each of the major types of detectives—a private investigator, a police officer, and an amateur detective. Her most recent novel, Fast Friends, *tells the story of two women on a desperate road trip. A founding member and past president of Sisters In Crime, her short stories have won two Anthony awards and a Macavity award.*

§§

"IF YOU MEET the Buddha on the way, kill the Buddha." The words keep traveling across the inside of my forehead like the big headline banner in Times Square. The accepted meaning of the metaphor is that any person seriously inter-ested in facing reality must discard beliefs, dispense with concepts, even, finally, the concept of concepts.

But that's not what's trailing through my mind at all. It's the kill part that keeps grabbing me. *Kill the Buddha.* Vin-cent Viola was sure not Buddha. And I didn't kill him. Not exactly.

No one believes I did. Not directly. But a guard on rounds in our lockup at two A.M. yesterday found the Mafia hit man dead. An hour later, my boss was on the horn to me. While he didn't exactly say my life was in danger because Vincent Viola's pals would think his arrest was just a setup to have him assassinated and they'd take revenge on anyone involved, I could hear the warning in his voice. I can still hear him, his voice strained from anger, frustration, and questions withheld. And fear. Honestly, I barely remember anything about the Mafia hit man, although my boss's voice rings in my head every once in a while.

Stress begets confusion; maybe that's the problem. Or I could be losing my mind. Or at least my memory. Or my ability to concentrate. I transpose numbers, and maybe worse. Making mistakes is not a good thing when you're a civilian clerk in a police station.

But I'm not supposed to be thinking about that now. That's the whole problem: my mind is where it shouldn't be. And so am I. I shouldn't be anywhere near the dead hit man's compadres—and they're everywhere.

Still, I have to focus. If I can't, nothing else matters. What I am supposed to be focusing on here, now, this Saturday morning, is sewing a Zen Buddhist priest's robe. Sewing this robe isn't like mending a hole in your pocket so that you don't dribble dimes all the way up the street. It's a very precise craft, requiring total concentration. Concentration is hardly my strong point, and normally I would avoid anything like this. But after this last week, any benign activity is a boon. An all-day meditation retreat with quiet strangers and some robe sewing struck me as just perfect.

Zen meditation is not about concentration per se. Any increased focus is a side benefit. In the meditation you notice your thoughts and let them go like clouds in a windy sky. I've sat in meditation other places but never at this meditation hall, this *zendo*, and never with such desperation. I trust this teacher. He's smart, accomplished, and, most important right now, kind. The one time I met him, he reassured me that I was doing the best I could, even if it didn't seem anywhere near good enough.

I hoped he would still think that when he heard I had arrived late because I'd misread 12th Street for 21st. I didn't know whether anyone was searching the city for me, so I had

stood huddled outside the *zendo* door, back to the street, until the bell inside had rung, and I'd stepped barefoot into a
white-walled room. The first thing that struck me was the
sweet woody smell of incense. On the altar at the far end,
the pale light of a lone candle flickered across the dark metal
statue of the Buddha. Black-garbed students sat on black
cushions on ledges along the other three walls. The silence
surrounded me like a hooded cloak. This was the last place
anyone would look for me.

Three periods of sitting were followed by a silent breakfast, a brief rest period (not that I dared close my eyes), and
then a work period. Work period, the sweet teacher had told
me, served to get done stuff like cleaning, cooking, and
sewing, and to provide students a chance to bring their
"meditation" awareness to a work situation.

This was confirmed when the woman who greeted me at
the *zendo* door, Marcia, or was it Marcelina, looked me over
carefully and then said she assigned jobs so a student could
deal with his own issues. A shy woman could be a crew
leader, a finicky guy could find himself as a toilet cleaner.

"You will sew the priest's robe," she said haughtily. "It
takes a great deal of focus to do that."

I was surprised, honored, and unnerved that she had
spotted my issue, my inability to concentrate, so fast. I had
only been here a few hours!

The robe to be sewn was the *okesa*, the priest's formal
outer robe used in the *zendo*, and at ceremonies. Draped sari-
like over one shoulder and tied with two black cords, it is
worn atop the black-sleeved kimono, and, in winter, long
underwear. A priest sews his or her first *okesa* for his ordination (with the help of his students) and is given others at
well-spaced occasions in his lifetime. Devoted students are
so anxious to help, there may be little left for the teacher to
do himself. They purchase several yards of silk, cut the cloth
into twenty-one separate pieces, and lovingly sew those
pieces back together into one, to symbolize a robe made of
rags. On rare occasions the robe is made in a hurry; then the

block of cloth is left whole and merely the frame, the decorative corner squares and the ties are sewn on. The robe symbolizes many things, but one is the esteem in which the community holds the teacher.

Still, I don't sew and this wouldn't have been my first choice of job, and the sewing room was definitely not a place I'd have picked. It's in the basement of the brownstone where any outsider could stoop down and peer in the windows.

Marcia or Marcelle, whatever her name was, spread the black silk over a large low table. "The *okesa* is the outer robe worn by the priest. Today we'll be finishing it up. Some of you . . ."

A robe lasts a long time, and I wanted to do a good job. Novice that I am, I needed to pay attention to Marcella. I tried. But all I could see was the front counter at the police station. Memories hung in my mind like a painting on veils. A tall patrolman leaning so far over the counter his nose was nearly against mine, whispering about a lead he'd gotten on Vincent Viola. About how it would make his career to collar Viola. That was Monday or Tuesday, maybe. By Wednesday, the rumor was all over; everyone in the station was wound tight. There had been lots of commotion on Thursday. But in a police station, there's commotion most days, not only when a Mafiosi checks in.

The newspaper said there was plenty of commotion early Friday morning when an upstart gang took credit for the hit man's murder.

Disjointed memories fluttered through my consciousness, but the actual booking was gone. Whenever I tried to grasp it, a gust blew, the veil fluttered, and the picture faded into fuzz.

The uproar must have died down by now—a day is an eternity in the news cycle—but I don't know for sure because I hadn't watched the news yesterday. What I'd done was sit in a chair trying to clutch that picture veil in my mind. But every time I grabbed, a wind inside my head jerked it away and flapped it riotously. By dusk it was in shreds.

It wasn't till dusk that I noticed the wind *outside* my head. Maybe winter winds always scrape the air as night approaches; maybe early dusk is always ominous then. Shutters on all houses may creak; shadows may slither across windows.

Maybe I should have stayed out of sight. Nowadays, I can't judge. I had to come to this *sesshin* today to try to see through the veil of my panic, thoughts, my fears, to see what's real. Nowadays, I don't know what's real and what I'm creating. The sweet priest said I was doing the best I could, but that is just not good enough. People are locked away who think more clearly than I do.

My mind-fuzz could be from lack of sleep. Last night I didn't sleep at all. The creaking got shriller, the shadows more solid, the moaning of the wind loud enough to mask the soft slap of steps. At five A.M., I was huddling outside the *zendo* door. I don't know where I'll go to find safety after the *sesshin* is over. I can't think that far ahead.

Thunder cracked. No, wait, there's no storm now, not today. It was someone coughing, here in the sewing room. I snapped my attention back to Marcella, the sewing teacher. She was holding up the yards of black silk that made up the robe, and saying something about running stitches.

Mentally, I'd been running since my boss's call yesterday morning. Actually, I'd been on a treadmill set too fast the whole time I'd worked at the police department. Civilian clerk was a wretched job for someone like me, prone to reverse numbers. Mistakes circled like mosquitoes. But I had been grateful for anything that gave me money every two weeks to pay off my ex's debts. The truth is my mind was already racing when I applied for the job, and even at the time I'd wondered what it said about the competition that the civilian authority chose me.

Paranoid as this sounds, I had wondered if they chose me not in spite of my flurried mind but because of it.

Embarrassed, I shook off the memory and stared hard at Marcella, who was standing in front of the windows, explaining the stitching requirements. She was a short woman, holding up a small black silk square, the decorative corner piece. Behind her, the uncurtained window exposed us all. Anyone lurking on the street could spot me. I took a deep breath, muttered silently: *Paranoia, just paranoia,* and refocused as she said, "Bring the needle up from the wrong side of the fabric. Your stitch should be an eighth of an inch across, like so." She held out the black fabric with the invisible black stitch. Behind her, something moved. Something at the windows.

But the flutter was only a toddler and his mother. She grinned as if this startling movement of his, which could have been any threatening thing, was cute.

Marcella hadn't paid any attention to the unnerving child at the window. She was still holding up the end of the black cloth. "Each stitch is no larger than an eighth of an inch, see? Each stitch is no farther than a quarter of an inch from the previous one, see? All stitches must be the same. All spaces between stitches must be the same."

My hand shot up into the silence. Marcella shot to my side. "I'm not that good a seamstress," I whispered, though in the silence everyone in the room could hear me, and a couple of people emitted burbles which could have been muffled gasps or laughs.

Marcella nodded. "Just do your best. Concentrate on each stitch. Remember the robe is for Vinnie, and we want everyone to have the chance to help with it."

"I heard about Vinnie Johnston and his achievements," I blurted. "I mean, actually from him . . . I was so impressed with him being not only a priest, but an accomplished cello or viola player and a Scrabble wizard to boot. He mastered all three—I mean they're so divergent . . . He had to know how to focus, right?"

He *had* to help me. I had realized that no matter how dangerous it was for me to be out on the city streets, this *sesshin* was the only chance I had to get some control of myself. I would be allotted one personal interview with the priest this afternoon. I had no idea what he could say that would be the magic bullet I needed, but I was sure that he would point me in the right direction. Then I would be able to part the veil of panic, speculations, fears, and see what was actually going on.

She patted my shoulder. "Just pay attention to what you're doing."

As if!

Maybe the danger wasn't outside the windows, but closer. Maybe it was Marcella I needed to think about. She seemed so familiar; had I seen her before? Maybe she had been to the precinct house. In which case she would have been hanging around, reading the wanted notices, the sheaf of municipal job specs, she, an island of calm in the maelstrom of our waiting room. But, more likely, it was her message rather than herself I recognized: *Just pay attention to what you're doing.* I nodded in response to her. As I had the many times I'd been given that instruction at the station.

A beady-eyed woman at the table passed me the thread and scissors. I cut my black thread, stretched it between my fingers and squinted at the hole in the needle, willing the twenty inches of thread to pass through.

"Make your stitches with care. We don't have time to go back and take out sloppy ones. Repeat, silently, *Namu kie Butsu*. With each stitch," she said slowly, as if she could read my panic. I hadn't even started the stitches, the black on black stitches, which had to be uniform in size. I couldn't figure why she seemed so familiar. And I hadn't even looked at the rest of the people here to see if *they* were familiar. Had I talked about coming here? After I met the priest, I was so impressed . . . had I told anyone he had invited me to this *sesshin*? Could my boss know? Or the Mafia?

She reiterated, "*Namu* as you insert the needle from the back side of the cloth. *Kie*, as you pull it through. *Butsu*, when you prick the cloth to begin the down stroke. *Namu kie Butsu.*"

Maybe I was being dangerously paranoid, but I heard the edge to her voice, a foisted-upon-forbearance, a tone I've heard often enough to recognize. I had been the one at the station who booked the priest, of course—I'm the only clerk and despite being a civilian, I handle the paperwork—but it wasn't my fault he was being booked. Legally, it was *his* fault. Too many outstanding parking violations will do that for you. And *he* wasn't upset with me. So why would Marcella be so put out? Plus, if he'd had to spend the night in custody, wasn't that because she hadn't rounded up bail money sooner?

My hands were shaking. With steely care, I pushed the needle down through the cloth. My stitch looked straight, petite, perfect. I took a breath and positioned the needle beneath the cloth an eighth of an inch farther along. But when the needle emerged it was closer to half an inch distant. I yanked it back and tried again. And again. And once more before the thread came up in the right spot. I sighed.

And glanced up into Marcella's gaze. Again I caught her a moment before she got her mask back in place. Her narrow-eyed, clenched-jawed look shocked me. It was exactly what I kept expecting to find on the face of some thug staring in the window. Not on the face of the Zen sewing instructor.

I was crazy to suspect her.

Still, what did I know about her? Nothing. Except that she was bearing down on me and my idle needle. To redirect her focus I grabbed the first thought that crossed my mind. "When is the ceremony?"

"The last period of *sesshin*."

"Today!"

She nodded.

"*Today!* I thought his ordination was going to be next month, or even later."

"Moved forward," she said through clenched teeth.

"There's no way we can get this done today."

She tapped the fabric. "*Namu kie Butsu.*"

I poked the needle through the underside of the cloth. I had to get it right. She was peering over my shoulder. Standing behind me, her hands could be poised on either side of my neck! I tackled the stitch as if it alone had the power to keep her at bay. The unseen diagonal stitch, that was the hard part. It had to emerge the expected eighth of an inch from its predecessor. My fingers were trembling. *Namu.* I pulled the thread all the way through. *Kie.* The stitch was perfect! Relief settled on my shoulders like a heated towel.

I was glad this stitch was proper, for the priest's sake. He had been a godsend Thursday. He strode quietly into the waiting room right after my boss had exploded about the transposed number thing. I'd been shaking, so chilled by his sarcasm that I couldn't do anything but just stand there. Then, suddenly, in front of me was this tall, sweet, shaven-headed priest, though I didn't realize the priest part until later because he was dressed in street clothes. Then he told me about himself—not at all pompously. I mean, if I had had all those artistic and musical talents plus being a Scrabble champion, I'd have had a neon sign in my apartment window. Flashing. But he was so matter-of-fact, like those things were only bonuses that came with his ability to *focus*. And even focusing was a by-product, not the point of Zen meditation. But he understood why I was caught by *focus*. He would do what he could to help. Anyone who made a serious, sustained effort could learn. *Anyone!* Even me. It was like I'd been in solitary and suddenly the cell door had flown open. I wanted to run out of the station and sign up for *sesshin*. When he said he'd sign me up, and then grinned and added, "As long as that's not considered bribing a public official!" I actually laughed. I didn't think I would ever laugh in the station again.

Marcella rapped my shoulder again. I just about dropped my little black square. In my relief, I'd forgotten she was lurking there. As I bobbled the square, I saw her face. If she could have stuck my needle through my eye, she would have.

I was so flustered I yanked my needle up through the fabric. It was a mile away from the last stitch. Panic spread across my back like oozing poison in a horror movie. Not cold or warm. Gravelly, as if it were gripping each cell of my back, tugging it relentlessly away from the bone.

She could be Mafia. There are hit women. They're as efficient as men. And with a lethal needle—

A bell rang. I jumped. But no one else moved. Not Marcella, not another soul in the room. The bell, I realized, was a reminder to us all to stop, to pay full attention to the sounds, the smells, the feelings in our bodies, to cease following thought after thought. It was the sweet bell they used in the *zendo*. And, surprisingly, it did cut through my panic. I felt the same calm as when I had been talking to the priest at the station.

Which had to have been *before* the Mafia booking, because no way would there have been any space for anything like calm after it. So there was no way that any of the deceased Mafiosi's associates would even know that the priest and I had discussed this *sesshin*, much less that I would be here. No reason why a hit man would be outside the window looking for me, and certainly no reason to assume Marcella was a made woman who just happened to meditate on the side, and do it where I just happened to come this one day. I really had followed my thoughts into fantasy.

The bell rang again. Cloth rustled; needles clicked.

I glanced up and again caught Marcella's expression. There was no mistaking her venom. But, if she wasn't connected, what was going on? Her pique had to be about the priest having been booked. Maybe her unwarranted anger was coming from her own guilt. I knew that pattern. Maybe she wasn't irked merely about the priest being booked; maybe it was *she* who was actually responsible for him going to jail. Like, maybe, she'd borrowed his car and hadn't paid that ton of parking tickets and hadn't told him.

The thing was, though, you don't put people in jail for not paying their parking tickets.

I poked the needle into the cloth somewhere on the square and jiggled it as if I was considering the spot.

My back tightened, as though all that toxic ooze was congealing. I had made mistakes before, but not on Thursday. I was sure of that. We were all primed for Vincent Viola's arrival and let me tell you, a prospective Mafia booking is way ahead of a priest's robe-sewing as an aid to concentration.

I pulled the needle out and moved it closer to the last stitch. Maybe no one would notice the half-inch gap between the previous two. I poked, pushed, pulled the thread through.

The priest had to have arrived at the station before the hit man, while we were all still hoping for the lead to him to pay off. I could see the sweet priest standing across the desk. Him telling me about the *sesshin*, about a Scrabble tournament, about playing the cello, or was it the viola?

The viola.

Vincent Viola.

I dropped the square.

My whole body clenched; I couldn't move. Vinnie Johnston played the viola. Vincent Viola. Had I . . .

Frantically I searched for excuses. Somebody else . . . But the station is small; I'm the only clerk. Besides, I could see the booking form as clearly as the needle in my hand.

Marcella rapped my shoulder and smacked the square back into my hand. "We have to finish this robe today!" she hissed.

Vincent Viola was dead, but Vinnie Johnston was going to be ordained today. We were making this robe for *his* ordination. A warm wave of gratitude surged through me. Every tense muscle relaxed, the door to every cell opened onto escape. Onto freedom. It was like sinking into a hot tub at the end of an icy night. A thousand times greater than that.

Whatever led to Vincent Viola getting whacked by gang

members didn't matter. Gangbangers are always offing each other. Vincent Viola had probably done it plenty of times himself. It was just his bad luck to end up in our cell with the brother of one of his off-ees. I shouldn't be so callous, but I could focus on that later.

Otherwise, things were fine. Like the times I had reversed numbers, this had all worked out. I felt awful to think any mishap of mine might have caused a problem for the sweet priest. But whatever happened, it was all over now. Soon the sweet priest would be ordained here. I wanted to run around the room hugging everyone here. I wanted to hug Marcella. Most of all I wanted to find Vinnie Johnston and hug him.

I would apologize, of course. He would forgive me. He was that kind of man. He had specifically invited me here because he knew I was desperate. He knew about the mistakes. He had invited me anyway. He wouldn't even care if my stitches in his robe were irregular. He'd know I was doing the best I could. But now I wanted my square to be perfect for him, to be the cloth embodiment of my wonderful relief.

I grabbed the scissors, clipped the thread and began pulling out the errant stitches. Even if I didn't get back into the *zendo* all day, even if I missed the rest of the meals for the rest of the day, what mattered was that this square on his *okesa* be perfect.

After all, it would be almost the only decoration on the robe. There weren't the normal sixteen pieces here. No one had cut them from the original piece of cloth; no phalanxes of students had sewn them back together making the normal pattern. Vinnie's robe would consist only of the edge piece and four corner squares.

Because his ordination had been moved up.

"Marcelina," I said aloud.

"Marcia," she corrected.

"Sorry," I whispered. Everyone was looking at me now, Marcia daggers. I took a breath. I wanted to get this question right. I could see where a night in jail might be enough to make a priest postpone his ordination. But not to move it forward. And why the rush? Why this hurried robe? "Marcia, why has Vinnie Johnston's ordination been moved up to today?"

"Ordination?"

I nodded at the robe.

It seemed like an eternity before she answered. No needles moved. No one seemed to breathe. Even the street noises stopped. It was the only time in my life I have experienced total silence.

She said, "He was ordained yesterday . . . as he was dying. This robe is for his funeral."

The curtain parted and the pure clarity of memory struck me then, and I realized that never again, no matter how much I longed for it, would I be able to lose focus and forget how a mind fuzzed and scattered can change everything.

ॐ

Sewing a Fine Stitch

Whether you're sewing an *okesa*, a quilt, a doll, or any other project that requires fine stitches, evenness and consistency are the most important qualities. As you practice, you can concentrate on making your stitches smaller—you may even reach the expert level of eight to twelve stitches per inch. The kind of fabric, thread, and needles all affect the outcome of your finished piece. Cotton fabric and cotton thread are good places to start. Quilters advise using shorter needles, especially for the running stitch. Cut a length of good cotton thread about twenty inches long, thread it through the needle, and make a knot on one end. Insert the needle through the back of the cloth, and pull up so that the knot is hidden.

The running stitch is a good choice when something

needs to be reversible, as a quilt. For a running stitch, pass the needle over and under the fabric several times. The upper stitches should all be of equal length; the lower stitches, also equal in length, should be half the size of the upper. Make three or four stitches, and then pull the thread all the way through. Repeat to complete the seam.

The ladder stitch is used in general sewing and especially in doll making to close up all stuffing openings. The ladder stitch is made by pulling the needle up on the left side of the seam, then down on the left; then up on the right and down on the right; then the pattern is repeated until the end of the seam. For the ladder stitch, or *kayakushi*, it might be helpful to repeat *namu* as you insert the needle in the back of the cloth, *kie* while pulling needle and thread through, and *butsu* with the insertion of the needle into the front of the fabric. The repetition helps the sewer to concentrate on the task and, in practicality, to keep the needle vertical as it goes through the cloth.

Madame de Farge, the most famous knitter in literary history, may have been the inspiration for a contemporary group of knitters who meet regularly to knit and discuss how to further what they call a revolutionary agenda.

Knitting, which is thought to have originated among nomads in the Arabian desert as long ago as 1000 B.C., has definitely come into the twenty-first century. In addition to buying supplies and finding instructions on the Internet, you can tap into the knitting community through hundreds of web logs, or blogs as they're commonly known, in which posters write regularly about the progress of their projects. Knitting blogs have even been joined together to form web rings, creating communities that may be separated by thousands of miles but whose members all share a passion for knitting.

STRUNG OUT

by Monica Ferris and Denise Williams

Monica Ferris is the author of nine mystery novels in the Betsy Devonshire needlework series, including Hanging By a Thread, Cutwork, and most recently, Crewel Yule. She lives in Minneapolis with her husband, who is a museum curator, and two cats.

Denise Williams works with art materials and yarn. She lives in Long Lake, Minnesota with her husband, three sons, two parakeets and a Samoyed. She designs needlework patterns, teaches flute and Russian language, and studies early music. This is her first work of fiction.

§◊

GARY HIKED HIMSELF higher against the headboard of his bed and focused on picking up two loops of yarn with his right-hand knitting needle. He was a thin kid, a little undersized for fifteen, with large, knobby hands and dark, unruly hair that shaded his gray eyes. He was decreasing the number of stitches in the row but trying to do it evenly. He was pretty good at knitting in the round, and had a good idea in his head how to do the decrease, but wasn't sure it would work on the actual sleeve—and he had diverged so far from the pattern in the book, he couldn't consult it for help. He rubbed his stockinged feet together and held the work up to see how it looked so far.

He was in his cluttered bedroom with two friends, Marcus and Redhawk, watching *Kill Bill* on his DVD player.

Redhawk was slouched in a beanbag chair, eyes on the screen. He was only three weeks older than Gary, but two inches taller and fifteen pounds heavier. A supremely self-assured young man, he wore his auburn hair cropped very short on the sides and back, and long on the top, as close as his parents would let him come to a Mohawk. He sometimes spiked the top when he was far enough away from home that he thought they couldn't find out. He had the light brown eyes that sometimes came with red hair, and a beaky nose he was vain about. He wore tan cargo pants and a black shirt buttoned all the way up so people might think he was hiding a rude tattoo. Redhawk was a nickname he had given himself years ago; none of his peers knew his real name.

Marcus was the oldest at sixteen, though he'd lost a year of school when he came down with mono a couple of years ago and so was a classmate of the other two. Thin and very tall for his age, with a broad pug nose and sleepy blue eyes, he kept his hair back with a grimy bandanna. He wore camouflage trousers and T-shirt under a green vest covered with pockets and loops. He was slow of speech and movement, and always smiling as if at some secret joke. He was sitting on the chair at Gary's little desk.

Meanwhile, on the screen, Vernita shot a gun through the bottom of a cereal box, missing her attacker and sending cereal flying. Her assailant nailed Vernita in the chest with a knife. Blood oozed, and Vernita gasped her last. Their fight had been a really violent one, and the walls and floor of the kitchen were well splattered with blood, the floor covered with cereal.

"That's right, hide your face, Gare," taunted Redhawk, because Gary was still holding up the sleeve. Marcus snorted in amusement.

"Nuts, I've seen it three times. Bill's just a creepy guy holding a sword," replied Gary. "Tell me when the anime starts." Gary liked Japanese cartoons. On the screen, the victor strode from the kitchen, crunching cereal underfoot. Gary resumed knitting the row.

"What is that, a hat? You gonna *wear* that?" queried Marcus, nodding at the fluffy white mass in Gary's hands.

"Hell no!" said Gary, beyond mere disgust at his friend's ignorance. "It's the sleeve of a sweater. It's for my sister." Marcie would be four in two weeks, he was knitting a cardigan in white angora for her. He already had the cardinal-shaped buttons for it. How Redhawk could think the sleeve of a child's sweater could be a hat for a fifteen-year-old guy was beyond him.

"Doesn't matter," said Redhawk. "Knitting's something a man shouldn't be doing anyway. That's women's work—no, it's *gran'ma's* work." He laughed loudly at the jest, rolling from side to side on the beanbag.

"It's men's work, too!" Gary retorted. "Soldiers knit. When they get shot and go to the hospital, they need to do something to get their minds off the pain and get their trigger fingers back in shape, so the nurses teach them to knit, y'know? They got medals on their chests and knitting needles in their hands, I've seen pictures of them. So just shut up, you ignorant doofus." Gary had a restless nature, and the only way he could sit through a movie was to give his hands something to do. Knitting was perfect, he could do it sitting down, and there was something useful at the end of it.

"'Ignorant *doofus'*?" Marcus drawled from the chair. "What kind of a word is doofus?"

"A word that describes a doofus named Redhawk, that's what!"

"You never even been shot *at*," Redhawk sneered, "much less shot. So you're no hero, *gran'ma*."

"I could take you in two seconds, doofus!"

"Oh, yeah, *gran'ma?*"

"Yeah!" Gary swung his legs over the edge of his bed and began to put his knitting down.

"Hey, shut up," said Marcus lazily, sliding farther down

his spine on the chair. "Here comes the big kung fu fight." He gestured at the screen.

That stopped the argument. The nameless swordswoman in a sleek yellow leather jumpsuit faced a man, then a girl wielding a mace, and finally a horde of masked thugs, and even those who had seen it before did not wish to miss it. Swords clashed, heads and limbs were severed, thugs were impaled, and blood spurted in great quantity. Gary went back to his knitting, glancing occasionally at the screen, where the scene blinked from color to black and white, and then to black silhouettes over blue lighting. Cool.

But all good things must come to an end, and finally, as Gary was just starting the cuff of the sleeve, the woman in yellow stood balanced on a high railing over the nightclub dance floor. She looked at the dead with satisfaction and shouted down to the dying writhing in pools of blood: "Those of you lucky enough to have your lives . . . Take them with you! However, leave the limbs you've lost. They belong to me now."

Marcus, noticing Gary was not avidly watching this brilliant scene, slipped off a shoe and tossed it at him. Gary, paying more attention than Marcus thought, twisted agilely and caught it between his feet. He dropped the knitting, grabbed the shoe, and threw it all in one motion—at Redhawk. Redhawk howled when it clipped him on the ear, and a real fight would have ensued had not Gary's mother rapped on the door to say it was time for Gary to wash up for supper.

Redhawk rolled off the beanbag, which he punched a few times to release tension. He snorted at it, as he would have at the ruins of Gary, stood and looked first at his empty hands then wildly around, then clapped his right hand on a back pocket.

"Looking for something?" drawled Gary.

"Nah. And I'm outta here, *gran'ma*," he sneered and left in a huff.

Marcus retrieved his shoe and put it on, then began to

hunt for his backpack. He found it under Gary's desk. It was old, a dulled blue, with a zipper that wouldn't close all the way and a buckle missing its tang. He lifted it onto his narrow shoulders, straightened to his considerable height, and started for the door.

Back when he was eleven, Gary had purchased a good-sized wooden box full of beads at a garage sale. It cost fifty cents and was full of wooden beads, plastic beads, glass beads, stone and clay beads ranging from an inch and a half in diameter down to a quarter-inch. He had spent much of his free time that summer stringing them into a curtain which he suspended from his door frame. Four years later the curtain remained intact, a rattling secondary barrier to the rest of the house that he refused to take down or modify. He called it his Dream Catcher—and the string of nightmares he'd been suffering from had stopped when the curtain went up, and even now were rare.

Marcus turned to wave as he went through the curtain, reaching with his other hand for the doorknob. Gary, busy taking the DVD out, said, "Here, take your DVD." Marcus turned the rest of the way around without realizing he had twisted a strand of the bead curtain into the top of his backpack.

"Hey, watch it!" Gary shouted, just as the strand tightened on the backpack.

Marcus jumped, turning again and thereby hopelessly tangling the strand into the open zipper—and catching another strand with his left ear.

"No, the other way!" yelled Gary. Marcus, trying to solve the puzzle, shrugged out of his backpack. The second strand rolled smoothly free but the first tried to support the weight of the backpack for a few seconds before it broke, sending beads bouncing and rolling. The backpack dropped with a thud, spilling books and papers.

"You jackass!" roared Gary, as Marcus squatted, reaching in all directions for his belongings.

"Sorry, man, really sorry," muttered Marcus. He stuffed

his things into the pack, then began crawling around on the floor with Gary, picking up beads. But the room was small and cluttered and the two kept getting in one another's way.

Finally, Gary said, "Forget it, butthead, I'll get the rest of them. Just go."

"All right, all right, man. Hey, I really am sorry."

"Whatever."

Gary put the beads into his underwear drawer, then went to supper. After, he resumed the search and found six more beads, and a test paper with Marcus' name on it, marked D+—he blinked at that; Marcus had been a B student until recently. He tossed the paper into his wastebasket, crawled around some more, and found three more beads, a knitting pattern he thought he'd lost, a knitting needle, and, half under the beanbag chair, a plastic bag stamped with colored leaves and what looked like the remnants of a sandwich in it. He put the pattern and needle on his desk, tossed the plastic bag into the basket, and continued searching.

He finally decided the only way to find all the beads was to clean the floor of his room. With a deep, sad sigh, he settled into the task. It took him all evening, but netted him nearly a dozen smaller beads. This cheered him up enough to change the linen on his bed—which got him another bead, a carved wooden one he really liked. He stuck it in his pocket and began clearing off his desk.

Gary had a one-track mind. He was still working on his room when his mother came in at eleven to send him to bed. She looked around in amazement at the order he had wrought. "God love you, this is wonderful!" she said. "Is your homework done?"

"Yeah—I did it yesterday, because I knew my friends were coming over."

"Better and better. Well, get to bed. I'll empty the waste basket and vacuum in here while you're at school tomorrow."

*   *   *

GARY CAME HOME Monday afternoon to find his father waiting for him in the living room. "Son, I want to talk to you," he said in the voice of doom that Gary had come to dread. He gave his conscience a swift examination and found, to his surprise, it was relatively clear.

"Sure, Dad." He followed his father into his den, a place he otherwise studiously avoided. His father was a retired army colonel, whose last assignment was teaching strategy and tactics at West Point. He retained the haircut and squared shoulders, the habit of barking orders, and the black/white mindset. Gary admired him—he was scrupulously fair—but had always been in awe of him, and was sometimes afraid of him.

But now he went into the study, lined with books, trophies, and awards, with no qualms.

His father went behind a carved wooden desk, clear on the surface except for a phone and pen set, and a plastic bag that Gary, surprised, recognized.

"Hey, why do you have that?" he asked.

"Your mother showed it to me. Talk to me about it."

"Looks like garbage, a leftover sandwich or something."

"Don't lie to me, son!"

"I'm not! That's what it is. See the sprouts?"

"You're damn' right I do! Your mother never made you a sandwich with *these* sprouts!"

"I know that! It's not mine, one of the guys must've left it in my room."

Gary would not have thought it possible for his father to stand even straighter, but he did. His chin went back and his neck swelled, a sign of full-bore rage. Gary felt his mouth drop open and made an effort to close it.

His father grated, "Don't try to throw this into someone else's court."

"Whaddya mean? Throw what? It's just trash out of my wastebasket, not something I threw in Redhawk's yard or something."

"You mean to stand there, look me in the face, and tell me this is just some worthless garbage?"

"Well, it is! I was cleaning up my room. Ask Mom."

"It was your mother who found it and told me what it is."

"Well, so what's the big deal?"

His father found a deep well of patience and carefully untwisted the wire fastener to open the bag and shake the contents out onto his desk. "Look at this. Tell me to my face you don't know what it really is."

Gary came closer. "Well, that's a paper towel, kinda juicy, and there's some alfalfa sprouts."

"That's not alfalfa."

Gary shrugged. "Then what is it?"

"You tell me."

He was starting to feel desperate. "I don't *know*! What did Mom say?"

"She says it's marijuana."

Gary bent sharply forward. "It is? Is that what it looks like?"

His father turned away, wiping his face with his hand— a very bad sign. "How long has this been going on?"

"How long has what been going on? I don't smoke marijuana, if that's what you're thinking, I never have!"

His father turned back. He looked older somehow, and sad. "Please don't lie to me. This isn't the kind you smoke, it's the kind you grow."

Gary felt himself giggling, he couldn't help it. "There's a *difference?*"

"These are sprouted marijuana seeds. You take these and plant them, and they grow into tall plants, which you harvest and dry, chop, and smoke."

Gary was amazed at his father's broad knowledge of the topic. "I didn't know that," he said. "Wait, you said *Mom* told you about it? Wow." His dad, Gary knew, got his broad experience from being a soldier. He'd been a soldier since before college, and he came from a line of soldiers that stretched back at least as far as the Civil War. Mom, on the other hand, had been an art teacher and was still pretty good with watercolors. But, say, weren't artists notorious for smoking dope? Wow, his own mother! With an effort, he didn't smile, but he suddenly felt almost cheerful.

"That's not the point here, Gary," said his father. "The point here is that you apparently have been around this stuff long enough that you've decided to go into business selling it."

"I have not! I told you, I never smoked it. I don't know who owns that, but it isn't mine! I found it when I was cleaning my room yesterday. I bet it belongs to Marcus, it was under the beanbag chair he was sitting on."

"I already warned you about trying to blame someone else for this!"

"I'm not! For Chrissake, Dad! Why would I lie?"

Of course the conversation went downhill from there. His father was threatening to call the police when his mother came in, drawn by the noise they were making. Gary was struggling not to cry and begged his mother to do or say something. She sent Gary to his room while she talked to his father.

He flung himself onto his bed, where he kept turning the pillow over when it grew too hot on his face. A lot of good it did him cleaning his room like a good kid, he thought.

His mom came in an hour later, exhausted, to say his dad had relented only to the extent that the police wouldn't be called at present. Gary was grounded "until he decided to tell the truth."

"But Mom, I really *am* telling the truth! C'mon, Mom. Please, *please*, you've got to believe me!"

THERESE DID BELIEVE her son—though she didn't say so to him.

Instead, she talked with her friend Betsy Devonshire,

who owned a needlework shop called Crewel World down
on Lake Street. Betsy was an amateur sleuth who had actually solved two murders.

"I know this isn't murder, but it's terribly important that
we find out the truth. If my son has really gotten so far into
drugs that he's thinking of dealing, then my husband is
right, and something very serious has to happen to divert
him from that path. On the other hand, if he's innocent—
and I think he is—then it's desperately important that we
prove that to his father."

Betsy was a middle-aged woman, plump despite all ef-
forts, with blond hair and keen blue eyes. Her smile was
sympathetic, but she said, "I don't know what I can do."

"You know about solving mysteries. Please, Betsy."

Betsy sighed and rubbed her nose. "I don't know anything about growing marijuana from seed."

"Well, as it happens, I know a little about it," said
Therese. "In college, I had two friends who were putting
themselves through grad school by selling LSD and marijuana. They bought the LSD from a Mexican guy, but grew
the grass themselves. They showed me how they sprouted
seeds by sprinkling them on wet paper towels kept in a
plastic bag, then planted them in big pots in a bedroom
with lots of full-spectrum lights. They grew some great
stuff with those lights, but that's what did them in. The
landlord noticed their electric bill was more than twice
what it should be. He paid the apartment a visit while they
were out, took one look at that room, and called the cops.
So when I saw that plastic bag, I knew right away what was
in it."

"Therese, I had no idea you had such an adventurous
youth."

Therese's smile turned wry. "You know, looking back, it
seems even to me that she was some other person. You
should have seen Frank's face when I told him about what I
found. He was as surprised that I knew what it was as he was
mad at Gary. So, will you help?"

"I know your son knits, because he buys his yarn here. He seems like a pretty good kid, but I don't know him well. Tell me, were you surprised when you saw the bag?"

"Yes. Yes, I was. Gary is a good kid, he's into computers, and he plays those elaborate games that get hundreds of people involved from all over the world."

Betsy frowned. "That would seem to mean he's smart. Or am I wrong?"

"No, you're right. He's very bright."

"Then why did he throw the bag into his wastepaper basket? Or does he empty it himself?"

"Almost never. Anyway, I remember telling him I would empty it and vacuum his rug." Therese brightened. "Well, thank you! Of *course* he didn't know what it was, or he wouldn't have left it where I could see it! But will Frank believe that? I don't know, but this might be a wedge into his closed mind. But do you see what that means? If it's not Gary's, then it's one of his friends. Smoking is bad enough, but if he's growing his own, I think we need to know who that is. Betsy, will you please talk to Gary?"

"All right. But don't tell him I want to question him. See if Frank will let him stop in to buy something. I imagine, without his computer to play with, he's knitting up a storm."

"Yes, he sure is. All right. Thanks."

GARY STROLLED TO the knitting yarn section of Crewel World and began rummaging in the basket that held the sale yarn. He didn't mind crumpled paper bands or even slightly soiled fibers. He also didn't care if the world knew he loved to knit—an unusual sign of maturity in a fifteen-year-old male. "Hey, Betsy!" he shouted from across the room, causing two other shoppers who hadn't realized he was there to turn and stare, "you got only one skein of this?" He held up the skein, which was a medium green sock-weight yarn with a single filament of white twisted into it.

The paper band around it looked as if it had been taken off, wadded up, then smoothed and put back on.

"All the yarn I have on deep discount is in that basket," she replied, starting his way. "But I may have more that's not on sale." She helped him go through the basket again—his method tended to send skeins rolling across the carpet, which Betsy hoped to forestall. There was no need to risk the yarn's last chance to recoup its cost—the next step down from this basket was the Dumpster.

There was only the one skein.

"What are you making?" she asked.

"I was thinking a pair of socks. For my mom."

"Maybe some other color?" she suggested, holding up two sky-blue skeins for his attention.

"Nope, it's gotta be green." He reached into a jacket pocket and came out with a clear plastic tube full of green seed beads and a packet the size of his palm held shut with a single staple. It was half-full of dark green beads in some pointed shape. "Check these out. I got them both for a buck." He handed her the packet, and she saw the beads were shaped like a cluster of narrow, serrated leaves. "Will your mother know what these are?" she asked, pinching one of them between thumb and forefinger.

"Sure, we've got it growing in our backyard."

"You do?"

"Yeah, Mom says a bird planted it. It's called a mountain laurel. I was gonna mow it down when it first sprouted, but Mom said leave it, so I did, and now it's a tree, with these orange berries on it. All kinds of birds come to eat them. She likes it a lot, so when I saw these leaves I thought I'd make her something with them."

"Fine. Do you need a book on knitting with beads?"

"Nah. Well, I mean, I tried it one time and the only big secret is to string the beads on the yarn first. But what I did is I found this crazy program on the Internet that uses a mathematical method to work out patterns, and I got to twiddling it, and I used it to design this pattern to put beads on a cuff."

"Cuff? Oh, the cuff of a sock."

"Or the cuffs on a sweater, or the bottom of a vest or anything where you make ribbing. They kind of drape, and it looks cool. All you need to know is how many stitches to figure how many beads. Anyone can figure out how to sprinkle little beads into a pattern, but when I tried using bigger ones, the twist of the yarn makes them want to lean sideways. So I figured out that if you put a little bead on each side of a bigger one, it kind of dangles. And with these beads, you see why I want green yarn."

"Yes, I do. Very clever of you. Could you bring the socks in when you finish? I'd like to take a look at it. Maybe it's a pattern we could sell."

"Really?" The boy brightened. "Sure! Wow!"

Betsy was perfectly serious. Gary had learned to knit in first grade, from a teacher who taught her whole class the art. He was probably the only boy who took to it, and kept it up even when it stopped being cool. But that meant he understood techniques as few could.

"Here, let's look around and see if I have any more of that yarn." Betsy found another skein of the green and decided, since Gary was a designer she was thinking of buying from, she'd sell it him for the same price as the bargain basket one.

At the checkout, Gary dug into his grubby pocket and pulled out a thin pack of singles. "My dad gave me an advance on my birthday money," he said.

"Before you leave," Betsy said, "can you show me something?"

"Maybe," he said, a trifle warily. "What?"

"I've been thinking of knitting with beads, and I'm one of those people who has to be shown something. I don't learn well from books. Show me how you string the beads."

"Okay. Sure."

Betsy led the way to the library table in the center of her shop. "Do you need a tray?" she asked.

"No, I just work right on the table."

He sat down and opened the tube and packet. Using his left thumb and forefinger to control the spill, he poured out a little group of seed beads. "See, I first make three sets of eight little beads." Using a short, two-ended knitting needle he pulled from an accessories holder in the center of the table, he began to maneuver them into three rows of eight beads each. Then he opened the packet and spilled out some leaf beads. "Now I make eight sets of a little bead, a big bead, and a little bead." Again using the needle he pushed some beads into that arrangement. "I need eight sets of this," he said quietly, and continued herding the beads into little groups along the edge of the table.

"Now I do a row of sixteen beads," he said. His voice had grown softer, as if he were talking more to himself than her. "And a row of thirty-two little ones, and then a row of sixteen." The way he said "little ones," he might have been speaking of children or pets.

While he was doing that, Betsy went into the box and found a pair of hair-thin beading needles on a card. She pulled one out and handed it to him as soon as he was finished arranging the beads.

"Do you put them on in reverse order?" she asked.

"No, this is the reverse order. You put them on this way, then they come along in the right order as you knit them."

"Yes, I see," she nodded.

He pulled out the end of one of the skeins of sock yarn and pushed a couple of inches of it through the needle. The needle was for very fine beads; these were heavier, so simply touching the tip of the needle to one tilted its open end easily onto the needle. The boy leaned forward, his mouth open a little, tip, tip, tipping them swiftly onto the needle. His other hand pulled them back onto the yarn as they accumulated.

Betsy hated to break into Gary's flow. The intent look,

the absence of awareness—a customer came to the table with a question about a counted cross-stitch pattern she wanted to buy, and Betsy answered her without breaking Gary's concentration—were indications Gary's mind had gone to a sweet, calm place as he skillfully threaded the yarn with the beads.

But she had agreed to help Therese with her son, so she said, "Gary, may I ask you some questions?"

"M'hmmm," he said, possibly meaning yes, but also possibly not knowing who she was, or even where he was.

Betsy knew about "flow," having discovered the deep, deep pleasure of falling so far into stitchery that the rest of the world dissolved into a distant mist. But she persisted.

"Gary."

"Yuh?" That was closer. She waited a minute more. "There," he said, picking up the last bead and sliding the last lot of them down onto the yarn. He looked around blinking, as if waking from a nap. "I'll have to wait till I get home, where my needles are." He looked as if he wanted to start for home right now.

"How long did it take you to figure out the pattern?" she asked.

"Maybe three days, or a week. The first time I tried my own pattern, I put way too many beads on the sock, and it was too heavy."

Betsy said, "Are you sure it was that fast? When I'm working out a variation on a pattern, time doesn't mean anything. I think it only took a few minutes, when it really took several hours."

"You get that, too?" He smiled with his whole face, and she suddenly saw that he was going to be a very handsome man.

"How did you figure this one out?" she asked.

He went into a long explanation that at first didn't seem an answer at all, about how he liked to use his computer to create pictures of people that looked like the characters in his computer games. "They have pictures of them, but sometimes I get a different idea of how they should look. And there's a program that uses like a mesh to make a three-dimensional object. You figure out where your points are, the high and low, and it draws lines and turns it into a drawing that has like a mesh over it."

"I don't understand. Do you mean like when you copy a drawing, you first draw horizontal and vertical lines over it to form a grid?"

"No," he shook his head. "Not a grid, it's a mesh. It's three-D. Made of triangles. It's hard to explain. But once you have the mesh, you can turn the figure around and see it from different angles. Scientists came up with the program, they used it to make a really detailed picture of the heart that looked like it was transparent so you could see the inside and the outside at the same time, and from any angle. All you need are enough points so you can draw the lines—like those connect-the-dots games in coloring books for little kids, only kinda way more complicated."

"And this helped you design a knitting pattern?"

"Sure. I used it to see what the pattern would look like finished. You know how it is, once you get how the pattern works, you don't need the instructions."

That was just starting to be true for Betsy, who came to stitchery late. For Gary, who could purl before he could read, knitting was as natural as walking. She had no doubt he could look at a sweater and understand how to replicate its pattern.

"I want to talk to you about that bag of marijuana sprouts your mother found in your wastebasket."

He straightened, eyes wide, wary and uneasy. "My mother told you about that?"

"Yes, she did. You probably know that I do a little crime solving. It's a talent I have."

He stared at her. "You do?"

"Yes, I do," she replied firmly.

"But why do you ... I mean ... I didn't commit a crime!"

"No, of course you didn't."

"You believe me?"

"Yes, I do. And so does your mother. That's why she came to me. She wants me to find out who really did it."

"Ah, for my dad." He nodded.

"That, too. But you see, if it's not you, then one of your friends left that bag of seedlings in your room. People who raise it from seed are generally planning to sell it. Dealing is a serious crime, and it doesn't help that he's careless about it. Your mother wants to know which of your friends doesn't care who he involves in this business. So, who left that bag in your room?"

"Well, it could only be one of two guys. They were the only ones there that night."

"Could someone else have left it earlier, on another day?"

"I haven't had anyone over for about a week. I think I would have noticed it by then."

Betsy nodded. The sprouts would likely have died if left for a week without care.

"So tell me about these two friends."

"Well, one's Marcus."

"What's his last name?"

"Lundstrom."

Betsy thought. Though Lundstrom was a common Scandinavian name, she didn't know anyone by that name.

"What's he like? Is he a good friend?"

"He's like my best friend. I like him 'cause he's laid back, easygoing."

"Is he a gamer?"

Gary laughed and picked up the needle to begin threading beads again. "No way. He isn't interested in anything that takes more than fifteen minutes, unless it's a movie with lots of stuff going on."

"What is he interested in?"

"Eating." Gary laughed again. "Well, that and gross movies. He's not fat, but when he's hungry, he can really pack it in. You should have heard him one time! He was describing Doritos like they were the best food in the world. He even liked the shape." Gary lifted his face, eyes closed, and drawled, "Man, they're so, like, *triangular*!"

Betsy chuckled. "What else does he like? Does he have a job?"

"No. Well, not any more. He used to work at Leipold's, but he never got to work on time. Mr. Leipold is a nice man, but even he finally had enough. I like Marcus, though, because nothing bothers him, even getting fired. *Everything* bothers me." That last was said in a very quiet voice.

"I understand your father is bothering you a whole lot right now."

Gary fell silent. Obviously, he preferred to keep his feelings about his father to himself. Then he stirred himself to say, "So, anyway, the other guy's called Redhawk Lieder-brod."

Betsy smiled. "You mean Elmer?"

"Well, Redhawk's last name is Liederbrod. You mean his real first name is *Elmer*? He always makes everyone call him Redhawk." Gary smiled, his eyes alight. "Oh, this is golden!"

"What does he do? I mean outside of school?"

"He plays electric bass. He keeps trying to start a band, but he can't keep it going because he gives everyone too much crap. He always has to be the boss, he won't listen to anyone but himself. He likes to game, like me—but when he's gamesmaster he's too strict, and he fights with the gamesmaster when he's not, so he doesn't play much any-more."

"Why is he your friend?"

Gary smiled. "We've known each other since kindergarten, for one thing. And, he's always got your back, y'know? Definitely there when you need him. Once, when my dad was being one huge butt nugget, I called him up real late one night, and he actually snuck out a window to come over, y'know, to talk and hang out for a while. Plus, I like him because he's a wild man, you never know what he'll try next. And that makes him fun, y'know?"

Betsy nodded. Often the tame ones like to associate with the wild ones. "Okay, that's very helpful. You're good at describing him."

They were interrupted by a customer with a plastic bag in her hand. "Betsy, I found this in the back. It seems to be a kit, but there's no price marked on it." It was a small, clear plastic bag with autumn leaves on it. Inside was a long rectangle of white Aida cloth, four lengths of Anchor floss in four gorgeous fall colors, and a folded piece of paper printed with a pumpkin pattern.

"It belongs in a basket by the cash register. Someone must have taken it out, then put it down when she changed her mind." Customers were always doing that; Betsy sometimes felt she spent half her time in the shop putting things back.

Betsy reached for it, but the customer lifted it high. "How much is it?"

"Five dollars," said Betsy.

"I'll take it."

Betsy stood to follow the customer to the checkout desk, then glanced over to see Gary staring wide-eyed at the customer.

Betsy handed the receipt to the customer, and waited until the door "binged" as she walked out. She turned back to look at Gary. "What is it?" she said.

"That bag, it's just like the bag I found in my room. With the paper towel and sprouts on it. Only they weren't sprouts. Well, not alfalfa sprouts."

Betsy said, "Are you sure?"

"Sure, I'm sure! I mean, it wasn't like those bags Mom buys at the grocery store to put sandwiches in, or the ones you put stuff in you're gonna freeze. It was like that one the woman there had, with leaves printed on it." He snorted. "Leaves. I think I hate leaves, they're nothing but trouble."

"I think this time the leaves are going to get you *out* of trouble. I know which of the two it is."

Gary stared at her. "You do?" He was impressed, then alarmed. "Are you *sure*?"

She nodded. "Mrs. Liederbrod bought two of those kits a couple of weeks ago. I suppose it's possible Marcus could have acquired one of those plastic bags somewhere else, but I don't know where. I bought them at a Dollar Store in Crystal last winter to use this autumn. Does Marcus shop in Dollar Stores?"

"No, he goes to Goodwill and Unique Thrift Store." He beamed at her. "You're pretty smart, you know that? Are you going to tell my dad about this?"

"Yes. And Mrs. Liederbrod, too, I'm afraid."

"I STARTED OUT sure it was Marcus," Betsy said to Therese the next day. "He had all the signs of being a marijuana user: slow and laid back, with attacks of the munchies. But Elmer—Redhawk—had the business head. Then Gary put the solution into my hand by recognizing the plastic bag. Funny," she looked sideways at Therese, "you must have recognized the bag, too."

Therese nodded. "Oh, I did. But it didn't mean anything to me. I guess nearly every woman I know stitches and shops at Crewel World. So I didn't think about the bag as an important clue."

"Did Gary's father apologize?"

Therese smiled. "Apologies come hard to Frank. But I know—and so does Gary. For penance, he's letting Gary teach him how to knit a set of covers for his golf clubs."

§§

Bead pattern for "Strung Out"

The beads should slide comfortably over the yarn, not too tight, not too loose.

Choose nice quality beads that have rounded holes so the edges of the beads don't wear through the yarn.

Changing the color of the yarn or beads can change the whole mood of the finished piece. The combination I chose is purplish blue metallic beads with ice blue leaves on black yarn. I'm also trying purplish metallic on violet yarn, and bluish green leaves on turquoise yarn. Experiment with different yarns and beads, make stuff up and have fun with it.

Some realities to observe (it's just the way things are):

- The beads have to fit over the yarn. This might seem obvious, but I drooled over some beads that just were not going to fit over the yarn I wanted to use.
- There's going to be some math. The beads have to be strung onto the yarn in order, and the pattern has to repeat over a multiple of eight stitches to come out even.
- Beads are surprisingly heavy, so use them as accents. My first attempt was very ambitious, and the cuff of the sock I started slumped under the weight of that complex bead patterning.
- The beads have to be strung onto the yarn in reverse of how they will be knitted into the pattern. The last bead you thread on will be first in line to go into its place in the knitting.

Materials for a pair of socks with a beaded cuff:

2 skeins black sock yarn

Size 6 seed beads

Bead threader (or strip the paper off of a twist tie and bend the wire into a threading needle, or use a length of strong nylon thread)

16 leaf or other decorative beads

Size 1.5 and 2 double pointed (dp) wooden sock needles (or size to get gauge)

Gauge = 7 stitches/inch

Beaded accent pattern:

String the beads onto the yarn in this order

8 + 8 + 8 +		24 +
(1 + leaf + 1) × 8 +	*or*	(1 + leaf + 1) × 8 +
16 + 32 + 16		64

On size 2 dp needles, cast on 64 (or multiple of 8)
Change to size 1.5 dp needles and rib 11 rows in twisted, k2 p2 ribbing.

Bead sequence
Change to size 2 dp needles.
Row 1: (k3, knit 1 bead into next stitch). Repeat to end.
Row 2: knit
Row 3: (knit 1 bead into stitch, k1). Repeat to end.
Row 4: knit
Row 5: k1, (knit 1 bead into next stitch, k3, end with k2.
Row 6: knit
Row 7: k1 (bead+ leaf+bead, k7) end with k6. To place the bead+leaf+bead, bring these three beads loosely to the front of the knitting, hold them in front, bring the yarn back to the back of the work, and knit the next stitch, making sure yarn is relaxed and the leaf bead hangs comfortably between the two outside beads.
Rows 8–14: knit
Row 15: k1, (*knit 1 bead into next stitch, k7*)
Rows 16–20: knit
Row 21: Repeat row 15.
Rows 22–30: knit

Row 31: Repeat row 15.

This completes the bead sequence.

Choose any yarn and beads and knit this pattern as an accent band of beaded knitting around the collar or cuffs of a sweater, or a hatband.

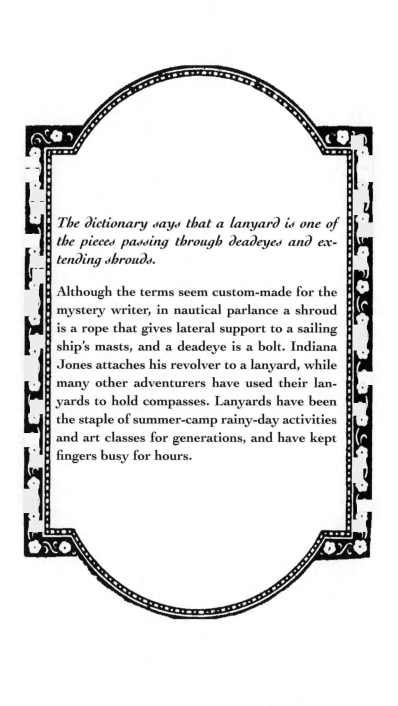

The dictionary says that a lanyard is one of the pieces passing through deadeyes and extending shrouds.

Although the terms seem custom-made for the mystery writer, in nautical parlance a shroud is a rope that gives lateral support to a sailing ship's masts, and a deadeye is a bolt. Indiana Jones attaches his revolver to a lanyard, while many other adventurers have used their lanyards to hold compasses. Lanyards have been the staple of summer-camp rainy-day activities and art classes for generations, and have kept fingers busy for hours.

OH, WHAT A TANGLED LANYARD WE WEAVE

by Parnell Hall

Parnell Hall is the author of the Stanley Hastings detective novels, the Puzzle Lady crossword puzzle mysteries, most recently And a Puzzle to Die On, *and the Steve Winslow courtroom dramas. Parnell, who lives in New York City, grew up in Wisconsin and used to weave lanyards while listening to the Milwaukee Braves baseball games on the radio.*

§§

HE HAD A blue and gold lanyard around his neck. If a whistle had been attached, it might have been the one he wore to coach his teams. But there was nothing on the hook at the end of the plastic woven strands. And the loop of the lanyard was not loose on his neck, the way it would be worn. Instead, it had been pulled tight like a noose, crushing his windpipe, and cutting off the flow of oxygen to his brain and to his heart. This had not been conducive to his health, and Coach Crandel had duly expired.

I was sorry to hear it. I was sitting in the bleachers of Valley View High, with my wife Alice, waiting for the game to commence. We were there to watch our son, Tommie, play soccer. Tommie doesn't go to Valley View, he goes to Riverdale. It was an away game, but at least a dozen Riverdale parents were there to cheer their kids on. Provided they could be heard over the hundred and fifty Valley View High parents assembled.

Tommie plays right wing because he can't kick with his left foot. Alice hates it when I say that. But it's the truth. Tommie's quite good with his right foot. He dribbles the ball down the right side of the field and launches long kicks across the front of the goal, which, on occasion, have been headed in by the center forward. Both occasions made the school paper.

Tommie can't do that from the left corner. This is not due to a lack of character, determination, or skill. It is merely because he is not ambidextrous.

Don't get me started.

Anyway, Tommie is quite adept at kicking from the right wing, and Alice and I were eager to see him do it.

Only the game was delayed. And it wasn't, as usual, that a referee was late. Both referees were out on the field. No, something else was going on, and it didn't take long for the news to ripple through the stands: Coach Crandel was dead.

Well, that certainly put a damper on the day. Not to be insensitive, but Alice and I didn't know Coach Crandel. The looks we gave each other conveyed our acknowledgment of the inappropriateness of our assessment of the situation: we weren't going to get to see Tommie play. With the equally inappropriate thought, "How long are they going to keep us?"

Actually, it was quite a while. First a middle-aged man in academic tweed, most likely a dean of some sort, stepped out onto the playing field and addressed the crowd in the inadequate speaking voice such men invariably have. I attribute the fault to the microphones on the lecterns today. Speakers don't have to project, hence they never learn to. I know, another inappropriate thought. But as an actor, I notice these things. Yeah, I'm an actor. At least I still consider myself an actor, even though I haven't acted in years.

Anyway, the dean told us there'd been an accident, the police were here, and we were all to remain in the stands. Actually, I couldn't hear a word, but he was accompanied by a uniformed policeman and nobody moved, so what else could it have been?

Shortly after that, more policemen crossed the field in the direction of the gymnasium. People in the stands may not have known that, since the policemen were in plain clothes. I knew at once because I'm a trained observer.

And I happened to recognize one of them. Sergeant William MacAullif. Of Homicide.

Which was a very bad sign. If MacAullif was here, it was unlikely the coach's demise was an accident.

Anyway, I recognized MacAullif, and he recognized me. At least I think he did, because he broke stride crossing the field. And it's not like MacAullif to break stride on his way to inspect a body. MacAullif is a big, beefy cop, who heads for a crime scene like a fullback smelling the end zone, brushing would-be tacklers aside.

Alice grabbed my arm. "Stanley! Isn't that MacAullif?"

"Yes."

"So this is a murder."

"Not necessarily."

"He's a homicide cop. He investigates murders."

"He investigates *potential* murders. Some of them turn out to be accidents."

"Don't split hairs."

I hate it when she does that. Alice is quick to point out hairsplitting in others. She, herself, could split the atom.

"All right, Alice. In all likelihood, it's a murder. In any event, the game is off. We're not going to get to see Tommie play."

"That's rather heartless."

"I know. I thought I'd voice the opinion so you wouldn't have to."

Alice refused to dignify that assertion with comment. "So, MacAullif's on the case. He's going to want your help."

I looked at Alice sideways. "Is that a dig? Are you needling me for the so-you-wouldn't-have-to remark?"

"Not at all. You're a trained investigator. You're good at these things. You might have some insight."

"I thought your opinion was I'm so unobservant I couldn't pick Arnold Schwarzenegger out of a Boy Scout troop."

"That's different. When it comes to figuring out a murder, you're practically an idiot savant."

"Thanks a bunch."

"MacAullif's gonna want your help."

"Trust me, Alice. MacAullif doesn't want my help."

A plainclothes cop hurried up. "Stanley Hastings? Would you come with me, please? Sergeant MacAullif wants your help."

THE CRIME SCENE was the home team locker room. The victim was the aforementioned home team coach. He was lying on his back with his eyes bulging out of his head. A blue and gold lanyard in a plastic evidence bag, clearly the murder weapon (the lanyard, not the evidence bag) lay on the bench beside him. Detectives were taking his picture. The medical examiner was shaking a gloomy head. An EMS team with a gurney was waiting to cart him off. The coach, not the medical examiner. I sometimes wonder if I would have succeeded as a writer if I hadn't had so many misplaced referents.

MacAullif sat on a bench in front of one of the lockers. His shirt looked tight in the collar. There was a bead of sweat on his brow. "What you got, Doc?" he asked.

"What you already know. He was strangled, probably within the last hour. No apparent contributing factors. I'll know more when we get him back to the morgue. Can we pack him up?"

MacAullif glanced at the detective with the flash camera, who nodded. "Okay, take him."

The medics carted off the corpse.

With the body gone, there seemed little reason to stay in the locker room.

"Can we go somewhere else?"

"Why?" MacAullif said. "The place freaking you out?"

"No, but it's hot in here. You're sweating like a pig."

"There's no ventilation."

I nodded. "Yeah. The elevated temperature will affect the medic's estimation of the time of death."

"You think?"

"No, I'm pulling your leg. Let's get the hell out of here. It's so hot I can't think straight."

"I'm not sure that has anything to do with the temperature."

We retired to the coach's office, which was air conditioned. It sported lockers, file cabinets, an oak desk, and a glass case, filled with trophies. On the walls were pictures of the coach, in better days. There's a stupid thing to say. Any day would probably beat his current condition. But I mean a younger coach, posing with his teams. Often with trophies, or victory banners. None featured the pudgy, out-of-shape man I'd just seen carried out.

MacAullif sat behind the desk as if it were his own. He probably could have passed for a college coach, if it weren't for the plastic evidence bag with the blue and gold whistle chain murder weapon that he flipped on the desk in front of him.

"Okay," I said to MacAullif. "You want my help. Can I assume that you haven't a clue who might have done this?"

"Not exactly."

"Well, what part of that is wrong?"

MacAullif grimaced. "Oh. Parsing one of your statements to separate the fallacies. What a dismal, time-consuming prospect. It would be so much easier to point out those rare instances when you're actually accurate."

"Do the other cops know you're literate? A guy your size could get into a lot of bar fights talking like that." I sat down, put my feet up on the desk. "I'm not going to argue with you, MacAullif. I figure when you get good and ready, you'll tell me what this is all about."

"I don't want you to tell me who did it. We *know* who did it. That's not the issue."

"What is?"

MacAullif took a cigar out of his pocket, drummed it on the desk. The cigar was a prop. His doctor made him give up cigars, but he liked to wave them around now and then.

I said, "Uh-oh."

"What?"

"When you start playing with a cigar, it's usually bad news."

MacAullif stuck the cigar in his mouth. If it had been his service revolver, he'd have been in serious danger of blowing his head off. "It's bad."

"What's the problem?"

"It's a kid on the soccer team."

"So."

"The kid's learning disabled."

"Uh-oh."

"Yeah. It's a public relations nightmare. You don't get credit for busting a learning disabled kid. No matter what he's done. The kid gets all the sympathy, and you're the bad guy."

"That's tough luck."

"I don't wanna be the bad guy." MacAullif raised his eyes, looked at me.

My mouth dropped open. "Oh, no!"

"That's right. I don't *have* to be the bad guy. I can cast you in the role. I'm gonna let you finger the perp. You're gonna listen to all the witnesses, and then you're gonna tell me who to arrest. Isn't that nice? You're gonna get your name in the papers. 'Private investigator, Stanley Hastings, whose son was playing in the game—that is why you're here, isn't it?—was able to point police in the right direction.'"

"That's ridiculous."

"Maybe so, but it gets me off the hook." MacAullif raised his voice. "Jenkins!"

A young plainclothes officer stuck his head in the door. "Yes, sir."

"We're gonna reinterview."

"Oh."

"What is it?"

"His mother's here. I was just about to get you."

"Is she the type to wait."

"No."

"Okay. Start with her."

MAXINE DORN LOOKED like she could have played soccer herself. Blond, lean, tan, muscular, she could have done Nike ads.

"Johnny didn't do it," she said as she came through the doorway. "Johnny wouldn't do such a thing."

MacAullif flipped open a notepad on the desk. "And you would be?"

"Johnny's mother. Maxine Dorn. You know that, because you sent for me. Now, let's stop playing games."

"Okay, Mrs. Dorn. Sit down, please. Let's have a little talk."

"It's *Ms.* Dorn."

"Of course. Please, sit down."

I stepped aside, offered her the chair in front of the desk. As she sat, I could see a jagged scar down her right cheek, marring her beauty. It was faint, only visible in the right light. When she turned her head it was gone.

"Who's this?" she demanded.

I flushed, embarrassed, as if she caught me staring, though it was probably just in my head.

"That's another investigator. He's also asking questions."

"Well, he's not asking the right ones if you think my son did it."

"Let's try some," MacAullif said. "You weren't at the soccer game?"

"No. I was at work."

"What do you do?"

"I'm a receptionist at J and R Lighting."

"You didn't take off for the game?"

"No. I need the money. I'm putting Johnny through school. Even with a scholarship it isn't easy."

"Johnny's on scholarship?"

"He's on partial scholarship. He's also on assistance from the Board of Education. He has learning disabilities. If you spoke to him, you know."

"What about his father?"

"Johnny never knew his father."

"Oh."

"No, *not* 'Oh,'" she said irritably. "There was a car accident. He was driving. I was in the passenger seat. The suicide seat, they call it. But I survived. He didn't. I woke up in the hospital four days later to the news.

"I was pregnant at the time. Eighth month. Doctors delivered the baby. Emergency C-section. They saved his life, but he was premature and brain-damaged. But he's a good kid, and he doesn't deserve what you're putting him through."

I stole a glance at MacAullif. No wonder he didn't want anything to do with this one.

MacAullif cleared his throat. "You say you weren't here when it happened? You were at work?"

"I don't *know* when it happened."

"It would appear it was just before the game was to start. You were at work then?"

She frowned. "Actually, I was out of the office. They called me on my cell phone."

"The police called you on your cell phone?"

"No. Ricky's mother. He's one of Johnny's teammates. She told me I'd better get on over. Here I am, and you tell me Johnny did it."

"I'm not the one saying Johnny did it," MacAullif told her.

"Well, who is?"

I found myself involuntarily shrinking into the wood-work. That sounded like MacAullif's cue to finger me.

He didn't.

He smiled, a sad, kindly smile. "Everyone." He sighed. "Even Johnny."

JOHNNY DORN LOOKED like his mother. Blond, ath-letic, muscular, handsome. I don't know what I expected. I guess I'm prejudiced. I heard "learning disabled," and I im-mediately figured Mongoloid features, cleft palate, dull stare.

Johnny looked perfectly normal. More than normal. He looked good. Or he would have looked good if he'd been feeling okay. At the moment he was frightened and upset, just as he should be.

He was also remorseful.

"I'm sorry," he mumbled. "I'm sorry."

"What are you sorry about, Johnny?" MacAullif asked.

"Coach Crandel."

"You killed Coach Crandel?"

"MacAullif!" I interrupted.

He looked at me in annoyance. "Yeah?"

"The kid should have a lawyer."

"He doesn't need a lawyer."

"He certainly *does*. You're asking him to incriminate himself."

"So what?"

"So *what*?"

"Yeah. What's the big deal? He hasn't had Miranda. I never read him his rights. Nothing he says can be used against him. We're just having a little talk. So, you killed Coach Crandel, Johnny?"

"I'm sorry."

MacAullif waited for more, but that was all. He referred to his notes. "You're a goalie, right?"

"Yes."

"Are you a good goalie?"

Johnny looked around like he didn't know how to answer.

"Yeah, you're a good goalie," MacAullif told him. "You're strong and you're quick and you dive on the ball and you kick it away."

Johnny nodded. "*To* someone." He said it firmly, with determination. I could imagine the countless times Coach Crandel had drilled that into his head.

"That's right," MacAullif said. "And you're good at it. But you don't play goalie."

"Sub."

MacAullif nodded. "Yes. You're the substitute goalie. You're the second-string goalie. You're the goalie who stands on the sidelines and watches while the other goalie plays."

With a faint twinge of resentment. "Kevin."

"Yes, Kevin. Tell me Johnny, are you better than Kevin?"

"I dunno."

"Is that why you killed Coach Crandel? Because he played Kevin and not you?"

Johnny didn't answer. A tear ran down his cheek.

"Okay, Johnny. That's all. Jenkins! Take him to his mother, bring me the other goalie."

Jenkins led Johnny out.

"I thought you brought me here to ask questions," I said.

"You want to ask questions?"

"No, but you didn't know that."

"Yes, I did."

Kevin Harrington III didn't look like an athlete. A pudgy boy, he gave the impression his only chance of stopping a soccer ball would be if someone laid him down in front of it. Coach Crandel's death had hit him hard. He looked like he was about to cry.

"Come in, Kevin," MacAullif said. "Don't be frightened. We just want to ask you some questions."

"I told you what I know," Kevin protested.

"Yes, you did. I'd like you to tell us again. You're the starting goalie on the team?"

"Yes." Kevin said it almost defensively.

"And Johnny Dorn is your backup goalie."

"So?"

"Does Johnny ever get to play?"

"That's up to the coach."

"Exactly," MacAullif said. "And if Johnny didn't get to play as much as he thought he should, that would be because of the coach, wouldn't it?"

Kevin said nothing, stared straight ahead.

"Is Johnny a good goalie?" I asked.

Kevin reacted as if he'd been stuck by a pin. "Who are you?"

"I'm an investigator. Trying to figure out what happened here. Is Johnny any good?"

"He's okay."

It was one of the most grudging compliments I've ever heard.

"You think it made Johnny mad sitting on the bench?"

"Yeah."

"Mad enough to kill the coach?"

Kevin said nothing, set his jaw.

"I know you don't want to accuse your classmate."

"It's his own fault," Kevin said sullenly.

"It's Johnny's fault, Kevin?"

"No. Coach Crandel."

"The coach? Why was it his fault?"

Kevin seemed interested in fiddling with his thumbs.

"Why was it Coach Crandel's fault, Kevin?"

Kevin stuck out his lower lip. "If Johnny was so good, he should have played him."

I frowned.

"You got any more questions?" MacAullif asked me.

"Yeah. Is your father here?"

Kevin appeared startled. "Yeah."

"Let's see him next."

*   *   *

KEVIN HARRINGTON JR. looked like Kevin Harrington III on steroids. He took up most of the coach's office.

He wasn't pleased to be here. "I don't know why you want to talk to me. I don't know a thing about it."

MacAullif looked to me.

"Did you know Coach Crandel?" I asked.

"Of course, I did. He's the coach."

"Ever talk to him?"

"I might have said a word in passing. No more, no less than anybody else."

"Ever give him any money?"

He scowled. "That's a vicious lie."

"It's not a lie. It's a question. I take it the answer is no?"

"Of course the answer is no. How dare you ask such a question."

"Your son got more playing time than he might have deserved. One wonders if it were bought."

"I never gave Coach Crandel a dime, do you hear me? Not a dime."

"And the school. What about the school?"

"What about it?"

"I notice they're breaking ground for a new gymnasium. I wonder if you gave any money for it?"

"All the parents gave money for the gymnasium."

"Yes, but some more than others. How much did you kick in?"

"That's neither here nor there."

"That may be, but I'd still like to know."

"I see no reason to tell you."

"If you pumped a lot of money into the athletic program, you might expect to see your son participate in it. You have any conversations with the coach in that regard?"

"How dare you!"

"How about the other way around? The coach ever come to you, say he's tired of playing your son, he'd like to try to win?"

The veins in his neck bulged out. "There's nothing wrong with my son!"

"I never said there was. But is it possible he's not the best goalie on the team?"

"Says who? Damn it, who told you that?"

I could empathize. I have a son on the soccer team. I'd be very upset if someone were bad-mouthing him.

Particularly if that someone was the coach.

"I didn't see you in the stands," I said. "Were you here at game time?"

It was hell of a bluff. I didn't know him. I'm not from his school. The chance of me noticing whether or not he was in the stands was slightly less than me winning the New York State lottery.

But he was too upset to notice. "There was a trustee's meeting. I got here late."

"The trustees of the school?"

"Yes."

"You're on the board of directors?"

"I'm a trustee, yes."

"You got out of the meeting and came to the game?"

"That's right."

"You come by way of the gym?"

His mouth fell open. "I don't know who you are, but you've got a lot of nerve. I happen to have friends on the force."

"He's not on the force," MacAullif said.

"Then what's he doing here?"

"I asked him."

"Why? You know who did this. And you know why. Why are you dragging this out?"

"We know who did this?"

"Yes, of course."

"And who would that be?"

"You know who. Johnny Dorn."

MacAullif nodded. "And what was his motive?"

"He wanted to play. The coach wouldn't let him."

"Every kid wants to play. And every team has a second string. Every team has benchwarmers. They don't kill the coach."

"Yeah, well, they're normal."

"Are you saying Johnny Dorn's not normal?" I asked.

"Have you talked to him?"

"Yeah, I've talked to him. Have you? Have you ever seen him play? Is he any good? How's he stack up against Kevin?"

"There's no comparison. My son is a starter. Johnny Dorn is a scrub."

"So there was no reason for him to resent the coach for not playing him."

Kevin's father shrugged. "He doesn't need a reason. He's not right in the head."

"YOU LIKE HIM for this?" MacAullif asked as the detective ushered Kevin Harrington Jr. out.

"A pattern is beginning to emerge. Here's a guy pumping huge amounts of money into the school. And, lo and behold, his son's the starting goalie on the soccer team. But the son is not that agile, and the backup goalie is, and the team's lost a few games."

"You know that for a fact?"

I did. The mother of our starting center forward knew the record of every team we played, and regaled us before each game. Valley View, despite a potent offense, had dropped the last two games, 4-3, and 3-2.

"So what?" MacAullif scoffed.

"Coaches like to win, MacAullif. Suppose the coach decided to play Johnny Dorn? Suppose he called Kevin's father to let him know?"

"You think that happened?"

"I have no idea."

MacAullif grimaced. "Oh. You know, it's tough to arrest

someone on the basis of 'no idea.' Prosecutors usually want a little more than that."

"Wusses. Who else you got?"

"The art teacher."

"What do you need him for?"

"The murder weapon."

MR. BAINBRIDGE, THE art teacher, was a gentle man with a kindly, paint-smeared face who was duly shocked by the current tragedy. "I can't believe it. I can't believe Johnny would do such a thing."

"Not the type?"

"Absolutely not the type. Of course—"

"Of course what?"

"You never knew what he was thinking."

"But he made the whistle chain."

"Yes, but as a gift, not a weapon."

"A gift for who?"

"Coach Crandel."

"So he made the whistle chain for Coach Crandel."

He flushed. "When you say it like that it sounds bad. He made it to please the coach."

"Please him? Maybe get on his good side?"

"I don't know what you mean by that. You make it sound scheming. Like an ulterior motive. Johnny isn't like that."

"Johnny wasn't getting much playing time. You don't think if the coach liked him better, he might have put him in?"

"I have no idea what the coach might have done."

"You don't think Johnny might have had that notion?"

"No."

"Why not?"

"It's an ulterior motive. I told you. Johnny doesn't have ulterior motives."

MacAullif was going around in circles. I said, "Tell me about the whistle chain."

"The lanyard is a standard item we make in class."

"I thought arts and crafts was more a camp activity."

"It's an art class. It's one of the less demanding art classes. For students like Johnny."

"Does Valley View *have* many students like Johnny?"

"No. But we have science nerds who need to fill their arts requirement." He flushed. "*Please*, don't quote me on that. Anyway, it's arts and crafts. We do painting and sculpture. We also have useful skills. The lanyard is one of them."

"How do you make them?"

"You start out with the hook, of course. Snap hook, you know the type I mean, that you can clip a whistle on. You snap the hook onto something solid. In shop we use an eye hook screwed into the table. Then you take your two strips of lanyard, in two different colors. Of course, you *could* make it all one color, but most choose two. Two colors is fun."

"Johnny's was blue and gold?"

"Yes. Those are the school colors. Kids often choose that when it's for a coach."

"Johnny always intended it for the coach?"

"That was my understanding."

"Go on."

"After you choose your two colored strands, you cut them to the right length, four and a half yards long, feed both colors through the end of the hook, and even them up. That gives you four strands, each eighty-one inches. You start with the diamond stitch. That's a round braid weave. Very easy. You do thirty-six inches of that. Then you do the box stitch. That's just what it sounds like. A square stitch that forms a rectangular box. You do that around your lanyard. See what I mean? You take the end that you've woven, loop it back on itself until it touches itself, facing the hook. Then you weave the box stitch around it in the direction of the hook. When you're done, the lanyard slides back and forth inside the loose box stitch. You put the whistle on the hook, and put the loop over your head."

"And that's what Johnny made?"

"Yes."

"For Coach Crandel?"

"That's right."

"Did he have any problem focusing on the work."

"No. He was most determined." He flushed. "I don't mean that the way it sounded. I mean he was intent on his project. He was concentrating on his work."

"But is that unusual for Johnny?"

"Actually, he often concentrates very well. But then it's hard to know what he's thinking."

"Uh-huh." MacAullif opened his briefcase, took out the plastic evidence bag. "Is this Johnny's lanyard?"

The art teacher seemed somewhat taken aback. "I don't know. It's the same colors. It's just *like* Johnny's lanyard."

I shot a glance at MacAullif. I knew what he was thinking—save me from the fair-and-impartial witness. The average guy says, "Yeah, sure, that's Johnny's," then it's up to the defense to break him down.

"So it *could* be Johnny's?" MacAullif persisted.

"It could."

"Were any of your other students working on a blue and gold whistle chain?"

"No."

"Then it's extremely *likely* that this is Johnny's. Would that be a fair assessment of the case?"

"May I see the lanyard?"

"What for?"

"Maybe I could tell."

"You can look. I'll hold the bag."

MacAullif came around the desk, holding the evidence bag up for him to see.

Mr. Bainbridge peered at the lanyard, then shrunk back. "Is that—is that blood?"

"It broke the skin," MacAullif said. "Damn strong stuff, your plastic lanyard."

The art teacher gestured with his finger. "Could you turn the bag around?"

MacAullif showed the other side.

Bainbridge leaned close. Sighed. "It's Johnny's."

"How can you tell?"

"There. Third row of the box stitch. The gold strand's twisted. Johnny never noticed. He finished it up, wanted to give it to the coach before the game. I didn't have the heart to tell him. He would have had to take out all those stitches. He wouldn't have had time. It was a small thing. I let it go."

I could see MacAullif reassessing his opinion of fair-and-impartial witnesses. "So, this stitch allows you to positively identify the whistle chain as the one that Johnny made for Coach Crandel?"

"I'm afraid so."

"And what did he do when he finished the whistle chain?"

"He ran out of class." He shook his head sadly. "To give it to the coach."

MacAullif beamed. "Thank you, Mr. Bainbridge. You've been a big help."

"May I ask a question?" I interposed.

"Be my guest."

"Are any other team members in your class?"

"I really couldn't say. I don't know who the other team members are."

"Kevin Harrington III, for instance. Is he one of your students?"

"Kevin's on the soccer team? I had no idea."

"You mean he never made a whistle chain?"

"No. He's a painter. Quite artistic. Is he on the soccer team? Funny. He never struck me as the athletic type."

I nodded. "Me either."

AFTER BAINBRIDGE HAD been led out, MacAullif said, "Well, you ready to make your recommendation?"

"I'm not happy about this, MacAullif."

"I didn't expect you to be happy. Just to help me out."

"I'll bet you did. Yeah, let's get them in here."

"Them?"

"Yeah, MacAullif. Johnny and his mother, and Kevin and his father. If they fit in the room, let's have 'em."

"It's gonna be tight."

It was. Jenkins brought folding chairs from the scorer's table in the gymnasium, and lined them up in front of the desk. The parents sat in the middle. The two goalies sat on either end.

The parents were not happy. Particularly Ms. Dorn. Johnny had apparently told her the type of questions he'd been asked, because she'd completely withdrawn her cooperation.

"He's not saying a word," she proclaimed. "You want to talk to him, I want a lawyer."

"Absolutely," I assured her. "We're not going to ask Johnny any questions. But if at any time any one of you should want a lawyer, just speak right up, and we'll see that you have an opportunity to contact one."

"You're not going to ask any questions?" Kevin Harrington Jr. said. "Then what do you have us here for?"

"To tell you what we know. If you'd care to correct any misassumptions we may have made, that's entirely up to you. You can also just sit there and listen."

I glanced at the two goalies. Neither appeared to be paying the least attention. Johnny was looking at the trophies on the wall. Kevin seemed fascinated with his wristwatch.

"Okay, here are the facts as we know them. Mr. Crandel was strangled by a whistle chain. It was pulled tight around his neck like a noose, cutting off the flow of oxygen. This required considerable force. The whistle chain actually broke the skin. There were traces of flesh and blood embedded in the plastic braid."

I held up the evidence bag. "This is the whistle chain in question. It was found around Coach Crandel's neck. A whistle chain of blue and gold, the colors of Valley View High."

At least that got the goalies' attention. I put the bag

back on the desk. "What else do we know? That Johnny Dorn was the second-string goalie on the soccer team. And, rightly or wrongly, he felt he was not getting enough playing time. Johnny felt, and, again, this is only his opinion, that he was just as good, if not better, than the starting goalie on the team."

I pointed at Ms. Dorn. "That view was shared by his mother, who is, however, a no-nonsense, practical woman, who does not consider soccer an important enough activity to be concerned about. Nonetheless, in the case of her son Johnny, it would particularly rankle to see him denied permission to do something in which he could excel.

"Ms. Dorn is lithe, athletic, and strong. And, by her own admission, she was not at work at the time Coach Crandel was killed."

Johnny gawked at his mother. "Mom?"

"Don't say a word, Johnny! He doesn't mean it. He's just trying to get you to talk." She stuck out her chin at me angrily. "And I think it's pretty low of you to try to trick the boy that way."

"I assure you, that was not my intention. I'm just trying to lay out the facts." I turned to Mr. Harrington. "In Kevin's father's case, we have a similar situation. He's large, strong, capable of the act, and cannot account for his whereabouts at the time of the murder. And if the coach intended to sit Kevin and play Johnny, that might be a motive."

"In your dreams!" Kevin Harrington Jr. said. "Coach Crandel never had any such intention. You know it, I know it, everyone on the team knows it. You find me anyone who says different, I'll show you a liar."

I put up my hand. "Once again, no one is claiming any such thing. I'm just demonstrating that, under such circumstances, you could have had just as much motivation to kill the coach as Ms. Dorn might have under other circumstances. I am not pointing fingers at anyone. However, taking the facts *as we know them*, and not as I can postulate they might hypothetically be—"

I looked around, realized I'd totally lost both goalies with that verbal construction. "Never mind. Here's what the facts are. According to the art teacher, Mr. Bainbridge, Johnny worked hard on the blue and gold whistle chain because he wanted to give it to the coach before the game. He finished it and went running out to the locker room. He was late. The other players were already on the field. He went to his locker and changed.

"Coach Crandel came looking for him. Johnny was delighted to see the coach. He gave him the whistle chain. The coach put it on.

"Johnny was happy. He thought he'd pleased the coach. He asked the coach if he could start the game. The coach said no, Kevin was going to start. Johnny couldn't believe it. After he'd been so nice. Made him a whistle chain. Johnny grabbed the whistle chain. Pleaded with the coach. The coach said no. Johnny pulled, tighter, and tighter . . ."

Johnny was rocking back and forth in agony, muttering, "No! No!"

Ms. Dorn grabbed Johnny, cradled him to her. "It's all right, Johnny, it's all right." She spun on me with eyes of steel. "Stop it! You *will* not do this! I *will* not let you!"

"Sorry," I said. "I don't mean to upset Johnny. No more of that, okay? I'm just trying to explain something. Let's all calm down."

Ms. Dorn still smoldered, but held her tongue.

"Okay," I said. "Let me tell you where we are. We know what happened here. We just can't prove it yet. We have the motive, as I've already discussed. We have the opportunity. And we have the murder weapon. We just have to connect it up."

Ms. Dorn said suspiciously, "What do you mean, connect it up?"

"Johnny made a whistle chain in art class. And a whistle chain is the murder weapon. It's the same color as the whistle chain Johnny made. But that doesn't prove it is."

"Who else's *could* it be?" Kevin's father scoffed.

"That's not the point. Even though we *know* it is, that doesn't *prove* it is. A blue and gold whistle chain. It could be anyone's."

Kevin mumbled something.

"What did you say?"

"He messed up. Johnny messed up. One of the weaves is twisted. In the square part. If it's Johnny's, it'll have that."

"Really? Let me see."

I picked up the plastic evidence bag, turned it around, looked it over. "Yes. Here it is. The weave is twisted. In the box stitch. Just like Kevin said. That proves it. The whistle chain is Johnny's. We can tell by the tangled stitch." I smiled slightly, recited, "'Oh, what a tangled web we weave, when first we practice to deceive.'"

They all stared at me. Even MacAullif. Even Ms. Dorn, who had been about to protest my linking the whistle chain to Johnny. "It's a quote, often attributed to Shakespeare, but actually from Sir Walter Scott. It seemed appropriate here. What with the miswoven stitch. And with the web of lies I've been forced to untangle."

"Web of lies!" Ms. Dorn cried. "How unfair! You want to say the whistle chain is Johnny's, fine, say it's Johnny's. But don't do it with some dramatic web-of-lies announcement. No one *lied* about it. No one said it *wasn't* Johnny's. You just said you couldn't prove it. Now you say you can. Big deal. But don't give me that web-of-lies bit."

"That isn't what I mean at all. When I say *web*, I mean *web*. Everyone here has lied, creating a veritable jumble of facts. That's what makes sorting them out so hard."

"Johnny didn't lie!"

"Oh, but he did. I'm sorry, Ms. Dorn, but that's so. I asked Johnny if he was a better goalie than Kevin, and he said he didn't know. That's a lie. It's a polite lie, but a lie none the less. He *does* know. He *is* better than Kevin, and he knows it. Isn't that true, Johnny?"

"Leave him alone!"

"Okay, I'll ask Kevin. Kevin, who's a better goalie? You told me you are, but I don't think that's true. I think Johnny is, and you know it. You could help me a great deal by telling the truth. Because Johnny being better and not being played is a strong motive. Only no one's telling me that. Which makes my job harder. You see what I mean? So, let's try again, and this time let's have the truth. Who's a better goalie, you or Johnny?"

Kevin avoided his father's eyes. "He is."

"There you go! And there's your daddy's lie. Your daddy said that was nonsense, that you were the better goalie, that he didn't have to pay the coach to let you play."

Kevin looked at his father in dismay. "You paid the coach?"

"Of course not," Kevin's father snarled. "He's the one who's lying. I never paid the coach a thing."

I nodded. "Right. We went through that. You just contributed to the school."

Kevin looked at me, then at his father. "Dad?"

"Don't listen to him, Kevin." Kevin's father turned on me. "Why are you doing this? I thought all you cared about was Johnny's motive for the crime."

"I'm telling you who lied. *You* lied about needing to bribe anyone for your son to play. Whether you *did* or not is another matter. But you lied about the *need*. That's your lie." I turned to Ms. Dorn. "Which brings us to you."

"I didn't lie," she said defiantly.

"Oh, but you did. You know what your mom's lie is, Johnny? She lied about not caring about the soccer games. She cares a great deal. She sneaks off from work to watch you play. She hides behind the stands where no one will see. She was there this afternoon when she got the call about Coach Crandel's death. Of course, she already knew. She had to hide out a half-hour before showing up, so it wouldn't look like she'd been there all the time."

Johnny's eyes were wide with horror. "Mom?"

I said kindly, "It must have been very frustrating for you, to watch all those games, knowing your son was better, not getting to see him play."

Kevin's father stared. "You mean—You mean it wasn't *him*, it was *her*?"

I smiled. "Nice try. But we know who it was, don't we? It must be very hard on you. I bet you were an athlete in school. And your father before you. You would have wanted your son to be an athlete, too. Particularly a firstborn son, who carried your name, and your father's. What a blow to find out he wasn't. Had no real interest in sports. You made him play anyway. Forced him into it. Made him try out for the soccer team. What a disaster! Big, slow, klutzy. Couldn't kick the ball. No way he makes the team."

"Except as a goalie. Goalie's different. You don't have to run. He can pick up the ball with his hands. So what if he's not the best goalie in the world? With a good team, the ball doesn't get to the goalie that often.

"So you make it happen. A sizable donation to the new gymnasium, and your son is goalie on the soccer team.

"The only problem is Johnny Dorn. A quick, agile, first-rate goalie who doesn't play.

"So what happens? You lose some tight games. The kids on the team begin to grumble. Why is Johnny on the bench, and your son in the goal?

"That had to be a lot of pressure on Coach Crandel. One can't imagine him taking it for long."

"So he told me he was benching Kevin and I killed him, is that what you're saying?" Kevin's father sneered. "I see what you're doing here. You tell us everyone lied, and then you go around the room and I'm last. So I must be guilty. Isn't that how they do it in detective books?"

"I wouldn't know about that. It's an interesting idea. But that was never my intention. That was never my plan, no matter how much you might wish it were."

Kevin's father, poised for an angry retort, choked on that one.

I nodded. "Yes, you see what I mean? Your wretched arrangement worked a huge hardship on everybody. Johnny. His mother. The coach. But there was probably no one it was harder on than your son. To go out there, game after game. Resented by his teammates. For messing up the big plays. For helping them lose. It's gotta be hell."

"Of course, Kevin doesn't know what you've done. He may suspect it, but he doesn't know. He's had a bad couple of games. He hopes the coach will come to his senses. He goes to the coach today, to ask the coach to bench him, to play Johnny instead. And there's a good sign. The coach has Johnny's whistle chain around his neck. Surely the coach and Johnny have come to an understanding. Surely Johnny will play."

"But, no, the coach is starting Kevin. Even though Kevin begs him not to."

"Kevin is astounded. Is he nuts? Is he crazy? Foolish old man. Why can't he understand?"

Kevin's father jumped up, put himself between me and his son. "Don't say a word, Kevin. He has no proof."

I nodded. "That's right, I don't. I thought Kevin might have marks on his hands from pulling the whistle chain, but he was wearing his goalie gloves. No help there. That's why I asked my questions as I did. Kevin told us about the twisted strand in the box stitch. And that's the key. Because, according to the art teacher, Kevin was involved with painting, and never went near Johnny's project. He didn't see that twisted box stitch in the art studio. He saw it in the locker room, when the whistle chain was around Coach Crandel's neck."

Kevin writhed in agony and shame. A tear ran down his cheek. "He wouldn't listen. He said I had to play."

I could feel for him. It wasn't entirely his fault. But a glance at his father assured me that the other culprit was suffering, too.

* * *

WHAT FOLLOWED WAS routine. Jenkins placed Kevin in custody. Kevin's father phoned for a lawyer. The police took Kevin downtown.

Johnny and his mom went home. She had her arm around him, her chin thrust out defiantly, stretching her skin tight, exposing her scar, daring the world to find fault with him or her.

MacAullif walked me back to the stands, where Alice was waiting patiently. Tommie was long gone with his team.

"Your husband put on quite a show, Mrs. Hastings."

"He usually does."

"This was a little more than usual. He quoted poetry. He went through a big spiel about how everybody in the room lied, then pointed out how they did."

"Is that right?" Alice asked me.

"Yes, it is." I cocked my head. "And, when I said everyone, I meant everyone, MacAullif."

He looked at me. "I beg your pardon?"

"You know why MacAullif wanted me?" I asked Alice. "He said it was because the kid who did it was learning disabled, and he didn't want to take the hit for accusing a learning disabled child. Only it turns out the kid didn't do it."

"He *said* he did it."

"He said he was sorry. He felt guilty for making the whistle chain. But he didn't kill the coach. You knew that, didn't you MacAullif?"

"Aw, hell."

"But guess what? The father of one of the other kids had connections downtown. The guy actually threatened us with them during the interview. And his son looked just as good for this as the other boy. Which you didn't bother to tell me, but let me find out for myself. That was the tangled web of lies I was referring to, MacAullif."

"You brought out the facts, I made the arrest. You know how far we'd have gotten with the guy's son if *I'd* been the one trying to bring out the facts?"

"Telling me what you wanted would have been too straightforward?"

"Would you have gone for it?" MacAullif asked. While I considered that, he added. "Well, you're right. *Everyone* in the room lied. Even you."

"Stanley lied? I find that hard to believe. What did you lie about, Stanley?"

"It wasn't so much a lie as a bluff. I said Kevin, the kid who did it, must have seen the twisted whistle chain around the coach's neck because, according to the art teacher, he never went near him in class. Of course, the art teacher never said any such thing."

"I'm sure that will make sense after you fill me in," Alice said.

"I'm sure it will, but it's not what I mean," MacAullif said. "I'm talking about an out-and-out lie."

"I don't know about out-and-out. I said Johnny's mother skipped work every game to watch her son play. I don't *know* that's a lie. It might even be true."

"That's not it, either," MacAullif said.

"Well, would you mind telling us what *is*?" Alice said impatiently. "Because, after you get through exposing my husband's devious nature, I'd kind of like to hear about this murder."

"Okay," MacAullif said. "Stanley was summing up the evidence, taking all the suspects in turn, and one of them said that's how they'd do it in a detective book. Stanley said he wouldn't know anything about that. I think that's an out-and-out lie."

Alice smiled. "That's for sure."

§§

Weaving a Lanyard

To weave a lanyard, you'll need a snap hook and two pieces of plastic lacing, (also called *gimp*), about twelve feet long each. Figure on using three times the length of the finished product for a basic round braid, or nine times the length for a box stitch. It's easier to visualize—and more fun to do—if the strands are different colors. Hang the snap hook with the small end down and pull both laces through the hook, making sure that all ends are even.

Let's say you've chosen blue and gold, as the boy in the story did. From left to right, we'll call the strands 1, 2, 3, and 4. When you start, blue will be 1 and 2, gold will be 3 and 4.

To make a basic round braid, first, place strand 4 under strands 3 and 2, then wrap it back over strand 2. Then, place strand 1 under strands 2 and 4, then wrap it back over strand 4. Pull strands tight. Keep repeating these two steps until you've reached the desired length. You can tie off the ends with an overhand knot, snip the loose laces, and your lanyard is ready to use.

If you want to add the box stitch, get someone who went to camp to show you how! It's really easy, but describing it here would make your head spin. Happy weaving!

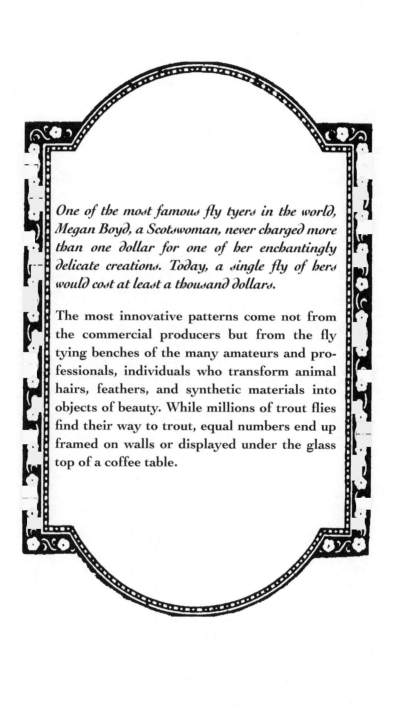

One of the most famous fly tyers in the world, Megan Boyd, a Scotswoman, never charged more than one dollar for one of her enchantingly delicate creations. Today, a single fly of hers would cost at least a thousand dollars.

The most innovative patterns come not from the commercial producers but from the fly tying benches of the many amateurs and professionals, individuals who transform animal hairs, feathers, and synthetic materials into objects of beauty. While millions of trout flies find their way to trout, equal numbers end up framed on walls or displayed under the glass top of a coffee table.

HOW TO MAKE A KILLING ONLINE

by Victoria Houston

Victoria Houston is the author of five books in the Loon Lake fishing mystery series, set in the north woods of Wisconsin against a background of ice fishing, fly fishing, and fishing for muskies, bass, bluegill, and walleyes. The most recent, Dead Hot Mama, *features ice fishing and illegal traffic in body parts. Also the author of six nonfiction books, Victoria lives in rural Wisconsin.*

MARTHA ESTABROOK PUSHED back from her worktable to study the results: Forty-five Hare's Ear Wulff trout flies. Sparse, sleek, not overdressed like so many commercial dry flies. And not bad for a day's work. Especially now that several of her custom patterns would sell for over a hundred dollars each—give or take a few bucks. One more reason to work just three days a week.

After a half-hour of sorting and stacking on the beat-up butcher block in her garage, she slipped the last of the tiny plastic cases into a Priority Mail envelope—marveling as she did every day around this time—at the change eBay had made in her life.

LESS THAN FIVE years ago, she was a minimum wage drone slogging through the day at a call center for a local pet supply mail-order company. Tying trout flies, an art learned from her grandfather, was strictly a stress reliever. Her income? Thirty thousand a year if she didn't get laid off and the taxes on her cottage didn't go up.

Then one of her coworkers, for whom she tied flies in exchange for venison, told her about selling his chainsaw sculptures on eBay for five times what the locals would pay.

"Martha," he'd said, "your trout flies are works of art. Heck, I always feel bad fishing with 'em. I'll bet you anything, you could make a killing online." And he arranged for his fifteen-year-old son to help her get started.

The teenager guided her through the purchase of a used PC (off-line) and a new digital camera (on eBay) and spent a week showing her how to use them. She set herself a routine and got started.

She would tie for two hours on the workbench nestled under the kitchen window facing the lake, then lay the tiny trout flies on a yard of black velvet, which she had draped over a cardboard box on a chair in a corner of her bedroom. After shooting the photos, she would load the graphic images into her computer. Her total investment before the big orders hit was less than $1,500. Within six months, she'd made ten times that.

After a year, encouraged by the same coworker, who was a dedicated fly fisherman and a collector of antique fishing lures and trout flies, she began to include some of her own designs. These were unique patterns that differed from the traditional as she tipped in tiny surprises of chenille, squirrel hair, and Hungarian partridge feathers.

Did they catch fish? Perhaps. More important, they caught the eye of fly fishing enthusiasts who appreciated the quality of her handiwork: the precision with which she wound her waxed threads, tied her whip finish knots, and the exquisite colorings she brought to the tiny sculptures.

One day, a buyer for a prestigious fly fishing supply house was cruising fly tying websites and fell in love with her patterns. He offered to feature them—and her photos—on their site alongside the products, names, and pictures of other famous fly tyers.

Within a month, she had more orders for her Black Minx, a smallmouth bass fly, than she could fulfill. The pattern was one that took longer to tie, which only sweetened the price. The limited inventory that she once sold for a dollar each escalated at auction to ten dollars per trout fly. Then twenty-five.

Now, two years later, she could count on a single Black Minx to sell in the range of $250. That one fly boosted the value of her entire inventory—as well as her sense of well-being: Never had she been happier. Never had she felt so relaxed and, finally, in control of her life.

It wasn't just that she loved tying trout flies, but the whole process couldn't be easier. And her income today? Over a quarter million dollars a year, and the business was continuing to grow. She still couldn't believe her bankbook: Thanks to low overhead, she had nearly a half a million dollars in her account.

Martha still lived in her two-bedroom cottage, which was on the lake where she had grown up. The rustic but winterized cottage was nestled into a glen at the end of a long road leading off the county highway. Though she had few visitors, she had no complaints: The solitude and privacy made for easy work hours.

But she wasn't a hermit, either. She made it a point to have lunch every Thursday with two friends from her call center days. Once a month, she took the family of the coworker who had helped her launch her business out for a nice dinner. Her only relative was a sister who lived outside Chicago, but they rarely spoke. All in all, a solitary but pleasant life.

As Martha put away the mailing supplies, she made a mental note to set up an appointment to see her bank's financial planner. It was a meeting she kept putting off. Too

much confusing information: Stocks, bonds, annuities, RE-
ITS—it all sounded so tiresome even though she knew she'd
graduated to the ranks of people who "need to make your
money work for you."

Checking her watch, she hit a button on the computer—
time to check the current eBay auction. While she auctioned
only twice a week herself, she had, in addition to the fly fishing supply house, two power sellers who bought from her
and re-sold at a slight markup. She decided to check e-mail
first.

After deleting spam, she had seven e-mails from satisfied
buyers and one of her own kicked back. No . . . wait . . .
Martha leaned forward. That was her name, all right, but
not the correct e-mail address. She opened the e-mail:

> *Hi, Martha,*
> *We have the same name! I Googled myself, and you came up.*
> *So we're both named Martha Estabrook. I'm thirteen, and I*
> *live in New York City—where do you live?*
> *Martha Estabrook.*

Well, isn't that interesting, thought Martha. A thirteen
year old in New York City, huh. I'm a fifty-four-year-old in
Eagle River, Wisconsin.

She sat up straight as she hit REPLY:

> *Hi Martha,*
> *What a surprise to hear from someone with the same name.*
> *But then I suppose it is fairly common. I live in northern*
> *Wisconsin, and I'm a good forty years older than you!*
> *All the best,*
> *Martha*

Assuming that would be the end of that, she put the
computer to sleep and drove into town to the post office.
That evening she checked her e-mail and was surprised to
find a response from the youngster:

Hey, Martha,
It's me! You're right. I found fourteen of us with the same
name. Isn't that fun? I'll be a freshman this year. How
about you? What do you do? Lots of water where you live?
I have a friend who goes to camp in northern Wisconsin.
Rhinelander. Is that close to you? When she's there she goes
fishing and rides Waverunners. I'll bet you have kids who do
that stuff, right?
Martha

Martha paused. She didn't feel right about this. How
many times had she heard about youngsters, recently one in
Eagle River even, being lured into sexual liaisons by preda-
tors lurking on line. This child needed to be careful.

She hit REPLY:

Martha,
Do your parents know we're corresponding? Since I'm a total
stranger, I would feel better if you would check with them be-
fore you e-mail me again.
Best,
Martha

The girl responded within minutes:

Oh, sure. But they're in Ireland right now, so it might be a
day or two before I hear back. They said they would check
the Internet at the hotel every day. I know they won't care.
They went to Ireland to track down my great-great grand-
parents. My mom is really into genealogy. I have an older
brother named Patrick—we're very Irish. What about
you—is your family Irish, too? Like when did your family
come to America? Wouldn't it be funny if we had the same
ancestors? My mom's mom was a Ryan from County Clare.
What was your grandmother's maiden name?
Your new friend,
Martha

Feeling she'd been a little harsh, Martha answered quickly,

I don't know my grandmother's maiden name. My mother was a McBride, and I'm not sure what county her family was from. She died when I was only six, and my father married again, so I've never thought to find out. To answer your earlier questions—yes, we have hundreds of lakes here and quite a bit of fishing. I don't fish myself—but I tie trout flies for a living. So I know lots of fishermen. If you're interested you can go on eBay, put in my/our name and you'll see photos of my work. Off to bed now.
Sleep well—Martha, Senior

She smiled at her sign-off. This was actually kind of fun. The one thing in life she had missed was marriage and a family. She didn't know much about young girls—it would be interesting to see what young Martha would think of her work.

Before she fell asleep that night, she wondered about the phenomenon of connecting with someone who shared the same name. Would they have anything else in common? Hair color? Eyes? Mannerisms? Likely not. She turned over and pulled the covers close to her chin. But she *was* half Irish, so they did have that.

SHE WOKE TO a lovely morning, the water on the lake outside her kitchen window bright blue and still. The eBay auction had gone well—everything sold. When she checked her e-mail, she had large orders from the two power sellers and a sweet message from the girl.

Omygosh—I can't believe you do that! Your fish things are so pretty. I really like that black one especially. Can I wear it as a pin? It is so cool. I'm going learn how to buy on eBay

so I can bid on one of those! I forwarded your stuff to my dad right away, too. Did I tell you he fly fishes? I'm sure he'll be impressed. Write me back and tell me all about how you do this. Maybe I can use it for a report in school.
Love,
Martha

Martha laughed out loud and typed back:

Don't you dare bid—that could cost you over a hundred dollars. Let me send you one. After all, you're my namesake. You're entitled to one.

After spending forty-five minutes on a detailed answer to the girl's question about how she worked, Martha looked long and hard at the e-mail before she hit SEND. If this girl was as nice as she sounded, maybe they could meet someday. It would be fun to show her the "dead animal room" that she kept stocked with wood duck flanks, wild turkey wings, squirrel tails, and deerskins. She decided to add a line to the e-mail:

Ask your parents if it's okay for you to send your snail mail address. If so, I'll send along a Black Minx.
Martha

Three days went by with no response. Martha cringed every time she read that last e-mail to the child: she must have stepped over the line, and the parents were upset.

The fourth day, just as she uploaded the images for the second auction of the week, she received an e-mail from New York City.

Hey Martha,
My dad called last night. He said no one pays a hundred dollars for a trout fly. He's sure you typed wrong and meant

*one dollar. I told him I thought you said a hundred but he
said that's outrageous. I told him if he didn't believe me, he
could check eBay when they get home tomorrow night. Oh—
he said it's okay to give you my snail mail. And guess
what—if you send me that Black Minx, he promises to take
me fishing so we can see if it works. Cool, huh?*

Martha sent the package off that afternoon, taking care
with the child's address. Just to be funny, she included a
stamped, self-addressed envelope "in case you don't catch
anything—feel free to return." She also slipped in a copy of
her brochure, which featured the other six trout flies that
she sold and very nice photo of her at work. As she sealed
the FedEx envelope, she couldn't help feeling just a little
smug: "Outrageous," huh? Well, this was one father who
was going to be surprised.

And he was.

*Hey Martha,
My dad is so blown away with the Black Minx. He wants
to order a bunch from you. Can you e-mail me everything he
needs to place a bulk order—like for maybe fifty? He said he
needs the Item Number and your tax number so his secretary
can place the order. I told him he would be impressed, and
boy is he ever!
Love,
Martha*

With great satisfaction, Martha sent off the information
for the order. She included a note stating that since she was
not incorporated (a process she kept delaying), her Social Security number would suffice as the tax number.

TWO WEEKS LATER, as Martha was right in the midst of
tying a new batch of Black Minx, she heard a knock at the

kitchen door. Glancing through the window, she was surprised to see a man she didn't recognize. He was wearing khaki shorts, a white T-shirt, and a baseball cap. Had to be a tourist who took a wrong turn.

"Yes?" she opened the door. He was a smooth-faced man of medium height with eyes that darted around the room behind her as he stepped forward, forcing her to back up.

"Excuse me," said Martha, irritated with the intrusion. "Do I know you?"

"You sure do," he said with a tight grin, "my name is Martha Estabrook."

She saw rather than heard the gun in his right hand as he grabbed her around the shoulders and pressed the barrel to her temple.

GREG JEFFERS HURRIED through the small house. He had enough information on the woman that he was confident she was not likely to have visitors during the two days he needed to accomplish his goal. He hit a key on the sleeping computer.

The first password he tried was her mother's maiden name. No luck. Next he put in Black Minx. Bull's-eye. People are so easy to figure out.

THE BANK EXECUTIVE assigned to Martha's account had taken two personal days off so he didn't notice the withdrawals until they had been underway for three days. What he saw then was alarming: every hour, an electronic withdrawal of $9,000 had been taking place—the money wired to an account at a bank in Minneapolis.

It wasn't until he was eating his dinner that night that the significance of the $9,000 dollar withdrawals hit him: Each electronic deposit to the new account would have been just under $10,000—the amount that triggers a money-laundering alert to federal banking authorities. He jumped up from the table.

By the time, he reached an officer with the Minneapolis bank, the account had been emptied and closed. Over four hundred thousand dollars gone. He called Martha Estabrook's home but there was no answer. He called the police.

Martha never showed up for her Thursday lunch date. Surprised and worried, her friends drove out to her cottage. The door was unlocked. They found the house looking as though Martha had just stepped out for a walk. Her fly tying tools and supplies were neatly organized on the worktable—one fly half-finished and waiting in the vise. The computer was off. No lights were on and none of her personal belongings appeared to have been disturbed. Indeed, the kitchen was spotless. Wherever Martha had gone, she had tidied up before she left.

It was the mailman who pinpointed when she'd left, as he knew she had not picked up her mail for four days. And unhappy bidders on her eBay auctions soon posted negative notices stating that she was not fulfilling orders.

When it was obvious that Martha was not likely to come home, her friends made sure to return the checks that had been arriving in the mail. Her sister closed down the cottage and paid the bills. Then everyone waited, hoping that she would show up with some kind of excuse.

Late that fall, a man hunting grouse through a dense screen of aspen two miles away stumbled over what the eagles had left of Martha. Right about that time, a young girl—a freshman in a private prep school in Manhattan—received an e-mail:

Hi, Martha,

We have the same name! I Googled myself and you came up—something about you in your school's newsletter. So we're both named Martha Estabrook. I'm fourteen, and I live in Los Angeles. My dad's in the movie business. He helps make the Harry Potter movies, and I had a small role

in one—just an extra but fun. What year are you in school?
Martha Estabrook.

Wow, thought Martha. Her dad makes movies? That is so cool! She e-mailed: *You are so lucky. My dad is a boring investment banker. We live on the Upper East Side and I'm a freshman this year . . .*

§ॐ

The Art and Craft of Tying Trout Flies

Nimble fingers are the first requirement of successful fly tying—that, plus a willingness to work up close and personal on something that may be less than half an inch long. But a lot can happen in that tiny space, which is why fly tying is an art with a long, rich tradition worldwide.

If you have never tied flies, a good way to begin is with a close reading of *The American Fly Tying Manual*, a full-color, fifty page guide by Dave Hughes, which costs only ten dollars and may be available at your local library or sporting goods store.

The manual, which my ten-year-old niece finds easy to use, has step-by-step instructions—clearly illustrated—that take you from tying the thread on the bare hook to cementing the head of a finished fly. Wonderful, large illustrations show every detail as you learn about dry flies, wet flies, nymphs, streamers, emergers, salmon flies, panfish flies—nearly three hundred of the most popular and productive flies.

Each fly is shown in full color so you can tie it exactly as it should be tied—with proper proportions and the correct colors. In addition, the author, who says, "You can tell a good fly tyer by their tools," lists every tool you will need along with recommendations on specific manufacturers.

Be aware that in order to tie a fly you must have or borrow an adjustable vise, scissors with fine points, a good bobbin that does not roll when hanging, good-quality hackle pliers, and a reliable bodkin for applying cement.

The following tips from Dave Hughes on how to get started will help you decide if fly tying is in your future:

- Find a tying area with plenty of room to spread out tools and materials and with a good light source that can be directed at the fly.
- Set your vise so that it holds the hook right in front of you.
- Adjust your bobbin so your thread spool turns before the thread breaks.
- Set your scissors, bobbin, hackle pliers, and bodkin to the right of your vise (to the left if you're left-handed) and within easy reach.
- Lay your materials—i.e. feathers, hair, quills, etc.— out in the order in which you will use them.
- Now read carefully about each new pattern before you begin to tie it.
- And as you set up to tie for the first time be sure you have learned:

    a. how to break your thread in order to understand tension.

    b. how to tie a soft loop (shown clearly in the manual).

    c. how to use your fingertip to roll a half-hitch onto the head of a fly.

    (Each step is shown clearly in *The American Fly Tying Manual*.)

Ready? Hooked on tying flies? Here's wishing you Tight Lines! (Fishing lingo for Good Luck.)

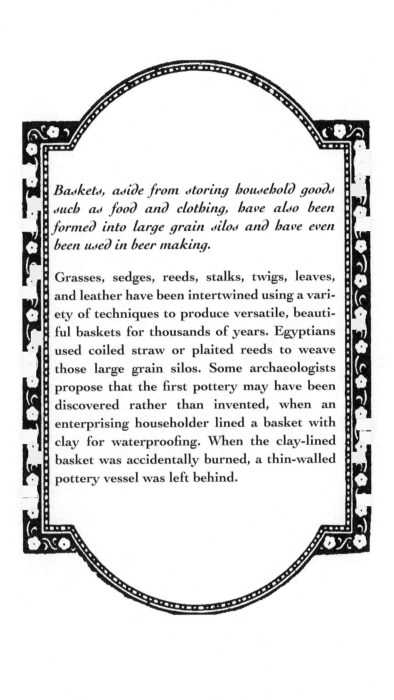

Baskets, aside from storing household goods such as food and clothing, have also been formed into large grain silos and have even been used in beer making.

Grasses, sedges, reeds, stalks, twigs, leaves, and leather have been intertwined using a variety of techniques to produce versatile, beautiful baskets for thousands of years. Egyptians used coiled straw or plaited reeds to weave those large grain silos. Some archaeologists propose that the first pottery may have been discovered rather than invented, when an enterprising householder lined a basket with clay for waterproofing. When the clay-lined basket was accidentally burned, a thin-walled pottery vessel was left behind.

THE *M* WORD

by Judith Kelman

Judith Kelman is the author of thirteen novels, including Summer of Storms, *which won the 2002 Mary Higgins Clark Award, and, with Dr. Peter Scardino,* The Prostate Book, *a nonfiction work for the general public on prostate cancer and other prostate diseases. Her work has been translated into twelve languages, and one novel,* Someone's Watching, *was adapted as an NBC Movie of the Week. Kelman mentors aspiring writers in the public schools, as a writing teacher, and through her award-winning website,* Judith Kelman's Writers Room *(JKelman.com).*

§§

DAWN BLOOMED CLEAR and optimistic on the day Gil Malvent drowned. Lottie Mossman peered up from her work to watch as the earth came awake. She tracked a solitary gull whose long, lazy passes seemed to sweep the last of darkness from the sky. A gaunt, bearded man in baggy shorts and an engineer's cap jogged around Baltimore's Inner Harbor as the sun chased the gloom behind him from the rumpled face of Chesapeake Bay. A few yards from where Lottie sat, he stopped short to avoid tripping over the rangy mutt that dashed up, trailing its leash, to bark an irate challenge at the serpentine paddle boats that bobbed amid their shrinking shadows near the shore.

By the glow of her portable torchlight, Lottie noted that

it was not yet six A.M. Restless eagerness had driven her from her room at the Renaissance Harborplace Hotel over an hour ago. As first to arrive, she'd claimed the centermost spot in the horseshoe of rectangular folding tables that had been arranged to accommodate the finalists. Lottie had filled her gray rubber basin from the hose set out for that purpose and started soaking the round reed she would use later on to carve rims and handles. For the basket proper, she had acquired fine specimens of the real thing, *scirpus lacustris*, from a little-known specialty supply house in New Hampshire. Late last night, before the second sleeping pill finally, mercifully, took hold, she had sprinkled the spokes and weavers with extravagant care and wrapped them to mellow in the soft, worn, woolen blanket she had brought from home. Her best tools were cleaned, honed, and scrupulously aligned on the table. Fondly, she stroked the slim slice of polished ivory bone, the red-handled shears, the antique draw knife she'd happened upon at a flea market, and the lucky knife that had been passed to her by Granny Mae.

Lottie lifted the knife reverently, enjoying the heft and balance of its smooth pearlescent case. A touch of the silver button near the shank launched the sharp, gleaming blade. The sight propelled Lottie back to the day decades ago when Granny Mae had beckoned her close, made sure she was paying full attention, and then slid the blade over her stained, calloused thumb. Granny had passed it with the gliding ease of a seasoned skater, but her thick flesh split like a ripe plum nonetheless. Lottie, only a kid at the time, had watched in rapt horror as the wound forged a bright scarlet trail. Soon, the oozing track bubbled up and spilled its banks, raining bloody droplets on the bile-colored linoleum. Without a word, the old woman had taught her proper respect for the tool. Granny Mae, rest her soul, had understood better than anyone how to get a lesson learned.

Leaning down, Lottie peeled back an edge of the blanket that swaddled the reed. She selected a pliant, evenly formed spoke and wove until it was seated hard in place. Eyeing her work from several angles, she assessed the size and symmetry of the base, made a few subtle adjustments, and decided the time had come to start the sides. The process of turning the spokes upright from the base was called *upsetting*, and it was, as the name implied, one of many stressful moments of truth that determined whether the creation would triumph or fail. Baskets were made of living things; splint pounded from the trunks of felled trees, roots, vines, needles, leaves, or in this case, majestic dried grasses. Living things were shaped by the sum of their experience, even in death; subtle scars from old insults and injuries remained. Every bit of material she used in the craft held hidden memories and opinions, and no one could predict with certainty what they were or how they might bear on the finished piece. Without warning, a spoke could crack or a weaver might go limp and ragged, most tragically when the basket was nearly complete. An unseen weakness could ruin a basket's balance, dooming it to tip, no matter how subtly, like someone burdened with a short leg or feeble spine. For the average hobbyist, such a flaw could be camouflaged or compensated for and forgotten. But for a master weaver competing for the craft's top honors at the national convention of the prestigious North American Basketmakers' Guild, nothing short of utter perfection would do.

Cautiously, Lottie dipped the finished base into the broad gray trough. Too much moisture would sap the reed's strength; too little would leave it stiff and headstrong. The glorious creation she planned would reflect the net sum of countless such small but crucial calculations.

As she lifted the base, Lottie caught the rhythmic slap of footsteps approaching from behind. Her heart quickened, knowing it could be Gil. Hoping it was. How many nights had she lain awake, staring at the shifting shadow forms on the cracked, stained ceiling of Granny Mae's cabin, dreaming of this day? How many hours had she spent mired in fantasy about the precious moment when she would finally get to see Gil again? She had planned for this in fevered detail, and it showed. Lottie knew when she looked her best. *Radiant*, she imagined Gil saying in that sultry voice that told her he wanted to taste her radiance; that he yearned to drink it in and feel the warm press of that radiance against his quickening flesh.

Blushing fiercely, Lottie smoothed the flowing flowered skirt and the delicately embroidered white peasant blouse she had scrimped for months to order from one of those fancy catalogs Granny Mae still got in the mail, even though she'd been dead almost a year. Lottie finger-combed her long dark hair, now free of wiry gray strands thanks to the colorist at a downtown Baltimore salon who had charged her an arm and two legs. The little money Granny had left her along with the cabin was fast running out, which set Lottie's stomach churning. But soon enough, she'd be with Gil, and he had more than plenty. In fact, as president of the Malvent Charitable Trust, his job was traveling around and giving gobs of his family's money away. So Gil knew how to live without fretting the way Lottie always had over every silly dime. He took all the dazzling things he had as a matter of course: fancy car, big house with his very own swimming pool, first-class travel, servants, the works. Lottie was determined to learn how to be blasé, too. Taking fancy things for granted was classy. That much, she knew.

Pulling a hard breath, she pinched color in her cheeks and ran her tongue over lips that suddenly had gone dry as chalk. She waited for the thrill of Gil's spicy breath against the back of her neck, shivering in anticipation of his touch. But instead of Gil, the footfalls delivered a chunky, pie-faced woman named Anita Jo Carsweiler, corresponding secretary of the guild's Missouri chapter.

Anita Jo dumped her things on the table to Lottie's right. From a quartet of canvas totes, she plucked tightly bound bundles of quarter-inch flat reed and half-inch flat oval. She laid out slim lashers to bind the rims and sturdy rounds, fat as knockwurst, for the handles. Next she set out gallon-sized Ziploc bags stuffed with clothespins, bulldog clips, and several blunt metal tamping tools, all amateurish shortcuts and crutches. Anita Jo even toted a pair of heavy metal weights designed to hold the spokes in place like an extra hands. Those things were intended for rank beginners, Lottie noted with no small measure of disdain. From the look of things, Miss Piggy planned to make the same ugly step basket that she had last year. From the sound, she was going to be every bit as chatty, meddlesome, opinionated, and annoying as she had been last year, as well.

"Well, aren't you the early bird?" Anita Jo said in her cloying honeyed drawl. "Better watch you don't catch yourself a worm."

With a dismissive shrug, Lottie focused on gently but firmly redirecting the spokes from the horizontal to a sloping uphill pitch. She treated each one as a reticent child that had to be coaxed like her daughter Lacy. Faced with something unfamiliar, the child had always been skittish, but once she'd gotten a push in the right direction she did fine. Lottie remembered now how Lacy broke through her shyness to dance like the beautiful angel she'd been tapped to portray in the Christmas pageant year before last at St. Mark's Elementary School. A sudden longing for the child struck Lottie like a gut punch. But she breathed through it and shifted her focus to Gil. Lottie had thought long and hard, agonized really, before concluding that she had no choice but to let Lacy go live with her daddy. Even when Ray got the new job and moved all the way to Detroit, which could have been Mars for how often Lottie was able to get there, she knew her decision had been right. Maybe someday down the road, when she and Gil were settled in and established, they could take the child on, but not now. First, they had to build their own solid base, just the two of them.

Anita Jo waddled over and planted herself smack in front of Lottie's table. Her squinty eyes scrunched small as steam slits. "So what are you up to, Lottie? Wait let me guess. Bet it's a Georgia pecan basket. That right? You going fixed handles or hinged? Planning to chase weave or what?"

Lottie responded with a stingy sideways nod, inviting the irksome busybody to disappear.

A stifling mass of time passed while Anita Jo just stood there, staring. Finally, she shrugged. "Guess I'd best get cracking. That five o'clock closing bell always sneaks up faster than you'd expect. Don't you think?"

Actually, what Lottie thought was that Miss Piggy was no competition. Neither was Nadine Truitt, the brash, self-important president of the Florida chapter, who arrived next and sat on Lottie's left. By seven, all the tables save one were occupied. Lottie recognized most of the weavers from last year's convention. Her memory of that life-altering week-end was as sharp as Granny's knife, especially every precious second she'd spent with Gil.

Lottie swerved in her seat and scanned the harbor, wondering where on earth he could be. Last year, his first as chief judge of the competition, he'd urged Lottie out of bed before sunrise, coaxing her up from the torpor she'd fallen into after a night of glorious lovemaking. Thankfully, her indolence soon yielded to a burst of creative energy that spurred her to produce an impeccable Cherokee gathering basket with a stunningly complex weave. At the end of the day, it seemed only natural when Gil called her name to come to the podium and receive the gold medal, and along with it, the raw envy of the other weavers and the heady adulation of the crowd. To seal the moment's perfection, Gil had embraced her warmly for the guild's photographer in a proud and courageously open declaration of his love.

Nadine was nattering now. "Hey there, Lottie. Had a good year?"

"Fine." That was all she said, her message as clear as a slammed door. But Nadine was too thickheaded to take the hint.

"You've got a little girl same age as my Alice. Name's Tracy. Isn't that right?"

"Lacy."

Nadine drew a sodden weaver from her pail and flicked it

as if she was casting for trout. "Lacy, right. And your husband's Ray, I remember. Nice-looking fellow. Solid type. Saw him in that family picture they ran in the newsletter. What's he do again, your husband?"

"Construction." Lottie pictured Ray now, driving home nails with a raw fury directed at her. Try as she had to explain things, poor old Ray simply hadn't been able to understand. His face went dead blank when she'd patiently described how she'd fallen in love, how Gil was her soul mate, her missing half. He'd stayed blank when she'd explained how these things simply happen and how they're beyond anyone's control. Lottie hadn't been looking for Gil. Far from it. When she won the state prize and the Michigan guild offered to pay her way to the convention, all she'd been able to think about was what to weave, how to win the national gold and make Granny Mae proud. The old woman had been failing for months, losing to the emphysema, and Lottie had wanted nothing more than to give her a reason to smile. The last thing she'd expected was to come here to Baltimore, to go away without Ray for the first time in their eighteen-year marriage, and fall hopelessly, completely in love.

Then, how could Ray begin to get such a thing when he was about as romantic as boiled eggs? Lottie's husband was the solid type all right, if what you meant by solid was a great big yawn. Everything with that man was routine. He had bacon on toast for breakfast every morning; dinner at six-thirty sharp. Ray had strict rules against shoes in the living room and wouldn't abide calls in or out of the house after nine P.M. He insisted they go to church every Sunday, no matter how bleak and miserable the winter day happened to be on their tiny frigid prison of an island off Michigan's Upper Peninsula. Lottie suspected Ray felt compelled to go to atone for the few minutes of perfunctory, predictable sex they had after the single glass of sweet sherry he allowed them every Saturday night. It was lights out; eyes closed; missionary position; mute, clumsy, flesh-bumping congress, after which each of them slipped from bed in the pitch dark and showered in turn, because Ray couldn't even think of sleeping until all traces of the shameful act had been expunged. Laundry sex, Lottie secretly called it; it was about as big a turn-on as sorting socks.

Nadine was still at it. "My Charlie's in construction, too. Sheet-metal contractor. Air conditioning mostly, but also some ductwork when it comes along. No point in turning down business, I say. Every bit helps. Your Ray work on his own or with a company?"

Lottie eyed her sternly. "Best to concentrate."

Nadine's ferret face went tight, and to Lottie's delight, she turned her attention to Franny Winkovsky, who was seated at her other side, struggling with the rebellious spokes on a fanny basket. "Some people take things way too serious, if you ask me," Nadine said, pointedly tipping her head Lottie's way. "Like a basket competition was life or death."

"And some people haven't got a clue," Lottie muttered under her breath. She knew the importance of being mindful in the craft, leaving nothing to chance. As the temperature and humidity built, wilting the morning's freshness, Lottie was constantly aware and made the necessary subtle adjustments. She noted the weight of the air and the harsh, unflinching testimony of the sun. She factored in the moisture rising off the bay and the thickening mass of tourists swarming the harbor, stirring the atmosphere with their idle thoughts and mindless chatter.

"Like it was life or death," Nadine repeated and puffed her lips. "Like this was as serious as a war."

Lottie released a loud, pitying sigh. Nadine was like Ray, simply incapable of understanding certain things, and that's why poor Nadine would never rise above mediocrity. Ditto for Franny and Anita Jo. Silly cows just couldn't see the light.

From the first time Granny Mae invited Lottie to try her hand at weaving when she was maybe four, she'd viewed the craft as a sacred trust. From that unforgettable day when Granny Mae sat her down, placed a bucket filled with scrap reed at her side and started teaching Lottie how to shape and tame the material into a simple napkin basket, she'd been humbled and awed. People understood things or they didn't, plain and clear. And thankfully, Lottie was one who did. She understood that she'd been blessed with a talent for weaving and doubly blessed by having Granny Mae to teach and guide her in that and all things. She knew that the so-called tragedy of her parents' dying in that car wreck when she was only two was actually fate's way of putting her in better hands. Lottie also knew, like she knew how to breathe, that Gil was as much a part of her destiny as Granny Mae. Sure, she was sorry to have to hurt Ray and leave Lacy behind, but that was simply the way it had to go.

Again, she peered around, searching for Gil. It was nearly nine o'clock now and there was still no sign of him. Last night, when she'd called, he hadn't answered in his room, but Lottie hadn't given that much thought. Maybe he'd checked in late after a long flight on one of the trips he was always taking. She imagined him exhausted from the time change and what-have-you, and falling hard asleep. Or maybe he hadn't arrived yet at all, and the hotel switch-board was simply mistaken. Gil's executive secretary arranged his travel and maddeningly often, that girl got things mixed up. Lottie had gotten used to the need for persistence when she wanted to hear Gil's voice. She'd just keep at it, ring him at home, at the office, and on his cell, and eventually, there he was.

He certainly had to show up well in advance of the luncheon today when he was scheduled to swear in the guild's president elect. And he had to turn up soon to supervise the competition in progress, given he was chief judge again.

She cleared her throat and mused aloud. "Wonder where Gil could be."

Nadine looked down her long, pinched nose. "Best to concentrate, Lottie. Isn't that what you said?"

"Gil?" Anita sniffed. "Where do you think?"

Lottie tapered a weaver with her shears, tracking a slow, gentle slope. "I'm just hoping nothing's wrong, that's all."

"Come now. Don't tell me you think Gil comes to these conventions for the basket making."

"Well, of course he does. Why else?"

Several of the women started tittering. "Hmmm. Let me think," Anita Jo said, venom dripping off her drawl.

"Saw him last night in the hospitality suite, warming up his flavor of the week. Girl looked barely past her teens," Franny reported.

"So this year he's going much younger," Nadine said with a pointed glance at Lottie. "She married?"

Franny snugged her weaving to the rhythm of her words. "Wasn't wearing a ring. Not that that tells all."

"Won't fly if she's not," Anita Jo said. "Last thing Gil wants is some chickie expecting happily ever after when all he's ever after is another notch in his belt."

Lottie lost control of her shears and lopped the taper blunt. "Shame on you, spreading a bunch of lying gossip like that!"

Anita Jo's brow climbed halfway up her broad forehead. "Whoa, girl. Easy now. Romeo doesn't need you to defend him, believe me. Man's not the least little bit ashamed of how he is."

"Ashamed? Hell, Gil's proud of it," Franny said. "Just look."

Tracking their gaze, Lottie saw Gil emerge from the hotel with his arm around the waist of a willowy, young blonde. She tried to turn away, but her gaze froze on the sight of them, and her heart thumped with terrifying intensity.

"Wonder how his wife puts up with it," Nadine mused.

Lottie's throat jammed. *Wife?*

Anita Jo rubbed her thumb against her fingertips, the sign for cash.

"Not me. No way, no how. There's not enough green on this good earth to get me to live with a man who can't keep his zipper up," Nadine said. "Gil ever try any funny business with you, Franny?"

Franny eyed the heavens, but a guilty smile gave her away. "Didn't give in though. Not completely, thank heaven."

"Amen to that," Anita Jo said, swiping mock sweat from her brow. "Can't say I wasn't tempted though. Man could charm the spots off a Dalmatian."

Both women turned to Nadine. "You're being awful quiet. Now spill," Franny demanded.

The ferret face went coy. " 'Fraid I'll have to plead the Fifth on that."

Anita Jo wagged an accusatory finger. "Naughty, naughty. Thought you couldn't deal with someone who couldn't keep his zipper up."

Nadine set her pointy jaw. "I said I couldn't be married to someone like that, and no way I could. This was nothing; a little midsummer night madness is all. Anyway, Lester never suspected a thing, so no harm done."

A wicked grin crossed Franny's face. "How was Gil's thing anyway?"

Nadine covered her mouth in mock shock. "You're bad!"

"You're terrible, all of you," Lottie said. "If you really knew Gil, you wouldn't talk such trash."

Anita Jo whistled low. "Best watch yourself, Lottie. You take a fall from way up on that high horse, it won't be pretty."

Lottie tuned them out and saw only Gil. The sight of him warmed her. That girl meant nothing. It was always Gil's way to flirt and flatter. Part of his charm. In her heart, Lottie knew Gil was one hundred percent hers. Otherwise, she certainly wouldn't have told Ray and Lacy good-bye. She wouldn't have spent the winter in Granny Mae's godforsaken cabin all alone with no TV, having to pump water from the well and heat it on the stove, having to go out in the frigid darkness to do her business in Granny's smelly old outhouse, spending nearly every last nickel she had to her name in fevered anticipation of this day.

Lottie caught Gil's eye and waved. He nodded, and then squired the young blonde to an empty table. Lottie watched as he pulled out her chair and then helped her arrange her materials and tools.

Pulling a breath, Lottie let her envy go. Gil was being a gentleman, that's all, acting sweet and thoughtful. The girl was new and knew nobody, so he was showing her the ropes, settling her in so she'd feel comfortable. Lottie smiled, thinking she could add that to the long list of things she loved and admired about her man. Gil was a prince.

She watched fondly now as he set out a large bundle of double pointed spokes and the weaving materials Lottie recognized as the makings of a Nantucket basket. Sure enough, Gil dug into one of the girl's collection of fancy totes and pulled out the nest of progressively sized Nantuckets that were ready to be inserted into the one she'd make today. The rules allowed for this, given the complexity of the form. Nothing in the craft was more difficult to pull off than a perfect Nantucket nest, precise in symmetry and descending size. Lottie, for all her experience and talent, could never have mustered the nerve to try such a thing in competition.

She chuckled to herself, keeping the smug smile at bay. So let the poor thing fall on her pert, little cup-hook nose. Let her learn the perils of too much ambition the hard way. Miss Nantucket was almost painfully young. She had plenty of time to figure things out and get them right someday.

Riding a fresh burst of resolve, Lottie set to work again. She tapered a weaver expertly and began to set her pattern. Her plan was to replicate the most famous and historically significant basket of all time: the Moses ark. Lottie had studied countless biblical references and interpretive texts until she was satisfied that she understood exactly how that legendary vessel had looked. Naturally, there were varying opinions around an event so ancient, but scholars agreed that the Hebrew baby who would someday lead his people out of bondage in Egypt had been spared annihilation when he was hidden by his mother in a basket made of bulrush (*scirpus licastrus*), which had been rendered waterproof with tar and pitch. That basket had altered the destiny of the Jewish people. Were there justice, the unknown person who wove the Moses basket would be central to the story. But no, the weaver's true identity did not even merit a footnote. Lottie hadn't even come upon any speculation about which craftsperson had been responsible for Moses's survival and in turn, should be credited with everything he accomplished from his infancy. Some scholars had suggested that his mother had simply thrown the basket together at the last minute, as if such a thing was no big deal. Obviously, they knew less than nothing.

Lottie worked with single-minded zeal, gratified as the basket developed a pleasing shape and impeccable symmetry. The bulrush was so utterly compliant it felt like a natural extension of Lottie's hands. For a time, she was virtually hypnotized by the weaving and unaware of everything, including the progress of the other competitors. When thoughts of Gil pecked at her concentration, she pushed them firmly aside. A central part of her plan for this day was to triumph in the competition. She wanted to carry that with them as they started their new life.

Less than an hour remained until the required lunch break. In that time, Lottie planned to weave at least halfway up the sides. Sculpting the rims and handles precisely and finishing the piece would take hours, and she didn't want to rush any part of the process. She could name the archenemies of perfection: rushing, a lapse in attention, galloping emotions, and, perhaps the worst, broken confidence, and she was not about to fall into any of those traps.

Not on this of all days.

Only a few times did she allow herself to glance Gil's way. Each time she found him hovering around little Miss Nantucket. Then *Nan*, as Lottie now secretly called her, needed all the help she could get. With almost half the day gone, her basket was going nowhere in a hurry. She hadn't even inserted all the pointed spokes in the wooden base, and once she did, she had hours of laborious weaving ahead of her. Silly, misguided girl was bound to face the indignation of having to present an unfinished mess after the closing bell.

Lottie smiled, and her imagination fast-forwarded to the winner's podium. She'd been planning her acceptance speech for weeks, and she loved how the theme came together. She was going to talk about all the essential *M* words in her life. She'd been born and raised in *Michigan* with the last name *Mossman*, and even when she'd married Ray, she hadn't given that up. Mossman was Granny Mae's name, and the Mossman tradition of excellence in weaving was what Lottie meant to carry on. *May* was another *M* word, and that was the month of Lottie's birth. There was her May fourteenth birthday and Granny *Mae Mossman*, blessed with a double *M* name, who had raised her up from age two. There was *M* for *mindfulness*, which Granny Mae had taught her along with the other crucial elements of the craft. And there was *M* for Baltimore, *Maryland*, where she had won the gold last year and met the love of her life. In keeping with the *M* motif, Lottie would explain why she'd chosen to weave a replica *Moses* ark. That basket had cosmic physical significance back in biblical days, and building it again seemed an appropriate tribute to the unknown, unheralded weaver responsible for Moses's salvation. The Moses basket worked on a symbolic level as well. Like Moses and his people, Lottie was being delivered from the slavery of Ray's suffocating existence and numbing routines to the Promised Land of milk, honey, and sweet freedom, which was Gil. Of course, she wouldn't mention that in her speech, out of delicacy. But that's what she would be thinking along with the fact that Gil's last name, *Malvent*, was an *M* word, too.

Chairs scraped around her as the time came to break for lunch. Anita Jo tossed a blanket over her lumpy step basket, and Franny stuffed her unwieldy mess of a fanny basket in a tote. Nadine, who made up in recklessness for what she lacked in skill, simply left everything. Lottie tenderly swaddled her entry in the blanket and carried it up to her room. True, someone from the guild stood guard during lunch, but she was taking no chances.

Entering the crowded ballroom, she searched for Gil. He would be seated up front, probably at the center table. Lottie spotted him quickly, but there was no vacant seat for her by his side. Every chair at that table was taken, and Gil was wedged between Nan and Mavis Barstow, who was moving up from executive vice president to president this year. Well, he had his responsibilities, and she could deal with that. The man would be all hers soon enough.

Lottie found an empty chair at the back of the room. She picked at her lunch, not all that hungry, and turned only half an ear to the endless speeches that followed. Naturally, Gil's introduction for Mavis Barstow interested her the most. He was captivating as always, and as he spoke about Mavis's dedication to the craft and long, distinguished service to the guild, all eyes were riveted on him, especially Lottie's. The sight of his tall, trim form, dark wavy hair, and blizzard-white smile turned her insides to mush.

When the luncheon was over, she waited for Gil outside the ballroom. He was among the last to trickle out. Little Miss Nantucket was practically glued to his side, and Lottie imagined he must be good and fed up with her by now. Boldly, she positioned herself directly in their path. She fixed Nan with an imperious look. "If you'll excuse us, Gil and I need a few minutes alone."

"Sure. Why not? Knock yourself out."

Gil stood stiffly, watching as Nan strode toward the exit, waggling her rump like a silly pup.

Lottie rolled her eyes. "You poor thing, Gil. Bet that little twit's been driving you right up the wall. Figured you must be needing a break from that poor, clingy girl by now. You can thank me proper later on."

"Thank you?"

Lottie blushed. "Well, in a manner of speaking, I mean.

Soon as the judging's over, we can go upstairs and pick up where we left off. Take all night if we feel like it. How ready are you for that?"

Gil seemed to rise up taller. "All I'm ready for is to have you disappear. Stalking is illegal, you know that? I could throw your crazy ass in jail."

Lottie dug a knuckle in her ear. "How weird, Gil. You wouldn't believe what I thought I heard you say."

"Don't play games with me, you nutty bitch. I tried to be nice to you, to give you time to get your damned act together, but that's over. Over, do you hear?"

"What are you saying, Gil? I don't understand."

"I'm saying you are to get the hell away from me and stay away. I'm saying that if you ever call me again, if I ever so much as see you looking at me, I'll turn your sorry butt in."

For a long time, Lottie stared at him in frozen horror. Then she burst out laughing. "My Lord, Gil. Good joke. You really had me going there for a minute."

He gripped her wrists and squeezed so hard she saw stars. "I am not joking! I'm dead serious. I've had it with you bugging me at the office, driving my secretary crazy, calling my house. I don't care what a pathetic, desperate piece of trash you are, I'm not putting up with your crap any more."

"Gil?" To her own ear, Lottie's voice seemed hopelessly small and far away. Time had stalled, and her heart didn't seem to be beating.

He pushed her away with such force; Lottie lost her balance and sprawled to the lobby floor. Instinctively, she held out a hand so Gil could to help her get to her feet.

He backed away as if she'd burned him. "Don't touch me! Don't come near me! You just stay the hell out of my face!"

Paralyzed, Lottie watched Gil leave. Through the glass face of the hotel, she saw him scoop Miss Nantucket up in his arms. He lifted the girl and twirled her gaily. Then he set her down, sliding her body over his like a shirt. Pulling back, he spoke awhile, gesturing dramatically, and then started to laugh. Soon they were both laughing raucously, streaming tears of hilarity, having great fun at Lottie's expense.

And what an expense! Numbly, she considered all that she'd sacrificed for that vile monster. Lottie had left the comfortable home Ray had custom built specially for her—three bedrooms, two and a half baths, a kitchen to die for and the beautiful paneled den where they spent so much good family time—and moved back into the primitive hell-hole of a cabin she'd grown up in with Granny Mae. She'd tossed eighteen years of marriage to Ray down the drain, pretty blissful years as she considered them now. Ray was a good man, *solid* like Nadine said, loving and reliable, and a God-fearing churchgoer to boot. Above all, she thought of her little sweetheart of a perfect girl: Lacy. Ray had told her how the child had cried and cried for missing her in the beginning. Poor little thing had been brokenhearted, inconsolable, wanting her mother, begging to have Mommy back. But nearly a year had passed since Lottie left to start divorce proceedings. Last time she called Ray a few weeks ago to check on their daughter, he had been only too happy to report that Lacy rarely even mentioned her any more. When Lottie asked him to put the child on so she could say hello, Lacy had flat out refused. Lottie heard her whining in the background as if she'd been ordered to eat liver. *I don't want to talk to her, Daddy. Don't make me, please!*

Lottie got to her feet and smoothed her skirt. She tucked the errant tail of her peasant blouse back in place. Squaring her shoulders the way Granny Mae always told her to do, she strode to the bank of pay phones down the hall. Her hand trembled as she keyed in the number of Ray's house in Detroit. But as soon as she heard his voice, she went calm and clear.

"Hi, Ray. Glad you're home."

"What's wrong, Lottie? You sound terrible."

A dry nervous giggle escaped her. "Nothing's wrong. I'm just fine."

"What then? This is not a good time."

"No problem, Ray. What I have to say will only take a sec. We can talk more when I get home."

"What is it then? Because if you're looking for more money, you'll have to take it to the judge."

"Nothing like that." She tuned her voice to that kittenish tone Ray always fell for. "I made a mistake, sweetie. I want us to get back together. So I was thinking I can come right from the convention to Detroit. I can get a realtor to sell Granny's cabin and send us the cash. Maybe we can use it to finally take that honeymoon we always talked about."

Silence bristled on the line, and Lottie thought they'd been disconnected. "Ray? You there?"

"You know something? For months after you took off, all I could think about was figuring out how to get you back."

"I understand, sweetie pie. But that's all water under the bridge."

"That's true, and the bridge has been demolished. I don't want you back, Lottie. I'm happy without you, and so is Lacy. The two of us have done just fine, better without all your craziness, if you want to know. Anyway, I met a wonderful lady at the church. Lacy's crazy about Roseanne, and if all goes well, we are going to make it legal the minute my divorce from you is finalized. Should be any day now."

There was a loud humming deep in Lottie's head. Had to be a bad connection. "I can't really hear you, Ray. Better cut this short. Will you pick me up at the airport, or should I take a cab?"

"Neither. You listen to me, Lottie Mossman. You're not welcome here. You made your bed, now you go lie in it."

"I'll take a cab then, Ray. No problem at all. Wouldn't want you to get Lacy out of bed at that hour anyway. See you tomorrow night, sweetie. Can't wait."

The humming was louder now, and Lottie realized they'd been disconnected for real. Well, she and Ray would be reconnected again soon enough. She'd see to that.

And she was not going home empty-handed. No way.

She was going to show that rotten snake Gil exactly what he was giving up. She pictured him weeping in remorse after she won top honors. How he'd beg to have her take him back. But too bad, she was going to tell him. You took too long to order, Gil baby, and the kitchen is closed. You made your stupid bed, now you can just go lie in it.

Lottie retrieved her partially finished Moses basket from the room. Then she crossed the lobby and left the hotel. The steamy harbor now swarmed with tourists, many slick with sweat and fanning themselves with colorful brochures from the visitor center. Lottie wove slowly through the swirling crowd, guarding her precious creation from accidental harm. Last thing she needed was some jerk with a lit cigarette to burn a hole in the reed or some flailing idiot to unseat a crucial weaver.

Finally, she reached the crescent of tables and took her place. Scanning quickly, she realized that all the craziness with Gil and Ray must have taken far longer than she'd thought. Most of the competitors were nearing the end of their weaving, preparing to fashion their rims and handles or carving them already.

She had to pick up the pace to make up for lost time. *Over two, under three . . .*

"Get a load of her," Anita Jo said. "Girl's going so fast you'd think her hair caught fire."

Nadine's thin lips puckered in distaste. "Where'd you get to anyway, Lottie? Figured you must be off having a nooner or something and forgot yourself."

Lottie kept weaving in a fury, frantically trying to keep count. If she wasn't mindful, she could breach the pattern or make some other embarrassing mistake.

"Lighten up, girl, for godsakes. Keep up like that, you'll give yourself a stroke." Anita Jo's tongue clacked in mock concern.

Over two, under three, pass one at the corner, pass two at the center side, over two, under three . . .

"She's right, Lottie. You look like a volcano fixing to blow. Whatever it is, it'll pass, believe me," Franny said. "Life's too short."

Over two, under three, pass one at . . .

Lottie was exerting too much force. The gentle outward slope she wanted began to veer toward the straight vertical. To correct that, she had to rip several rows. Frantic now, she overcorrected so the sides flared too wide.

Over two, under three, pass one at the center side, pass two at the corner . . .

Down the row, she heard Gil's seductive voice followed by the trill of Nan's coy giggle.

Over one, under two, pass two . . .

The little twit's satisfied giggling went on and on, building to a clanging cacophony in Lottie's head. So loud, she thought she'd scream. The thought of screaming was so real, her throat went raw.

Next thing she knew, Anita Jo was clutching her shoulders and shaking her.

"Quit it! Let me go!"

"Sssh, Lottie. I was just trying to calm you down, honey. You were screeching like a hoot owl. Looking all wild in the eyes."

"I'm fine," Lottie said, puffing the rumpled sleeves of her peasant blouse.

Nadine was at her other side, stroking her hands and gently prodding them away from her basket. "Time to quit now, Lottie. Contest's over. They rang the bell."

Lottie blinked. "Can't be over. I'm not done."

"It's fine. Just fine. Don't you worry." Anita Jo slipped her hands under Lottie's armpits and nudged her out of the chair.

"I'm not worried. Not in the least." If the contest was over, that meant the winner would soon be announced, and she'd have to make her speech. "I should probably go freshen up."

"Good idea. You do that," said Franny. "We'll see to everything here."

The crowd parted as if by magic to let her pass, and Lottie drifted toward the hotel. In the room, she touched up her makeup and fixed her hair. She checked her image in the full-length mirror and smiled. She was ready.

The spectators stood three deep. Lottie reached her table just as Gil took the microphone and began to speak. His voice reverberated over the speaker system. "Ladies and gentlemen, now is the hour. These talented people have worked tirelessly for years, even decades, to master this highly challenging craft, and today, they have given it their all in hopes of winning the highest honor conferred in the weaver's world: the gold medal from our national guild. So with no further ado, I'm delighted to announce that this year's winner is—"

Lottie sprang to her feet in anticipation.

"—Melanie Marshack from Deer Hollow, Vermont. Come on up and tell us all about yourself, Melanie. Join me in a round of applause for the creator of this magnificent nest of Nantucket baskets. Let's hear it for Melanie Marshack!"

Nan shrieked with glee and trotted to the podium. Gil twirled her around again and lifted her high in the air. Then she stepped to the podium, and the crowd fell silent.

Lottie's voice rang clear and true. "Seems only fitting that I should win my second consecutive gold medal with a Moses ark. Words beginning with the letter *M* have always had great meaning in my life. *M* for Mossman, like my name. *M* for my Grannie Mae and the month of May and, of course, for Moses himself. *M* for mindful, too. Let's not forget that."

A noisy murmur rose from the crowd. Lottie heard rude snickering and catcalls. *Shut up and let the winner speak, lady.*

"Let's not forget manners, either," Lottie said angrily. "Manners like your mother should have taught you but obviously did not!"

Anita Jo and Nadine each took her by an arm. They backed her away from the table and started walking her toward the hotel. "Wait! I'm not finished!" Lottie shrilled.

"Hush, sweetie. You need to rest now," Anita Jo said.

"That's right," said Nadine. "And we'll have a doctor come look at you, maybe get you something to calm you down."

"But what about my medal?"

"Don't bother yourself about anything," Anita Jo said. "Just try to relax."

The hotel doctor shone lights in her eyes, tapped her knees with a rubber mallet, ran a pin across the sole of her foot, and asked her a bunch of silly questions. Who was the president of the United States? What city was this? What was the date?

Lottie answered to humor him. "Look. I'm fine, doctor. Plus, I have to get ready for the party. Can't exactly have the celebration without the winner, now can they?"

"I think you should stay quiet for awhile, Mrs. Mossman. You've obviously been under a lot of strain."

"That's all behind me now. Water under the bridge. So if you'll excuse me."

After he left, Lottie took careful stock and prepared. She ironed the wrinkles out of her skirt and blouse and freshened up her makeup yet again. She was perfectly clear now about what had happened, and she accepted it with striking calm. Miss Nantucket was the winner, and this would be her night. Can't win them all.

The phone rang. "Hey, Lottie. It's Anita Jo. How are you doing, hon? What did the doctor say?"

"It was a shock, but I'm over it. This is not a matter of life or death after all. Life's too short."

"Good for you. That's exactly right."

"See you at the party then."

"You sure you're up to it?"

"Absolutely. Wouldn't miss it for the world."

"Okay, then. See you there."

Lottie fairly floated into the ballroom on a newfound cushion of calm. Moments later, the bar waiter appeared with the champagne she had ordered. Lottie pointed out Gil and little Miss Nantucket, and watched as he delivered the bubbly along with the mysterious note she'd written and the other very special surprise she'd tucked inside while no one was looking.

She had splurged on a bottle of Dom Perignon, Gil's absolute favorite. Though it would eat up too much of the precious little money Lottie had left, she hadn't hesitated for an instant. No matter what it took, Gil would get what he deserved.

As she'd known he would, Gil steered Nan out to the deserted terrace where he could share the bottle with no one but her. Lottie stood out of sight near the terrace door, watching. Soon after the bottle was drained, Gil started to fade. His spine sagged and he settled heavily in his chair. Nan dropped her head on her hands and fell fast asleep on the table. Before Gil could follow suit, Lottie went out to him and practically lifted him out of his seat. He leaned heavily on her as she guided him out a rear exit and ferried him out of the hotel. Gil was bobbing and weaving like one of the serpentine paddle boats on the bay.

"That champagne sure got to you, didn't it, sweetheart?"

"Wassat? S'gwin onere?"

"I just put a little something in the bubbly to relax you, honey. That way you can settle back and enjoy the long journey I've planned for you."

"Zis?"

"Hush now, Gil. You're not making a bit of sense. You wait like a good boy, and Momma's going to tell you a nice story soon as she gets back."

She found the basket where she had left it in the shadows behind the tourist office, swaddled in the blanket. Lottie ferried her Moses ark to the now-deserted distant end of the harbor where she had propped Gil with his feet dangling in the water.

"Moses's mother loved her little boy, and she couldn't bear to think of casting him away as the pharaoh had ordered, so she hid him in a basket on the Nile. She told her daughter Miriam to watch over her baby brother. Soon, the pharaoh's daughter came to swim in the river and found the baby and took him home where he could be raised as a prince."

Lottie lowered the basket in the bay and then slid Gil feet-first into the woven ark. By now, he was so perfectly pliant, she could shape him with ease. No matter that he was bent nearly double with his knees pressed tight against his face to fit in the meager space. Half a bottle of champagne filled with Lottie's crushed sleeping pills had sent him off beyond discomfort to the land of who-gives-a-damn.

She went on. "And in the palace, Moses grew big and strong, and eventually he learned who he really was and became the liberator of his enslaved people. And while some say that his mother wove the basket that saved Moses and altered the destiny of mankind, in fact no one really knows who the weaver was."

The basket strained under Gil's weight and, poorly built as it was, almost immediately began to sink. Hurriedly, Lottie used Granny's knife, the lucky one with the pearlescent handle, to carve a large *M* on his back. The knife sliced easily through Gil's jacket and shirt and split his flesh to the bone. As Lottie watched in fascination, scarlet tracks spread in an *M* shape on the cut fabric of his suit coat. "And murder is an *M* word, too, Gil. Let's not forget that."

He murmured something incomprehensible and smacked his lips.

"So back to the story. What we do know is that Moses was saved because the basket was perfect. It was coated with tar and pitch and completely waterproof. The craftsperson who made that basket remained utterly focused. There was no breach in her mindfulness, no rush to finish the work, no distraction, no ruinous emotion, or break in her self confidence. And so that very special baby stayed safe and survived."

Gil stirred at the shock of the water on his skin. He flailed comically, jerking his limbs as if to shed tight bonds. As his face began to submerge, he pulled a reflexive breath, but instead of air, he drew a mouthful of water. Sputtering, he coughed and struggled harder. But in seconds, the top of his head went under and the last few bubbles his lungs put out rose up and broke into nothingness. The surface of the Chesapeake went smooth as a sheet of cool black glass that reflected the radiant glow of Lottie's smile.

She returned to the ballroom. Someone had spirited little Miss Nantucket away to sleep it off. The wine was flowing freely. The band was playing a salsa tune. And the party shifted into high gear.

Anita Jo peeled off of the dance floor and trundled her way. "Hey, Lottie. How nice to see you all smiling and with some roses in those cheeks for a change."

"I feel great. Honestly. Couldn't be better."

"That's the spirit. Keep your chin up and don't let the bad guys get you down. Plus there's always next year."

Lottie smiled ruefully. Chances were she'd be a guest of the state of Maryland next year, and quite possibly for the rest of her life. But there were worse things. And there was a definite upside. She certainly wouldn't have to worry about money anymore. Money or men. In a way it was comforting to have all that uncertainty behind her. Peaceful really.

Nadine appeared at her other side and curled her scrawny arm around Lottie's waist. Anita Jo's chunky hand scrawled soothing circles on Lottie's back. Suddenly, the music stopped and a hush descended. There was a flurry of activity near the door, and Lottie braced herself for the rush of stern-faced cops. She awaited the frisking hands and the harsh bite of handcuffs on her wrists.

"Don't worry. I'm ready for this."

Anita Jo looked skeptical. "Just hang in there."

Eyes closed, Lottie waited. A stifling mass of time passed, but nothing happened. Then, from the distance came a voice. "Ladies and gentlemen, please join me in a round of applause for our gold medalist, Melanie Marshak."

Bristling with disbelief, Lottie opened her eyes. She watched little Miss Nantucket strut toward the stage on Gil Malvent's arm. Melanie Marshak was as perky as a cherry fizz, and Gil didn't have a drop of moisture on him. No sign of the bloody *M* carved in his suit jacket either. He was utterly, obscenely alive.

Terrified, Lottie clung fast to Nadine and Anita Jo. Waves of dizzy horror washed over her. She was imagining things, and that meant something must be terribly wrong with her mind. Thank goodness she'd brought her family along for moral support. All she had to do was go up to the room and talk about her crazy conjuring. In the cool light of day, this would all seem like nothing but a bad dream. Sweet little Lacy would sit on her lap and love her up, while solid, sensible Ray heaped her with practical advice and assurances. And Granny Mae would know right off exactly the right thing to do. Good thing that old woman was as healthy as a horse. Lottie couldn't imagine how she could ever get by for a single day without her Granny.

Napkin Basket

To make a napkin basket you'll need:

> 25 feet of half-inch flat reed for stakes and base fillers
> 45 feet of quarter-inch flat oval reed for weavers and lashing
> 4 feet of three-eighths inch flat oval reed for rims
> 2 feet of #6 round reed
> scissors; spring-type clothespins; bone folder or basketry packing tool

- Cut three stakes 22 inches long and seven stakes 18 inches long from half-inch flat reed. Also, cut two base fillers 10 inches long from half-inch flat reed. Soak these in warm water until pliable, about two minutes. Make a pencil mark on rough side at center of each piece.
- Lay one 22-inch stake beside a 10-inch base filler at

the pencil mark. Continue alternating until you have three 22-inch and two 10-inch pieces.

- Then, weave the center 18-inch stake over the 22-inch stakes and under the 10-inch fillers. Next, on each side of the center stake, weave another 18-inch stake, this time under the 22-inch stakes and over the fillers, spacing stakes half an inch apart. Continue until all seven stakes have been woven.

- Soak the base in warm water for two minutes. At the edge of the base on all four sides, gently "upset the basket" by creasing each stake and each base filler upward at a right angle to the base.

- Trim the base filler pieces so that they are one and a half inches from the crease, then cut each piece down the middle to the crease. Spread the two ends and tuck each piece under the second 18-inch stake.

- Soak a long piece of quarter-inch flat oval reed—the "weaver." Fold it in half. Begin on a side where you have seven stakes—start at the third stake from the left and place the folded weaver around the stake. Using one piece of the weaver, weave behind the fourth stake and outside the fifth stake, continuing around one row. Next, using the other half of the weaver, weave outside the fourth stake and behind the fifth stake, and weave around. Hide weaver ends behind the uprights.

- Continue to weave rows, using even tension, until the basket is about 5 inches high. Weave a final row of quarter-inch flat oval around the top and overlap the ends. Starting at the bottom of the basket, "pack down" the rows of weaving so all rows touch each other.

- Soak the extended ends of the stakes in warm water. Find the stakes that have the last row of weaving on the inside and tightly fold each of these to the inside of the basket (every other stake will be folded). Tuck each folded stake over the top weaver and under the third weaver from the top. Cut the remaining stakes even with the top of the basket.

• You can use a variety of lashing and finishing techniques to make the rim of your basket look finished. One simple edging consists of laying a strip of reed or even long pine needles or leather along the rim and using an overhand stitch at a diagonal to secure it to the basket.

Basket making is a satisfying and engrossing activity, with many possibilities for materials, colors, textures, shapes. These instructions offer newcomers to the craft an idea of the process.

In some cultures the wreath was a signal to a prospective lover — a birch wreath meant acceptance, while a hazel wreath meant rejection.

During midwinter festivals in ancient Rome, evergreen branches were formed into wreaths and brought indoors to serve as symbols of an enduring life and to ensure a fruitful year, while in ancient Persia and Greece a wreath worn on the brow of a bonnet denoted royalty. It wasn't until the fifteenth century that ordinary people used wreaths to honor religious holidays and mark special occasions.

BEWREATHED

by Margaret Maron

Margaret Maron is the author of twenty novels and two collections of short stories that have been translated into a dozen languages. Winner of most of the major American awards for mysteries, her works are on the reading lists of various courses in contemporary Southern literature. Bootlegger's Daughter *is numbered among the 100 Favorite Mysteries of the Century as selected by the Independent Mystery Booksellers Association. She has served as president of Sisters in Crime and of the American Crime Writers League, and she is the current president of the Mystery Writers of America.*

OKAY, SO I wasn't freezing in Times Square waiting for the big apple to fall at the stroke of midnight. Nor was I in Raleigh waiting for the brass acorn to fall and listening to Dwight Bryant grumble about it being cold enough to freeze similar objects off brass monkeys.

Instead, I was standing on a rise overlooking my brother Robert's back fields, watching Robert try to get a pile of stumps and scrap lumber—soggy scrap lumber I might add—to burn while four of my other brothers made helpful remarks like "Ain't you got no kerosene, Robert?" or "Didn't I see a can of gas under your tractor shelter last week?"

It wasn't even all that cold The night air was cool and damp, invigorating without winter's usual raw chill.

All the same, this wasn't how I'd visualized spending my first New Year's Eve with Dwight. We had talked about going to Raleigh's First Night celebration with some friends, and I'd even bought tickets back before Christmas. Then Dwight, who heads up Sheriff Bo Poole's detective squad, got caught shorthanded with two deputies in bed with flu and a rash of break-ins across the county.

As a district court judge, I know first hand that crime doesn't take a holiday, but court does, and I've always packed a lot of playtime in the week between Christmas and New Year's, so I was disappointed that Dwight couldn't come play, too. I gave the tickets to one of my nieces and was prepared to throw myself a solitary pity party when April called to see if they could borrow a suitcase. April teaches sixth grade, and she and my brother Andrew were taking their kids to Disney World over the school break next week. As soon as she heard Dwight had to work, she insisted I come along with them to Robert's.

"You want a wreath, don't you?"

"So?"

"So Robert pruned his grapevines today and saved the cuttings for me." My sister-in-law is so creative she could probably knit a tree if she'd only slow down long enough to find the right yarn. "We'll build a bonfire, roast hot dogs, start you a wreath, and see the new year in together, all at the same time. Minnie and Seth are coming, Haywood and Isabel, Zach and Barbara, too," she said, naming others of my brothers and their wives who still live out here on the family farm along with her and Andrew. "Robert says Doris has even bought a bottle of champagne." (Despite France's battle to keep Champagne from becoming a generic term, here in Colleton County, any white wine that sparkles is automatically called champagne.)

I had to smile. "One bottle for a dozen people?"

"Well, you know Doris."

I did. Robert's the oldest of my daddy's eleven sons, and his wife is one of the most conflicted hostesses I've ever seen. She truly wants to be generous, but she can't help counting the cost—the heart of a bon vivant housed in the body of a miser.

"We're going to do a loaves and fishes on her," April said, laughter bubbling in her throat. "You got anything fizzy in your refrigerator, Deborah?"

"Two bottles," I told her. "Count me in."

"Andrew says we'll pick you up around nine."

I CALLED DWIGHT to let him know where I'd be in case he could get away before midnight. He was in and out of our house so much when we were growing up that he knows Robert and Doris about as well as I do and is equally amused by them. "At least I won't have to worry about you getting too much to drink," he said.

"Don't count on it," I said. "How's the surveillance going? Any sightings?"

"Nothing so far. I've got patrol units out all around Cotton Grove, but hell, Deb'rah, we're probably not going to hear about any break-ins till the owners get home to tell us."

With its easy commute to the Research Triangle, Colleton County's experienced such a population boom in the last few years that we now have our share of the usual misdemeanors, petty felonies, and yes, the burglars who would rather steal for a living than work.

From sitting in court, I've learned that their victims will often have a pretty good idea of who's ripped them off. It will be the friends of their teenage children, itinerant repairmen, or a pickup laborer who cased the place while cutting grass for the homeowner's lawn service.

Beginning at Thanksgiving, though, there had been a systematic looting of eight or ten homes over the past few weeks, and nobody had a clue. At each house, the owners were away for at least three or four days, either on vacation or traveling for business or pleasure during this holiday season. All were within the same five-mile radius of where we live. All were without burglar alarms, in middle-class neighborhoods, and entry was always by breaking through a rear door or window. The only items taken were money, jewelry, and small electronics that were easily fenced. So far, there were no fingerprints and nothing to indicate whether it was the work of a single person or a whole gang. Trying to figure out how the perps knew which houses would be empty was driving Dwight crazy.

At first, he thought that dogs might be the link since the first four houses did shelter canine pets, and all four had boarded their dogs in the same kennel. That theory went bust when the next three break-ins were at dogless homes.

Now people are often careless about the little things that will let a thief know if a house is empty. Mail will pile up in the mailbox, newspapers will litter the driveway once the box is too full to hold more. In summer, the grass will go uncut. Winter's a little harder to read since we seldom get enough snow to bother with shoveling the drives. But these latest victims had taken all the sensible precautions. They had stopped delivery of mail and newspapers, they used timers to turn lamps on and off at normal hours, they even alerted nearby neighbors to keep an eye out. Unfortunately, nothing seemed to be working.

"Could it be loose lips at the post office?" I had asked. "A mail carrier would know as soon as someone on the route suspends their mail."

Dwight reminded me that our area is serviced by two separate postal zones.

"Well, what about newspapers?"

"Same thing. Billy says that the *News and Observer* has at least three different carriers out in this part of the county." (Billy Yost is a neighborhood kid who's been delivering papers to the farm ever since he got his driver's license.) "Plus separate carriers for the local weeklies. He thinks that all told, we're looking at six or seven carriers, at least. In fact, one of them's his grandmother's friend, Miss Baby Anderson, and you know good as me there's no way Miss Baby is part of any burglary ring."

"Good lord! Is she still delivering the Cotton Grove *Clarion*?" Miss Baby Anderson is a scrappy 82-year-old poor but proud grandmother who has always lived near poverty level.

"Every Tuesday afternoon," Dwight said. "I guess she needs to supplement her Social Security."

The sheriff's department had issued warnings through all the little weekly papers, but Dwight fully expected to hear of several more incidents when people got back from their Christmas travels, and he wasn't looking forward to their unhappy complaints about poor crime control.

"Maybe you'll get lucky tonight," I told him.

"I certainly hope so," he said, and from the leer in his voice, I realized that we were no longer talking about his work.

"I'll save you some champagne," I promised.

SO HERE I was on New Year's Eve at the edge of Robert's small vineyard, watching Robert try to get his bonfire started while Doris set out hotdogs, buns, chili, and coleslaw on an ancient picnic table Robert had hauled out to the site. We'd had a rainy autumn, but these logs and boards looked as if they'd been dredged from a swamp the day before.

"Where the hell did you get this wood?" asked Zach, one of the "little twins" next up from me in age.

"Part of it's the old strip house the last hurricane knocked down, the rest are stumps out of that bottom land I drained this fall," Robert admitted.

He sloshed gasoline over the pile and lit another match. There was a brief splutter of flame, then nothing.

"First time I ever seen even gas too wet to burn," muttered Haywood, one of the "big twins."

My brother Seth dangled his truck keys out to Haywood's son Stevie, the only nephew to elect to see the New Year in with us rather than drive into Raleigh. "How 'bout you run fetch me my blowtorch?"

"I'll ride over with you," I said. Stevie's my favorite nephew, and I hadn't seen much of him over the holidays. His girlfriend was off somewhere with her family, and he was at loose ends this weekend, so this gave me a chance to ask how life was treating him.

"Pretty fine," he said as we navigated the back lanes from Robert's part of the farm through a shortcut to Seth's workshop. Stevie and Gayle had been together since high school and would probably marry after they finished college.

"What about you? What's monogamy like?"

"You ought to know," I told him. "You've been monogamous a lot longer than I have."

He grinned. "That good, huh?"

"Yeah," I said happily as we rooted around in Seth's shop for his hand torch.

"So how come Dwight's not here tonight?"

I described the break-ins and how the sheriff's department was stretched thin with two deputies out sick. Like me, Stevie immediately suggested that Dwight should look at the people delivering the mail or the newspapers.

"Way ahead of you," I said. "Some of the burglaries were committed in the Cotton Grove postal zone, the others in the Dobbs zone. And Billy says there are several paper routes in this area."

"Billy Yost?"

"That's right, you and he were in school together, weren't you?"

"Before he flunked out. Life's not fair, is it, Deborah?"

"Never has been," I agreed.

"I mean, here I am, halfway through college, and he's still delivering papers."

"Somebody has to."

"Yeah, but Billy's smart. Smarter than me. He shouldn't've

had to work so hard that he couldn't stay awake in class."

We both spotted Seth's blowtorch at the same time, hanging from a nail on the side wall. When we were back in the truck, I said, "So if Billy was that smart, why didn't he just ride the schoolbus?"

"You think the only reason he worked three jobs was to support a car?"

"A lot of kids do."

"Not Billy. His grandmother raised him, and she didn't have anything but Social Security to live on. He felt like he owed her. He used to say there wasn't enough money in the world to pay back the old women who step in and take over when their sorry children can't hold it together."

I remembered the details now—no father, abused by a mother on crack and whoever she was sleeping with at the moment—no wonder he'd want to repay his grandmother for taking him out of all that when he was six or seven.

"Speaking of old women, Dwight says Miss Baby's still delivering the *Clarion*," I said, and Stevie shook his head as he maneuvered the truck around a fallen tree.

"North Carolina lets her drive? Isn't she about a hundred and ten now?"

BACK AT ROBERT'S, a lopsided moon had risen over the treetops that rimmed his lower fields. It was a week past full but still cast a cold blue light across the landscape. Through the far trees, a good quarter-mile away, we could see the streetlights of yet another new housing development. A light breeze blew up from the bottom, bringing a clean smell of damp earth and the promise of a new seedtime and new beginnings.

Using Seth's blowtorch and the rest of the gas in Robert's can, my brothers finally got the bonfire going, and Doris kept urging us to take another little sip of her ersatz champagne. "My, these bottles hold a lot, don't they?" she marveled.

By then, we had topped her bottle off at least twice without her noticing. She also hadn't tasted any difference between her $2.69 Food Lion bubbly, April's Corbel, or my
Roederer Estate.

April had piled the grapevines on the back of their
pickup, and she sat on the tailgate to start coiling a wreath
while the men scrounged for fallen limbs out in Robert's
wood lot. My other sisters-in-law came over to watch.

"If these weren't freshly cut, I'd have to soak them
overnight in warm water," April said as she gathered up
several vines and began bending them into a circle. When
the circle was as thick as her slender arm, she deftly wove
the loose ends back onto themselves and soon had a nice
tight wreath. I'm not into cutesy, but I thought a rustic
grapevine wreath on our back door might get me a few
points for domesticity, maybe keep people from feeling so
sorry for Dwight. Securing the vine ends was harder than it
looked, and my wreath was nowhere near as tight as April's
when I'd finished.

"If it starts to fall apart, you can just wire it back together or hit it with some hot glue," April said reassuringly.
"What sort of theme you want?"

"Theme?"

"You know—winter? Spring?"

"Valentines," Doris teased; and Isabel said, "How about a
pair of little turtledoves for you lovebirds?"

"Oh, please," I said.

Barbara laughed. "I have some wooden hearts and a can
of red paint."

The bonfire was burning brightly now, and they'd all had
enough sips of sparkling wine to begin feeling a New Year's
glow.

"Little gold cupids!"

"Lace and red foil!"

"Shiny packs of Trojans!"

"Forget it," I said firmly as the suggestions grew
raunchier.

From beyond the fire, Robert suddenly called, "Hey! Who you reckon that is?"

We looked down the hillside to where he pointed. Off in the distance, car headlights swept through a cut in the woods that led from the road to his back lower fields. The lights shone straight across the bare land, then suddenly went dark. The moon wasn't quite bright enough to let us see the car, although we could hear the engine as it continued on course as if the driver knew exactly where he was going and the moon was all the light he needed.

Robert and Haywood immediately reverted to form. Ask a farmer for permission and he'll let you dig dogwoods and willow oaks out of his woods. He'll let you hunt rabbits or doves. He'll keep you in watermelons and sweet corn all summer, let you cut Christmas greenery in winter. But pick a single wildflower, shoot a single rabbit without asking, and he'll bristle up and invite you to get the hell off his land, often at the end of his shotgun.

"Come on, Haywood," Robert said, lumbering toward his Chevy pickup. "Let's go down and chase 'em!"

"Aw, now, honey," Doris protested. "What are they hurting?" Every one of us had parked down at the end of deserted farm paths in our time, and we murmured in agreement when Isabel said, "Oh, let 'em celebrate in peace."

Robert and Haywood were too bullheaded to listen though, and they roared off together in Robert's pickup. Andrew, Seth, and Zach just shook their heads and piled more limbs on the bonfire.

From our vantage point, we watched Robert's lurching headlights leave the lane and strike a diagonal across the field.

"I don't think that's a good idea," said Zach.

"It's okay," said Doris. "He's got four-wheel drive."

"Yeah, but the land's real low back there," said Seth.

Zach turned to Andrew. "Didn't one of the tractors bog down there last winter?"

Andrew nodded. "Took three others to pull it out."

I crawled up on top of the cab of Seth's truck and perched there cross-legged to enjoy the show. Sure enough, it wasn't long till we heard the high-pitched *rrrr-rrhrr-rrrhrrr* of spinning tires going nowhere fast, then the slamming of truck doors. A flashlight bobbled across the field as Haywood and Robert made their long muddy way back up the rise to us.

"I reckon we gave 'em a good scare, though," Robert said smugly.

Haywood stomped the mud from his boots. "They probably slipped out while we was driving down there."

"I think they were further back," I called from atop Seth's cab.

"Naw, shug," said Robert. "I got four-wheel drive on my truck, and if *I* got stuck up to the axle, ain't no car could've gone further."

"Uh, Robert?" I pointed down behind him.

He whirled in time to see a glow in the far field resolve into car lights as it zoomed straight along the field's bottom lane, back through the woods, and out toward the safety of the road.

"Well damn!" Robert said. Then he shrugged. "All the same, I bet that was the shortest loving *he* ever got."

"Spoilsport," said April.

"Never mind about them," said Doris. "That fire looks about ready, don't y'all think?"

We threaded bright red hot dogs on wire coat hangers that Robert had straightened out, and we held them in the bonfire till they were charred on the outside and warmed through the middle, then popped them into buns and spooned on the onions, chili, and coleslaw. Even though Doris had bought the cheapest brand sold, everything combined to make those hot dogs taste like gourmet sausages.

It was ten minutes till twelve and I was fixing myself a second one when Dwight pulled in.

"Just in time!" Doris called to him happily and waved

her heavy green bottle in his direction. "Still plenty of champagne here. Nobody seems to be drinking it but me."

All around the neighborhood, colorful bottle rockets shot up in the sky, and firecrackers popped as the old year wound down. Zach and Stevie set off a few fireworks of their own, and I gave Dwight my hotdog and a cup of the good stuff. Robert had his pocket watch out to count down the minutes, Andrew cranked his truck radio up so we could hear the announcer in Times Square, and all my brothers began to edge closer to their wives. Dwight set his hotdog down on a paper plate.

"Ten! Nine! Eight!" chanted the crowd from New York, and we joined in. "—four—three—two—one—Happy New Year!"

Dwight's kiss was long and satisfying. He smelled of woodsmoke, onions, champagne, and aftershave, and I could have taken him right there except that we were suddenly in the middle of an exuberant group hug with my brothers and sisters-in-law, who were tipsily singing "Auld Lang Syne." Somewhere in the distance an iron farm bell rang, and more rockets exploded overhead in a cascade of bright sparks.

DWIGHT AND I slept in the next morning and were finishing up a late breakfast when April came by to drop off my wreath. She and Andrew were on their way back to Robert's to help pull his truck out of the field. Dwight offered to help with a length of heavy chain. I wasn't going to stay home and miss the fun and besides, it would give me a chance to find stuff for my wreath.

Seth was already out in Robert's muddy field with one of the tractors when we got there; and while the men debated whether it was better to haul the truck out frontwards or backwards, April and I walked down the far lane to pick up gumballs. Sweetgums are a nice shade tree, but they shower down hundreds of prickly walnut-size seed balls every winter and make walking such a hazard that nobody lets them grow in the yard. We found clumps of silvery gray dried moss, hickory nuts, and some small pine cones, too. Then, because our eyes were searching the ground for seed pods and other woodsy objects, we saw where that car last night had turned around. We also saw fresh shoeprints in the soft earth, prints that began at the car and disappeared through the hedgerow.

April giggled. "He must have had to answer a different call of nature."

"I don't think so," I said.

The hedgerow here backed up to the new development; and beyond the bare twigs and scraggly bushes, thin morning sunlight reflected off a broken rear window of the nearest house.

"Watch out where you walk," I told April. "That was no horny teenager last night."

"Good eyes," Dwight said after he went across to check on the house. It had definitely been broken into, and no one seemed to be home. He called for the crime scene van to come out and record the tire and shoe prints we'd found, and he got the owner's name and holiday vacation phone number from a hungover neighbor across the street who was supposed to be keeping an eye on the place. "Who the hell expects somebody to break in on New Year's Eve?" the neighbor asked plaintively.

It didn't take Dwight long to learn that the mail was delivered by one of the Cotton Grove carriers, that the Raleigh daily paper was delivered by a reformed drunk named Sam Parrish, and that the *Courier* was delivered by "some sweet little old lady."

"Miss Baby Anderson?" he asked.

"That's her name," said the neighbor's wife. "I don't know how she keeps going, out driving in all sorts of bad weather. It's a wonder she's not been sick more this winter."

When Dwight told me that, I started thinking about Miss

Baby. She was almost as poor as Billy Yost's grandmother, yet when I ran into her at the grocery store a week or so earlier, her basket had held a large rib roast—"Everybody's coming to my house for Christmas dinner," she'd said happily, "and they're tired of turkey, so they've all chipped in."

"Sounds like you're going to have a big time," I said.

"Oh, we are." She beamed. "A real party. I'm even going to ask Sarah Jeffers and her boy to come eat with us, too. Billy's been so good about helping me this winter. I owe that boy a lot."

Like Billy's grandmother, Miss Baby was another who had stepped in to help raise the children of her children. Her winter coat was old and frayed at the wrists, but when she reached out to pat my arm in parting, I had noticed that she wore an expensive designer gold watch.

Billy was so good to her?

"Let me see your checklist of stolen goods again," I told Dwight.

IT WAS THE second night of Andrew and April's vacation trip, the second night that Dwight and I had turned out their lights at ten-thirty and waited in their darkened living room. Normally, none of us bothers to stop our mail or newspapers because there's always a sibling willing to empty the boxes, but April had agreed to my plan and had made the necessary calls before they left.

Dwight thought that staking out their house was a waste of time. "Nobody who knows this neighborhood's going to rip off one of my brothers-in-law," he'd argued. "And even if they do, you shouldn't be here."

"It's my idea," I said stubbornly. "And my brother. And I don't care what Miss Baby might think. Her new watch didn't come out of any yard sale."

Reluctantly, Dwight had admitted that such a watch had indeed gone missing from one of the burgled houses.

We were snuggled together on the couch under one of April's patchwork quilts, my head in his lap, and both of us were half-asleep when the sound of breaking glass brought us instantly to our feet. I grabbed the flashlight on the table and Dwight drew his gun.

We tiptoed down the hall and into the kitchen where we saw a slender figure silhouetted against the outside security light. A gloved hand reached through the broken door pane and turned the door knob. A wave of cold January air flowed over us.

As soon as the door opened and the burglar was all the way into the kitchen, I hit him with the light and Dwight said, "Game's over, Billy."

"Oh, dear!" said Miss Baby Anderson.

"MISS *BABY*?" ASKED April when we were telling her and Andrew about that night. "But we're not even on her route."

"No, but you're on Billy's," I said.

"Billy Yost and Miss Baby were working together?"

"Billy didn't have a clue," said Dwight. "His car tires didn't match the those in Robert's field the other day, but we still thought he was our perp because Deborah noticed that he or Miss Baby delivered to every house that was hit."

"She and Billy's grandmother are close friends," I said, "so I asked around and learned that whenever she was sick this winter, Billy would fill in for her. That's why I was so sure he'd know her schedule and know when she'd been told not to deliver the *Clarion*."

"Instead, it was the other way around," said Dwight. "He kept a copy of his schedule on the refrigerator so his grandmother would always know where he was if she needed him in an emergency. Miss Baby started checking it out whenever she was over there, noting down which houses would be empty and easy for her to break into."

"But why?" April asked.

We could only repeat what Miss Baby had told us while we waited for a squad car to arrive. The watch was the one piece of jewelry she'd kept. The rest had been fenced for food, medicine, and small luxuries.

"I've worked hard and lived poor my whole life and I was flat-out tired of doing without," she'd said. "Then my heart pills went up again right before Thanksgiving, and that was the last straw."

Her belligerent attitude took me by surprise, but I was cynical enough to know that by the time her case came to court, she would again be a sweet-faced, silver-haired little grandmother who would tug at a jury's heartstrings and earn herself a suspended sentence. Zack Young would probably defend her *pro bono*, and I could see a defense based on the high cost of prescription drugs so that the country's whole health care system would be on trial, not just Miss Baby.

As we stood to go, I asked April if I could borrow her glue gun to finish my wreath.

"Sorry," she said. "I lent it to Doris this morning. She and Isabel and Barbara are working on something."

Two days later, when Dwight and I got home from work, we discovered what that something was. An enormous heart-shaped wreath hung on our back door. It had been wrapped in black and white ribbons to look like a convict's striped uniform. Hot-glued to it were a couple of toy pistols, some star-shaped sheriff's badges from Bo Poole's last election campaign, and a small wooden gavel. A pair of toy handcuffs dangled from the bottom of the wreath, and each cuff framed a picture—one of Dwight, one of me. White letters had been glued to the black ribbon stretched across the front: "Life w/o Parole."

Dwight grinned.

"Works for me," he said.

§§

Valentine Wreath

Supplies needed:

> Grapevine wreath, 14–16 inches in diameter
> White enamel spray paint
> Small wooden hearts
> Red enamel
> Paintbrush
> Hot-glue gun and glue sticks
> 4 or 5 silk roses
> A packet of children's inexpensive Valentine cards
> A pair of 4" white turtle doves (optional)
> Large red-and-white polka dot bow
> Craft wire
> (Other symbols of romantic or carnal love are optional)

- Spray the wreath white, less spray for a rustic look, more for the polished look of white wicker.
- Paint the wooden hearts red, let everything dry.
- Hot-glue several brightly colored Valentines around the wreath. Overlap and intersperse them with the wooden hearts.
- Form the roses into a cluster, twist the wires around each other, then tuck the ends into the lower right quadrant and secure from beneath.
- Wire the bow to the bottom center of the wreath so that the ends trail down.
- Position the doves as you like and either wire or hot-glue into place.
- Avoid hanging your wreath where it will get rained on.

Some Native Americans believed that the first urine of first-born sons was the best medium for indigo dyeing.

An important dye in Japan, West Africa, Thailand, and the Americas, indigo is temperamental, non-water soluble, and requires great care, giving rise to stories all over the world about how to ensure good dyeing. In England, an arsenic compound was added to the dye vats. Among the Yoruba of Nigeria, tribute was paid to a patron deity, Iya Mapo, to ensure success. In Thailand, drops of rice whiskey were added to the fermenting leaves of the plant, and women told stories to entice the spirit goddess to watch over the dye pots.

THE DEEPEST BLUE

by Sujata Massey

Sujata Massey is a former journalist who left Maryland to teach English in Japan and try her hand at writing fiction. The Salary-man's Wife, *published in 1997, launched Rei Shimura, who hunts for upscale antiques and murderers in Tokyo, San Francisco, and Washington, D.C. The books, most recently* The Pearl Diver, *illuminate Japanese history and cultural traditions ranging from Zen Buddhism to kimono dressing. The series has been honored by Agatha and Macavity awards and nominated for the Edgar®, Anthony, and the Mary Higgins Clark awards. Sujata, the mother of two young children, has returned to Baltimore.*

Lucy Diggs, who wrote the dyeing instructions, lives on a ranch near Healdsburg, California. She is a writer and a quilter who makes quilts entirely from hand-dyed fabrics, using natural dyes and methods that have been used from the time of the ancient Egyptians until the latter half of the nineteenth century.

§§

I HAVE PLENTY of my own reasons for needing to spend time in Buddhist temple gardens, but on that Sunday afternoon on the Japanese island of Shikoku it was all about business. Amid the gentle gongs of the temple bell and the hum of chattering tourists, I was following up a lead I'd

gotten from a German textile curator I'd met the previous
week at a wine bar in Tokyo.

The deepest blue, she'd said. She was trying to describe
the exquisite depth of an indigo textile as somewhere between a Kamakura blue hydrangea and the early evening
sky. It was an intensity of blue she'd seen nowhere else, even
in the land where blue and white reigned as the most ubiq-
uitious color combination.

As I walked past the temple's great wooden hall to a side
garden, I realized that I looked like a blue and white
groupie myself, wearing a patchwork blue and white halter
top and blue denim shorts. Very casual, but it was the kind
of outfit most young women tourists were wearing on the
hot and humid island—even to visit a Buddhist temple.

I rounded a bank of purple-blue hydrangeas and found
myself facing the strange sight the curator had raved about.
Before me was a regiment of bronze statues, identical images of *Jizo*, the gentle Buddhist sub-deity who protects lost
children. At least three-quarters of them were dressed alike
in tiny smocks made of indigo.

My friend had told me that the smocks were on temple
statues, but she hadn't known what it meant. But I did, and
as always was the case for me, these days the sight of those
small figures made me want to cry. When a Japanese woman
loses a baby, she might commemorate her private loss by
buying a *Jizo* statue. All those small figures, about the size
of a large doll, were representatives of lost children.

I turned away for a minute, trying to remember why I'd
come: for business. I was the dealer who would bring this particular indigo fabric to my friend Simone, and she would make
exquisite, yet practical cushion covers and kimono jackets to
sell at her textile boutique in Omote-Sando and beyond.

I took a steadying breath and walked into the midst of
the bronze statuettes. Closer, underneath the blue smocks, I
could see the remnants of each mother's original gesture to
her child; a knitted hat, a scarf, and other kinds of doll
clothing. It was unusual for so many of the statues to have

an identical blue smock; after all, mothers bought and dressed their statues privately, not wanting to share their grief with the world. But Japan was all about groups behaving as one—from school children to company employees. Maybe this philosophy had come into play for this group of dead children, too.

Carefully, I fingered one of the smocks. It felt like real indigo, a fabric hand-woven of linen and flax and dyed in a vat filled with the fermented leaves of the indigo plant, along with sake, lime, and lye. After the fabric was lifted out and exposed to air, it turned blue. Indigo dyers worked obsessively for years to get the fermentation right, and then dyed fabrics over and over until the desired shade emerged. This cloth, I decided, looked natural; there was a slight hint of white between the deep blue threads, which spoke of the fabric's response to persistent rain and sun.

AT THE TEMPLE office, I made an offering of five thousand yen—about fifty dollars—to the head monk, and then I introduced myself as Rei Shimura, an antiques and textiles dealer from Tokyo. After the niceties had been completed, I asked him to tell me about the tiny indigo smocks.

The monk shook his head—a gleaming, bald pate that reminded me of the *Jizo* statues outside. "Indigo dyeing and weaving is a life mission that leaves time for nothing else. We spend our time in service to Buddha, not indigo."

I paused, wondering whether he was challenging me with some kind of unanswerable Buddhist riddle. "Who in the community, may I ask, brings these little smocks to you, and why are they on most of the statues?"

He was still for a moment, as if deciding how much to tell me. I began regretting wearing the halter top; it probably made me look too frivolous. But to my relief, he answered my question. "The smocks were made by Mizuno-san, a local woman indigo dyer. Every month she brings a box of smocks. These are just for us; she does not sell them. We put them on the statues whose owners haven't come for a while . . . knitted and woven cotton clothing wears out, as you can imagine. But indigo is stronger. It is a fabric for eternity."

I nodded. "I have a great admiration for indigo dyeing. It would be a privilege for me to pay my respects to Mizuno-san. Does she live nearby?"

He pressed his lips together. "I'm afraid that she and her husband—he is the one who raises the indigo crop—do not have their own place. They work for Miss Toshiko Takayama."

"Oh!" I exclaimed, stunned by this connection. Miss Takayama was one of Japan's so-called Living National Treasures, a tiny, select group of artisans the government recognized with a decoration akin to a knighthood. Miss Takayama was an elderly woman artist whose boldly dyed indigo work had been displayed at a special exhibition at the Smithsonian in Washington, D.C. years ago. I'd known that her home was somewhere in Japan, but I had never thought much about it. Now my head was spinning with new possibilities. If the indigo artist worked under Miss Takayama, the cloth would be even more valuable. Simone couldn't possibly cut it up for cushion covers, but maybe what could be sold were one-of-a-kind kimonos . . .

The priest's gentle voice broke into my train of thought. "Have I answered your questions fully? If so, I shall return to my duties."

"I apologize for the interruption," I said quickly. "One last thing. Where is Miss Takayama's place of business located?"

"She works privately at her home set in the indigo fields about six kilometers up Mount Fukamo. But you must not travel there," he added with a serious expression. "She is quite a private person."

"Of course," I said, reminding myself that I wasn't after an interview with Miss Takayama, just her gifted underling.

"Now that you have what you asked for, perhaps you would care to take a charm with you. We have many special charms made here at the temple that will protect you on your journey back to Tokyo—and indeed, through the rest of your life." The priest gestured toward a glass case that stood between us, a case filled with tiny, brocade-wrapped items about the size and shape of a pocketknife. Each charm cost a sum between a thousand and ten thousand yen—ten to one hundred dollars—the higher prices being for harder-to-grant prayers.

I found myself gritting my teeth while I rooted through my backpack for the extra yen he'd expected in exchange for that last piece of information. What was the value of a name and place? At least another five thousand yen. For that, he handed me a shiny red brocade charm that I slid into my pocket before bowing good-bye.

It was only when I was on a public bus with broken-down air conditioning hauling its way up the mountain that I had a chance to examine the charm he'd made me buy. It was for the conception and safe delivery of a baby.

WHEN I DISEMBARKED from the bus at the halfway point, the first thing I saw was a field covered by the short, dark green leaves of the indigo plant, rustling gently in the warm afternoon wind. I found a rough dirt path to follow through the field's center. In the distance I saw a series of tiled roof buildings that I guessed were Toshiko Takayama's indigo business.

But before I reached the house, a man wearing *mompei*, traditional wide-legged, cotton farmer's pants, and a conical straw farmer's hat, rose up from where he'd been crouched. He was sorting through a few indigo leaves in one hand—a hand that was blue. Involuntarily, I looked down at my ankles. No, they weren't blue after having brushed against the plants. The living indigo plants were dark green, not blue. The color blue emerged only after fermentation.

The farmer was so involved in the inspection of his leaves that he didn't notice me until I was a few feet away. I cleared my throat and told him I was looking for Mizuno-san.

"I am he." His voice was rough from unuse. So this was the husband, and I was at the right place.

"My name is Rei Shimura. I am a great admirer of indigo work. I've come from Tokyo to speak with the great artist whose work I saw at the village temple." I gave him my deepest, most courteous bow.

He bowed back, but when his face came up, it was frowning. "I'm very sorry but Takayama-*sensei* cannot be disturbed. Her farm and studio are closed to outsiders."

He'd called his boss *sensei*, the word meaning "teacher" that was used for scholars, significant artists, and other kinds of leaders. He hadn't understood that I meant his wife.

"I actually wanted to meet your talented *wife*," I said, smiling. "She is the one who makes the generous donation of the little smocks for the *Jizo*-sama statues at the temple, isn't she?"

"Yes, during her free time." But instead of smiling back, he looked at the dirt path between us.

"Those smocks are made of extremely beautiful and re-silient indigo. I wanted to talk to her about her talent, and also some new opportunities for her."

He looked back at me and something flickered across his weather-worn face; an expression of sorrow and longing. "I'm sorry, but you cannot speak with her right now. She is working with Takayama-*sensei*. In fact, I was just going in-side to show *sensei* the condition of the leaves."

"I understand. I'll return this evening then, when your wife has finished her work. Is seven o'clock fine?"

"Circumstances are difficult . . ."

As he began to recite the standard excuse Japanese people used in place of the word *no*, I cut him off. "Would it be bet-ter for us to meet in town? I would enjoy taking both of you to dinner . . . and your children, of course."

He was looking even more pained. "We are not able to visit the village except once every weekend. I'm sorry."

The *sensei* sounded like a real control freak. "I'll come to this field, then. Please. I came all the way from Tokyo to see her work . . ."

I must have worn him down, because he finally agreed to let me come back to the same place at seven-thirty. And if his wife were to be finished with her work by then, he'd take me to her.

I SPENT THE rest of the afternoon kicking around the village, where I found a small museum devoted to indigo. The townspeople had farmed and dyed indigo for the last six hundred years, although production had declined greatly since the rise of synthetic dyes. Most of the natural indigo dyers were gone, but Toshiko Takayama, the fifth generation of her family to pursue the craft, had emerged as one of Japan's last famous indigo artisans.

The museum showed pictures of indigo artists over the years. One of the earliest, a grainy photograph from the 1920s, showed a man identified as Hiroshi Mizuno at work in an indigo field, and I imagined he was a grandparent of the indigo farmer I'd just met. There were also shots of the interior of Toshiko Takayama's house that had been taken in the 1970s. The Living National Treasure was shown crouched over the dyeing vat, a large ceramic urn sunken into a tatami-mat floor.

From the museum exhibit, I learned that the room containing the dyeing vat was called the bedroom, and the mats that covered the vat's opening were known as the bedclothes. If the homespun thread that was dipped within the vat didn't take the color well, indigo dyers said the baby had caught a cold. Obviously, for these artisans, growing the delicate leaves, fermenting them correctly, and then introducing fiber into its mix was like raising a child. Maybe the charm the monk had given me was the right one, after all.

Over dinner at a nearby noodle shop, I spoke with the waitress about Miss Takayama's operation.

"Nobody around here buys from there. Far-away muse-

ums, yes, but none of our shops." Then, leaning forward
conspiratorially, she added, "There are stories that the fabric
brings bad luck."

When I asked why, the woman shrugged. "I don't know
exactly. It's an old place, you know. My grandparents told
me that in the old days people here believed in demons, and
that the reason Takayama's blue is so deep is because of a
dyer, long ago, who was having trouble raising the baby—
you know, getting the right color. As her tears fell into the
vat where the leaves were, the color changed to the color she
had wanted all along. She pulled her thread out and re-
joiced, but after it dried and she began to weave it, a demon's face appeared in the finished cloth."

"Go on," I said when she paused. "Please!"

"She was frightened, of course, and tried to burn the
cloth, but the demon only jumped out and went back into
the vat. There it stays, but they say the face emerges from
time to time in the pieces that Takayama-*sensei* dyes."

In a sense, I knew what she was talking about. Miss
Takayama used a form of resist dyeing called *tsutsugaki* to allow white images to dance across the deep blue background.
I'd seen examples of flowers and vegetables in the museum,
but all these images were free-form; the villagers could easily consider them demon faces if they liked. Gently, I
pointed this out to the waitress.

She nodded solemnly. "I don't think the stories can be
true, but the fact is that local people don't go there anymore. When she first became a national treasure, in the
nineteen seventies, there were tours, but then there was
some trouble. I don't know what happened exactly, but
from then on, the tours stopped."

I thanked the woman for the delicious meal and paid,
then made my way to the village grocery, where I bought a
$60 muskmelon in a fancy lavender-colored box. That in
turn went into a shopping bag, which I carried carefully to
the bus stop, where the mountain bus arrived exactly on
time. Even outside of Tokyo, life in Japan remained pre-

dictable; buses came on time, and every town had a place where you could buy an overpriced melon.

AS I RODE up the mountain, I mulled over what I'd learned. The legend sounded typically Japanese; I wondered if Takayama-*sensei* hadn't encouraged it along so she could have her solitude—near-solitude, I corrected myself. She still had Mr. Mizuno to farm the indigo for her, and Mrs. Mizuno to do the spinning of the thread and fermentation and dyeing. Miss Takayama, I guessed, probably just did the weaving and the design of the *tsutsugaki* images.

At seven-thirty, I was briskly walking the dirt path that led through the indigo fields. Mr. Mizuno was waiting for me outside the tiled roof house, no longer with the straw hat on his head. He was wearing a clean shirt, proper khaki trousers, and had his hands folded in front of him.

"Thank you for waiting for me," I said when I was within earshot. "I'm very eager to speak with your wife."

"I don't know how much she has to say. She's not used to talking with others."

"I understand. I just want to express my admiration for her work, and I also have something that I'd like to give her." I patted my backpack, which contained the melon gift along with some photocopied articles about my work in Japanese antiques and historic preservation.

In a cool flagstone entryway that smelled of something I couldn't quite define, I slipped out of my shoes and into the indigo patchwork slippers that Mr. Mizuno gave me. He put a finger to his lips and motioned me to follow him down a long hallway. Sliding doors half-open revealed a succession of rooms; the first, a grand sitting room with a traditional alcove to showcase a changing display of art and flowers. Here, it was wild roses, but in a handmade earthenware vase; and the wall hanging over it was indigo with a *tsutsug-aki* design of a loose, exaggerated spray of flowers, no doubt made by the National Living Treasure herself. The next room was what I guessed was the workroom, because I saw many spools of coarse blue thread in baskets, a spinning wheel, and a large opening in the *tatami*-mat floor that was covered loosely by a straw mat.

The scent I'd caught in the entryway was very strong here. I looked up to a see a small Buddhist altar mounted close to the ceiling, a tiny golden Buddha with a tiny, plastic baby doll in front of it, and a smoldering stick of incense. Now, Mr. Mizuno was introducing me to his wife.

His wife! I had missed seeing the woman crouched behind the spinning wheel. She was tiny; about the size of an eleven-year-old, I thought, as she placed her blue hands on the floor and bowed before me. I guessed that she was in her fifties, although her face was completely free of lines, save for a furrow between the brows. The furrow of concentration, of never leaving the house, I thought—if she'd been out of doors like her husband, she'd have forehead lines, too.

I bowed back, though not on the floor, and gave her my name and held out the melon I'd brought from the village. She refused it twice. I expected her, after my third entreaty, to take it as was the usual custom in Japan, but she wouldn't.

"I am not the *sensei*," she said. "Takayama-san is, and she will not accept that because she does not accept any visitors, you see. It is a firm rule here for many years. My husband should not have brought you."

"But if you are the one who makes the exquisite indigo smocks in the temple garden, you are the *sensei* I have been searching for." I explained the idea I had about her either providing the fabric for, or actually making child-sized kimonos and jackets to sell in Tokyo and through Simone's Internet catalog. I concluded by bringing out some articles about the past adventures I'd had uncovering lost and stolen Japanese antiquities and the Internet catalog pages for Simone's pretty little shop in the Azabu-Juban neighborhood. Both of them studied these things for a few minutes.

At the end, Mrs. Mizuno said, "But an apprentice is not able to sell."

I was disappointed to see her husband nod in agreement, so I said, "After twenty years of work, how can you call yourself an apprentice? Surely, you are a master dyer. And I think you may have some time, because you found the time to make all those smocks for the temple. The monk told me he has more than enough waiting for his next—" I stopped short, realizing that "customers" was not an appropriate word for the bereaved women, but unable to figure out any other substitute word in Japanese.

"For the temple, it is allowed, but I cannot do anything else," she said.

"I'm sorry," her husband said in a low voice. "I could have explained this earlier if you had been clear about your intention."

I should have expected this, but I was still disappointed. I thanked them in a subdued voice and had just started to turn around when I caught sight of a witch at the door. Not a real witch, I realized after a second; just a wizened old woman in a blue-black kimono, her back curled by osteoporosis. Her sunken eyes seemed to burn with rage as they regarded first me, and then the Mizunos.

"I see you invited a friend to visit," she said in a voice that was smoky with age and malice.

Recalling what the Mizunos had said about apprentices not being able to earn their own money, I decided I'd better not clarify my exact reason for being there. I played dumb, bowing deeply, mumbling my name, and saying how pleased I was to get a chance to see her, the honorable *sensei*. How I hoped she hadn't heard most of what I'd said.

"Why?" she spat at me.

"I am a great admirer of indigo. I—I saw the exhibition at the village museum and understand you are a Living National Treasure." As I spoke, my eyes went to her hands. They weren't blue; did that mean the Mizunos were the ones doing all the work?

"I'm known much farther than that patch of mud at the bottom of the mountain."

"Yes, I first saw your work some years ago in Washington, D.C. I never forgot the impact. Now I run a business with Japanese antique textiles and furniture in Tokyo." I was trying to offer the kind of details that might reassure her.

"My work is not going to be sold at some little antique shop. I have dealings with an exclusive gallery."

"*Ah so desu ka,*" I said, trying to fake disappointment that she wouldn't be interested in working with me.

"We take no visitors here, because people distract us from our work. We have no need for anyone." Her voice was contemptuous.

"I see." I had to struggle to figure out what to say next. "Anyway, I apologize for the intrusion, and I must say my visit here—taught me so much about indigo dyeing. All the business about the bedroom and the baby in the dyeing vat, it's so fascinating . . ." As I rambled on, I noticed Miss Takayama's face alter its sneer into a curiously still expression.

"You told?" Miss Takayama's words seemed directed at Mrs. Mizuno, who was cowering on the floor.

"No, no!" she said in a barely audible voice.

"Nothing," Mr. Mizuno added with vehemence, and coming to his wife's side. "Certainly nothing!"

"As you know," Miss Takayama said, her gaze fixed on the couple, "you are the last independent indigo farmer and farmer's wife in the area. It's a very special relationship we have. One built on trust."

"That is so," Mr. Mizuno said hurriedly. "We trust *sensei* to know what is best."

"Send her away," Miss Takayama ordered Mr. Mizuno. "And make sure she doesn't come here, ever again."

I DIDN'T BOTHER waiting for an escort. An unseen force was propelling me out of the room, down the hall, and into the entryway where I stumbled into my Asics running shoes, not bothering to lace them up until I'd gotten halfway down the path to the field.

As I stopped to tie up the laces of my shoes, I glanced back at the house and saw Mr. Mizuno running after me. My head had been so full of the sound of my own pounding blood that I had not heard him at all. Now I noted that he was waving his hands over his head as if it was urgent for me to remain in place.

"I won't hurt you," he said in quick gasps as he caught up with me. "I am not dangerous."

"I can see why nobody visits." I tried to make a joke, but still kept a close eye on him lest he suddenly reach out and grab me. There was something horrible about the farm; unseemly, unknown things could happen here, despite its placid and traditional appearance.

"I shall walk with you to the bus," he said.

"I'll really be okay," I protested.

"No. You must tell me how you learned." His eyes implored me, and I was no longer afraid.

"It's just like I told you. I saw the indigo smocks at the temple and had a business idea. I thought I could make some extra money for your wife, and maybe a little for myself and my friend who owns the shop." I paused to take a deep breath and still my racing heart. "Obviously, it won't work. I'm sorry for the trouble I caused."

"No, I mean, how did you learn about—the baby."

The baby. What had I said about a baby? Oh, yes. I'd set off Miss Takayama when I'd made the comment about indigo cloth fermenting in the vat. Was it because, as I suspected, she didn't do any of her own dyeing work anymore?

"I noticed her hands weren't blue, but I didn't mean to let her know that. I think I said something about baby, just that I thought indigo language was so interesting—"

He cut me off. "About the baby. How did you guess?"

I paused, confused. Surely, Miss Takayama hadn't thought I was talking about a real baby, had she? I looked at

Mr. Mizuno's tired, careworn face, and I thought again about the gift of smocks to the Jizo-sama statues, and the altar in the workroom that had a baby doll in front of it.

"Did—Did Miss Takayama lose a child a long time ago? Is that why she's so bitter?"

"Not her," he said softly.

Suddenly, I got it. I said, "I'm very sorry for your lost child."

As I spoke, his eyes filled, and I knew that I had made the right assumption. I ventured, "Takayama-*sensei* doesn't want people to disturb you. Does this mean she doesn't want you to try with your wife for another child?"

"Jun-chan was a healthy little boy. Lively, happy. Too much for her." He paused. "She made it clear we should not have another. It's hard for a husband and wife in our kind of work to find another place to live and work, and we could never afford our own land. As she said, our family has worked for hers for several generations. There is a relationship. And if we ever tried to say anything about—about what happened—she would twist it to her own ends . . . and everyone would believe her, because she is so great and famous."

So she'd forbidden them to have more children, after they'd lost the first one. But a question still bothered me; if Jun-chan was a healthy little boy, why had he died?

I thought back on the way that Miss Takayama had reacted to my words, and a chill gripped me, despite the warm evening weather.

"Jun-chan fell in the dyeing vat, didn't he?" I could practically see it. The deep pit filled with lye and lime and sake and mashed up leaves, a baby lifted out, turning blue as his parents tried desperately to save him.

"Jun-chan was just five months old—he couldn't even crawl. *Sensei* said she would watch him one afternoon when my wife was so tired she had to sleep. I was sent out to check the leaves on every plant in the field. I was not there." He bowed his head.

"She must have not watched carefully," I said. "What a terrible accident."

"It wasn't an accident. She didn't want us to have a child. And she didn't want us to leave for another place, either, because we were the only ones who understand her special recipe for blue."

"But—how did she get away with it?" I was transfixed by the horror of what he was telling me.

"The police came, and they filed a report finding an accidental death by drowning. They weren't suspicious, because nobody dares to speak directly to a Living National Treasure."

"I could say something. I mean, she must not get away with this—"

"It cannot be proven." He paused. "We thought about leaving, you know. But that was when land was becoming so expensive that we could never have afforded our own farm. And we must stay together, the Mizunos and Takayamas. It is a family tradition."

The bus was coming up the mountain. I wanted to take Mr. Mizuno's blue hands into my own, but I knew that would make the stoic Japanese man who'd gone against tradition by explaining so much to me uncomfortable.

"Why—why did you tell me this?" I asked.

"So you wouldn't try to find out by yourself," he said. "I saw those newspaper clippings about—about what you do. It must remain our own private sorrow, do you understand?"

"I'm very sorry for all the trouble that I've caused," I said again, then bowed and boarded the bus, feeling so dejected and disoriented that I almost forgot to pay. I hastily scrambled through my backpack, pulling up the temple charm and enough coins to pay for the bus fare for everyone aboard.

I dropped two hundred and ten yen in the conductor's box, then made my way carefully down the aisle. It was the same bus I'd ridden much earlier in the day, with the broken air conditioning.

It was late, so the bus was half-empty, and I had two seats

to myself. A few rows ahead of me, a woman cradled a baby against her shoulder. The baby's small, pink face with shining eyes peeped at me, first curiously, then sleepily. When the baby's eyes closed at last, my own began to water, and I looked out through a blurry haze at the beautiful fields of indigo slipping past. I still had the brocade fertility charm nestled in my palm. After a minute's contemplation, I stretched my fingers through the open window, and I let it go.

§¿

Dyeing with Indigo

To dye with indigo, you need:

4 ounces of indigo
one package of sodium hydrosulfite (available in most groceries as Rit Color Remover)
lye (also available in most groceries as Drano, Red Devil Drain Opener, etc.)
Heat-resistant jar with lid
a large receptacle (five or ten gallon bucket or wastebasket)
rubber gloves
an outdoor space (or other area where drips don't matter!) for hanging dyed items

The following recipe will dye about a pound — three T-shirts, or a T-shirt and a pair of long cotton pants, or one to two yards cotton cloth. The fascinating thing about indigo is that it is not water soluble, and therefore dyeing with indigo has a magical quality to it, because it's different from what common sense would lead you to expect.

In hot water (as hot as you can get from your tap, 110–140 degrees) in the quart jar dissolve two level teaspoons of lye, two tablespoons of indigo powder, and two tablespoons of Rit. Stir (gently, not vigorously — in all cases you want to mix in as little oxygen as possible) until thoroughly dissolved. The surface color will be purplish violet with a coppery sheen. Now put the lid on the jar, place in a container of hot tap water, and set aside while you go prepare the vat (aka the bucket). Fill it nearly full with hot tap water, add ⅛ teaspoon of lye for a five gallon bucket, two teaspoons of Rit, one teaspoon of detergent, and stir.

Check out the contents of the jar in which you dissolved the indigo, etc. Within an hour it should be a clear amber color, very similar to a nice English ale. Take it out to the vat/bucket and, holding the jar close to the surface, pour the contents of the jar into the bucket. Stir slowly and carefully. Now go read a story or two from *Murder Most Crafty*. When you come back (in about an hour), the dye bath will be yellowish-greenish. The easiest way to check the color is to take up a little in a white Styrofoam cup.

Now comes the fun part. Indigotin (the dyeing agent which is blue) is not soluble, so what you have done is dissolved it in the lye-Rit solution which reduces it chemically to indigo white (leucoindigo). This is why the dye bath will not be blue. Take your cloth and lower it gently into the bucket (with your rubber gloves on). Leave it submerged for at least ten minutes, then withdraw it gently from the bucket and squeeze it out over another bucket which you have set beside the dyeing bucket. Then pin the cloth to your clothesline. Within a minute or two, sometimes sooner, it will turn from yellowish to blue. The leucoindigo, which has been taken up by the fabric fibers while it was in the vat, combines with the oxygen in the air and turns them back into indigo blue. It's like a miracle! It's magic! It's really, really fun.

This recipe should render a medium blue. If you want a darker blue you can redip it. It's a good idea to dip it at least twice, no matter what color you desire, just to make sure that the color has penetrated well. Successive dippings will render your cloth a successively darker color, up to a point. With this recipe you won't get anything much darker than a medium royal blue.

Hang for at least an hour once you have achieved the color you desire. Then fill another receptacle with water and add a cup of vinegar. Soak your cloth in this solution for at least an hour, then remove, squeeze out, and wash. The purpose of the vinegar (mild acid) soak is to counteract the alkalinity of the lye. This type of vat, commonly called the lye-hydrosulfite, is historically the most recent, but it's the easiest to use and most efficient. It is, however, difficult to get very dark shades of blue with this recipe. For very dark blue you need to use the zinc-lime vat method, which is what they use in Japan for the near-black indigos.

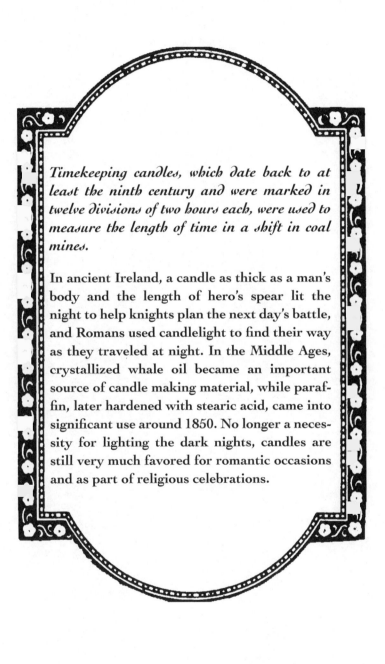

Timekeeping candles, which date back to at least the ninth century and were marked in twelve divisions of two hours each, were used to measure the length of time in a shift in coal mines.

In ancient Ireland, a candle as thick as a man's body and the length of hero's spear lit the night to help knights plan the next day's battle, and Romans used candlelight to find their way as they traveled at night. In the Middle Ages, crystallized whale oil became an important source of candle making material, while paraffin, later hardened with stearic acid, came into significant use around 1850. No longer a necessity for lighting the dark nights, candles are still very much favored for romantic occasions and as part of religious celebrations.

WAXING MOON

by Tim Myers

Tim Myers is the award-winning author of over seventy short stories, as well as three mystery series. The first of the lighthouse inn mysteries, Innkeeping With Murder, *was nominated for an Agatha. The first of his candlemaking mysteries,* At Wick's End, *was an Independent Mystery Booksellers Association national bestseller. Tim's third series, the soapmaking mysteries, will debut with* Dead Men Don't Lye.

ॐ

"HARRISON, I FEEL like I'm going to die."

I looked at Millie Nelson's face, and I could see that she meant every word of it. Millie runs The Crocked Pot, a café located in the River's Edge complex I hold title to, along with my candleshop, At Wick's End.

"What happened?" I asked as I steered her away from the crowd gathered in her café after-hours for a rehearsal reception. Millie catered outside events to supplement her restaurant business, and she was more than happy to host private parties and receptions in her café, if the price was right. She'd asked me to help serve that night, and I was perfectly willing to dress up and circulate through the room with a tray of appetizers in my hand. It was often an interesting way to kill an evening, and I took my pay in barter for baked goods, so everybody won.

"I've been such a fool," she said.

"What happened?"

When she wouldn't elaborate, I said, "Millie, I can't help if you won't tell me what this is about."

"I can't talk about it here. Let's go into the kitchen."

I followed her to the back, where Mrs. Quimby—another temporary hire for the evening who usually worked for Heather at The New Age—was taking a cookie sheet full of hors d'oeuvres out of the oven.

"Harrison, you know I haven't been all that conscientious about updating my security here. Now I wish I'd listened to you when you told me to get a real safe."

"You're not still keeping your deposits under your mattress, are you?"

"No, but I probably would have been better off if I had. My money had to have been safer there," Millie said as she pointed to a strongbox bolted to the shelf under one of the preparation stations. "Somebody robbed me tonight, and whoever did it is still in there at that party."

I saw Mrs. Quimby's eyebrows go up, so I knew she'd heard. It was too late to warn Millie not to say anything in front of her. Mrs. Quimby was a sweet, older lady, but I knew that sometimes sweet, older ladies could steal, too.

I looked down at the strongbox and saw that the keyed padlock on it was open. I pulled the lock off and flipped the lid up; the box was completely empty. Whoever had stolen from her had even taken the checks and credit card receipts stored inside. "Please tell me you went to the bank before the party."

The sick look on her face was enough to tell me she hadn't. "Harrison, what am I going to do? I can't call the sheriff. Even if he investigates and finds out who did this, it will ruin my business. Would you want a caterer who had her guests interrogated by the police?"

"It's better than losing the money, isn't it?"

"No," she said. "I'm just going to have to deal with this loss and update my system so it doesn't happen again."

I put my hand on her shoulder. "Don't give up yet. Let me think about this." I studied the lock closely and could see that it hadn't been tampered with. Whoever had opened it had used a key. "Do you still have your key?"

She nodded. "That's the first thing I checked. It's right in my apron pocket, just where it always is."

I lowered my voice and asked, "Are there any copies?"

"No," she said, "I lost the only duplicate I had years ago. I don't know how this happened."

"Are you sure you still have the right key?"

She reached into her pocket and pulled out her ring of keys. "It has to be the right one. How else could I have opened the padlock? The box was locked when I checked it earlier."

"Okay, let's think about this. Have your keys been out of your sight at any time in the last couple of days?"

"Harrison, you know I never take my apron off when I'm working, and the keys are always in my front pocket so I won't lose them." A cloud of concern covered her face for a moment. "Wait a second, that's not entirely true."

"What is it?"

"Yesterday when I was going over the last few details for this party, I took my apron off so I'd look more professional. When I did that, my keys fell out. I laid them right here." She gestured to the counter over the strongbox. "But nobody broke into my strongbox yesterday, Harrison. This just happened ten or fifteen minutes ago."

"Who came by?"

Millie thought about it for a second, then said, "There were four of them. Let's see, besides the bride and her father, her brother came, and her maid of honor was here, too."

"Were any of them alone in the kitchen?"

She frowned. "I can't be sure, but I'm willing to bet that any of them could have come in here at one time or another."

I was starting to worry that Millie might be right about the thief succeeding. If she wasn't willing to have her guests interrogated by the sheriff, she might have to lose more money than she could afford to.

"Was this room ever empty tonight?"

Mrs. Quimby spoke up. "I had to leave to feed Esmeralda fifteen minutes ago. Heather knew she was going to be late on a buying trip, so she asked me to take care of Her Highness."

"Where were you then?" I asked Millie.

"I was circulating with the platters. This all happened just before you came, so I had to serve the guests myself."

"So then everybody at the party had access to this room. I just wish I knew how they unlocked the strongbox."

Could someone have taken Millie's key, had a duplicate made, and then returned the original to her ring, all without her knowing it? At the moment, it was the only explanation that made any sense at all. I knew what I had to do next. As I headed for the door, Millie asked, "Where are you going?"

"I need to interview our four suspects and see if I can figure out which one has your money."

"Harrison, they mustn't know what you're doing or I'm ruined."

"I promise I'll be discreet, Millie, but I'm not about to let someone steal from you."

I grabbed another tray on my way out and started looking for my suspects.

As I moved in and out of the crowd, I thought about the possibility that Mrs. Quimby had chosen that moment to steal the money while there were other suspects around, but I couldn't bring myself to believe it, not even for a second. It wasn't that she couldn't be the thief, no matter how unlikely it seemed. But if she had been the one to take the money, I couldn't imagine Mrs. Quimby trying to shift the blame onto someone else. No, it had to be one of the four people in the wedding party who had visited Millie the day before.

But which one?

Millie had pointed each of our suspects out to me from

the kitchen, so I knew who to look for. I didn't think I'd have much of a chance to get the bride alone, but she was actually the first one I spoke with. She wore a tight peach-colored dress that clung snugly to every curve, and the young woman carried a clutch purse so small I couldn't imagine what practical function it served. I offered her my tray, then said, "Nice party, isn't it?"

As she took an appetizer, I noticed a brand new Band-Aid on her finger. "What did you ask me? Oh, yes, the party's fine. Have you by any chance seen the groom?"

"No, I'm afraid not. That's bad luck," I said as I gestured to her bandaged finger.

"This? I got a paper cut reading my vows during the rehearsal this evening, can you believe that?"

Staying near her, I said, "All of this must have cost you a fortune."

She waved a hand in the air and pointed in the direction of the bar. "Daddy doesn't mind paying for it. He's been saving up for my wedding for years." Suddenly she called out, "Jonathon, I'm over here." As soon as the young man approached, she shoved her clutch into his hands. "Hold onto this. I've got to visit the little girl's room."

"Come on, Debbie, don't make me hold your purse. We're not even married yet."

"You'd better get used to it, Jonathon." His frown must have registered with her on some level. She snapped, "Fine, give it to Shelly to hold, I don't care. I really have to go."

And that was the end of my interview with her. I found the bride's father firmly planted by the bar, and from the glazed look in the man's eyes, I figured he needed something to eat to soak up some of the alcohol in his system. His suit looked brand new, and his hair had recently been styled by someone who knew what they were doing.

As I offered him the tray, I said, "It's a beautiful spread, isn't it?"

"That's easy for you to say, you're not footing the bill," he said, slurring his words slightly.

"Your daughter just told me you've been saving up for years."

He leaned closer to me, and I could smell the wash of alcohol on him. "I put her wedding fund in tech stocks. They all went right in the tank. I know how I'm going to make some of it up, though, believe you me. Shh, don't tell anybody."

I lowered my voice. "How are you going to manage that? Or have you already done it?" I was hoping he was drunk enough to confess the theft.

The father of the bride leaned even closer inside my personal space and said, "I've got a horse tip that's going to pay off big time, my friend." He winked at me, then grabbed a handful of food from my tray. "Gotta load up on all these I can. After all, I'm buying, right?" For some reason that started him laughing so hard and loud that everyone in the room was suddenly staring at us. A nice-looking young man in a rented tux joined us from the table piled high with early wedding presents.

"Dad, I told you before, you've had enough to drink."

"Davey, my boy, it's my money, and it's my booze," the man said.

David said, "Come on, let's get you outside."

He put an arm around his father, but the two men still nearly stumbled as they moved toward the door. I put my tray down on the bar and took the other side. "Let me give you a hand."

David nodded, so we walked his dad out of the party and into the night air. There was a waxing moon above us, barely producing enough light to show the way. We couldn't make it to the steps that led to the Gunpowder River, so David and I gently guided his father to one of the chairs in front of Millie's. Twenty seconds later, the father of the bride was soundly sleeping it off.

"I'm tempted to let him stay right here until the party breaks up. I hate it when he gets like this," David said as he slumped down in the chair beside his father. "I don't care what Debbie says, if this little get-together isn't over in half an hour, I'm going to pay a cabbie to take him home myself. It doesn't matter what my sweet sister says about any of us leaving the party early."

"Does your dad do this often?"

"No, it's just all the pressure he's under right now."

I leaned against a post. "I can understand that. It's not every day a man's daughter gets married."

"You're kidding, right? He's been looking forward to this for years. It's the money that's driving him to drink. I just wish there was some way I could help him."

"I guess you could always chip in yourself," I said, before I really looked at his threadbare suit and worn shoes. It looked as though he'd tried to polish his wingtips, but there was a spot the size of a quarter he'd missed on one, and I noticed a button was ripped off his jacket. The bride's brother was badly in need of a haircut, but at least his face was cleanly shaven.

He shrugged. "I would if I could, but I don't have that kind of money. Listen, thanks for helping with Dad, but you'd better get back to the party."

"It's time for my break anyway. I don't mind."

When he ignored my repeated attempts at more conversation, I finally gave up and went back inside. There was just one suspect left. I found the maid of honor, elegant in a strapless blue dress and designer shoes. I approached her with the tray after I collected it from the bar. "So, how does it feel to watch Debbie get married?"

She looked startled by my sudden appearance but managed to regain her poise. The maid of honor took an offering, tasted it, then spit it out into her napkin. "How do you know Debbie?"

"Funny, I was just going to ask you the same thing."

"We were roommates in college." She spread out her hands, gesturing to her dress. "How do I look?"

"Like a million dollars," I admitted.

She nodded her thanks. "I like to look nice, but you should see what she's got me wearing tomorrow for the ceremony. It's too hideous to even discuss. So tell me, is that any way to treat your best friend?"

"I know mine wouldn't stand for it," I said.

"So we agree about that." She gestured to the tray. "Honestly, isn't there anything better than this? I know what Debbie's dad is paying that woman. You'd think the caterer could at least come up with something edible."

I ignored the crack about Millie's offerings. "You were here yesterday, weren't you?"

"So what? I wasn't the only one here. There were four of us."

"Hey, I was just asking."

The maid of honor said, "Sorry, I'm a little on edge."

"It's not because you're hiding anything, is it?"

"I was wondering when somebody was going to say something to me. I didn't mean to knock that plate off the counter. It shouldn't have been sitting on the edge like that, do you know what I mean?"

"So that's why you've been so touchy."

"I'm perfectly willing to pay for it," she said. "It couldn't have been all that expensive."

The bride called out, "Shelly, I need you over here."

Before I could ask her anything else, she deserted me.

I'd spoken to all four of my suspects, but I still didn't have a solid clue about who had stolen the money, or how they'd done it.

I looked toward the kitchen and saw Millie staring at me through the opening. She gestured for me to join her, so I slid the tray on a table and walked back into the kitchen.

"Harrison, did you have any luck at all?"

"I'm not sure yet," I said.

"If you're going to solve this, you'd better do it quickly. They're getting ready to leave."

I considered everything I'd learned, then asked Millie, "Did anything else unusual happen during their visit yesterday?"

"Not that I can think of." She hesitated, then added, "No, that can't mean anything."

"You're not talking about the broken plate, are you?"

She shook her head. "No, I saw that happen. It was comical watching the maid of honor trying to shove the remnants of that plate under the counter."

"Did anything else happen?"

"I'm sure it's nothing, but after they left yesterday, I was cleaning the bathroom, and I found the oddest thing. Actually it concerned one of your candles."

"Go on, you've got my attention."

"I keep that beautiful blue candle you made me in the powder room as a decoration, but someone actually lit it. It was burned enough to make a difference in its height. No, that can't be connected to this mess."

That gave me an idea. "Hang on, I'll be right back."

I made my way to the bathroom, hoping that the party-goers would stay long enough for us to figure out which one had stolen from Millie. Someone was ahead of me in line, but in four minutes I was inside. I checked the candle, and it had indeed been burned. There were traces of black soot along its upper edges. The hazy ring on the lavatory's surface confirmed what I suspected. I walked back into the kitchen, and Millie looked as if she was ready to burst into tears.

"It's hopeless, isn't it?"

"That depends. Would you settle for full restitution, or do you want the thief to go to jail?"

"Honestly, Harrison, I just want my money back."

"Then I might be able to help."

I excused myself, had a brief conversation with one of my suspects, then returned to the kitchen.

I handed Millie the cash and receipts. "You can count it, but I'm pretty sure it's all there."

She looked at me with a stunned expression. "How did you do it? I don't believe this."

"Let's just say the theft dealt with my area of expertise."

As she clutched the money to her chest, she said, "You've got to tell me how you figured it all out."

"Let's get through the party, and I'll tell you afterwards."

After all of the guests were gone, including Mrs. Quimby and our four suspects, Millie deadbolted the front door. "Harrison Black, I'm going to scream if I have to wait one more second. What happened, and how did you figure it out?"

"Let me see your key first."

I took the offered key from her and examined it closely. "Do you see this?"

She studied the key, then said, "I don't see anything."

"Look closer. It's right there."

"You mean that fleck of blue paint wedged between those two teeth?"

"It's not paint, Millie. It's wax."

"Don't make me guess. What happened?"

"The person who stole your money tonight took your keys when you weren't looking yesterday. They opened the strongbox, but you'd already made your deposit yesterday. That's when it got tricky. The thief carried your keys into the bathroom. They lit my candle, puddled the wax on the vanity top, then made an impression of the key. The wax must have hardened pretty quickly, and after that, they peeled it off and filed a duplicate key."

"So who was the culprit?"

"Do you really want to know?"

"You'd better believe it."

I took a deep breath. "At first I thought it could have been the bride. She had a bandage on one finger, and I thought she might have burned herself melting the wax. Then I realized that she had nowhere to hide the money and receipts. Did you see how small her purse was, or how that dress clung to every curve? She wasn't hiding anything. Then I talked to her father, but frankly, I didn't think he had the intelligence or the nerve to pull it off. I knew the maid of honor was nervous about something, but as soon as she confessed to dropping that plate, she was fine. That left David, the bride's brother."

"Sweet David? I can hardly believe it. What gave him away?"

"There were a couple of things. He was obviously too broke to get a haircut for his own sister's wedding, but then outside he suddenly offered to pay for a taxi for his father. The real giveaway was when I looked at his shoes, though. When David melted the wax, a big blob must have hit one shoe. He managed to scrape it off, but there was enough residue left behind so that the polish wouldn't touch it. That's when I knew it had to be him, and as soon as I confronted him, he broke down and confessed. David felt so guilty that he couldn't afford a present for his sister that he decided to rob you. He said he'd come by tomorrow after the wedding to apologize himself and thank you in person for not turning him over to the authorities. He swore to me that this was a one-time deal, and I think he's telling the truth."

"Harrison, I don't know how to thank you. I can't believe you came up with the solution."

"Well, I had an advantage. After all, when it comes to candles, it's hard to fool a candlemaker."

§§

Candlemaking Tips for Twisting Dipped Candles

Dipping candles is great fun, and once you've mastered the basic technique, there are lots of variations to experiment with. After your melted wax reaches the proper temperature, the layers build up on your wick at a satisfying pace. You can add scents and dyes to your wax, too, yielding endless combinations.

One of my favorite things to do with a freshly

dipped candle is to twist it. The wax needs to be warm and flexible for this technique, so it works best on a brand-new candle. If you can't wait to dip an entire candle, take one you've already dipped and dunk it into melted wax eight or ten times to warm it throughout. This process is called overdipping.

Take the warm candle and place it on a hard surface like the back of a cutting board. Use a rolling pin or any round piece of wood to flatten the middle part of the candle. You need to press firmly here to get the wax flat enough for a pretty twist, a little under half an inch thick after it's rolled out. Working quickly, pick the candle up, grasp the top edge of the flat section with one hand and the bottom of the flattened area with the other. Then gently twist the candle until you've got a shape you like. Gently knead the wax as you twist it, keeping it smooth and even all along the spiral.

After you've got a shape you're happy with, check to be sure the candle's base will still fit in a holder, then look to be sure the candle is straight. Set the candle aside until it cools, and then light it! Twisted candles give off a good light, in spite of their flat centers.

Have fun, and don't be afraid to experiment.

Happy candlemaking!

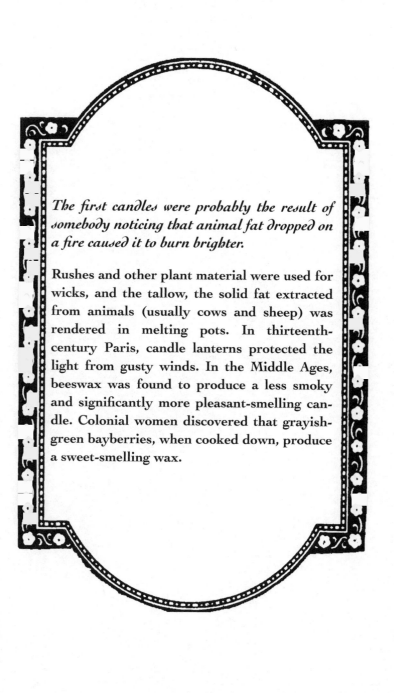

The first candles were probably the result of somebody noticing that animal fat dropped on a fire caused it to burn brighter.

Rushes and other plant material were used for wicks, and the tallow, the solid fat extracted from animals (usually cows and sheep) was rendered in melting pots. In thirteenth-century Paris, candle lanterns protected the light from gusty winds. In the Middle Ages, beeswax was found to produce a less smoky and significantly more pleasant-smelling candle. Colonial women discovered that grayish-green bayberries, when cooked down, produce a sweet-smelling wax.

LIGHT HER WAY HOME

by Sharan Newman

Sharan Newman is a medieval historian and the author of the Catherine Levendeur series set in the twelfth century, most recently The Witch in the Well. *Sharan, who lives in Oregon, is also the author of a nonfiction book,* The Real History Behind the DaVinci Code.

§§

EDGAR OF WEDDERLIE, merchant of Paris, looked up from the silver wire he was trying to thread around a piece of deep golden amber.

"Catherine," he asked his wife, "where are you going with six of our best candles?"

Catherine started. She'd been hoping to leave without him noticing. She stopped with a sigh. He'd find out sooner or later.

"Margaret and I are taking them to St. Lazare," she told him. "As an offering for the prayers of the anchoress."

Edgar shook his head. "One candle is more than her prayers are worth," he said. "Everyone knows that the woman spends more time gossiping at her window than on her knees."

"Edgar, that's not true!" Catherine answered with indignation. "Petronilla can't help it if so many people come to her for prayers and advice. She spends much of the night reading her psalter and asking Our Lady to help us. That's why she should have good candles."

Edgar knew he would lose this one, but he wanted one more sally. "And just why do we need help?" He grinned to show he was now teasing. "Don't I keep us all fed and housed? And won't you soon have a lovely new amber necklace?"

Catherine nodded. "You take good care of us," she assured him. "But this is not the only world. This is for *your* soul," she counted off the candles. "This for Margaret; three for the children, and this one," she gave it a caress, "is for the soul of our poor Heloisa."

The mention of the baby that had died ended the pretense of argument. Edgar turned his face back to his work, his pale hair hiding his expression.

"Be back by dark," he said. "And make sure my sister remembers to wear her warm scarf."

It was only after she left that he realized that she had not taken a candle for prayers for herself. He shook his head. They could have spared one more.

CATHERINE AND EDGAR'S sister, Margaret, hurried through the streets up to the abbey of St. Lazare. It was late autumn, and the black mud of Paris stuck to their wooden *sabots,* so that each step made a sucking noise. The hems of their robes were soon heavy with it. Around them, other women had tied up their skirts between their legs to be able to move more easily. Catherine wished she had done the same before they left the house.

The two women made their way to the edge of the city, where the monks had built a hospital as a refuge to care for lepers. There seemed to be more of them since King Louis had taken so many knights and soldiers to fight in the Holy Land. Of those who returned from the east, there were few who had escaped some illness or injury. The lepers were the saddest.

It was against the chapel wall of this hospital that the anchoress Petronilla had chosen to build her cell. It was only a frame-and-plaster building of one chamber. A slit in the back wall allowed her to see into the church, participate in the mass, and receive the Host. A small window on the other side was to allow her communication with the world. Each day food and other provisions were delivered and the waste bucket taken out and emptied.

Catherine felt it a slander to say that the anchoress spent all her time in gossip. On the contrary, Petronilla kept her own counsel better than many priests. People came to her to unburden their hearts and souls of their troubles. They asked her for prayers and advice. Pilgrims came from miles away to speak with her. It was said that Petronilla had the gift of solace. Many left her with grateful tears. What deep secrets Petronilla had been told, she never revealed.

As they neared St. Lazare, Catherine and Margaret noticed that even in the autumn rain, there were a few supplicants waiting to speak with Petronilla.

"Perhaps we should just leave the candles with the porter," Catherine suggested. "He'll have her confessor deliver them along with our message."

"I don't mind waiting," Margaret said. "I'd like to speak with her."

Catherine gave Margaret a worried glance. What did a girl of seventeen have to confess?

"Are you thinking of retreating from the world?" she asked, keeping her voice light.

Margaret laughed. "If I were, I'd go back to the convent, not build a hermitage at a crossroad."

But something had been troubling Margaret ever since she had returned home at the end of summer. Catherine suspected the cause but was too afraid of the answer to question her. Perhaps Petronilla could give Margaret wiser guidance than the family was able to.

When their turn came, Catherine hoped that Margaret

wouldn't be too long. She was shocked at how wan the anchoress looked.

"God save you," the woman greeted them.

"And you, blessed sister," Catherine answered. "Forgive me, but are you well?"

Petronilla smiled. "I am a bit tired, nothing more."

She glanced over Catherine's shoulder. Catherine turned to see the man who had been there before them trudging disconsolately away. Catherine turned back to Petronilla, who sighed,

"My confessor warns me not to exceed my strength, but I know that God will give me what I need to continue," she said.

"Of course," Catherine took the candles out of her basket. "We made these from the best bees' wax and scented them with lavender to soothe the spirit. May they be of some use to you."

"You are very kind." Petronilla accepted the gift. "I shall pray for you and your family. I admit that it is easier to concentrate on the psalms with the odor of lavender and honey in my nostrils rather than the meaty smell of tallow candles."

She sighed. "If I were truly as devout as people believe, I could make my devotions in the middle of a slaughterhouse and not notice."

"But there is no need for that," Catherine said. "You are afflicted enough with visitors to test your steadfastness."

"You are not an affliction, Catherine," Petronilla assured her. "And even the most worrisome of those who come to me remind me of how fortunate I am to be able to remain in my cell rather than face a daily struggle just to survive."

Ah, that's it, Catherine thought. *She is weary from the cares of others, not her own.*

Margaret must have felt this, as well, for she didn't ask for a private moment with Petronilla as planned. Or it may have been because of the rain, now turning to sleet. Catherine was relieved that they could leave, for her felt hat was sodden. Water dripped from the brim into her scarf and down her cheeks. Warm wool helped, but the chill found its way in.

Twilight was settling in as they left. Catherine was fretting about the rain and the chances of getting back before darkness made the twisting streets unrecognizable. She didn't see the figure waiting to speak to the anchoress, but Margaret noticed in time to pull Catherine aside before they collided.

"Who was that?" she asked as they slipped and slid back to the house.

"A man, I think," Margaret answered. "There was a sharp smell to him. I could have sworn it was the same one who was there when we arrived. Did you notice?"

"No, nothing but the rain running down my neck," Catherine said. "Oh, my hands are freezing!"

As soon as they entered the house, they threw off their damp woolen cloaks, slipped out of the rough wooden shoes, and hurried to the hearth. The dying light had stopped Edgar's work, and he was waiting for them impatiently.

"Have the children been fed?" Catherine asked as he handed her a bowl of egg and cabbage soup.

"Long ago," he answered. "They're upstairs with Martin, probably destroying something."

Catherine nodded. She knew her children.

Margaret gave her brother a kiss. "Don't scold us, Edgar. We had to wait to see the anchoress."

Edgar poured a cup of wine and gave it to her, then filled his own.

"I don't understand why this woman draws so many to her," Edgar complained. "I've heard about her at the merchant's meetings. She's the daughter of a money changer. Her brother keeps the changing window on the *Grand Pont*. I bring my coins to him to weigh. That's not exactly a spiritual beginning."

Catherine shrugged. "Who knows why God chooses some for a contemplative life? I go to her because . . ." She paused. "Now that I think of it, I don't know why. Petronilla gives me a sense of peace. There is an air about her. She listens, smiles and nods, promises to pray for me, and I go home feeling better. That sounds rather silly, doesn't it?"

Margaret had been silent up until then, warming her face and feet at the fire. Now she spoke up.

"I don't think so," she stated. "She makes me feel that way, too. I don't care that she comes from money changers. When we talk, my problems seem easier to bear."

"Well, then," Edgar closed the conversation. "That alone is worth the cost of the candles."

WINTER CLOSED IN early that year. The earthen streets of Paris were crisscrossed with wooden slats to keep carts from sinking into the mud. But these were soon slick with icy rain so that, even in solid wooden *sabots*, people slid from one end of the town to the other, grateful if they did not break a parcel or a limb in the process.

Catherine and her family stayed in much of the time. With three small children and a large dog in the house, she often thought wistfully of Petronilla's solitary cell.

Without warning, there came a clear day. The sun shone warmly, drying the streets. Everyone hurried out to the market for supplies and gossip.

The crowd was thick around the honey and wax stall, voices high with distress. Catherine stopped at the edge to learn what was causing the commotion.

"Dreadful! Just dreadful." Josta the ribbon seller was wiping her eyes. "The poor dear saint!"

"Catherine!" Her neighbor, Hervig, caught at her arm. "Have you heard? There was a fire last night at St. Lazare. Petronilla is dead!"

"What? A fire? But how?" The horror of being trapped in a doorless cell hit her all at once. Catherine felt short of breath.

"No one knows," Hervig said. "Perhaps a lamp spilled or a candle came too near the curtain."

"There's a corner of the roof all burned away," Josta added. "And one wall is down. They say a man coming home from a tavern saw the flames and tore down the plaster walls to pull her out, but it was too late."

"Her body is lying in the chapel," someone volunteered. "I'm going to pray before it as soon as the shopping's done. I've no doubt someone will receive a miracle even before she's buried."

Catherine didn't participate in the discussion of Petronilla's almost-certain sainthood. She was overwhelmed by the tragic circumstances of her death.

Margaret had been several steps behind Catherine, struggling to keep the two oldest children, James and Edana, from wandering off. She arrived just in time to hear someone announce, "They say her hands are scraped bloody from trying to claw her way out of the room. Poor Petronilla! How awful to be burned to death!"

"Petronilla! No! It can't be." The last sentence was hardly more than a whisper. Margaret's hands slipped from those of the children as she struggled to remain upright.

"Margaret!" Catherine dropped her vegetable basket as she reached out to catch her sister-in-law. "James, take your sister; run straight home and get Papa." She rounded on the crowd. "Where is your respect? We should be on our knees instead of standing about telling stories of such horror."

In Catherine's arms, Margaret gave a gasp and then began crying so piteously that many of those around felt ashamed.

"My dear," Catherine hugged her. "It's dreadful, I know, but you mustn't take this so much to heart. I'm sure Petronilla is now in Heaven."

Margaret wiped her eyes on her sleeve. "Please, take me home," she begged.

Everyone stared as the two women made their way across the market square. But they immediately returned to their business as Edgar came running toward them. He was known in the city as a man not to cross.

They got Margaret home and to bed. As they came back down into the hall, Edgar looked a question at Catherine.

"I don't know why she reacted so strongly," she answered. "I didn't think Margaret knew the anchoress that well. Certainly not enough to be so distraught even at such a sudden death. She's exchanged no more than a few words with Petronilla."

"Can you ask her when she wakes?"

Catherine shook her head. "I'm not sure that would be wise. She's been very reticent since she came home. When I try to find out what's bothering her, she only smiles and denies any worry."

They entered the hall, empty but for the smoldering charcoal brazier that only took the edge off the chill in the room. Edgar poked at the coals, then added a few more from the bucket.

"Perhaps," he spoke slowly, his eyes on the glowing coals. "Perhaps we should join those keeping watch on the body in the church."

Catherine looked at him in surprise. She knew he was worried about his sister. Catherine was, too. Margaret had only two choices, to enter the convent or accept a husband chosen by her powerful grandfather. Neither of these appealed. But Margaret was nearly eighteen, the age when the convent would accept her, and well past the age for marriage. Something had to be decided soon.

Edgar must be more concerned than she thought to grasp at the chance of a bit of overheard gossip enlightening them.

But she had planned to visit the church in any case, to add her prayers for the soul of the anchoress. "I would welcome your company," she said.

He looked at her and smiled. "A walk alone together with no children hanging from our sleeves? I would enjoy that, too, despite the occasion."

They set out later that afternoon, the pale sun still hanging just above the rooftops of the city. It was a long walk to

St. Lazare. No one wanted a hospice for lepers in the center of Paris.

The church was ablaze with light and full of people. Monks stood around the body to be sure no one tried to take a piece of clothes or hair or even a finger or two as relics.

Catherine and Edgar shuffled forward, stepping around people lying flat on the stone floor, wailing their sorrow.

To Catherine's relief, Petronilla did not look as though she'd been through a fire. Her short hair had been washed, and she'd been placed in a white robe. The only signs of burning were a bright redness around her mouth and across her nose and her torn and bruised hands.

They both crossed themselves and said a prayer for the poor young woman. Then they made their way out to the porch of the church, where several people had already gathered.

"That's the brother, Radulf," Edgar whispered, nodding toward a man in his thirties. He had an air of prosperity and wore a rich fur cloak held closed by a golden brooch.

The man was standing next to a woman whom Catherine assumed to be his wife. Both were weeping, dabbing at their eyes frequently with handkerchiefs. Around them, people patted their shoulders ineffectually.

"Should we speak to him?" she asked Edgar.

"Let's wait a bit and listen," he answered.

Catherine wondered how long they would be able to keep from being pushed out into the road by the flood of people coming and going. She leaned against the wall of the porch and dug in her heels.

Next to her, two men were talking.

"Terrible accident," the younger commented. "God's will is beyond my understanding."

"Well, that's a surprise," his companion said. "Did you get anything?"

"Just a bit of burnt rush from the roof of her cell," the younger complained. "I know those monks. They'll be tighter than mussels with the relics."

The first sighed. "Well, we might get some more of the roof and sell pieces to the pilgrims when they come."

Catherine turned away from them with distaste. The men went on talking.

"Good thing for Radulf, though" the young one said, picking something out of a back tooth. "He gets the changing house and a sainted sister."

"I wonder if he has anything of hers at his house," the other man said. "Maybe we could get some old robes cheap and cut them up to wrap around the charred rushes."

They finally moved off.

"Edgar," Catherine asked. "What did they mean about Petronilla's brother getting the changing house? I thought it was already his."

Edgar rubbed his eyes. The smoke from a hundred candles was slithering out onto the porch.

"I think I heard something about that," he answered. "Radulf's father left the building to Petronilla. I don't think he trusted Radulf to take care of her. At least that was the rumor."

"Then he didn't pay for her maintenance in the anchorage?" Catherine was surprised.

"I think she paid her own way from the rent on the changing house," Edgar said. "But it's no affair of ours, Catherine."

"I know," Catherine said doubtfully. "It just seems a strange situation."

"Edgar!"

As they pushed their way out, Edgar had come nose-to-nose with a man trying to enter the church.

He grimaced. "God save you, Maurice."

"And you," Maurice laughed. "The last person I'd expect to see here."

He glanced at Catherine and smirked. "Ah, now I understand."

Catherine started to giggle. Edgar gave her a sharp nudge.

"I don't believe you've met my wife, have you, Maurice?" he said. "Catherine, Maurice is a trader in leather."

Catherine had guessed that from the faint odor of urine he carried with him. She bowed.

"Oh, of course!" Maurice said. "God save you, *ma dame*," He tried to cover his embarrassment. "My wife sent me to help stand watch. She's ill, or she would have come herself."

"I shall pray for her recovery," Catherine said politely.

"By the way, Edgar," Maurice continued. "I met your sister last night, not far from here. She may have told you that I offered to escort her home."

"You must be mistaken," Edgar answered coldly. "Margaret did not go out last night."

"Edgar, I may not know your wife, but I've seen your sister," Maurice insisted. "That red hair is striking enough, along with the scar across her cheek. If you didn't know she was out then I'm sorry to have to tell you, but I'm sure you wouldn't want to be kept in ignorance."

He didn't appear sorry. Catherine was torn between alarm at his news and a strong desire to strike him. By the tension in his body, she knew that Edgar felt the same.

They left before they could act on their impulse.

"Do you think he really saw Margaret?" Catherine asked. "I was sure she had gone up to bed."

"So was I," Edgar answered shortly.

His anger sizzled in the cold air. Catherine said no more until they reached the house. She put her hand on Edgar's arm as they entered.

"If it's true," she pleaded, "I'm sure there's a good reason."

"Not good enough to put her life in danger," Edgar said.

MARGARET WAS SITTING alone by the dying embers of the charcoal brazier. She lifted her head at the sound of their steps.

Edgar was prepared to chastise his sister harshly, but one look at the abject despair in her eyes and his anger melted.

She sighed deeply.

"I was afraid Maurice would speak to you. I would rather have told you myself," she told them quietly. "I had to see Petronilla. She told me that it would be the last time we could speak."

"What do you mean?" Catherine knelt next to her. "Did she prophesy her own death?"

"I don't know; I never saw her. I was going to, but there was someone with her," Margaret told them. "I thought it might be her confessor in the church, but it sounded as though he were right in the cell with her."

"But how?" Edgar asked. "The man who tried to rescue her had to rip out the wall."

"I don't know," Margaret lowered her face. Her voice was barely a whisper. "He was shouting at her. I couldn't hear all the words. As I came close, he yelled, 'You cursed her!' and she cried, 'No, it was your sin that did it!'"

Edgar looked at Catherine. "That doesn't sound like a talk with her confessor."

Catherine's forehead creased with thought.

"Margaret," she said at last. "We need to talk with you about the reason you felt it so necessary to go out after dark to see Petronilla."

"Yes, I know," her voice wavered. "But first, Catherine, you must find out who killed her."

THE NEXT MORNING, Catherine and Edgar stood before the remains of the anchorage. There was a hole waist high in the wall, guarded by a burly lay brother of St. Lazare, leaning on a thick staff.

"The abbot has authorized me to strike anyone who tries to enter," he said. "He's been appalled by you relic hunters."

"We want no relics," Edgar said. "Only to look."

The man allowed them to approach but stayed nearby, tapping the staff meaningfully.

The walls inside the cell were streaked black with soot. One corner of the roof had burnt away entirely. The floor was littered with charred bits of fallen rushes. Edgar stared at them for some time.

"Do you think Margaret was right?" Catherine asked him. "It seems impossible. Even if someone wanted her dead, how could they have entered?"

"I know how," Edgar said, still examining the floor of the cell. "How the killer entered and, I think, how she was killed. The real question is why."

"She knew many secrets," Catherine considered. "Someone might have regretted confessing to her. If that's true, I don't see how we'll ever know who, unless they were seen."

"As Margaret was?" Edgar reminded her.

Catherine felt a shiver run down her back. Edgar had thought farther ahead than she had. If they announced that Petronilla had been murdered, the first suspect might be Edgar's sister.

"What can we do?" she asked.

Edgar chewed his lip, still staring at the debris inside the cell. Finally, he turned back to Catherine.

"This was a horrible murder, both cruel and sacrilegious," he said. "It is our duty to find the killer and bring him to justice."

Catherine agreed that this would be the best course. She also pointed out that discovering the one who had killed the anchoress and proving it might entail a great deal of work.

"Then we had better start now," Edgar said. "First, I want to examine the body more closely."

"Good luck with that! The monks won't let you near her," Catherine reminded him.

"I know; that's why you'll have to do it. I'll tell you what to look for."

They went around the hospital to the church and found that the crowds had thinned as the day waned. In a few moments they were standing in front of the mortal remains of Petronilla.

"Please let me through," she begged the guard. "I only want to kiss her good-bye."

"And snip a bit of her robe or a bit of her skin." He moved to block her way.

"Only a kiss and a blessing," Catherine promised. "She was my friend."

The guard made the mistake of looking directly into her eyes. They were startlingly blue against her olive skin and sparkling with tears.

"Very well," he said. "Keep your hands behind your back and be quick."

Catherine did as told. As she bent over the body, Catherine murmured a prayer and then kissed the bright red cheek, inhaling deeply as she did so.

"Thank you," she told the guard, giving him a coin. "For the poor."

By the time they got outside, she was shaking.

"You were right," she told Edgar.

He nodded grimly. "I think that the first thing in the morning, we need to pay a visit of condolence on Petronilla's brother."

RADULF THE MONEY changer was at his window on the bridge soon after dawn the next day. He forced a smile as Edgar and Catherine approached.

"Lord Edgar, my Lady, God save you," he greeted them. "Brought me more coins from foreign parts?"

"Only some *sous* from Rouen and Toulouse." Edgar handed him a small bag. "I don't like the look of the Norman ones. I fear they're light weight."

Radulf shook his head. "It's a sorry world," he said with feeling.

He took out a metal dish to put the coins in. "The silver seems good, if a bit light." He balanced them in his palm, a dozen pieces, each no bigger than a fingernail. His hand shook.

Catherine gave a sympathetic sigh.

"The death of your sister must grieve you terribly," she said. "We plan on attending the funeral Mass tomorrow."

"It's kind of you," he said. "Petronilla and I didn't always agree, but I shall miss her. Still, I hope you're not one of those who insist that she's a saint."

"Well," Catherine wasn't certain how she should respond. "Petronilla was a pious woman who gave her life to God . . ." she began.

"But no more. Nevertheless, those monks will ensure that she has a shrine and a few miracles by spring," Radulf continued. "Now that she's left them this house."

"She gave your home to St. Lazare?" Edgar asked in surprise.

"For our sins, she said," he told them sourly. "She might have asked if I wanted my sins forgiven and no place to work. The prior was here yesterday to tell me they're doubling my rent."

He finished testing the coins and gave Edgar their equivalent in money of Paris.

"I'm looking for a place near the road to St. Denis," he told them. "I hope you'll come find me."

"IT SEEMS HE had every reason to keep his sister alive," Catherine said as they walked back toward their home.

"I was afraid it wouldn't be so simple," Edgar agreed. "You don't think someone from St. Lazare could have . . ."

Catherine was horrified at the idea but forced herself to examine it.

"Murder for the sake of the rent on a building?" she said. "It's not as if the hospital is poor."

"What about murder for the alms that they will now receive in memory of the saint?" Edgar asked. "And the increased numbers of pilgrims."

"That would be a stronger reason," Catherine admitted. "But I can't help but think that the monks would be more subtle."

They had reached the house. Edgar stopped at the gate.

"What should we tell my sister?" he asked.

"Everything we know," Catherine took his hand. "Maybe she can help."

THEY CALLED MARGARET in at once.

"You weren't mistaken," Edgar told her. "There was someone in the cell with Petronilla just before she died."

"Are you sure?" Margaret asked.

"The roof was burnt entirely through at one corner," Catherine explained. "But the hole was made before the fire. The thatch on the floor was still whole."

Margaret nodded. "Mother Heloise always told us that a convent, or an anchorage, were kept unharmed more by the power of belief than stout walls. Someone hated her more than they feared God."

"Or feared her," Edgar said. "I think whoever it was wanted her to keep silent. Perhaps he tried to frighten her."

He paused and turned to Catherine. "Shall I tell her?"

"Of course," Catherine answered.

Edgar took a deep breath. "Petronilla had burns on her face, but they were light, in a ring around her mouth and over her nose. You'd think the monks would have wondered."

"When I bent to kiss her, I saw a sheen of wax at the edge of the burn," Catherine added. "And there was the scent of lavender."

Margaret's eyes grew wide with horror. "He used our candles!"

"I didn't find her cooking pot," Edgar said. "I think he dropped a candle into it, held her down, and poured the melted wax over her nose and down her throat. She didn't burn; she was smothered."

Margaret closed her eyes and moaned. Suddenly, her head jerked up.

"It was on his hand," she said. "The leather seller. When he caught up with me and offered to take me home. He gave me his hand, and it smelled of lavender. I thought he used scent to cover the stink of his occupation."

"Maurice? But what reason could he have had?" Edgar found it hard to believe. "Did he even know her?"

"Yes," Catherine said. "He was there when we brought the candles. Margaret remarked on the smell of his clothes then. And why else would he have been at St. Lazare that night? He probably saw Margaret from the window and chased after her."

"He must have killed her right after I started home," Margaret shuddered. "The voices stopped while I was trying to decide what to do. I must have made a noise."

Edgar and Catherine both embraced Margaret, each realizing how close she had come to being the second victim. She was still preoccupied with the cold-bloodedness of Maurice's actions.

"And after he decided I hadn't seen him," she went on, "he returned to set the fire. If someone else hadn't come by and pulled her out, no one would have known how she died."

Edgar reached for his cloak.

"Where are you going?" Catherine asked in alarm.

"To the provost," he said.

"But we still don't know why Maurice killed her," she said.

"I think it has to do with his wife's illness," he said. "How long has it been since anyone has seen her? Didn't Maurice travel with the king to the Holy Land?"

"You think he brought back a disease?" Catherine knew there were other things beside leprosy that were also caught through sin. "And his wife told Petronilla?"

"The king's men will find out," he told her. "Whatever

sin he was trying to hide, he has committed a greater one. I am more concerned to see him captured before he realizes that we know what he did."

Catherine had one more worry. "Before you go, Edgar; Margaret, can you tell us what you needed to talk to Petronilla about?"

Margaret sighed. "I had nothing to confess, if you were fearful. I only wanted her to help me to face what I know I must do. I have no calling to be a nun. I wish I did. Therefore, I am going to tell my grandfather that I will marry whomever he chooses for me."

"Oh, my dear!" Catherine said. "There must be something else you can do."

Margaret smiled sadly. "No, there isn't. You both know that. But Grandfather has promised not to make me go too far from those I love. Petronilla made me see that duty need not be sacrifice. I shall miss her."

As Edgar went out to inform the provost of Maurice's crime, he reflected that nothing the man might have done could have been worse than depriving the world of a woman of such wisdom.

NOTE: There really was an anchoress at St. Lazare named Petronilla. She owned the house on the bridge where her brother was a money changer. As far as I know, she died a natural death.

§§

Lavender-scented candles

There are a number of ways to make candles. If you lived next door to Edgar of Wedderlie, the first thing you'd need would be something to put a wick in. You could go to your local slaughterhouse and see about getting fresh tallow, sheep or beef, your preference.

Then you would render it and toss out the crunchy bits.

If you wanted something finer and more expensive, you could get a beekeeper to sell you some bee comb, after she'd taken out the honey. This also should be rendered and dead bees tossed out. Or sometimes the comb just can be rolled tightly about a wick.

The wick is a piece of string that has been soaked in the wax or tallow.

These days you can also go to the store and buy paraffin, an oil by-product.

Okay, you have a wick and some liquid wax substance. Tie the wick to a rod (I use a chopstick) and balance it over the center of a candle mold. You can buy metal molds at a craft shop or use a can or old milk carton. Put a few drops of essence of lavender into the melted wax. You can also add some sprigs of fresh lavender. Pour the wax over the wick into the mold and let cool. Slip the candle from the mold, clip the top of the wick, and light.

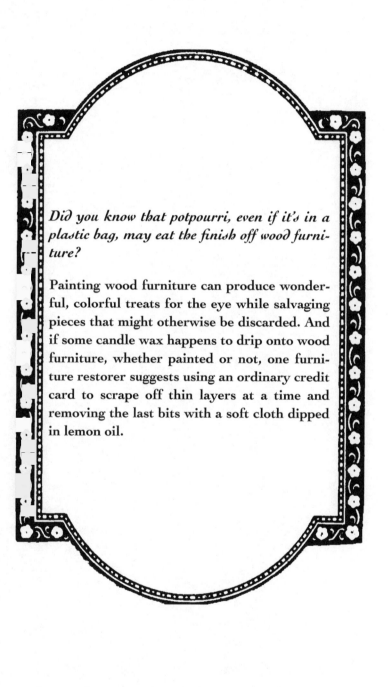

Did you know that potpourri, even if it's in a plastic bag, may eat the finish off wood furniture?

Painting wood furniture can produce wonderful, colorful treats for the eye while salvaging pieces that might otherwise be discarded. And if some candle wax happens to drip onto wood furniture, whether painted or not, one furniture restorer suggests using an ordinary credit card to scrape off thin layers at a time and removing the last bits with a soft cloth dipped in lemon oil.

ELLIE'S CHAIR

by *Gillian Roberts*

When Gillian Roberts relocated from Philadelphia to Marin County, California, it allowed her to indulge in bicoastal crimes. Beginning with Anthony award–winner Caught Dead In Philadelphia, *schoolteacher Amanda Pepper has appeared in twelve outings, most recently* Till The End of Tom. *Meanwhile, on the left coast, in* Time and Trouble *and* Whatever Doesn't Kill You, *PI's Billie August and Emma Howe are occupied with the darker side of California. Roberts has also written* You Can Write a Mystery, *and, under her given name, Judith Greber, has written four criminally-challenged mainstream novels. She teaches at the MFA in Writing Program at the University of San Francisco.*

§§

I MAKE SOME people uncomfortable and I don't care.

It was happening right now. I was driving Carrie Brigham to a garage sale. It was Saturday, so Carrie was home, rather than in a high-rise in the city selling bonus awards to corporations. She has a big title, something like Very Important Director of Something and Senior VP in Charge of Many Things.

I barely know her. This expedition was by way of seeing if we had bonding potential, though I doubted it. Sometimes, most of two people are incompatible but a little wedge of personality overlaps, and that's enough to form a friendship. We were trying to become flea-sale buddies. Carrie collects. She loves the hunt and the trophy, and almost anything can serve her needs: silver napkin rings, rocking horses, samplers, portraits (what anybody wants with a mediocre painting of somebody else's ancestor is beyond me), quilts, tin wind-up toys, cookie jars, perfume bottles, heavy pre-electrical irons that needed to be heated in the fireplace, perfume bottles, Depression glass—almost anything. If it's underpriced and decorative by her lights— it becomes her prey.

She's an acquirer who loudly prides herself on being a "self-actuated modern woman," as she puts it, and who has barely disguised contempt for women who don't live precisely the same life she does. I wondered if she saw the irony in how passionately she snatched up the leavings of those women she disparaged who saved scraps and created the quilts she coveted; the women who baked the cookies that filled the jars she found so quaint, who pushed those god-awful irons across the clothing they'd sewn themselves.

En route to the flea market, in the course of the conversation I'd let slip that I was an alumna of an Ivy League college. I regretted saying it instantly, because no sooner were the words in the ether than she recovered from her shock and zoomed into preaching her personal gospel.

"Don't you think . . ." she began, and the muscles at the back of my neck tightened. "I mean, with an education like that, do you ever . . ."

"—feel as if I'm wasting my expensive and extensive education." I kept my eyes on the road, away from her. "The answer's no. I'm a happy woman, and I like what I do."

"Of course," she said quickly. "But with so many talents and abilities—"

Here's what bothered her: I, Genevieve "Jenny" Watson, do not work to what Carrie considers capacity. I'm self-employed, and I don't punch a time clock. Besides, my work feels like play, so how can I time it? Still and all, by her lights, I am refusing to "have it all" because I'm not living the way she is, donning a power outfit and commuting in rush hour to an exhausting job. For some reason, that makes Carrie and too many others to count uneasy, confused, and obsessed with proselytizing. They're like unhappy people on a perverse and extreme diet. They're so uncomfortable with their regimen they feel obliged to have you restrict your diet precisely as much as they do. "You'll feel so much better!" they insist, although you're already feeling quite well.

I'm traveling to the market with Carrie to find discarded furniture to fix, decorate, and sell through my website, mostly. "The Furniture Orphanage" is a genuine business, albeit not the kind that makes it into the Fortune 500 or hires people like Carrie.

"Crafts are nice and all as hobbies," she said. "For people with free time, but . . ."

I didn't bother to respond. I have never understood the mild disdain for "crafts," and in fact, have never understood where the fuzzy border lies between "arts" and "crafts." "Fine" arts versus—what? Unfine art? Rough art? Unrefined art?

Just because most of what craftsmen produce is useful, does that make it less "art"? I've had many happy moments at museums paying homage to ancient pottery vessels and sculpted soup ladles and inlaid furnishings—all the brilliant handiwork of long-ago craftsmen. Maybe we have to be dead for hundreds of years to get respect from the Carries of the world.

"Don't you ever yearn to be part of the bigger world?" She softened her voice to make her words less offensive.

"I ship my pieces all over the globe. I had an order from Singapore this week. Everything I make is one of a kind."

She waved away my comment. "Whatever. You could write down one of your favorite one-of-a-kinds and find inexpensive labor elsewhere—in fact, go to your Singapore office instead of shipping one item there. Imagine it! Wouldn't that be better?"

"No."

She looked over at me as if I'd just insisted the world was flat.

We weren't going to bond. I probably disappointed her as much as she bored me. "I'm part of as big a world as I can handle," I said. "I don't want it one inch bigger. I think we've lost a lot with our busy lives today. I think we've lost community."

"What do you mean? We're going to a community flea sale, for heaven's sake!"

"When I was a kid, my mother knew the birthday of every kid in the neighborhood—and most of their mothers', too. And every one of those occasions was celebrated. And bad behavior was chastised. If somebody was sick, or going through a bad pregnancy, or going crazy with a houseful of children, or caring for an ill relative, other people knew, and they pitched in as much as they could."

"You're romanticizing," she said. "Your mother and her friends were probably stir-crazy most of the time. How gratifying can another casserole or cake be?"

I have fond memories of watching my mother experiment with the techniques of cake decorating, or making greeting cards. She was proud of what she called "spiffing up the calendar"—garnishing the ordinary face of our days. To me, that's a lost art. Not for lack of wanting it, but for simply having no time to do it. Instead, we go to flea sales and buy evidence of other people's lives—people who lived that way.

"Not that I mean anything negative about your choice," Carrie said. "I envy you the free time you have, the leisure . . ."

I tuned out her condescension. People like Carrie never invite me to comment in return on the quality of their lives. I'd have a lot to say, but politeness is among the endangered civilities I treasure.

I pulled into a long driveway. "Eureka," I said, "the motherlode." Carrie promptly stopped worrying whether I was fully evolved and turned her eyes toward "The Community Attic," a group sale that had infinite possibilities. She was almost salivating, and even I was excited by the prospects.

With over a hundred families taking part, the parking lot and playground of the elementary school was a solid mass of tables, boxes, trunks, cartons, and anything that could be dragged onto this lot.

Carrie and I drifted apart. As always, I looked for the odd, the misshapen, and the downright ugly. The more convoluted, lumpy, bumpy, busy, and downright ridiculous a piece is, the more fun I have with it, the more surfaces and angles there are to transform until, perhaps, there's a face peeking from behind an ill-executed rosette, a rainbow on the picket fence of a chair back, a stenciled design on ill-fitting drawers that makes their lopsidedness an asset, a homely table painted in gorgeous and surprising color combinations so that time and time again, the swan emerges from the ugly duckling. Furniture's fairy-tale ending.

I love pieces nobody else wants, the lepers and homeless rejects of the world of interior design. I restore their egos, give them value and self-assurance, and I turn a pretty penny, too.

While I sand and paint and seal, I think about the history of the chair or table or trunk I've adopted, about the hands that shaped their curved legs, and often my primary thought is: whatever did they have in mind?

It was a great flea market, and within an hour, I had filled the back of my pickup with three carved picture frames that would look great around mirrors when refinished, a hall table with a centipede's worth of legs and supports—I could see a prism across those eventually—a trunk that looked as if something had gnawed its base for too long, and a ridiculous tall and narrow chest, each drawer capable of holding one pair of socks. I hadn't found a chair yet, however, and so back I went to the market.

Chairs are my favorite paintables. They offer so many op-

portunities with fronts and backs, arms sometimes, legs
that can be amazing surprises in their shapes and ornamen-
tation, and seats that can be recovered in bright new colors.
All that sounds simple-minded, but every surface and angle
is a new canvas for me—a facet that gets its own attention,
an opportunity to do something inventive.

I saw a rocker that had possibilities, but you can go just
so far with a rocker. The ones with nursery-based themes
sell best, and I wasn't in the mood for that kind of sweet at
the moment.

I was about to leave when I saw it. In the world of or-
phaned furniture, this one was positively Dickensian. It sat
amidst fussy furniture of the generic "old-lady" type. This
chair had "doomed" written all over it and was destined to
become kindling if I didn't take it home. It had never been
fine and was made of cheap wood that had too easily become
dull and nicked. It's seat cover was faded and frayed. But
some well-meaning craftsman had attempted to carve what
I thought were meant to be lovebirds on its back. They'd
turned out more like amoebas bumping into a swollen
heart, but you knew that desire, if not skill, that had gone
into them.

The young woman selling it didn't hide her surprise at
my choice. "Really?" she asked. "You want that?"

"You'd be surprised—with t.l.c. and imagination . . ."

She raised her eyebrows. One of them had a silver ring
through it. She was in her twenties at the most, around my
kids' age, and while she junk-sat, she was reading a textbook
and running a yellow highlighter over passages. "I'd love to
see what you see in it," she said. "My cousin asked me if I
wanted any of Eleanor's furniture. I loved the woman, and
there sure was a lot, and since I'm in grad school, your basic
starving student, and need just about everything . . . but
even so . . ." She shuddered. "Too depressing. Why did people back then have such dark, heavy things around them? I
even once asked her about that specific piece. She said it was
special. Her own chair, made for her by her husband." She

shook her head, her curly hair bouncing with each move-ment. "He wasn't much of a carpenter."

But I was envisioning those lumpy birds painted a soft blue-gray, their wings detailed, their heads and eyes more clearly defined, and the heart made a high-gloss burgundy. I saw other places for burgundy highlights against shades of pearl and steel and the color of a day when the fog hasn't yet completely burned off the bay. "I'll give it an extreme make-over," I said. "The works. You won't recognize it." I pulled out one of my cards. "Here," I said. "Check out my website and you'll see what I do."

"The Furniture Orphanage," she said. "Cute." She almost smiled. She had another ring on the corner of her upper lip, and I wondered if her solemn expression was fear of the pain of stretching into a smile. A pity. I found myself imagining how I could do her over, and squelched the thought. There's a reason for my attraction to wood. It's quiet and amenable to suggestion and would never willingly stick rings through its sensitive parts.

"I'll check it out," she said. "I'm an art historian, or I will be someday. This—what you do—sounds interesting."

"Your grandmother, Eleanor—"

"My cousin's husband's great-aunt, Eleanor," she cor-rected me.

"Would that be Eleanor Darby?"

"How did you know?"

I was immediately flooded with the conflicting emotions that Eleanor Darby's name produced in me since her death. Sorrow for the loss of her, love of the memory of her, guilt at not having been there for her near the end, and an implaca-ble anger at the young couple who shared her house, an un-provable conviction that they were involved in her untimely, rapid decline.

"It's not that large a town," I finally answered.

"You knew her?"

"Years ago, mostly. When my children were young. And then, of course, when we'd bump into each other. We stayed in touch, but didn't see each other that much recently. I never was in her house—never saw this chair before."

"I gather she . . . well, you know. She was old, and she failed." She made it sound as if there'd been a life test, and Eleanor had flunked it.

"But you knew her, you saw her?"

"Only a few times after my cousin moved in. She seemed okay. A nice woman and then—" She shook her head.

"I tried to visit, but your—"

"My cousin. Or her husband, you mean?"

I nodded. "He told me she was upset and disoriented and ashamed to be seen that way." And he'd told it to me in a voice with a chill in it as loud as a warning siren. Ellie didn't matter to him.

I didn't like him or trust him. Joe, my husband, says I'm too quick to judge people, but I don't see the point of being slow about it. I come from a long line of people who were quick to size up other people's true motives. That's why we aren't extinct the way the slow sizer-uppers are.

Ellie didn't matter to him, but she had mattered to me by epitomizing that civility Carrie thought was my day-dream. Ellie Darby had materialized on a day when I was nearly hysterical with my two-year-old twin sons and my own ineptitude. We were in the park, Roddy sobbing with a scraped knee, Peter behaving like a manic dervish in the sandbox, screeching, whirling, and spraying sand in a little girl's face, so I had Roddy on my hip, my free hand trying to calm Peter and the sobbing little girl—and her furious mother—and all of me failing so miserably I burst into tears of frustration and failure.

And suddenly, almost as if we were in a fairy tale, Ellie materialized, counseling patience and the long view and a solid sense of humor.

She sat down on the edge of the sandbox, an elegant woman who looked en route to somewhere other than a playground in her tailored suit and chic shoes, long, mani-cured hands gesturing, drawing pictures in the air as she smiled and spoke softly to my crazed son, a diamond set inside a gold many-petalled rose catching the light on her ring finger.

I watched the ring. There was something hypnotic about the way it caught the sun with each gesture. In any case, the sight of it calmed me. Years later, Ellie said she was leaving me the ring, and though I protested, she insisted. "My daughter doesn't even like it," she said, "but it always reminds me of that first day we met. I saw you watching it."

Ellie talked Peter back into rationality, calmed the huffy mother and her little girl, and even the sobbing Roddy was too intent on the stranger to think about his injuries. I saw it happen, but I still don't quite believe or understand it, except to acknowledge that Ellie had a calm intensity, if there's such a thing, and children recognized it.

About a week later, my doorbell rang and she was there, looking nervous. "I hope I'm not being rude or imposing," she said, "but I couldn't get you or the twins off my mind. And I thought . . . well, my grandchildren live eight hundred miles away from here, and I have all these grandmotherly impulses going nowhere. I think it's unhealthy, so I wondered if you would be so generous as to let me share your children once a week or so?"

Nothing could have been more welcome—or presented more diplomatically. I was obviously falling apart. My father had died, and my mother had moved to Florida where she cared for her older sister, and here at my doorstep was emergency assistance presented in a way that saved face for me.

And so once a week, sometimes more, Eleanor Darby came to the house and spent time with the boys while I was given time out. Mostly I did errands and kept appointments, but I also often sat on a park bench and breathed deeply as I listened to the quiet.

She claimed the boys were her therapy. She'd lived alone since her husband's death, and her daughter lived several states away. The boys adored her. Together they baked cookies, made gingerbread houses at Christmas, created secret clubhouses, and played word and music games. She loved presenting puzzles, and she was fond of saying, when someone solved it, "As I said, it's Ellie-mentary, my dear Watsons!" The boys always laughed at the line, no matter how often it was repeated.

Best of all were the stories. "Don't you just love fairy tales," she said. "Everything always turns out right—you know the person in trouble is going to be heroically rescued, even if takes a little magic." She'd winked at me. "I want to believe real life's like that, too."

The twins, with their strange gift of simultaneous thought, looked at her and said in unison, "We'd rescue you if you needed it."

"Me, too," I said.

"I know," she solemnly replied. And then she winked. "And you know how I know?"

"It's Ellie-mentary, your dear Watsons," the boys said.

As it turned out, I hadn't rescued her. None of us had, though we'd have wanted to with all our hearts. Of course, Joe says there was nothing that needed rescuing, that, to use his favorite term, I was "looking at the picture from the wrong side." His point was that you can't be rescued from pure old age and debilitation, but I have never been convinced that a natural process was going on in that house.

Of course, once the boys began school, Ellie's visits became less regular, fitting into their ever-lengthening and more complicated schedules, and eventually, we became special-occasion friends, although she spent holidays with her own grandchildren more often than not, and we became more and more casually entwined, phone-call friends.

And on one phone call, I was surprised to learn that her nephew and his wife were sharing her home. It was a barn of a place, she said with a laugh that sounded less vital than I remembered, and the great-niece and her husband had money troubles, so the arrangement was good for all of them.

I'd heard Ellie talk and laugh and read stories in a variety of tones that fit the situations. The voice I heard that day didn't convince me that she meant what she was saying. It almost sounded like code, like deliberate bad acting, like one of her puzzles for me to figure out. "I'll come soon," I said. "Next week, okay?"

"Yes," she said with real enthusiasm.

I had two orders I had to fill before I could make the date, and I knew Ellie would understand. She was the first person who bought a piece of mine, a telephone table lacquered in soft lavender tones. She'd encouraged me to turn my hobby into a business.

"You'll come rescue me, as promised," she added.

I thought she was joking. Or maybe I just needed to believe that.

When I phoned to make the date, her nephew used that frozen voice to inform me that Ellie was "failing." It did not ring true. A week earlier, she'd sounded mildly depressed, but otherwise normal. "What's wrong?" I asked.

"She's old. It happens."

"What does the doctor say?"

"Mrs.—"

"Can I help? When you're at work, could I—"

"We're usually here, and we've taken care of the times when we aren't."

I wondered why they were usually there. They were in monetary straits—weren't they working, trying to get back on solid ground? "Would you tell her I'll be by as soon as she's ready for company?"

He sighed, as if conveying a message was an impossible burden, but with prompting, he promised.

I didn't like him, and I still don't. Joe might say I'm too quick to pass judgment, but he also admits I'm seldom wrong.

WHEN I PHONED again, I was told she couldn't have visitors for the foreseeable future, that her health, along with her mental faculties, was in decline and she was frequently agitated. I sent a card and a note, and flowers, and a box of cookies made with her recipe. My boys phoned and wrote, too. There was no response.

Despite Joe's objections, I eventually phoned her daughter, because I felt she should fly in and check the situation. But Ellie's daughter and son-in-law were celebrating their silver anniversary with an extended trip to Europe, staying in touch via e-mails and a barrage of cheery postcards. I didn't want to interrupt their trip, which was going to end in two weeks in any case.

And then one week later, the obituary was in the newspaper. "The whole thing happened too fast," I said.

Joe shook his head. "Maybe you're looking at this from the wrong side again. Think how it must have been, then work forward, not backward from a conclusion you've reached."

I folded my hands over my chest and stood there silently, shaking my head.

"Surely a doctor was in attendance," Joe said, "and would have known if anything was wrong. She was a terrific person, but life isn't fair, Jen. Probably a blessing that she went so quickly." And so we left it. He went to Ellie's funeral with me, as did the boys, who came in from their schools for the occasion, and so did her daughter and grandchildren, all of whom seemed stunned and incredulous.

The niece and her husband, the squatters, remained aloof and chilly. But Joe, being Joe, reminded us all—again—to look at it from the other side. That always means his side, and his point of view. They were in mourning, he said, probably upset this had happened on their watch, and so abruptly, so they were not likely to be jolly and hail fellow well met.

I saw no evidence of grief, only of an impatience to get the service over with. The cuckoos, I still thought of them, occupying somebody else's nest. And, in fact, they stayed in that nest, which had been left to them by their kindly great-aunt. I never heard from them about the ring, and the one time I phoned and attempted to find out, the wife, Deeanna, informed me briskly that she didn't know what I was talking about and that Ellie had lost her ring just as she'd lost everything because her mind was gone. Furthermore, she said in a voice as cold as her husband's, I was harassing them, and she'd have an injunction taken out against me if I bothered them again.

"An injunction!" I stormed to Joe. "All I wanted was . . ."

"I know," he said, "but the police don't know you. They won't know your interest has nothing to do with any worth the ring might have, that it's about sentiment."

"You mean I'll look like a grave-robbing type, a . . . a—what those cousins are!"

He let me rant, but the bottom line was that this chair and my memories would be my souvenirs of Ellie. This was one orphan that would never be put up for adoption.

Carrie saw me staggering to the truck with Ellie's chair and rushed over, saying she was ready to leave. "Look!" she said. "Look at this!" She'd found a delicately made cut-crystal cake stand, its base and top ringed with wide black, spotty bands. "A steal," she said, "and when it's resilvered it'll be good as new."

"Lovely."

She nodded happy agreement, then she observed my haul, frowned, and bit at her bottom lip so I could notice with what difficulty she was controlling what she wanted to say about the chair.

"I have this fabulous porcelain tiered cake," she said instead. "I bought it at a flea market in Paris. Mountains of white china icing and tiny pink roses, and I've never known what to do with it, but now—I'll set it on this. Won't that be something?"

I nodded. Happily, she didn't ask me what that something was. The cake stand was like the one my mother used to use to show off her celebratory creations. It had been a real stand for real cakes. Now, it would be a still life in Carrie's fantasy of home.

I ANNOY PEOPLE because I am content, and they translate that into dull and wrong. Dull, maybe, but not wrong. I like the feel of rescuing old things and delight in their second chances. One of the many things I like about them and the process is the great stretches where time's forgotten and I am lost in a swirling hum of color, texture and design. There's a silence inside old things, a deep well of history and the memory of human touch, a story, if you listen, a record of time and usage, attention and neglect, functionality and frivolity.

I'm lucky that Joe understands and is a kindred soul. He even wired the garage for sound, because music and good talk don't interfere with the silence I hear in the pieces, and he put in heat and often as not, he joins me and sits on "his" rocker, the first piece I ever refinished. His immediate enthusiasm, along with Ellie's, was the reason I continued on into a business. His rocker's a pale honey color with deep green cushions and fine evergreen accents etched into the crevasses on the armrests.

The whole idea of those pleasurable lazing-by times would drive Carrie Brigham up the wall. She's told me so on earlier outings through quiet "tsks" because I hadn't caught the new TV sitcom, or we hadn't seen the movie that just opened. And most times, the books we're reading aren't the biggest, loudest best-sellers, either.

"She's so . . . so noisy," I told Joe that evening. "I don't mean loud—but did you ever know somebody who could deafen you without opening her mouth?" I was finishing up a chest of drawers that had been a pretentious wannabe Louis the Fourteenth number in its previous life. All white streaky finish and gilded edges. Now it glowed in muted blue-violet trim, and its bellied drawers were a subtle green-grayed yellow I don't think has a name. I was enjoying putting on the final touches, but my eye kept wandering to the chair.

"That was Ellie Darby's," I told Joe, who was rocking in his chair and frowning at the newcomer.

"Looks torturous," he said. "Not the best way to show your love."

"I think it is. The woman saved me, and I'm saving her chair. Not an equal trade, I know, but the best I can do, given the circumstances."

"I meant not the best way for Mr. Darby to have shown her his love. He must have made this. No professional furniture maker could have done this and lived to do another."

I finished up the faux-Louis's claw and ball foot, tempted as always to paint the toenails bright red. Why put animal feet on a bureau? Was there something appealing about the idea that your chest could walk away?

"You couldn't have done anything for her, you know," Joe said, reading my mind.

I sighed. "No fairy-tale endings in real life, are there? No heroic, magical rescues." I checked that the back of the claw foot was completely painted and declared the piece finished. "Makes me furious, though. Still does. I know that those two—those two—"

"Let it go, Jen. You're an otherwise sane woman."

"Are you insinuating—"

"Not at all. I'm saying it straight out. On this one point, you're irrational. Even if you were right, and there's no evidence for that, you'd never be able to prove it, so let it go. Make a big fuss, and people will think you're angry about the ring, greedy for it."

"The ring has nothing—"

"Let it go, Jen."

His skepticism and dismissal seemed another weight on the scales, making the balance of justice completely out of whack. Nothing felt Ellie-mentary.

*   *   *

I SPENT THE next morning thinking about Ellie's chair. Since I knew it was going to remain mine, I wanted to make it as personal as possible, so that the story lady, and the puzzle maker, and the fairy godmother in the park would stay alive with me as long as I could see it.

First aid first. I put on music I enjoyed and began sanding and smoothing, starting at the top, the section that required the fewest body contortions on my part. The pine had nicks and scratches, bangs and even purple marks, as if someone had swung a felt-tip pen too close to it. I sanded and remembered, until the back was close to finished, and the morning was over.

After lunch, I started in again, turning the chair onto its side so I could work on the legs. I saved the seat frame for last, because it looked like a real pain with its curves and grooves.

I worked and remembered Ellie, and felt that rush of mixed emotions again and hoped that by the end of this project, I'd have resolved all that.

I started at the bottom of the legs—no claws on this one—and worked my way up the front legs, then repeated the process with the back. Sandpapering is my least favorite part of the process, and this nicked and battered piece had need of so much of it that my mind had time and opportunity to wander, and I had almost smoothed an upper portion of a back leg when it registered that a patch of wood was worn and dull, and considerably paler than its surrounds. The front of that leg looked all of a color, and I couldn't think what could fade a part of the furniture that never saw direct light.

Actually, I could think of what might have done it, but I didn't want to. I turned the chair around, and looked at the front again, shined a light on it to double-check. It definitely did not have the same coloration. Had I paid too little attention and sanded it away?

I checked the other back leg. I hadn't touched it yet, but

there it was—a light patch on its backside at about the same height as the worn patch on the other leg.

I took a deep breath. I did not want to jump to conclusions, be called a fool or a meddler by Joe, let alone anybody else.

The phone interrupted my attempt to list everything that could possibly cause those light patches. "Mrs. Watson?" a young voice said, and without waiting for an answer, continued in a rush: "This is Lacey, the girl from the flea market. You gave me your card, and I checked out your website, and it's great. I'm interested in folk art, and I wondered if I could interview you, watch you at work, something like that. For this paper I have to write, but also, because I'm interested."

Folk art. I thought maybe I'd just been promoted up from craftswoman to cultural artifact, but I'm still not sure about those blurred lines. In any case, it was flattering to have somebody want to study me, so of course I agreed to a few hours observation. "I have a question for you," I said, thanking fate for the good timing of her call. "You know the chair I bought. You'd seen it at Eleanor's house, correct?"

She agreed.

"Could you tell me where it was located, and whether it was in use?" Maybe it had been stored upside down on a table, on . . . I was grabbing at straws, but also trying to not rush to judgment.

"I stayed over one night and passed her bedroom, and she was sitting on it, reading. It looked uncomfortable with that funny back, and I think I said something like that, and she insisted that it was her favorite chair, and that her husband had built it so that it fit her perfectly. Hard to believe. For starters, no arms, and a hard back with lumps that would hit you uncomfortably."

The lovebirds and the heart. Perhaps to Ellie, they were a constant reminder, a gentle pressure recalling her husband's actual touch and a comfort in themselves. I thanked Lacey, confirmed our date, and resumed my pondering.

"What could make these marks?" I asked Joe before dinner. "These light patches."

"Uneven sanding."

I raised my eyebrows.

"Not yours, of course, but maybe the guy who built or
refinished it?"

"I think it was a different kind of sanding. I think it was
rubbing, a slow sanding by somebody tied up."

"For God's sake—"

"Otherwise, explain how they're precisely where the
wrists would be tied—and the ties would have gone around
the front on her skin, so there aren't any marks on that side
of the legs. But as she tried to jiggle her hands, keep the circulation going or escape, slowly, slowly, those marks were
made."

Joe was silent for a long time before he spoke with great
deliberation. "This is frightening, this obsession of yours,"
he said. "But I'll tell you what. You get any corroborating
fact, proof that we could take to the police—and I'll go with
you. I'll back you up. But it has to be more than a wild idea
without foundation."

"The young girl who saw the chair in Ellie's house said it
was her favorite. She'd be the person sitting on it. Maybe
her torturers would deliberately choose that chair, in fact.
Besides, it doesn't have arms, so it's easier to tie somebody
up. Poor woman. Poor, poor woman! I think they starved
her to death. She declined too quickly, too . . ."

He took another deep breath. "A real fact, Jen. A tangible something."

I understood what he meant, and I'd have loved one, but
outside of fairy tales and ghost stories, people do not provide clues from beyond the grave, not even a person who
seemed half a fairy-tale creation herself.

I SPENT THE next three days working on the old chest,
transforming it into something that could be a coffee table,

or a hope chest—did anyone have such things anymore? Whatever it would be, under its current layer of urethane, it was now populated with an imaginary world's worth of wish-granting fairies and sprites, creatures I could have used to help with the riddle of Eleanor Darby.

"I'm sorry," I told my memory of the woman. "I wanted to be your hero, but I don't know how." I had never been the one to solve the puzzle, to be the Sherlock who could say, "Ellie-mentary." Instead, I was the dear, dull, Watson. I needed her smarts, and they were gone.

The next day I considered the upholstered seat cushion on Ellie's chair. The gingham must once have been charming, but now the blue was faded and the white was gray and all of it was frayed. I contemplated what texture and color I wanted, and as I sat looking at it, I noticed a thin edge of bright, ungrayed white at the edge of the seat.

A crumpled piece of paper had been shoved inside a tear in the gingham. I unfolded it carefully and read a printed fragment that looked ripped from a book. ". . . in the night, and then it became obvious to Rapunzel that . . ." It was mostly margins, and the other side told me even less. "In that day, it happened that . . ."

I stuck my finger into the rip and wiggled it, but nothing crackled. No more messages. No more paper.

"RAPUNZEL," I TOLD Joe over dinner. "Locked in a tower."

" 'Let down your long hair,' is what I remember," Joe said.

"So I might climb up your golden stair," I said, finishing the story's request.

"So it might be taken to be a symbol about sneaking a guy into your room, or about excessive hair growth," he said. "Or not a symbol at all. A scrap left at any point in the chair's long life. When could she have done it, anyway, if her hands were bound?"

"They had to let her out now and then, don't you think? To use the bathroom?"

"They couldn't have let her loose often—if any of your theory is true. Otherwise, why wouldn't she call the police?"

"Do we know if she had a phone in her room? Who knows what the threats and restraints were? But she had books—children's books—used to bring some to the boys when she came—and even if she'd be out for a minute, she could grab an appropriate one, rip out a page—"

"Any page?"

"If needs be. There's a rescue or test on almost every page of one. But maybe there was time to flip and rip, then hide it in her hand and—"

Joe shook his head again. He considered my obsession with Ellie Darby's death my inability to face my own mortality. As much as I wanted to bring postmortem justice to Ellie, I wanted as well to earn an apology from my beloved, whose attitude toward my concern was enough to drive me to contemplate murder myself.

Nonetheless, the storybook scrap was not, I admit, something that the police would consider evidence.

Give me something else, Ellie, I pleaded. Forget the fairy tales. Give me something real.

And then I heard myself, and I realized how stupid this quest of mine was, and how futile. Don Quixote had nothing on me with his windmills. I saw stories in chairs and asked them to reveal secrets, to work magic.

I was a rapidly aging fool, turning guilt in having not shown enough concern for a dear old woman into someone else's having murdered her. I was ashamed of myself.

THE NEXT MORNING, I took a long walk that took me to Ellie Darby's street. I stood looking at her house, thinking about her and about Rapunzel. I had been sure I'd see bars on the bedroom window—perhaps disguised as a fancy grill, but a jail-like bar all the same.

Instead, the windows were no more than glass panes and wood trim, and so I returned home.

Today I was ready to tackle the wooden band that cradled the seat cushion. Someone had varnished the piece a while back and had done an inept job of it, so that hard beads were trapped in the grooves Mr. Darby had cut around the circumference.

I was almost all the way around, brushing away bits of stuffing leaking out of the seat cushion, making the wooden band as smooth as possible, thinking again about color combinations that might work, when I noticed a certain regularity in the scratches on the right side, close to the back. Straight lines, curves, none of the lines bold and definitive—scratches; no more, no less. I was afraid I was once again reading a great deal into something that was in essence nothing.

But they were something. They were letters.

w-p-n-p and a curled thing at its start that looked like the ribbons that symbolize AIDS and breast cancer, etc., only upside down . . . I wasn't sure that any of it was truly intentional, most of all that little ribbon.

w-p-n-p? Will you please not . . . Who put nifty pepper . . . Wipnip? The call letters of a radio or TV station? Western Pennsylvania National . . .

I was overreacting again, living in my fantasy once more. Even if it was a scratched message, even if there was the slightest possibility they'd allow Ellie an instrument so sharp it could scratch the wood, even if she'd wanted to leave a message—it wouldn't be an unintelligible series of letters.

I didn't intend to say anything about it at dinner, but Joe saw that I was upset, and bit by bit, he got it out of me. "Don't you dare say I'm looking at it from the wrong side," I snapped. "I am so sick of that ex . . ." And I stopped. I was quiet for so long that Joe thought I'd had a stroke, and he jumped up and rushed to me.

I put my hand up signaling him to halt. I needed to think. In fact, I needed to write.

Little upside down ribbon. *wpnp*. "Thanks," I said.

"For what?"

"For clichés about looking at things the wrong-way round. They say expressions become clichés because they're truisms, and that one was."

"I hope you're going to say something that makes sense, or I'm dialing the paramedics. Maybe that really was a little stroke."

"Stroke nothing." I turned the paper to face him. "*w-p-n-p*," he said.

"And the ribbon."

He nodded.

"What if I said 'you're looking at it from the wrong side'?"

"I'd promise to stop saying that and know I deserved to be made fun of."

"No. Do it. Look at it from the other side. Turn it around." From where I sat, while it faced him, it made perfect sense.

"*d-n-d-m*—and a lower case *e* in script?"

"She was trying to write it—that's why those rub marks. She pushed her hand forward until she could scratch out a message. It was facing her, upside down when read normally."

"*d-n-d-m-e*?"

"Say it."

"Dee End—"

"Deeanne, the cousin. Dee."

Even he had to give me a grudging "maybe."

"Dee En Dee Em EE?"

"I think it's a combination of 'Dee End Me.' Deeane is ending her, killing her." I was practically jumping out of my seat, eager to get on, to prove this.

"Interesting. Really."

"She loved words and games—and this is the most efficient way of spelling out what would otherwise be too long for a tied-up hand."

He looked at the letters again.

I couldn't sit still another minute. "You wonder—don't you?—what cut those feeble letters into the wood, and I think I know. If I'm right—then that message definitely was for me. She knew I'd come. I said I was. Sooner or later, she knew I'd try to rescue her. Even if it was too late to save anything except the truth."

I pushed back my chair and headed for the garage. I heard him following me. I refused to believe I could be wrong—I couldn't. I knew Ellie, and she knew me, and she knew I believed in community, in ties that bind, in doing the right thing—and in promises. And we'd had more than one conversation about old furniture, and the stories those pieces could tell.

Ellie Darby had written me her story, exquisitely.

I ripped off the gingham covering and pulled out stuffing, digging my hand in more deeply than I'd done earlier when I was looking for more of the paper. It didn't take long—after all, she'd had to work on it while tied up, with only so much give. "The ring," I said. "They really did think it was lost. She got thin enough for it to come off with little help, and she used it to scratch out the message, and then she buried the ring she left me. She knew I'd find it.

"They killed her, Joe. Tied her up and starved her until she was so enfeebled that of course she 'failed.' That's probably when the doctor was brought in—if then. I'm willing to bet that if we check—"

"If the police check," Joe corrected me. "Your job is restoring furniture."

"If the police check, they'll find no evidence of doctoring until she was close to death."

"It's still so speculative," he said.

I shook my head. "Even if they untied her now and then, there was no phone in her room, I'm sure. But I wondered why she didn't open a window and scream for help, even during the middle of the night. I walked there this morning and there are no bars on the windows. Tell the police to check for evidence that they'd been nailed shut or otherwise secured. She couldn't open them. She was Rapunzel, imprisoned in her tower."

THE POLICE CHECKED doctors' records (none) and sealed bedroom windows (hers still had the marks of the nails, plus a mesh barrier so the small panes of glass couldn't be broken) and after that, Ellie's chair became evidence for a long time, as well.

Now the cuckoos are in prison and Ellie's house is up for sale. Her daughter plans to give the entire proceeds to the library, all for the children's collection.

Carrie Brigham phoned me, quite excited, when the news made the paper. "This is incredible publicity, and you shouldn't waste it," she said. "I've got a group in the city with whom you must network. Sales will boom and—"

I didn't want booming sales. I didn't even try to explain myself. Once again, I upset Carrie Brigham. Once again, I didn't care. We did not bond.

Lacey, the future art historian, came and watched me work and took pictures of Ellie's chair. I'm to be in a slick magazine soon. As a folk artist, of all things.

And Joe has never again—not once—told me that I was looking at anything from the wrong side. That's about as good as it gets, so I'm as contented as I can be, given that my triumph was too little and too late. But it was something.

I wear the ring every day and look at it when I want to remember what is important and what is not.

Ellie's chair is back home after successfully 'testifying' in its own fashion. As Joe and I like to say, "Most times, people get the chair, but sometimes, if you're Ellie's chair, the chair gets people."

I've decorated it—all but the place where she'd scratched her message—with memories of her. Children's faces peep around a slat, fairy-tale bookjackets adorn the other side, the lovebirds are clear-eyed and shining, embracing the heart together, and the seat is covered with a blue the color of dreams.

Around the band of wood that surrounds it, I've written, in the most delicate of letters, almost as if a rose-shaped ring had cut them into the pine: "Ellie-mentary, my dear Watsons."

❦

To adopt and transform your own orphaned furniture

First, clean the piece with soap and water, a degreaser solution and/or steel wool. Then, make simple repairs, e.g., fill holes and cracks with wood filler, remove old nails, replace damaged hinges, or mend wobbly legs.

Gently sand the surface to provide tooth for painting and either proceed to painting if it's already been painted, or prime with appropriate material (acrylic wood primer or a flat latex undercoat, all available at any paint store).

And then for the fun part: add imagination, as much as you like. Paint it, stencil it (patterns available in paint, craft, and hardware stores), rub a woodwash color—or two—over it, decoupage collected images onto it, lacquer it, stamp it, crackle it, gild it—there truly are too many possibilities to list. Happily, there are many books on furniture facelifts and transformations. Thumb through them for ideas and then experiment to your heart and home's content.

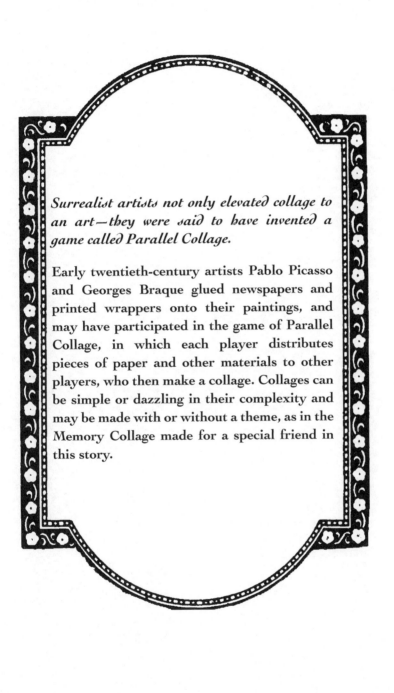

Surrealist artists not only elevated collage to an art—they were said to have invented a game called Parallel Collage.

Early twentieth-century artists Pablo Picasso and Georges Braque glued newspapers and printed wrappers onto their paintings, and may have participated in the game of Parallel Collage, in which each player distributes pieces of paper and other materials to other players, who then make a collage. Collages can be simple or dazzling in their complexity and may be made with or without a theme, as in the Memory Collage made for a special friend in this story.

MOTHERWIT AND TEA CAKES

by Paula L. Woods

Paula L. Woods is the author of the Charlotte Justice mystery series, most recently Dirty Laundry. Inner City Blues, *first in the series, won a Macavity award and was nominated for Edgar® and Anthony awards, and was named Best First Novel by the Black Caucus of the American Library Association. She edited the groundbreaking anthology,* Spooks, Spies, and Private Eyes: Black Mystery, Crime, and Suspense Fiction of the 20th Century. *Also a book critic, Paula lives in the Los Angeles area.*

ॐ

NELLIE WHITCOMB SHIFTED uneasily in the leather seat of her daughter-in-law's Explorer, squinted into the sunshine, and tried to count her blessings. She'd gotten a respectable price for her soul food restaurant, Mother Wit's. She'd leased the top floor of her brownstone in Harlem to a couple of nice young men for a good price. And, unlike many seniors she knew in New York, she was in tolerably good health and had family who wanted her to spend her golden years with them—family who needed her almost as much as she needed them.

So if she was so lucky, why was her stomach coiled tighter than one of her famous cinnamon rolls?

Her son Mack and daughter-in-law Connie meant well, she told herself, when they convinced her that it was too much trying to run Mother Wit's alone, that at seventy-two she deserved a rest and winters where she wasn't sidestepping ice patches and PETA fanatics trying to throw blood on her full-length mink. Couldn't even wear a mink most days in Los Angeles, Nellie thought as she peeked below the car's sun visor to see where they were headed.

She must have muttered this last bit aloud, because her daughter-in-law Connie laughed uneasily and replied, "But it's a nice introduction to California, wouldn't you say, Mother Whitcomb?"

Nellie rolled her eyes away from her daughter-in-law and wondered if the girl had lost her natural mind. A nice introduction would have been her furniture arriving on time instead of delayed in a snowstorm in Ohio. A nice introduction would have been finding a church within walking distance of the house that offered services in English, instead of Korean or Russian or that New Age mishmash with an integrated choir. A nice introduction would have been her dear Mack meeting her at the airport with flowers instead of her taking a bouquet to him at the hospital or later at the cemetery when he didn't survive the sudden heart attack he'd suffered the day before her arrival.

So here she was, living with a daughter-in-law who she had never liked much anyway, despite the fact she was the mother of two of the most wonderful grandchildren ever to walk the earth. Sneaking a peek at Connie's sharp profile, the way her lips had thinned to a russet-colored slash, the way she fiddled angrily with that gold pendant around her neck when she should have both hands on the wheel, Nellie clutched the plate of homemade tea cakes in her lap and thought—this time she made sure only to herself—*I'm in deep dish doo-doo now.*

CONNIE KLEIMAN WHITCOMB was having similar thoughts herself. Moving her mother-in-law to Los Angeles had seemed the right thing to do when Mack was alive—in fact, she was the one who'd insisted on it—but the thought of having to face Mother Whitcomb's tight-lipped disapproval of how she was raising the kids or running the agency had left Connie exhausted and more jittery than a pickpocket at a police convention. And on top of it all, the old woman had become a bitter party of one—just sat around complaining about how everything from buses to butchers was better in New York.

The Golda Meir Senior Center was a last-ditch effort to snap her out of it. It was around the corner from C&M Investigations, the detective agency she and Mack had started when he retired from the LAPD. The seniors Connie had seen going in and out of the center seemed energetic, active, and she found out they even had a few African American and Latino clients when she'd called for information.

Connie pulled into a parking lot bordered by the center on the left and a conveniently located medical group on the right. She unconsciously fingered her black pearl and amethyst necklace—the last birthday present her dear Mack had given her—along its chain as the old woman laboriously gathered up her things and got out of the car.

"You're going to have a great time, Mother," Connie said, forcing a hopeful note into her voice.

"So you say," was the curt reply.

A YOUNGISH WOMAN of about fifty with a hennaed hurricane of hair took Nellie's raincoat, hat, and gloves and asked some impertinent question about Nellie's circulation. Her nametag said "Marjorie Engel, RN, MPH, Executive Director." "We're a little sad around here today," Mrs. Engel explained, her eyes directed across the large multipurpose room. "Mrs. Guttendorf's had a death in the family."

Nellie's heart wrenched at the thought, and her mind flew to the loss of her beloved son Mack. She sadly took the intake forms Mrs. Engel handed her as her attention was drawn to a silver-haired, mousy-looking lady roughly her own age. She was being comforted by four other similar-looking captives of the center while she balanced a picture frame facedown on her lap.

"Danny was all I had left," she lamented. "How could they be so cruel?" The other women clucked sympathetically, although Nellie noticed one of them edging away to grab a handful of party mix from a nearby table. Mrs. Engel led Nellie in that direction to put down her tea cakes. Two older gentlemen, their backs to Nellie and Mrs. Engel, were surveying the spread. Or so Nellie thought.

"I kept tellin' Sophie she needed to keep a closer eye on Danny," the black one said with a harrumph as he ran a yellow bandanna over his bald head.

"He was so old, he was always wandering away," the taller, white fellow said, teeth clacking in agreement like dominoes on a card table.

Nellie figured it would be rude not to stick out her hand when Mrs. Engel made the introductions, but she was somewhat put off to hear how the two men were jawjacking about poor Mrs. Guttendorf behind her back. But they changed their tune when they spotted the plate of tea cakes. Nellie removed the plastic wrap and passed the plate to Mr. Schneider first. He peered through darkened post-surgical glasses, took a couple of tea cakes, and sent the plate on to his buddy. "I couldn't help but overhear," Nellie began, watching Mr. Calhoun get crumbs all over his mustache. "Did Mr. Guttendorf have . . . Alzheimer's?"

Both men looked at her blankly, then Mr. Calhoun—Roscoe, he insisted—set down the plate and let out a huge guffaw, drawing the ire of Mrs. Guttendorf and her silver-haired cronies. One of them frowned, snatched the photo out of Mrs. Guttendorf's lap, and placed it carefully on a table filled with photographs and craft paper in the center of the room. Nellie couldn't quite make it out from that distance, but she got a better look when one of the other women passed out the instructions for their project.

Below a lovely written tribute, Mrs. Guttendorf's Danny

looked up from the picture at the top of the instruction sheet, the hair on his face almost completely white, a big goofy smile plastered all over it and his tongue lolling to one side.

Danny was a Jack Russell Terrier.

RUN OVER BY a car, Roscoe and Mr. Schneider—Harold—told her, after hours while he was leashed up right in front of the center. "Sophie had just run across the street to the bakery and *bam!*" Roscoe explained, sounding just like that Cajun chef on the Food Network.

"I took down the license plate," Harold said, pulling a wrinkled Lotto ticket out of his pocket. "It was a silver Mercedes, I think."

Mrs. Engel's eyes lit up, and she reached out a hand. "Good work, Harold. We should turn that in to the police."

"My daughter-in-law owns a detective agency," Nellie offered. "Maybe she could look into it."

Harold's eyes sparked. "Good idea," he said, handing the ticket over to Nellie.

Mrs. Engel was about to say something when Mrs. Guttendorf joined them, a limp handkerchief balled up in her left hand. "I'm sorry about your loss," Nellie offered, not knowing what else to say.

"First it was my husband Morrie last summer, and now Danny," Mrs. Guttendorf said, the tears coming again.

Mrs. Engel put an arm around her shoulder. "I'm going to ask Dr. Silverblatt to prescribe something if you don't stop upsetting yourself like this." The older woman looked at Mrs. Engel as if she were going to faint, her step faltering as she backed away. "Sophie, are you alright?" Mrs. Engel asked, leading the older woman to a chair.

"I don't need to see Dr. Silverblatt," Sophie Guttendorf said querulously.

"I know dear, but maybe we should take you over there anyway, get your blood pressure checked."

While Mrs. Engel went to call the doctor's office, Nellie asked if the medical group next door was a good one. "My daughter-in-law says I'm getting more forgetful lately," she confided to Mrs. Guttendorf. "Maybe Dr. Silverblatt could tell me why."

"University West ain't no medical group," Roscoe retorted, giving a disdainful snort in the office's direction. "Just Dr. Silverblatt and a bunch of doctors who float through there different days of the week. And don't let the fancy name fool you into thinkin' it has sum'n to do with USC or UCLA, either."

"I think they took their name after the University West Hospital down the street," Mrs. Guttendorf offered timidly.

"I like Dr. Silverblatt!"

Roscoe patted his friend's back. "I know you do, Harold. I just think old Eagle Eye Engel's a little too quick in sendin' folks over there all the time.

Harold tapped his glasses. "But I was getting cataracts!"

"And I *have* had a couple of spells," Mrs. Guttendorf conceded softly.

"Did Dr. Silverblatt find out what was causing your spells, Mrs. Guttendorf?"

"Call me Sophie, dear," the other woman reminded Nellie, then she shook her head. "He thought it was my blood pressure, so he put me into the hospital for some tests. But they didn't find anything."

"You mean they spent all that money and didn't give you an answer?" Roscoe asked incredulously.

"That twenty-six thousand didn't come out of *my* pocket," Sophie said, the relief evident in her voice. "Medicare paid for everything."

"Still, twenty-six thousand dollars," Roscoe said with another snort. "I haven't spent that much at one time since me and my wife bought twin Cadillacs twenty-some-odd years ago." He looked at Nellie and added pointedly, "My *late* wife," and took another tea cake.

"Where are you from, Mrs. Whitcomb?" Harold asked.

"Harlem, USA," Nellie said proudly.

"Well, Mrs. Whitcomb, I hope you're not one'a those New Yorkers who never forgave us for stealin' the Dodgers," Roscoe broke in, a twinkle of mischief in his eye as he reached for another tea cake, " 'cause I'm sure hopin' you'll share this tea cake recipe with me. I ain't had tea cakes since I was a boy."

"If I can call you Roscoe, you should call me Nellie," she replied, aware of the warmth on her cheeks as he offered her his arm and led her to a seat at the table.

THE DAY'S PROJECT, Mrs. Kassem, the activity director informed them, was to create a framed collage in memory of Danny that would hang in the center. "I hope everyone brought something that reminds them of Danny."

"I brought a patch from his raincoat," Sophie offered, holding up a scrap of fabric that looked to Nellie like her own Burberry.

"I brought a package of Beggin' Strips," Roscoe said. "Danny would dance across the floor on his hind legs for one'a them things."

A couple of people offered their own memories—a photo of his favorite tree, another of Danny in costume from the center's last Halloween Party—while others selected pictures from dog magazines and other materials provided by Mrs. Kassem. While everyone else sorted and cut the items to fit a small square, Nellie wrote out her tea cake recipe, one for the collage and another for Roscoe, to which she added a note at the bottom with her phone number in case he ran into any problems with the instructions.

Motherwit's Old-Fashioned Tea Cakes

½ cup butter or margarine
½ cup plus 1 teaspoon sugar
1 egg
1 teaspoon vanilla
2 cups flour
2 teaspoons baking powder
¼ teaspoon baking soda
¼ teaspoon salt
¼ cup buttermilk
¼ teaspoon ground nutmeg

Beat butter and ½ cup sugar in a large bowl until light and fluffy. Blend in egg and vanilla. Combine dry ingredients together and add to bowl, alternating with buttermilk. Mix well after each addition. On a lightly floured surface, roll dough to ½-inch thickness; cut with 2½-inch round cutter or drinking glass. Place on greased cookie sheet. Combine 1 teaspoon sugar and nutmeg and sprinkle over cookies.

Bake at 375 degrees, 8 to 10 minutes or until lightly browned.

Makes about 1 dozen.

When their spirits lagged, Harold moved to the piano, where he played a few tunes in memory of what must have been the center's unofficial mascot. And although everyone was singing along by the time he got to *Oh, Danny Boy,* the room grew quiet when a man in a white lab coat entered the center. "That's Dr. Silverblatt," Roscoe whispered to Nellie, "director of the medical group."

Nellie didn't understand Sophie's reluctance to visit Dr. Silverblatt because he sure wasn't hard on the eyes—tall, curly-haired, boyish but with enough gray at the temples for you to know he wasn't a baby. He sat down next to Sophie, who was sitting on the other side of Roscoe, and put his hand over hers reassuringly. Nellie caught the glint of an expensive watch beneath his French-cuffed shirt and was reminded with a pang of what a sharp dresser her son Mack had been.

"Mrs. Guttendorf, I warned you something like this could happen," Dr. Silverblatt said softly.

Sophie flinched and looked away, but to his credit Dr. Silverblatt didn't withdraw his hand, just continued to comfort her and speak to her quietly.

And although Nellie was suitably impressed with Dr. Silverblatt's bedside manner, she couldn't hold a candle to Mrs. Engel, who, soon as she saw him, flew out of her glass-walled office, whispered something in his ear, and seemed pleased as punch when he nodded. She flitted away, returning in a moment with a wheelchair, which soon had Sophie Guttendorf in it and on her way to the medical group's office.

Harold continued playing half-heartedly for another thirty minutes before Mrs. Engel returned. As soon as he spotted her, Harold got up from the piano and followed the center's director to her office, Nellie and Roscoe Calhoun bringing up the rear. "How's Sophie?" he asked anxiously.

"They're going to run some more tests," Mrs. Engel told them.

"Was it her blood pressure?" Nellie asked.

"They're not sure yet, Mrs. Whitcomb."

"*Zei gesunt*," Harold said with feeling, "she should live and be well."

Mrs. Engel came over and patted his shoulder. "I'm sure she'll be fine, Mr. Schneider."

"Well, at least she's got health insurance," Nellie said to the group.

"Thank goodness for Medicare!" Harold exclaimed.

MOTHER WHITCOMB WAS the most animated Connie had seen her since she moved to California. She talked a blue streak all the way to the kids' school in Santa Monica, and as they made their way back across town to their home near the Hollywood Bowl. Problem was, none of what she was saying made any sense. "Slow down, Mother Whitcomb, and run that by me again."

"There's something strange about that Mrs. Engel at the center," Mother Whitcomb repeated as they inched their way through traffic. "Roscoe told me she's taken nine of the center's seniors over to that medical group in the past month, and seven of them ended up being hospitalized. I think she's putting something in the food to make them sick."

"Or it could just be the flu." Carefully choosing her words, she said, "Plus, when one gets to a certain age—"

"Poppycock! I'm telling you, Connie, I think Eagle Eye Engel is up to no good."

"Eagle Eye?"

"Common sense would tell you that a woman in her fifties who dyes her hair *that* bright is hiding more than just some gray," Nellie went on. "And the way she acts when that Dr. Silverblatt is around is obscene!"

"Now, Mother Whit—"

"Motherwit is *just* what I'm talking about!" the old woman retorted, bristling at the tone of her daughter-in-law's voice. "And motherwit tells me something's wrong."

Connie took a deep breath. "Honestly, Mother . . ."

"All I'm asking is for you to check into Danny's death. If you won't do it, I will!"

"One of them *died?*"

Nellie nodded, pulled the instruction sheet for Danny's collage project from her purse, and thrust it at Connie. The younger woman glanced at it and thought, *Heaven help us, we are talking about a dog.* Maybe this senior center wasn't such a good idea.

Turning into the driveway, Connie could see her mother-in-law's profile in the passenger seat, see the firm set of her jaw, the determined glint in her eye. Her heart fluttered at how much Mother Whitcomb at that moment looked just like her husband when he was in hot pursuit of some case despite the odds against him. She wondered now, what would Mack do?

She held out her hand. "Let me see that address," she said with a sigh and thought, *You owe me for this one, Mack.*

CONNIE FELT LIKE an idiot, calling for this kind of a favor from Larry Richardson, Mack's old partner on the LAPD. Larry was a lieutenant now, running the detective table out of the Hollywood Division, but he could still have a check run on a car, which he reluctantly agreed to do when she explained the suspicions Mother Whitcomb had laid out for her the night before.

"We've got a Senior Abuse Unit at Parker Center. Maybe I can call in a favor with one of the guys I know over there." They shared a laugh about the challenge of having elderly parents before Richardson's tone grew serious. "How are you holding up?"

"I've got so much on my mind, Larry, I honestly don't know." Connie ran a hand through her hair and fought back tears. "With the kids and Mack's mother, I'm getting pulled in three directions at once." She sighed before saying softly, "I'm thinking about selling the agency. I'm not sure I can to do this alone."

"Well, let me get on the phone and have that plate run for you. At least you won't have that to worry about."

ARMED WITH DIRECTIONS she got from Roscoe, Nellie sneaked out of the center at one and took the bus six blocks south to the Fairfax Dog & Cat Hospital. There she met with Dr. Vielma, the vet who had attended Sophie Guttendorf's dog. "My friend is still very upset about Danny, so she asked me to come and talk to you," she told him, hoping God wouldn't punish her for the half-lie.

Dr. Vielma had soulful dark eyes that regarded Nellie

with concern. "If I recall correctly," he began, "Danny had been badly injured when Mrs. Guttendorf brought him in. We did everything we could for him."

"My friend's not upset about that—we just wondered if maybe Danny met with foul play." Nellie looked up at him and gave him her sweetest, most grandmotherly smile. "Is there any way you can tell if that happened?"

"I'll take a look." Dr. Vielma smiled indulgently, left the room, and came back with a manila folder. "As it turns out, the bump from the car did less damage than the leash," he began. "I made a note in his chart that Danny had marks on his neck and across his body . . ."

"Like he'd been choked?"

"More like he was struggling to get away from whatever was coming at him," the vet said gently.

"Would he have made a lot of noise?"

"I'm sure," Dr. Vielma replied. "Terriers are a very vocal breed."

So poor Danny saw his killer coming at him in the parking lot, yelped, and tried to get away, but was run over anyway. Nellie shuddered. How could they be so cruel?

As she waited for the bus to take her back to the Golda Meir Senior Center, she remembered with a shock that that was Mrs. Guttendorf's exact phrasing as well.

ALTHOUGH SHE HATED to admit her mother-in-law was right, after talking to Marjorie Engel for ten minutes, Connie Whitcomb concluded the center's director had a serious case of what her kids would call "the hots" for this Dr. Silverblatt. When Connie had found out that it was the doctor's car that had run over Mrs. Guttendorf's dog, she'd decided to talk to Mrs. Engel privately, and see what was the best way to approach the situation.

And she was met with the brick wall of the woman's denial. "Oh, I'm sure there's been some mistake," she had said with a simper that made Connie's stomach turn.

"Well, one of your clients saw Dr. Silverblatt's Mercedes pull away from the scene—"

"That would be Mr. Schneider, but he was recovering from cataract surgery! He couldn't be sure of what he saw."

"Nevertheless, Mrs. Engel," Connie said firmly, sliding a card across the other woman's desk, "I'd appreciate it if you'd call Dr. Silverblatt for me and let him know I'd like to talk with him."

Engel had reluctantly compiled, grousing all the while that she hated to accuse a doctor as fine and upstanding as Dr. Silverblatt of something so cruel. "Maybe Arthur didn't realize he'd hit poor Danny," she had argued.

"Maybe not," Connie had agreed for the hell of it.

But now, in the presence of the object of Mrs. Engel's infatuation, Connie knew in her gut that Marjorie Engel was more impressed with Arthur Silverblatt's good looks than by his good character. And while Connie had to admit he *was* handsome, Jewish men had never been her type, even though she was Jewish herself. This one would have been a turn-off from the start, with his expensive clothes and transparent lies.

At first he feigned ignorance, then grew indignant. "You don't think I would have seen a dog?" But when Connie looked him dead in the eye and agreed that she hadn't understood that herself, the truth came slithering out. "Maybe I did hear something," he conceded, unable to look Connie in the eye. "But I was on the way to the hospital on an emergency and talking on my cell phone, so I probably just didn't pay it any attention."

"I see." Disgusted, Connie gathered up her purse in preparation. "Where's my mother-in-law?" she asked Mrs. Engel.

"She'd be in yoga class," Mrs. Engel said. "I'll go get her."

After Mrs. Engel left the room, Connie stared at Dr. Silverblatt until he offered to make restitution to Mrs. Guttendorf. "Buy her another damn terrier and send me the bill if it'll make you happy!"

"It's not about me, Doctor, it's about Mrs. Guttendorf. But I'm sure your stepping forward will help cushion her loss." *You putz.*

"Just call my office and let me know the cost," he said, shaking his gold link watch down on his wrist and making an excuse to leave.

"I've got to go, too." Connie rose and looked questioningly at the just-returning Mrs. Engel. "Is my mother-in-law ready?"

And watched all hell break loose because Nellie Whitcomb was nowhere to be found.

NELLIE'S HEAD WHIRLED with questions as the bus lumbered through afternoon traffic. The veterinarian had confirmed that poor Danny had been choked, but who would do such a thing? And what was that Mrs. Engel doing to make poor Sophie sick? She was so lost in her own thoughts that she almost missed the stop for the Golda Meir Senior Center. She was getting off the bus right in front of the center when she realized Connie's Explorer was already in the parking lot. Her daughter-in-law emerged a moment later, deep in conversation with Mrs. Engel, Dr. Silverblatt right behind them.

Connie saw Nellie approaching and rushed over to her. "Mother Whitcomb!" Connie said angrily. "Where have you been?"

Dr. Silverblatt was frowning at her, boyish charm gone with the wind, while Mrs. Engel added, "Yes, Nellie, you've had us all worried half to death," oozing sympathy and concern.

Something had happened, but Nellie couldn't figure out what it was. Maybe they'd been talking about her behind her back, discussing her memory lapses. Suspicious and angry now, she dimly saw Roscoe standing behind them in the lobby of the center, making hand gestures, pantomiming that he would call her later.

"I was just practicing catching the bus," Nellie said irritably and stomped off to the car. "You said you wanted me to start learning the city, didn't you?"

NELLIE WAITED BY the phone in Connie's kitchen until it rang at seven. It was Roscoe and Harold, on one of those three-way calls Roscoe engineered himself. Nellie started off by relating her conversation with Dr. Vielma, which cast a pall over the conversation. Harold was the one to break the silence. "So the poor bastard choked himself to death," he concluded.

"Or some person choked him," Nellie said ominously.

"Why d'you say that?" Roscoe wanted to know.

"My daughter-in-law found out who hit Danny."

"Who was it?" they asked in unison.

"Dr. Silverblatt," she said, and ran down Connie's version of the confrontation with the good doctor.

"Figures," Roscoe concluded. "I never liked that man. Too touchy-feely for me."

She could hear Harold's teeth clatter. "But you can't blame him. He's a busy man, and Sophie knew better than to leave Danny in the lot that way."

"And you're willing to let it go at that?" Nellie asked.

"It was an accident," Harold insisted. "No point in bothering Sophie with it, in any case. She's got enough weighing on her mind, being in the hospital and all."

"That is, if she doesn't already know," Nellie said.

"What do you mean?" Harold asked.

"Nothing, I'm just babbling," Nellie replied quickly and added, "So what's this about Sophie being in the hospital? Did you talk to her?"

"We went to see her," Roscoe corrected. "She's over at University West Hospital, and she's scared to death."

"Her husband Morrie died in that hospital just this past August," Harold added.

That was only five months ago. Although Nellie had

buried two husbands some years ago, she knew how grief could sap the life out of a surviving spouse. "Is her condition that serious?"

"Could be," Harold replied. "They say the blood flowing through this big artery to Sophie's brain is partially blocked. They've got her scheduled for surgery."

"If this could happen to Sophie, fit as she was, why am *I* exercisin' every day?" Roscoe asked. "Just so I can die healthier?"

Nellie started to laugh until she heard the catch in Harold Schneider's voice. "Dr. Silverblatt said Sophie was lucky they caught it in time," he said, covering his emotion with a cough. "She could've had a stroke. So Mrs. Engel wasn't wrong to keep taking her to the doctor's office after all."

"I guess there's some good that comes out of everythang," Roscoe reasoned.

"But why couldn't Dr. Silverblatt figure out what was wrong with her the first time they put her in the hospital?" Nellie wanted to know. "They spent all that money."

"Maybe it came on her suddenly," Harold said.

"Well, it just sounds fishy to me," Nellie insisted, "and I'm going to find out why. Anyone want to join me?"

"What you got in mind, Nellie?" Roscoe asked.

"I don't know yet, but I will by the time I see you tomorrow."

THE MEDICAL GROUP office was very busy that next afternoon. A light rain had brought out patients suffering with everything from flu to phlebitis. Two dozen of them filled the seats or stood close to the exquisite Japanese prints on the walls, exchanging germs and advice. While Roscoe and Harold waited in line, Nellie found a seat closest to the receptionist's station, gathered her raincoat about her, and pretended to sip the artificial lemonade she'd brought over from the center. Her eyes went to a television mounted high in one corner that was showing a video from the place where they had Sophie. It seemed University West Hospital was owned by some conglomeration that was full of happy, upbeat employees who assured her, "It is our pleasure and privilege to care for you." If Sophie had to sit watching this thing every time she waited for the doctor, no wonder she was scared to death to go to that place.

Nellie's accomplices finally got to the head of the line, Roscoe holding Harold under the elbow. Nice touch, Nellie thought, but Harold seemed to be fussing, muttering something, and jerking away from Roscoe as if he were angry. After a few words from Roscoe, Harold finally signed in, turned, and walked toward a seat on the opposite side of the room.

Walked *perfectly* to a seat on the opposite side of the room.

This was not a part of the plan she'd worked out with them. Harold was supposed to stumble, pretend to faint, cause a diversion. They'd rehearsed it three times that morning, and Harold swore he knew his part, even though he complained it wasn't manly for him to be the one doing the fainting.

So now he was balking, like some kind of petulant diva. Roscoe threw Nellie a panicked look over his shoulder. Nellie gestured frantically, looking around to see if anyone noticed. But the patients were all riveted to the television screen, where a perky little Stepford nurse was explaining University West's admitting process.

Roscoe hurried in front of Harold and stuck out his foot, sending the taller man sprawling over his chair and into the lap of a large woman seated next to it.

"Vat the——" she exclaimed.

"You *tripped* me!" Harold yelled at Roscoe, struggling to his feet.

"Naw, man, your shoelaces are untied," Roscoe replied, pointing.

A stern-looking black woman in blue scrubs slid open

the glass partition. "Is there a problem out there?" she asked, a Caribbean lilt to her voice.

Harold took a swing at his friend. Roscoe ducked, and Harold hit a bewigged woman instead. The woman shrieked, and all eyes turned toward the scene in the waiting room, something finally more entertaining than the endless video.

The nurse closed the partition, and soon appeared in the doorway that separated the waiting area from the examination rooms and offices in the back. "What are you people doing out here?" she demanded.

Harold was still trying to swing at Roscoe, the woman who got hit was clinging to Harold's arm, and the woman in the chair was shouting at the top of her lungs in a language Nellie couldn't begin to understand. Dr. Silverblatt and another doctor shouldered their way past the Caribbean nurse to untangle the mess.

They were so busy, not one of them noticed the elderly black woman, wearing a watch cap and raincoat, slipping inside the door.

NELLIE HID IN the ladies room first, where she poured the rest of her lemonade into a small plastic cup sitting on a shelf over the toilet. Armed with her paper-wrapped alibi, she emerged from the lavatory, acting like she was looking for a place to deposit her specimen. She moved briskly down the hall, eyes searching right and left, until she found the records room in a large windowless office in the back of the building.

The G's began near the front of the second aisle of shelves, a few feet above Nellie's head. She found a stepladder, quietly dragged it over, and stood on the first rung to get a better look.

There were Garrisons and Gleimans, Grahams and Grangers, Grants and a Grisham—not the writer, she was disappointed to learn—and a bunch of Guiterrezes. Twice

Nellie heard someone coming her way, but thankfully they walked on. The third time one of the nurses actually came into the records room, causing Nellie to leave her specimen on the shelf where she was searching and crouch behind some boxes piled high with files in a corner, her heart fluttering against her ribs. But the nurse only dropped off some files on a small table by the door and exited quickly.

Nellie tiptoed back to the stepladder and hurriedly resumed her search. Finally, she found a medical record for a Guttendorf, but it was Morrie Guttendorf, Sophie's deceased husband. Hoping it was a file for the whole family, she took it to the corner and, balancing it on top of the boxes where she'd hidden earlier, flipped it open.

But she was mistaken, because there were visits listed for this Morrie Guttendorf as recently as last week, when Dr. Silverblatt paid a house call to monitor his congestive heart failure. And while Sophie's Morrie had died in August, looking through the chart, Nellie noticed Dr. Silverblatt had been visiting this Morrie Guttendorf twice a week for a year.

How many Morrie Guttendorfs could there be?

Nellie hurriedly fished a pen out of her pocket, but couldn't find any paper. She looked around and ran up front, grabbed her phony specimen, and used the paper towel to scribble down the home address and other information from the face sheet of the chart.

She was almost finished when she looked up to see the Caribbean menace coming through the door, some files in her hand. Nellie crouched behind the boxes, her heart doing somersaults and her mind emptying of everything. She could hear the woman coming closer, as if she were a homing pigeon and Nellie was the cage. "What are you doing here, ma'am?" she asked harshly.

Nellie straightened up, sweeping the contents of Morrie Guttendorf's and the other medical records to the floor. "Uh . . . I . . . uh." What was she supposed to say? She grabbed her specimen container. "I stopped in here to write down my name on the cup, and I guess I forgot what I was doing."

The woman eyed her suspiciously and put a firm hand on her elbow. "I don't remember checking you in. What's your name again?"

Nellie tried to twist away, felt the pudgy hand clamp down on her as she was forced into the hallway. "Let me go, young woman! You're hurting my arm."

"Are you trying to sneak in here and get some drugs?" the Caribbean Demon asked, eyebrow raised.

"How dare you!" Nellie raised her voice to cover the pounding she could feel in her chest. "I'm an old woman, and you're hurting my arm. Stop it right now, or I'll call the police!"

Just then Dr. Silverblatt rounded the corner. "What now?" he said in exasperation. His face hardened when he saw Nellie. "Mrs. Whitcomb, isn't it? You're that private investigator's mother-in-law. Where did you find her, Mrs. Collins?"

"Hiding in the records room."

"I was waiting in the lobby to talk to you when the fight broke out," Nellie hurried to explain. "I got scared, so I hid back here."

"With a specimen cup?" Mrs. Collins asked suspiciously.

Nellie held it out. "I thought he'd want to have it. My doctor back home always does."

Dr. Silverblatt smiled and gestured for the nurse to take the cup. "You wanted to talk to me?" he asked, thrusting his hands in his pockets.

Nellie nodded eagerly. "Sophie Guttendorf told me about you. She said you could help me with my memory problems, maybe get me some tests or something. Then when my daughter-in-law told me about Danny and your generous offer, I thought maybe I could help you find a new dog for Sophie, and you could help me find out why my brain gets so addled."

"What is she talking about?" the nurse asked.

"Nothing," Dr. Silverblatt replied, his face reddening. "Why don't you wait for me in my office, Mrs. Whitcomb? We can talk about it in there."

Nellie looked at her watch. "I've got to meet my daughter-in-law right now. Can I make an appointment with you for tomorrow?"

"Sure," he agreed, seeming glad to be rid of her. "In the morning," he told Mrs. Collins.

The woman only slightly loosened her grip on Nellie's elbow as she marched her to the lobby. "You may have fooled Dr. Silverblatt, Mrs. Whitcomb," she said, "but I've got my eye on you."

Nellie mustered up the nerve to glower back at Nurse Collins. "And I've got my eye on you, too."

The nurse put the specimen on a countertop, and turned toward the appointment book. Nellie slipped behind her and removed the paper towel and put it in her pocket. She then stood making an appointment she knew she'd never keep when her daughter-in-law entered the reception area. Nellie waved to her through the open window. Connie scowled at her and motioned her to hurry. "Don't forget to put my name on that," Nellie said, gesturing to the cup.

"When you come back, we'll start a chart on you and take another specimen then," the nurse explained.

"Well, if you're not going to use it, put some ice in it. It makes for a very refreshing drink."

Her jaw hanging open, Mrs. Collins muttered to herself, "That old woman's brain damn sure is addled."

IT BECAME CLEAR that Nellie, Harold, and Roscoe couldn't go back to University West Medical Group or have any contact with the people at the Golda Meir Senior Center for a while. So in the days and weeks that followed, they met at Canter's up the street for lunch, went to the three-fifty matinee at the Grove, or played pinochle at Roscoe's Park La Brea apartment until Connie gave them the word that they could go back to the senior center one more time.

It was a special occasion for the three would-be sleuths, one they wouldn't have missed for the world. Nellie was pleased to see that Connie had called Sophie Guttendorf, too. She was waiting for them in the Golda Meir lobby, beneath the matted and framed collage of Danny they had worked on during Nellie's first visit to the center. Sophie looked like a million bucks since she'd changed doctors and started taking a new blood thinning medication. "The credit should go to your daughter-in-law, Connie," she told Nellie, taking her and Harold's hand. "If she hadn't come to the hospital to warn me about Dr. Silverblatt's bad intentions and helped me get a second opinion, no telling where I'd be."

Connie had also tipped off Larry Richardson about what Nellie had found snooping into the medical group's patient records. Larry had in turn called the U.S. Attorney's office, which had initiated an investigation that was culminating, three months later, in the morning's action.

It was eight o'clock by the time the four of them got settled into their seats, although hearing a presentation on Bush's pharmacy plan was the last thing on their minds. "Bunch of smoke and mirrors, if you want my opinion!" Roscoe grumbled.

At eight-thirty, two vans pulled up and a half-dozen green-jacketed FBI agents clambered out, armed with warrants and dollies and cardboard file boxes. As other seniors arrived that morning, they were treated to computers, medical records, and business files being removed from the building and, in the grand finale, Dr. Silverblatt and four of his colleagues being escorted out of the building for interviews at the Federal Building.

They all went outside to watch him being led away. "*Gonif!*" Harold shouted and spat on the ground in front of him.

"He's worse than a thief," Sophie added, tears in her eyes. "I could have died having that surgery!"

Nellie put an arm around her. "He's going to have plenty

of time to think about that and all the other people he and his buddies have injured."

Not to mention the U.S. government, Nellie was to find out. A month later, she and Roscoe were in Nellie's new favorite deli, reading in the *Los Angeles Business Journal* that it was one of the biggest Medicare billing fraud schemes in the city's history, while the *Times* reported there had been arrests of a dozen physicians, the administrator of the University West Hospital who had been giving them kickbacks, and, in a separate raid, the Golda Meir Senior Center's executive director.

"Guess Mrs. Engel thought she could buy Dr. Silverblatt's love," Roscoe chuckled.

"She should've known a man doesn't love a woman just because of what she gives him!"

"Now, I don't know about that, Nellie," Roscoe said, and slid a little closer in the booth. "If you gave me a little kiss, I might be persuaded to throw some love your way."

"You old fool!" Nellie said, and swatted him with her napkin. "How are Sophie and Harold doing?"

"Sophie bought a new puppy with her share of the whistleblower money from the government. Harold helped her pick it out. He's probably over at her house playing with him right now." Roscoe sat a little closer. "Which reminds me, when am I going to get an invitation to your house, Miss Nellie?"

Nellie blushed and said, "Well, my cooking utensils finally arrived, so I can prepare a decent meal. But it can't be during the week 'cause I'm going to start helping my daughter-in-law part-time at her detective agency. How's this Sunday?"

"Long as you make some more of those tea cakes, I'm a happy man," he said, and stole a kiss before Nellie could stop him.

৪৮

Memory Collage

This project is the perfect way to commemorate a loved one's life, or an event like a going-away party, graduation, anniversary, special birthday, wedding, or baby shower.

1. Ask participants to bring one or more flat items that are of special significance to the person being celebrated — an old photo, a piece of fabric from an old item of clothing, an old or new greeting card, mounted ticket stubs, wrapping paper from a previous gift, the front panel of a package of dog treats (in Danny's case), or anything else. Remind guests that their item(s) should be cut into a square at least 4" × 4."

2. After the event, assemble all of the items and trim them to a square that measures 3" × 3."

3. Arrange the trimmed squares into a pleasing rectangular grid, adding extra pieces of colored art paper, fabric, mounted stickers, or other items to achieve the desired size. You should also make a square panel with the date of the event, (Ann's Going-Away Party, June 10, 2005), or the dates of the person's life (Jack Russell Danny Guttendorf, 1994–2005).

4. Mount the squares, side by side, on a colorful piece of art board, leaving a uniform border of one inch around the collage.

5. Once the collage is completed, go to a frame store and add a matte, glass, and frame. Be sure the matte is positioned so that the edges of the art board are visible. The result is a double-matted, one-of-a-kind keepsake to be treasured by the guest of honor or their family for years to come.

APPENDIX

Museums and Artisan Centers

Museums and artisan centers are great places to see noteworthy examples of various handcrafts. As a character says in the Gillian Roberts story in this anthology, when you see some of these pieces it's hard to understand why people make a distinction between art and craft.

American Craft Museum
40 West 53rd Street
New York, NY 10019
(212) 956-3535

Fuller Craft Museum
455 Oak Street
Brockton, MA 02301
(508) 588-6000

Museum of Craft and Folk Art
Fort Mason Center, Landmark
Building A
San Francisco, CA 94123
(415) 775-0991

Ohio Craft Museum
1665 West Fifth Avenue
Columbus, OH 43212

Kentucky Artisan Center at
Berea, off exit 77 of Interstate 75
P.O. Box 280
Berea, KY 40403
(859) 985-5448

Artisans Center of Virginia
601 Shenandoah Village Drive
Waynesboro, VA 22980
(877) 508-6069

Folk Craft Museum
441 Mt. Sidney Road
Witmer, PA 17585
(717) 397-3609

Carolina Foothills Artisan Center
Highway 221 and Highway 11
P.O. Box 517

Chesnee, SC 29323

Wheeling Artisan Center
1400 Main Street
Wheeling, WV 26003
(304) 232-1810

American Museum of Fly
Fishing
4101 Main Street
P.O. Box 42
Manchester, VT 05254

Shows and Festivals

To appreciate what contemporary craftspeople are doing, attend a craft show or festival to see some superb examples. Start your own collection, buy holiday or special occasion gifts, and be inspired. Check local newspapers and online listings for information about the thousands of such events in the U.S. each year.

Crafts at Rhinebeck
June and October
Dutchess County Fairgrounds
Rhinebeck, NY
(845) 876-4001

Mountain States Arts
and Crafts Fair
July
Ripley, WV
(800) CALL-WVA

New Mexico Arts and Crafts Fair
June
New Mexico State Fairgrounds
Albuquerque, NM
(505) 884-9043

Saturday Market
8th and Oak Streets
Eugene, OR
(541) 686-8885

Renegade Craft Fair
September
Wicker Park
Chicago, IL

Piedmont Craft Fair
M.C. Benton Convention Center
Winston-Salem, NC
(332) 725-1516

www.sugarloafcrafts.com

www.craftshowyellowpages.com

www.artandcraftshows.net

Sew, Quilt, and Embroidery
Festivals
(800) 472-6476
www.pcmexpo.com

Publications

So many magazines are devoted to crafts that it would take pages and pages to list them all. Here are just a few of the publications available.

Shuttle, Spindle & Dyepot: Handweavers Guild of America

American Craft

Crafts

The Crafts Report

Fiber Art

The Gourd: quarterly journal, American Gourd Society

Guilds and Organizations

For the serious craftsperson, belonging to a guild or organization is a vital way to share information. Local and specialized craft guilds abound. You can find one in your geographical area and/or area of interesting by checking with one of the Internet search engines.

The magazine *The Crafts Report*, available online at craftsreport.com, is a wealth of information about various crafts, and lists crafts organizations by region and by medium.

American Craft Council
72 Spring Street
New York, NY 10012
(212) 274-0630
www.craftcouncil.org

American Gourd Society
P.O. Box 2186
Kokomo, IN 46904–2186
www.americangourdsociety.org

Federation of Fly Fishers
P.O. Box 595
Bozeman, MT 59771
www.fedflyfishers.org

International Women Fly Fishers
www.intlwomenflyfishers.org

Northeast Basketmakers Guild
www.northeastbasketmakers.org
(Many other regional basket makers guilds exist.)

Craft supplies and instructions

Nothing substitutes for being able to touch the fabric, see the colors of the yarn, feel the heft of the paper or the lightness of the gourd. In addition to offering those opportunities, local stores are also likely to offer classes, personal instruction, a place to meet like-minded people, and helpful hints that add to the pleasure of making things by hand. I heartily encourage crafters to patronize their local stores whenever possible.

Not everyone lives in easy reach of such stores, however. Luckily, most folks can take advantage of the current interest in crafts by making use of one of the resources listed below. I've offered just a few samples for each of the crafts in the anthology; I don't endorse any of these places but I did want to give readers an idea of the wealth of possibilities that are available across the country and online. If you can, talk to others, whether in person or via the Internet, to open new vistas of craft information.

General craft supplies:

Michaels Crafts Stores
Sam Flax Art Supplies

Earthguild: tools, materials, and books for traditional and contemporary handcrafts
33 Haywood Street
Asheville, NC 28801
(800) 327-8448
www.earthguild.com

Papermaking:

www.papermaking.net

www.botanicalpaperworks. mb.ca
Classes, supplies
Winnipeg, Manitoba, Canada

www.arnoldgrummer.com
> Projects, supplies, dealer
> listings

Gourds:

www.welburngourds.com
> Gourds, tutorials

www.wuertzfarm.com
> Gourds

www.sycamorecreek.com
> Sycamore Creek Trading
> Company
> Leather dyes, etc.

www.mhc-online.com
> Mountain Heritage
> Crafters
> Woodburning tools

Mosaics:

www.mosaicmatters.co.uk

www.mosaic-witsend.com
> Wits End Mosaic
> Supplies, classes
> Tempe, AZ

www.monstermosaics.com

Fine sewing:

www.threadart.com

www.kathyneal.com
> Both sites have informa-
> tion and instructions, and
> sell fabric, thread,
> needles, and other
> notions.

Knitting:

www.knitwitts.com

www.berroco.com

www.yarn.com
> All offer yarn, needles,
> patterns, and
> instructions.

Lanyard weaving:

Pepperell Braiding Company
22 Lowell Street
P.O. Box 1487
Pepperell, MA 01463
(800) 343-8114
www.pepperell.com

Fly Tying:

American Fly Fishing Co.
3523 Fair Oaks Blvd.
Sacramento, CA 95864
(800) 410-1222
www.americanfly.com

www.onflyfishing.com
> These folks have a great
> quote on their website.
> Paul Scullery says, "Call-
> ing fly fishing a hobby is
> like calling brain surgery
> a job."

Basketry:

www.basketmakers.com
> Supplies, tutorials, links
> to local guilds

Arnies. Inc.
3741 W. Houghton Lake
     Drive
Houghton Lake, MI 48629
(800) 563-2356
www.arnies.com

www.basketpatterns.com
  Instructions, supplies

Wreath making: www.marthastewart.com

Dyeing: www.fabricstodyefor.com

www.dharmatrading.com
  Both sites feature dye,
  instructions, helpful
  hints.

Candlemaking: www.peakcandle.com

www.craftcave.com

www.candlewic.com
  All three sites offer
  candlemaking supplies,
  tutorials, and soapmaking
  supplies.

Furniture painting: www.furnitureknowledge.com

www.refinishfurniture.com

www.antiquerestorers.com
  All three sites are loaded
  with information about
  preparing, restoring,
  refinishing, and caring for
  painted furniture.

Collage making: www.collageart.org

www.talbot1.com
  Both sites feature a vast
  array of paper, adhesives,
  suggestions, and other
  helpful hints.